Dancing with the Devil

Best wishes

Elara Rose

Dancing with the Devil

Elana Rose

JEREZMIN

ISBN 978-0-9563607-2-4

Printed and bound in the UK by
CPI Antony Rowe, Chippenham SN14 6LH

First published in the UK in 2011 by

Jerezmin
9 Hillfoot Road, Romford, Essex RM5 3LP

Dedicated to my special friend Mary,
my lovely copy typist Rachel,
and everyone who has had faith in me.

AUTHOR'S NOTE

Whilst mention is made of real bands and performers, in the interest of nostalgia and authenticity, all the characters in this novel are entirely fictitious. Any resemblance to actual persons, living or dead, is entirely coincidental and unintentional.

Chapter One

Rush Green Hospital 1983

'Push, Rosie, push, I can see the baby's head,' cried Ray.

'Take deep breaths,' said the midwife, 'it helps.'

Rosie was in agony. After having five children she'd thought that this birth would be a doddle but it was anything but. The comments from either side of her weren't helping either; her hair was glued to her head with sweat and her body wracked with pain. She gazed at the clock on the wall, it was seven o'clock in the morning and she'd been here for what seemed an eternity. Ray had tears in his eyes; he couldn't wait for this baby to be born. Rosie's tears were falling too; this baby appeared to be in no hurry to arrive. She recalled her father cracking jokes about childbirth to his brother many moons ago. He'd stated that giving birth was no more than a bad bout of constipation. His brother had replied that he imagined that it was a bit more like trying to stretch your lips over the back of your head. Rosie was now starting to believe that her uncle had a point.

Ten minutes later, the baby's head was out. 'Baby's almost here, it will soon be over,' said the midwife. Rosie was now in the process of pushing the baby's shoulders out, and that was no pain free exercise either. 'Push Rosie, just one more time,' the midwife's voice was echoing in her ears. She took a deep breath and a push to end all pushes, and the baby shot out between her legs.

'It's a boy, and he's huge,' cried Ray.

'Great,' replied Rosie. All she wanted to do was sleep.

Ray hugged her. 'You have made me the happiest man in the world, thank you for giving me such a beautiful baby.' His tears splashed onto her face; he was overjoyed at the latest edition to his family.

A cry from her newborn son jolted all of her maternal feelings to the surface. 'Is he okay?' she asked the beaming midwife.

'Fine.' The baby was placed into Rosie's arms and put to her breast.

'You are such a beautiful big boy,' said Rosie, cradling him in her arms. 'Your brothers and sisters will love you.'

'Gary's outside,' said Ray, 'he's a bit jet lagged, but he can't wait to see our new arrival.'

'Oh, Ray, send him in,' cried Rosie, forgetting that both she and her baby needed cleaning up.

The midwife took the baby from Rosie. 'Not yet,' she cried, 'this young man needs a bath before he can receive visitors, and you need to freshen yourself up. What a hunk that young man is outside. I wish I was twenty years younger.' She placed the baby against her shoulder and rubbed his back; he let out a massive belch and was sick all over her. 'Third one today,' she laughed, 'come on, young man, let's clean you up and get you weighed.'

'Ray, I need to clean up,' said Rosie, 'go and keep Gary company.'

'Okay,' replied Ray, leaving the room with a spring in his step.

About fifteen minutes later, Rosie and baby Raydon were deemed presentable for visitors. Gary, her eldest son, entered the room armed with a bouquet of flowers plus a huge teddy bear. Rosie was full of emotion; she hardly saw Gary any more, as he lived in Los Angeles with her ex-husband. He was in his late teens with an athletic build and was extremely handsome. Rosie opened her arms to him.

'Look at you, all grown up, I suppose you'll be making me a grandma soon.'

'If I did, you'd still be mistaken for my older sister.'

'You smoothie.' Rosie ran her fingers through his glossy black hair. 'You're just like your father when he was younger; tall, dark, and handsome with that devil-may-care look in your eyes.' She inhaled his aftershave, it smelt expensive. They shared a hug and then Gary turned his attention to his baby half brother.

'He's smiling at me. Can I hold him?'

'It's wind, all babies smile when they have wind and of course you can hold him, but be prepared for him to be sick though; the midwife caught the last lot.'

Gary took the baby from his cot and seated himself on the chair beside the bedside. Baby Raydon clenched Gary's finger and gurgled. 'Was I this big?' asked Gary. 'He's huge.'

'No, thank God, up until now, you were the heaviest. You weighed in at eight pounds, but this little devil weighed nine. I thought I'd never get him out. How's Barry?'

'He's okay, he seems happy. He's sorting Vic Lee out tomorrow; acts are not getting paid, so he's obviously cooking the books again. Dad's sick of having to fly back and forth across the Atlantic, but you know how he runs the stateside half of the agency; he takes pride in his work and won't suffer Vic's dodgy dealings.'

'So Barry's here too.'

'He certainly is. We're staying at the Dorchester but I wouldn't mind spending a few days with you if Ray doesn't mind.'

'You're very welcome to spend your time over here with us; our house is large enough. I haven't seen Barry in ages. Why waste money on hotels? Norma gets worse every day, but I'm sure that the girls and Bobby would love to spend some time with their big brother,' said Ray. He couldn't care less who came to stay with them now that he had Raydon. He knew that the baby was his, unlike baby Bobby whose parentage had always been in doubt.

'But Ray, Barry might not want to stay with us,' said Rosie taking Raydon from Gary and cradling him in her arms.

'Well, the offer's there if you want it. How long are you here for, Gary?'

'Two to three months. It's a lovely offer, I'll tell Dad about it when I get back to the hotel. Actually I should go now, I've been here ages.' Gary got to his feet, leaned over his mother, kissed her and then left.

'I suppose you'll have to go soon. Ada's had the kids and Norma for over twenty-four hours now; maybe you could bring the kids to see me tomorrow.'

Ray's eyes were fastened on his son. 'Okay,' he said, 'Raydon looks just like me, shame Bobby doesn't.'

'Ray, don't spoil things.'

'Sorry, you're right, it's time that I left. I've got my Polaroid camera with me, so I'll take some snaps; you and Raydon make a lovely picture.'

He took his camera from a bag and trained it on Rosie and Raydon. He felt guilty about his remarks, but lately the doubt over Bobby's parentage was eating away at him. He idolised Rosie; she was still beautiful with her long blonde hair, sensual mouth, big green eyes, and her curvy body. She gave him everything, including a red hot sex life. Now she'd given him his beautiful son and he was griping away about Bobby. It had to stop.

'Smile Rosie,' he said, 'I love you.' He took snap after snap using the whole film up, then he put the camera down and took Raydon from his wife. 'My perfect son,' he said. 'I want to take you and your mummy home now; I don't want to leave you but I have to. I'll be back tomorrow with your brother and sisters, plus Nana Ada, and Grandad Alf will probably put in an appearance too with the rest of my nutty family. Nana Norma's lost the plot but she's a very nice lady.' He glanced over at Rosie; her eyelids were drooping. She'd had a hard labour and looked exhausted. Placing Raydon back in his cot, he tucked him in and then kissed his wife. 'See you tomorrow, Rosie,' he said, 'I love you.'

'Love you too, Ray,' replied Rosie, happy in the knowledge that the pain was over and her oldest son was back in her life for a while.

Someone who was not happy about Barry and Gary's visit was Vic Lee. He'd been perfectly happy sitting behind his desk, with his mouth full of vanilla fudge and his secretary on her knees full of him. The sight of Barry storming into his office made him choke on his fudge and ejaculate. Kerry, his secretary, spluttered. She hadn't been prepared for Vic's sudden loss of control. She got to her feet and fled the room. Vic tried to regain his composure. 'Barry,' he cried, 'how wonderful to see you; to what do I owe this pleasure?'

Barry stared at the short, fat balding twat in front of him. 'There is no pleasure in being in your company, Vic; every time I see you, I want to vomit.'

Vic picked up his box of fudge. 'Have some fudge,' he said, offering it to Barry, 'one of my girlfriends brought it back from Devon.'

Barry knocked the box from Vic's hand, scattering fudge all over the floor. 'I'm sick of flying to and fro across the Atlantic,' he yelled. 'Whenever you're left in charge, there's chaos.' He grabbed Vic's tie and yanked him to his feet. Vic went blood red; he was choking.

'Barry, I don't know what you're talking about, everything here is fine.'

'Fine, so how come over twenty acts haven't been paid. You're even short-changing the Z Tones; poor Kevin Howard hasn't been paid for over three months and he's the front man. The only one who has been paid is Romany, I wonder why?'

'Rubbish,' retorted Vic. Barry was choking him, and his horn-rimmed glasses were steaming up. 'The only reason that Romany has been paid is because he's heavily in debt, and good lead guitarists are hard to find.'

'There are plenty of good lead guitarists out there, but none that want to work for you.' Barry let go of Vic's tie and the little fat man crashed down into his chair, red in the face.

'I'm thinking of replacing Kevin Howard with Mick Fraser, who was the original front man when they were the Shelltones.'

'He wouldn't work for you, he's got more sense.'

Vic's mouth was so dry, he couldn't spit a sixpence. 'Let's have a drink,' he said. He was having difficulty swallowing. 'I'll close the office; it'll be like old times.'

'I don't want a drink; you're treating Kevin like shit. He's been raising Ed Gold's son since his demise, and Gerry the keyboard player is a family man with a wife and kids to support, and as for the drummer in the band, I don't even know who he is any more. You sack every drummer that you take on; if I were Kevin, I'd walk.'

'That would be breach of contract,' said Vic smugly, removing his horn-rimmed glasses and wiping them on his shirt.

'So is withholding money that the band has worked for. I've had to leave my wife in Los Angeles to run the business.'

'Another wife, that's wife number three. What happened to you and Rosaleen? You must have been mad splitting up with her,' said Vic, putting his glasses back on.

Barry walked behind Vic's desk and spun him round in his chair, then he dragged him toward the open window. 'How would you like to view Soho upside down? We tried it in Los Angeles, didn't we? I think the blood must have rushed to your brain and put some sense into you because just afterward, your work improved. Shall we try it?'

'No,' screamed Vic. He remembered the episode well and didn't want to repeat it. He'd pissed himself, and could feel the urine trickling down his legs. 'No, I was going to pay Kevin a visit later this week; I've got his money now.'

'So get your cheque book out and send it today; do it now or we will repeat our Los Angeles feat.'

'Okay, okay,' cried Vic. His trousers were soaked and he was sitting in his own piss. Barry was still a force to be reckoned with even though he was in his late fifties. Vic was no force at all; he never exercised apart from having sex, and he even found that tiring these days, preferring blow jobs instead.

'Cheque book,' yelled Barry, dragging Vic and his chair back to the desk. He suddenly noticed Vic's wet trousers. 'Getting incontinent these days, are we?' he laughed. 'Maybe you should wear nappies.'

'Very funny,' replied Vic, taking his cheque book from the drawer. He was fuming; he owed Kevin and Gerry a fortune and he knew that he couldn't put a stop on the cheques as Barry was going to be around for a while obviously. 'How long are you staying in the UK, Barry? Maybe we could go out one night.'

'About two or three months, so if you're thinking about putting a stop on those cheques, don't even go there because if I need to dangle you out of the window again I might lose my grip on your ankles this time.'

'So where are you staying? I might need to contact you.'

'You won't. I intend to come here every day until the business is up and running properly again. I'm in the Dorchester at present, but Gary tells me that Ray and Rosie have offered to put us up.'

'Much better than hotels,' smirked Vic, 'and anyway, if Ray goes out to work, you never know your luck, your ex is a dish.'

'My name is Barry Grayson, not Ed Gold,' retorted Barry. 'I have principles, and Rosie is devoted to Ray, so don't sully her name.'

'You just sullied Ed's. Was he a problem?'

'He was a problem to everyone.'

'I always thought that your daughter Susie looked like him.'

'Shut it, Vic, and sign those cheques.'

Vic obeyed and smirked knowing that he'd hit a nerve. Kerry was summoned by Barry and told to ring both Kevin and Gerry. 'Waste of a phone call,' said Vic. 'My phone bill's sky high. I'll put these cheques in envelopes and they can be sent.'

'No, Gerry can pick his cheque up himself, he only lives in North London, it's not that far. You need to see him face to face, Vic, and apologise and, as for Kevin we'll ring and tell him we're on our way over, because in his case you need to grovel. Kerry can take care of the office in our absence.'

'I only work on Mr Lee's instructions,' snapped Kerry.

'Not while I'm here. I'm your boss now and you will do as you're told or you will be replaced. I'm a good boss to work for and you don't have to give me blow jobs.'

Kerry blushed to her boots and stared at Vic, waiting for his approval. Vic shrugged. 'Do as he says; he's in charge until he returns to Los Angeles. Oh and call Romany and tell him that I can't make it tonight.'

'After you've rung Gerry and Kevin and told them the good news,' said Barry. He was enjoying bringing Vic to heel.

Vic picked up the scattered fudge. 'Are you sure that you don't want any, it's wrapped?'

'No,' replied Barry, 'it'll take more than that to sweeten me up.'

Kerry was still hovering, still uncertain of who to take orders from. Vic shot her a killing look. 'Well don't just stand there, you stupid cunt, do as Barry says, ring Kevin, Gerry, and Romany in that order, and if anyone rings while we're out, tell them to ring back tomorrow morning.'

'Fine,' replied Kerry and left the room.

'And now,' said Barry, 'I need to see the accounts.'

Chapter Two

Vic and Barry drew up outside Kevin's home, which was a large mansion previously owned by the superstar Eden Gold. Cathy, Ed's wife, had inherited it, but a year after his demise, she had committed suicide leaving it to her son Eddie, a bright little boy. Kevin had been left to raise the child, aided by Ed's brother and sister-in-law when Kevin was touring.

Barry had only visited the mansion twice, once with Vic, and once with Rosie. Ada Shores, the housekeeper, invited them in and went to find Kevin. She found him in the garden feeding the koi carp in their swimming pool-sized ornamental pond. He made his way back to the house, and once he was in Vic's company found himself being suffocated by the little fat man who stunk of moth balls.

'Kevin, my boy, long time no see, how are you? I've got your money, and I've just signed a contract for you and the band to tour the West Country.'

'Will we get paid for this tour?' asked Kevin, taking the cheque that Vic had thrust into his hand.

'Of course you will; would I lie to you? This is Barry Grayson; he runs the agency from L.A.'

'I know. We spoke on the phone just over a week ago. I rang to ask if there was a hold up on the cash front as I'd received no money for ages. I'd wondered if the American promoters were responsible.'

'That's right,' said Barry, gazing at the young man who could have been mistaken for Ed's younger brother, 'and I told him that you'd been paid, Vic.'

'An oversight,' replied Vic, 'secretaries are useless these days. They can't type, their short hand is non-existent and they can't even take down dictation.'

Barry stifled a chuckle. Vic's secretary had certainly been taking down something when he'd breezed into the office earlier – Vic's trousers. 'Well, look,' said Kevin, 'if you hit another cash flow problem, I'd like to terminate my contract. I need regular income, and rumour has it that Romany has been paid.'

Vic went bright red. 'Who told you that?' he bellowed.

'Romany did; he was pissed one night and it all came out,' said Kevin.

Barry burst into laughter, with Romany everything always came out, and off. The magnetic stud showed no sign of slowing up. 'You're a great improvement on the last front man in every way,' he said.

'Thanks,' replied Kevin, 'but Vic wouldn't agree with you; I don't do drugs or sleep around.'

'You have to have a hell raising image,' snapped Vic. 'Ed took drugs and always had one or two women on his arm; he had a great image.'

'Well you can keep that image. He had a wonderful wife in Cathy but he still played the field; he was an arsehole.'

'And so say all of us,' laughed Barry. 'If you have any more problems, ring me and I'll sign you up if you leave Vic.'

Eddie came running in from the garden, his face all flushed. 'Wacky's got out and I can't find the gardener, can you help me to get him back into his stable?'

'Okay,' replied Kevin, 'I'll sort Wacky out. You sit down and tell Uncle Vic what you want for Christmas.'

'Okay,' said Eddie, seating himself facing Vic who looked very uncomfortable.

'I'll come and help,' said Barry, 'I've never seen this tortoise; I'm told that it's huge.'

'It is,' snapped Vic. 'Every time that I've encountered it, it's rammed my ankles, so I'm not going near it.'

Eddie turned his eyes on Vic. 'I think Wacky keeps getting out because he wants a girlfriend. All boys want girlfriends; have you got one, Uncle Vic?'

'Not at the moment; why, have you?'

'Yes,' replied Eddie, his bright blue eyes sparkling. 'She's my half sister, her name's Deanne Rose but I call her Dee Dee.'

Vic was gobsmacked. In 1977, Ed had recorded a version of the Troggs *Little Girl* and dedicated it to Deanne Rose.

'Have you got any other sisters?'

'Yes, Susie, but she's older than me. Sometimes Aunty Rose stays here and sometimes I stay at her house in Havering. I like Aunty Rose, she looks like Mummy. I like Ray too but he gets angry a lot. He calls Bobby a nasty name when he rows with Aunty Rose, and I don't like it. I can't tell you what it is because I'm not allowed to say it.'

'What else does Ray say when he's angry?'

'He calls my daddy an even nastier name.'

'Really?' Vic was intrigued. 'Have you got any photos of your sister and Bobby?'

'Yes,' and getting to his feet Eddie removed a large photo from the sideboard. He handed it to Vic. 'This is Dee Dee, this is Susie, and this is Aunty Rose and Ray. I'm cuddling Dee Dee; she's pretty isn't she?'

'Is that Bobby that Aunty Rose is holding?'

'Yes.'

'How old is your girlfriend?'

'Two months older than me.'

'How old is Bobby?'

'I don't know but his birthday is in August.'

Vic was wracking his brains. If Deanne was two months older

than Eddie, she must have been conceived while Ed was supposedly pining for Cathy, which meant that while he'd been trying to placate his suicidal superstar, the bastard had been playing happy families with Rosie. As for Bobby, the child must have been conceived just before Ed died. Out of the mouth of an innocent child had come a wealth of information which he could store and use to his advantage. Even in death, Ed was creating havoc, so much for the devoted caring husband. He was a complete bastard, just Vic's type of person. He wanted a closer look at the children, and if Barry stayed with Rosie, Vic had every reason to pay her a visit.

'If I marry Dee Dee, will you come to my wedding, Uncle Vic?'

'Of course, now what do you want for Christmas?'

Eddie took the photo back and placed it on the sideboard. 'A nice girlfriend for Wacky.'

Vic groaned, wishing that he'd never asked.

'Please, Uncle Vic.' Eddie gave one of his most appealing looks.

'Okay,' replied Vic, 'I'll get him a girlfriend.' His mind was going into overdrive; tomorrow he would seek out a good reptile expert and find out how much baby Sulcata tortoises sold for. He could offer to take any eggs off Eddie's hands, hatch them and give him a small portion of any profits made from sales. Vic loved making money at anyone's expense other than his own. 'They'll have babies, Eddie,' said Vic.

'Baby tortoises.' Eddie was jumping up and down with excitement.

'Yes, won't that be fun?'

'Kevin bought me a book about tortoises but you have to have an incubator to hatch them in and a vivarium for the babies to live in; I think they cost a lot of money.'

'No problem, young man, your daddy would have wanted you to have the best and I'm going to make sure that's what you get.'

'Thanks, Uncle Vic,' cried Eddie, throwing his arms around Vic.

'That's okay,' replied Vic with an evil glint in his eyes. 'Now tell me a bit more about your sisters and Bobby.'

Forty eight hours later, Rosie left Rush Green Hospital with her precious bundle. There was a welcoming party awaiting her at home; there was the entire Lynne family, her own children, and Norma. Balloons and banners adorned the main living area, plus many cards with the greetings 'Congratulations on the Birth of your Baby Boy' written on them. Everyone applauded as Rosie made her entrance with Ray and Raydon, making her feel like royalty.

Norma was shocked. 'Not another baby,' she cried, 'take it back; how could you, Rosie?'

'This is your new grandson, Mum.'

'Oh, is it? Nobody tells me anything these days.'

Ada Lynne took the baby from Rosie. 'He's the image of you, Ray,' said Alf, Ray's father, 'good strong stock.'

Bobby was screaming and rattling the bars on his playpen. Rosie went to him and picked him up. 'How's my wonderful boy?' she crooned.

Bobby smacked her in the mouth, incensing Ray; he stormed over, snatched the child from his mother's embrace and deposited him back in his playpen. Bobby clenched his little fists into balls and screamed even louder. Rosie was about to pick him up once more when Ray yelled, 'Leave him, he's got to learn that he can't always be the golden boy, you've got another baby to take care of now.' Rosie noted how he emphasised the word 'golden', knowing that it was just another dig at Ed.

'He's probably missed me,' she said.

'So have the girls, but they're not smashing you in the face.'

'It was an accident.'

'Rubbish, that child demands your attention twenty four seven.'

Rosie ignored him and picked Bobby up once more, cooing, 'Mummy's home, come and see your new baby brother.' She soothed him and the child stopped crying.

Deanne and Susie were delighted with their new baby brother and a demented Norma kept asking everyone who the baby belonged to. Ada Lynne had made a sumptuous spread aided by the girls and Norma. Everyone tucked in and then the party started in earnest. Later that night, Barry rang telling Rosie that he would be delighted to take her up on her kind offer of putting him and Gary up for the duration of their stay in England. Rosie was very happy, she'd have her handsome young son in her company for the next couple of months or longer. The only cloud on the horizon was Ray's attitude to Bobby, it was bothering her.

At the end of the week, Barry and Gary arrived and moved in. Rosie had made a roast dinner for everyone, and Barry remarked on her cooking skills. 'You're turning into a real little domestic, Ray must be good for you.'

'He is, he gives me everything I need.'

Barry sighed. 'I tried to but there was always someone else in the way,' he replied, gazing at his ex-wife. She was just as beautiful now as she had been when he'd first laid eyes on her, in fact she looked better now; she'd filled out a bit, her curves were irresistible and her face was more sensual than ever. He hadn't wanted to divorce her, he'd worshipped her and had forgiven her for her indiscretions with Ed until he found out that Susie wasn't his daughter. Furious, he had sent her and Susie packing knowing that if the child hadn't had her horrific accident and needed blood, he would never have known the truth. His passing shot to Rosie was, 'I've conceded defeat, you and Ed will always find a way to get together.'

He was right, as shortly after her return to England, Rosie and Ed met up again and before long little Miss Deanne Rose made her entrance into the world. It was no good dwelling in the past; he had Iris now and a wonderful life in Los Angeles.

'How's things with Vic?' asked Gary noticing that faraway look in his father's eyes.

'Hard work, he's hopeless. I don't know why he bothers to get up in the morning, he lives in a world of his own. I'm trying to sort out his mess and he's got his head buried in a book about Sulcata tortoises.'

Ray pushed his plate away, having demolished everything on it. 'Some money making scheme, I suppose,' he said, 'one where someone gets ripped off.'

'Eddie has a Sulcata tortoise,' said Deanne, 'his name's Wacky.'

Rosie stared at her daughter's plate. 'Eat up,' she said, 'you're not getting down from the table until you've cleared your plate.'

'But, Mummy, I hate greens.'

'I don't care; if you don't eat them, you can sit here all night.'

'But, Mummy.'

'Don't but Mummy me, eat up, we've trifle for afters.'

Deanne wrinkled her little nose up and pushed her greens around her plate with her fork. 'My daddy wouldn't have made me eat my greens, he loved me.'

'Well, I'm your daddy now, so do as your mother says,' snapped Ray.

Deanne burst into tears. 'I loved my real daddy, and he loved me,' she sobbed.

Rosie sighed; this dinner was turning into a nightmare. 'Eat up, Deanne, or you're going straight to bed,' she said.

Gary put his arms around his young half sibling. 'Dee Dee,' he said softly, 'eat them up for me, you'll grow big and strong. Wacky eats his greens, and look how strong he is.'

Deanne dabbed her eyes with a napkin. 'Okay,' she said, 'I'll do it for you, but only for you. Can we go out tomorrow to Bedfords Park?'

'Only if you eat your greens.'

Deanne picked up her knife and fork and demolished her greens in record time.

'I think you should move in permanently, Gary, she listens to you; I must be losing my touch. Maybe it's because I'm approaching forty and she sees me as an old fuddy duddy. I suppose I am, I've got no patience lately; yep that's it, I'm getting past it,' laughed Ray.

'You're a spring chicken,' chortled Barry, 'I'm almost sixty.'

Rosie smiled and poured some more wine. 'Let's raise our glasses to present company,' she cried.

The toast given, glasses raised and emptied in the space of seconds bringing more laughter and then everyone tucked into some delicious trifle.

A short while later, a game of Monopoly ensued. Barry was the outright winner, making piles of money.

'Always had the Midas touch,' laughed Rosie.

'What's the Midas touch?' asked Deanne, brushing back her blonde curls.

'Well,' said Barry, 'Midas was a king and everything he touched turned to gold.'

Deanne clambered onto his knee. 'Even his dinner?'

'That's right.'

'But if you've got the Midas touch, why doesn't everything that you touch turn to gold?'

'It's just a saying, Dee, it means that I make a lot of money.'

'So maybe you should call it Barry's touch,' giggled Deanne.

'Maybe, Dee.' Barry tickled the little girl, making her giggle more. She was a beautiful child; a younger version of Susie, blonde hair, big green eyes which she'd inherited from her mother, full lips, a small nose and a smile that melted your heart.

'Bedtime, Dee.' Rosie was on her feet, extending her hand.

'But, Mummy.'

'I said bedtime.'

'And Bedfords Park tomorrow,' said Gary. 'We might even have a picnic on the village green later, would you like that?'

'You bet,' and getting down from Barry's knee, Deanne said goodnight to everyone and took Rosie's hand.

Chapter Three

A week later, Kevin paid Rosie and Ray a visit with Eddie. Gary showed great interest in the Z Tones, stating that he'd seen the line up many times with Ed as front man but never with Kevin in his place.

'Well, if Rosie can spare you, you could catch us on our tour,' said Kevin.

Rosie bustled into the room with a tray of coffee and a plate of biscuits. 'I can spare him for a couple of weeks, as long as you keep him away from Vic and Romany; they're both pure poison. I remember Romany as a kid, as little Roy. He was a nasty little sod then but now he's developed into a nastier version called Romany. As for Vic, the words evil and vile don't even come close.'

'You can say that again,' said Barry, 'he's the spawn of the devil.'

Later that evening, the man in question turned up about nine o'clock unannounced. He was bearing gifts consisting of flowers for Rosie, a bottle of scotch for Ray, Z Tones latest album for Susie, sweets for Deanne, and teddy bears for the two youngest members in the Lynne household. He feigned surprise at seeing Kevin relaxing in an armchair even though he'd been informed by the housekeeper as to where he was. Rosie was glad that dinner was over; she didn't need a dining guest like Vic.

'Rosaleen,' cried Vic, 'long time no see.' He threw his arms around her and planted a smacker on her cheek. Rosie was suffocating in this horrible creature's embrace. Ray looked on in disgust, wanting to brain Vic with the bottle of scotch that he'd just been given.

'Uncle Jim,' cried Norma, 'where's Ivy, I wanted to go to the Hills and Steele in the market. We were going to go shopping and then onto the Rex Cinema to see *River of No Return.*'

Confused, Vic released Rosie. 'I'm Vic,' he replied, extending his hand, and staring at the demented lady before him.

'Oh are you, why do you keep changing your name, Jim?'

Vic became aware of someone tugging on his jacket. 'You mustn't hug Mummy, or kiss her, only Ray can do that,' chastised Deanne.

Barry roared with laughter. 'That put you in your place, Vic.'

Vic stared at the little girl whose face had that same defiant look that he'd witnessed from Ed over the years. 'What's your name, little girl?' he asked.

'Deanne Rose, but my friends call me Dee Dee. Who are you? You can't just come in here if you don't say who you are.'

The child's eyes were boring into Vic. 'I'm Uncle Vic,' he stuttered, 'I've brought you some sweets, do you like chocolate?'

'Yes, but why are you here?'

Vic was angry; everyone around him was trying not to laugh, and he was lost for words. 'Well I work with Barry and I needed to speak to him, plus I'm Kevin's manager.'

'Well you're not a very good one, are you? You haven't paid him for ages, so maybe you're too old to manage anyone any more. I should give up if I were you.' Deanne giggled and snatched the sweets from Vic's hand. 'Thanks,' she added, 'I'll share these with Eddie, see you later,' and she scampered off upstairs.

'She might have a point,' laughed Kevin. Barry was crying; he'd laughed so much that tears were streaming from his eyes and down his cheeks.

Susie emerged from the kitchen. 'Ray, can you help me with my homework? I'm stuck.'

'Well, if you're stuck, but how do you expect me to know the answers? I was at the back of the queue when brains were given out. Come on then, I'll give it a go.'

Vic's jaw had dropped. 'Is that your daughter, Barry?' he spluttered.

'Yes,' replied Barry. He wasn't letting on that she wasn't.

'Come here, darling, do you remember me?'

Susie shook her head. Vic's blood pressure was rising; the girl was the image of her mother. She had beautiful blonde hair, a slim body and long legs. 'Vic Lee at your service,' said Vic, 'I've got the latest Z Tones album for you. The last time that I saw you was when I was dressed as Father Christmas at Ed Gold's mansion, though you were much smaller in those days. You've grown into a gorgeous young lady; how old are you?'

'Thirteen, thank you for the album,. I don't want to be rude, but I have to do my homework,' replied Susie.

'Of course, my dear, run along,' and he watched as Ray and Susie left the room.

Barry was in his element. 'Deanne made you look a right twat,' he said, 'and you can put your tongue away now Vic and stop perving after my daughter.'

Vic was now focussing on the photos that adorned Rosie's polished sideboard, where there were countless photos of Ed and the girls. He picked one up and studied it; it was of Rosie and Ed, and Deanne who was astride a pony. Rosie looked on; she wanted this creep out of her house as soon as possible. 'Thanks for the flowers,' she said, 'I'll go and make some coffee.'

'That would be nice,' replied Vic replacing the photo on the sideboard.

There were sounds of a baby crying so Rosie gave up on coffee and hurried upstairs. The men in the lounge began to discuss the Z Tones forthcoming tour, and there were many arguments until Norma piped up. 'Uncle Jim, I'm getting very angry; when is Ivy going to turn up? It'll be too late now to go to Hills and

Steele and if she doesn't get here soon, we'll be too late for the evening performance at the Rex Cinema.'

Vic went blood red. 'Where the fuck is Hills and Steele? I thought that the Rex Cinema was closed, and who the hell is Ivy?'

'Your wife, you cheeky blighter, and don't use language like that in this house or I'll get my husband to sort you out.'

'The answer to your question, Vic, is Hills and Steele went and British Home Stores took its place. The Rex Cinema is now Tesco, and my father is dead, so he won't be sorting anyone out,' said Rosie entering the room with Bobby in her arms. 'Here, take Bobby and I'll carry on with the coffee.'

Flustered, Vic settled Bobby on his knee and presented the child with his teddy bear. 'Hello, young man, I'm Uncle Vic,' he said.

Bobby gurgled with delight and cuddled the bear to him. Norma was irate. 'Well that's my plans gone up in smoke. You wait until tomorrow, I'll give Ivy a piece of my mind. Oh well, I suppose I could go to L F Stones instead.'

'Which is now Debenhams,' shouted Rosie from the kitchen.

Eddie and Deanne had come downstairs, and Deanne eyed the photos on the sideboard. 'Someone's moved my photo,' she said, glowering at Vic and standing with her hands on her hips.

'Hi, Uncle Vic, have you got a girlfriend for Wacky yet?' asked Eddie.

'It's not Christmas yet,' replied Vic, 'plenty of time.'

'If he's your uncle, then he must be mine and I haven't got any uncles apart from Uncle Rusty.' Deanne walked over to Vic, got up close and gazed at his face. 'He's too old to be an uncle; he could be a grandad but I haven't got one of those either apart from Grandad Alf.'

'Well, I'm more like a kindly grandad or great grandad,' replied Vic, 'but I thought uncle sounded better.'

He smiled at the inquisitive little girl who was now touching his face. 'But you can't be a grandad either, or a great one, because there's nothing great or grand about you. Did you move my photo?'

'Yes.' Vic was really pissed off now. The child was humiliating him in front of everyone and they were laughing.

'Why did you move my photo? It's my favourite one; I'm riding Mr Ed. Daddy took me and Mummy to London Zoo and we went to the pets corner, that's where the photo was taken.'

'Two Eds,' cried Norma at the top of her voice, 'and neither of them talk, well apart from at night when one of them visits me.'

'What is she talking about?' Vic's head was spinning.

Eddie was in hysterics, he'd never seen Vic look so lost. Deanne perched herself on the arm of Vic's chair. 'The pony is Mr Ed; they call him that because he looks like the horse on the television series. It's not on these days but you must remember it, my nana does, she's always singing the song. The other Ed is my daddy; he was famous, did you know him?'

'I did for many years.'

'Oh, did you work for him?'

'No,' snapped Vic, 'he worked for me.'

Deanne got down from her perch. 'Well there's no need to be so rude,' she cried, 'I'm only a little girl. I didn't know, did I? You're a guest and you should behave like one.'

'I loved the talking horse,' cried Norma, and burst into song.

Barry threw back his head and laughed. 'Who needs to go out,' he said, 'Deanne's all the entertainment we need; she's a star.'

Ray entered the room followed by Susie; the homework session had ceased. Vic fixed his lecherous eyes on Susie and began to fantasise until an ominous squelching noise omitted from Bobby.

'Pooh,' cried Deanne, 'Uncle Vic's farted.'

'I think he's becoming incontinent,' said Barry, 'he wet himself in the office the other day.'

Eddie and Deanne were in fits of giggles, and both collapsed on the floor; soon they were both rolling around, with Norma looking on. 'That looks fun,' she said and she joined the children on the floor. When Rosie entered the room with the coffee, she couldn't believe her eyes. The children were rolling around the floor with her mother, Vic was holding Bobby at arm's length whilst gazing up Norma's skirt, and looking traumatised. Ray helped Norma to her feet.

'Spoilsport,' she cried, 'I was enjoying myself.'

'Yes, but you were flashing at Vic.'

Norma's face was a picture. 'So what?' she snapped. 'I've got knickers on, look,' and she hiked her skirt up showing everyone her pink drawers that had ridden up her crutch.

Rosie was fuming. 'Eddie, Deanne, get up, go and play upstairs, and as for you, mother, pull your skirt down, the world doesn't want to see your underwear.'

'Then I'll take it off. Why is Uncle Jim holding Bobby like that?'

'He's had an accident,' laughed Ray.

'Told you Vic was going incontinent; my sides are aching with all this laughter,' said Barry.

Norma sat down with her mouth set in a firm line. 'I was only having fun,' she said, 'you're a miserable lot, especially Uncle Jim, I can't think how Ivy puts up with him.'

Suddenly there were sounds of another baby crying over the baby monitor. 'Susie, will you hand out the coffee, I've got to go to Raydon, he must want feeding.'

'Okay,' said Susie and started to hand the coffee around as Rosie left the room.

Ray took Bobby from Vic and shouted up the stairs. 'What about Bobby? He stinks.'

'You'll have to do him.'

'I get all the rotten jobs.'

'Yes, but my tits are full of milk and they're bigger than yours,' shouted Rosie. Vic overheard the last remark and now started to fantasise about Rosie feeding her baby. He didn't want coffee, and hoped that Ray would open the bottle of scotch and share it round. Ray left the room with Bobby. 'God,' he said, 'no baby should smell like this, its evil.' Bobby chuckled, quite unfazed by everything and everyone around him.

Later, Vic asked if he could have a brandy. 'I always have a couple this time of night,' he said.

'No,' replied Rosie, 'you're discussing business and you need a clear head for that, and also if you get pissed you'll be unable to drive. I have no intention of putting you up for the night, as you arrived without an invite.'

Vic feasted his eyes on Rosie's ample bosom. 'I suppose Kevin's staying,' he said.

'Yes, but he and Eddie were invited and, as Barry and Gary are staying here, you will be the only one getting behind the wheel, in fact, I'd appreciate it if you'd leave within the next hour. I'm tired and Ray has to get up early for work.'

'I only wanted one brandy,' grunted Vic.

'Yes, but one becomes two, and two becomes three, and it goes on until you're unfit to drive. But I'll make you another coffee if you like.'

Vic shook his head and grunted again. Rosie sure had a way with words. Turning to Kevin, he said, 'Now, let's talk some more about the West Country tour.'

Chapter Four

Gary and Barry's stay flashed by, and soon Gary was leaving to meet up with Kevin in Truro. When he arrived, he was met by Kevin at the railway station. The two men had bonded, and Kevin had promised Rosie that he'd keep Gary away from both Vic and Romany and he kept to his word. All went well until the second week of Gary's stay with Kevin. Romany had been in a foul mood. He wasn't used to getting knock backs from women, and the whole episode was made worse by the girl coming on to first Kevin and then Gary. Kevin wasn't interested but Gary was keen; he loved the look of the girl. She wasn't beautiful, and she dressed tarty, but she had something and as the week went on the couple found themselves falling in love.

Romany was furious, he was used to girls falling at his feet. His other reason included his feet; he'd seen a pair of shoes in town and told Vic that he wanted them. Vic had agreed; they were classy and went with Romany's new image. Vic left the band and returned hours later laden down with clothes and shoes. Everyone was happy apart from Romany. When he tried his shoes on, he found that Vic had bought him odd shoes.

'You fucking idiot, Vic,' yelled Romany, 'one fits and the other doesn't; can't you get anything right?'

'What's up?' asked Kevin, watching as Romany tried to force his foot into a shoe.

'He's got me a six and a nine,' snapped Romany.

Gerry saw the funny side. 'That's apt,' he said, 'you like that number, don't you?'

'Not this kind, you pratt, Vic, now what am I going to do?'

'The shops are closed now,' said Vic, 'you'll have to wear your old ones.'

'Call yourself a manager, my prick could manage the band better.'

'You've got tiny feet, Vic,' laughed Kevin, 'what size are you?'

'Six,' replied Vic sheepishly.

'Problem solved,' said Gerry, 'you can go onstage together with your legs tied like a three legged race.'

The rest of the band fell about laughing, and Gary joined in. Romany shot Gary a killing look, he hated this newcomer; he was young, handsome and still in his teens, plus he was bedding the groupie that he wanted. He fixed his hard calculating eyes upon Gary; he was going to get him back big time. Romany had always been the looker in the band, his hair that was now streaked with grey had once been black and glossy as a raven's wing and his gypsy features and lean lithe body had knocked every girl out with desire. He still had his fair share of girls as he was an ace lover, but his looks were beginning to go and he knew it. Once a girl was in his bed, he'd give her a night to remember, but lately it was getting harder and he envied Gary who wasn't out of his teens yet. Gary looked away; he felt unsettled, and felt much worse when Romany ambled over. 'You moved in on my tart, and nobody does that to me; you'd better watch your back.'

'Leave him alone,' said Kevin, 'the girl made her choice.'

'So says the girl of the band,' mocked Romany, 'you're not fit to step into Ed's shoes, Kevin bloody goody two shoes, probably still a virgin. Oh no, you can't be, you fucked Cathy. Ed was barely cold in his grave when you moved in.'

'I looked after her when she was ill, and yes we were an item just before she died; we were planning on getting married.'

'How romantic,' said Candy, the little groupie. 'Cathy was a lovely soul, wasn't she?'

'She was a whore,' yelled Romany. 'I had her, Vic had her, and Christ knows how many others did.'

Vic had gone bright red; he hated his dirty linen aired in public. Kevin swung a punch at Romany who sidestepped making Kevin fall to the floor. 'Boys, boys, we have a show to do,' cried Vic.

'Okay,' retorted Romany, 'but this is not over.' Romany leered at Gary. 'Your mother was a whore too,' he goaded, 'sweet little Rosaleen who almost drove Ed out of his mind.'

'They were friends,' cried Gary, 'until my father divorced her.'

'And you know why they divorced, don't you?'

'My father had an affair with his secretary.'

'That what they told; I could tell you plenty.'

'My mother is a lovely woman; I won't have her spoken about like that.'

'You know nothing, and as for those shoes, Vic, you can take them back, I don't even want them now. Get another size six and you'll have a matching pair.'

Romany stormed out of the room, and there followed a deathly silence. Shocked, Gary turned to Kevin. 'What does he mean?' he cried.

'Nothing,' replied Kevin, 'your mother is a lovely woman and so was Cathy; this is just a Romany strop.'

Vic ran after Romany. 'Watch your mouth,' he yelled, 'that is Barry Grayson's son, and you could find yourself out of a job.'

'Do you think that bothers me? I could go to Los Angeles tomorrow and work with my brother Rick. I don't need your management or your fucking band, I'm the kind of guy who will never be out of work.'

'Gary's going home in a few days, so just try and control yourself until then.'

'I'm making no promises; I won't have anyone taking my tarts away from me.'

'Ed did in the late sixties; he used to procure women for you I'm told, and he helped himself sometimes before you got them.'

'That was before he was famous, and anyway they only slept with him to get to me, he was just the gateway.'

'And I believe your tart may be doing the same; Kevin was her first choice.'

'Really, she wants a pouf instead of a man. I think Kevin needs to come out of the closet; since Cathy's death, there hasn't been a woman in sight.'

'He still mourns Cathy.'

'What a mug, Ed was the only one that she wanted.' Romany shot Vic an evil grin. 'But she had needs though, both you and I know that; you may have made her a star but you helped yourself to her now and again. Me and Rick had a threesome with her in Los Angeles; we made her snort coke and it was a hoot. We got Ed out of his head, helped him to bed and took Cathy to ours.'

'She didn't do drugs, she wouldn't snort coke.'

'She had no choice, Rick told her that he'd fill her veins with heroin if she didn't snort it. Coke was the softer option. We had her every way possible, even made a sandwich of her, she hated that and screamed and cried telling us to stop. Trouble was that excited us more and we really gave it to her; I don't think she'd had it up the arse before.'

'Well whatever you did, I need you to apologise to Gary; calling his mother a whore is not exactly a good idea, he repeats everything to his father.'

Romany frowned. 'I guess I shouldn't have said that; she was never a whore, and Ed adored her. He said that she's given him his first blow job when she was only fifteen, the lucky bastard. He also told me that a few months later they'd graduated to sixty nines. He was an idiot cheating on her and then fucking off to France because once he'd gone Barry moved in for the kill and married her. Now she's married to Ray, even though three of her kids are Ed's.'

'So you think so too.'

'Yep, they all look like him, especially Bobby.'

'But Bobby was conceived just before Ed died and he was living happily with Cathy at that time.'

'Yes, but he had to visit his daughters, didn't he, and sometimes babies have a nap in the afternoon, so maybe Ed and Rosie did the same. I asked her for one once.'

'What a baby?'

'No you pratt, a sixty nine.'

'And what happened?'

'She slapped me, and when Ed found out he punched me on the nose. I suffered that night and I never got one.'

'Got what?'

'A sixty nine, which brings me back to those shoes; you're useless, and I'm seriously considering leaving but before I do, I'm going to wipe that grin off Gary Grayson's face.'

'Romany, I'm begging you, he'll be gone soon, keep calm.'

'Fuck off, Vic.'

'Romany, please.'

'I said fuck off, Vic, go back and hold girlie Kevin's hand; I think what I said about Cathy hit home. You want a good show tonight, don't you?'

'Romany, I'm warning you.'

'No, Vic, I'm warning you, now fuck off.'

Vic was beaten. Romany was unpredictable, and anything could happen.

The show that night was a good one; both Romany and Kevin performed as if they were best buddies but once the show was over the tension was back.

'We have a score to settle,' said Romany, leering at Kevin.

'We'll settle it next week, once Gary's left.'

'Babysitting, are we? How sweet. How's Rosie paying you, in kind?'

'Come on, Gary, we're leaving.'

'I'm not going anywhere until he apologises about the things he said about my mother.'

'Leave it, Gary, he's all mouth; he's made a living out of talking shit. If Ed were here, he'd kill him.'

'He was my best mate and I didn't even apologise to him.'

Vic was intrigued. 'About what?'

'Don't you know, you fat twat? You remarked on my cut and bruised face the day after Ed died.'

'You said you'd been involved in a fight.'

'I said nothing; you drew your own conclusions. I used to use Ed's place for shagging tarts now and again. I thought he was at the hospital visiting Cathy, but he'd come home and I hadn't heard him come in.'

'I'm off,' said Gerry. 'I don't want to listen to this shit.'

'Neither do I,' said Bill, the latest drummer. 'I'm going home to get stoned or pissed or both.'

Vic didn't notice them leave; he was really intrigued now. Romany folded his arms. 'I took two birds back to Ed's place that night, they were both useless. I'd had a bit to drink and started boasting about my conquests. Unfortunately I mentioned Cathy's name, but the birds didn't believe me especially when I told them that I'd screwed Cathy and Ed's stuck up fiancée on the same night. Ed had overheard the lot; he packed the girls off home in a mini cab and then almost beat me to a pulp. I kept telling him that I'd been saying it just to impress the girls but he kept coming at me. I tried to make it up with him but he wouldn't, so I told him that I'd also had a threesome with her on his American tour. I really got to him when I told him about Rick giving it to her up the arse while she was screaming for him to come and save her; his face was a picture, he was almost in tears.'

'You're vile,' cried Kevin, 'my poor Cathy.'

'Poor Cathy, she was a whore.'

'Enough,' yelled Vic, 'it's late and we've got another show to do tomorrow.'

Kevin shot Vic a disapproving look. 'You disgust me too, I don't want to breathe the same air as you. Come on Gary, let's go.'

'Not until he apologises,' cried Gary, 'he called my mother a whore.'

'No way,' scoffed Romany, 'your mother was a prick teaser. She drove Ed nuts for years, and when she was married to your father she was cheating on him with Ed. Over and over she told Ed that she'd leave Barry, but she dangled him on a string because she had no intention of leaving, she loved the Hollywood lifestyle too much.'

'You liar,' screamed Gary, and flung himself at Romany who brushed him aside as Kevin dragged him away.

'Yes he is,' cried Kevin, 'don't let him wind you up. A few words to your father should do the trick, and you'll have a written apology by the end of the week.'

Vic was petrified. Romany's job was on the line, maybe his was too. 'Leave now, Romany,' he ordered.

Romany grinned; he'd upset Gary and Kevin just as he'd wanted to. He felt good and the night was still young. His gear was already packed away so, putting on his leather jacket, he left. Candy had made her way to the ladies and, throwing the car keys at Gary, Kevin said, 'I need a few words with Vic in private.'

'Okay, tell Candy where I've gone.'

'You're really into her, aren't you?'

'We're in love. She's a sweet little girl and, groupie or not, when I leave I'm taking her home to meet Mum.'

'That sounds serious.'

'It is. She told me that she's in love with me too. It was love at first sight for both of us.'

'Great, I won't be long.'

Gary left the building and made for the car park; it was almost empty. As he headed for Kevin's car, he felt as if he were being watched. The car was parked over the back of the car park near the kerb. Many thoughts were coursing through his brain. He'd had a great time with the band and had acquired his first serious girlfriend. Romany was just a trouble maker, and there was no truth about Ed and his mother. Ed had always been kind to him; true Deanne was the issue of Ed and Rosie's relationship but they'd both been free agents at the time. He could hear footsteps, plus the sound of a car door opening and closing, but there was nothing unusual about that, it was a car park after all, then the car drove away.

As he put the key in the car door, he heard another set of footsteps approaching. They were coming his way, maybe it was Candy. Suddenly an arm snaked around his neck and he found himself gasping for air as the arm pressed onto his windpipe. He was blacking out and losing his balance, but summoning up all of his strength he elbowed his attacker in the groin. He heard his assailant yelp and stagger but he retained his grip on Gary. Gary repeated the process and this time there was a louder yelp and his attacker lost his grip. Losing his balance, Gary staggered and then fell backwards, he crashed to the ground, striking his head on the kerb. His attacker dropped to his knees, stole Gary's wallet and then fled to his car, driving away seconds later.

Minutes later, Candy, having freshened herself up, headed for Kevin's car; she spotted it and skipped towards it. She could see a body lying on the ground and heard loud moans. It was the kind of moan that she once heard coming from an injured dog that she'd seen run over one day. Thinking that the body on the ground was a drunk, she kept on walking towards the car. As she drew level with the drunken fellow, she screamed, it was no drunk it was Gary. She knelt down crying, 'Gary, what happened?'

There was no answer, just long drawn out moans. Candy attempted to sit him upright, and cradled him in her arms. Suddenly she realised that her arm around the back of his shoulders was wet and sticky; realising that it was blood, she crooned, 'it's okay Gary, I'm here, I'll get help.'

She had to keep calm for his sake although she didn't know if he was aware of her presence, as he just stared straight ahead of him appearing to see nothing. Taking off her coat, she made a pillow of it and placed it under his head, it was a cold night and she knew that she had to keep his body temperature up. The keys were still in the car door lock, so opening it she removed a fleece blanket from the back seat. Covering Gary up with it, she kissed him saying, 'I love you Gary, you'll be fine, I promise you.' Her brain was doing somersaults. What had happened, had he been attacked or had he fallen? Whatever had happened, he needed help fast. Her legs didn't want to hold her up, they were like jelly. She half ran and half staggered back to the building to get Kevin. Finding him still locking horns with Vic, she screamed, 'Kevin, Gary's hurt, he's bleeding badly, ring for an ambulance, I think he's dying.' A shocked Kevin dialled 999 and asked for the ambulance service. Vic was shitting himself; not only had there been a fracas in the dressing room earlier which could cost him his job, but now Barry's son was in the car park, possibly bleeding to death. 'I'm going back outside to be with Gary,' said Candy, 'he needs someone with him while we're waiting for the ambulance to arrive.'

She hurried out of the room leaving Kevin on the phone and Vic a shivering wreck. If Gary had been mugged, the police would be involved. He wanted the ground to swallow him up. Kevin was off the phone now and ordering Vic to come with him to see how Gary was. Meekly, Vic obeyed, he prayed that Gary wasn't hurt too badly, because if he was, heads would roll and one of them would most probably be his. Suddenly he heard a loud scream followed by an even louder one. Gary had opened his eyes fully, gazed at Candy, tried to speak and pulled her to him. 'What are you trying to say, Gary, who did this?' cried Candy.

Gary could only make sounds and then he cried, 'I love you.'

'I love you too, Gary, the ambulance is coming.' She could see the flashing lights of the ambulance. Candy clung to Gary and prayed that he would live. He began to moan louder and then let out a terrific scream and lost consciousness. The scream that followed was Candy's and then she broke down completely.

Chapter Five

Back in Havering, Rosie was screaming for another reason; her screams were of ecstasy as she received a multi orgasm delivered by her husband Ray. Their sex life was amazing, and it got better every day. Ray could never get enough of Rosie; the kids were staying with his mother apart from Raydon who was a model baby. He was a happy little soul and rarely cried unless he was hungry or needed changing.

As soon as Norma was in bed, Ray had suggested an early night and Rosie had been only too happy to oblige. Their marriage was rock solid and they delighted in each other. Ray thought that he wasn't doing too bad for a guy in his late thirties, and gazed up at his wife who was astride him screaming 'more, more' as the multi orgasm overtook her. She was beautiful. Ray felt so lucky to have her and increased his efforts.

As she relaxed and smiled down at him, he rolled her over onto her back. 'Do you really want more?' he asked, his blue eyes sparkling with fun.

'You bet,' said Rosie, and smiled as Ray entered her once more.

In the next bedroom, Rosie's screams were keeping Barry awake. He shuddered, recalling the earlier stages of their marriage. Rosie had been his pride possession, and sexually she knew exactly what buttons to press. She used to deliberately make him angry knowing that it turned him on, filling him with lust and making their sexual union extremely passionate. She'd talk dirty to him too, inflaming him even more, but at the end of the day her heart belonged to Ed. They'd grown up together and become childhood sweethearts. Later, Ed had cheated on her and cleared off to France, becoming part of a mysterious cult. Rosie had almost disappeared whilst on a trip to France with Barry. She'd been drugged by the High Priestess, and been involved in a ceremony in which she lost her virginity. Barry had had a vision of the whole thing but was powerless to rush to her aid as he'd had a stroke and was paralyzed. Francine the High Priestess wanted Rosie as her successor and needed her kidnapped, but Ed had been paramount in her escape and she'd returned to England with a baby in her belly. As soon as he was well, Barry had married her but it wasn't enough for Rosie, and once Ed was back in England they began an affair that had lasted right up to her divorce.

After the divorce, both Barry and Rosie kept up the pretence that Susie, their daughter, was Barry's, not knowing that Ed had revealed the truth to the girl. Gary still believed that Susie was his blood sister. Rosie wanted Susie to keep quiet about it and, wanting to please her mother, she kept schtum. Barry decided to go downstairs and make a coffee; there was no way that he was going to get any sleep.

Downstairs, Barry made himself a coffee and settled down in front of the television. There was an old Marx brothers film on; he loved the old movies and recalled the days when he, Rosie, Gary, and Susie had sat watching them. He gazed around the room. Nothing had changed much since the days when he had lived here. Rosie had always been the one to decide what furniture she had, plus colour schemes for furnishings. He'd had very little input at all, but he'd liked it that way. She made him happy and that was all that counted, but that was the old days and better forgotten. He needed to stop thinking about the 'if onlys' and concentrate on the film. He watched most of 'Go West' and then fell asleep in front of the television. It was the telephone that awoke him, and he decided to answer it thinking that it might be Gary. He'd had a letter from him that morning stating that he was bringing a girl home to meet him and Rosie. He'd said that he was truly in love for the first time in his life and that he couldn't wait to introduce her to his family, adding that probably Deanne would give Candy the third degree. Smiling, Barry picked up the receiver and listened.

'Could I speak to Barry Grayson?'

'Speaking.'

'It's about your son; we think he's been mugged as his wallet is missing. He has a bad head injury, and we need your permission to operate.'

'Is he in danger?'

'He will be if we don't operate.'

'Then you have my permission; give me the address of your hospital and I'll be on my way.'

The address was given out and Barry replaced the receiver with a feeling of dread. He had to wake Rosie and tell her what had happened.

Ray had heard the conversation; the phone had awoken him so he'd picked up the bedside phone as he didn't want the raucous ringing to awaken Rosie. He replaced the receiver and got out of bed as quietly as he could. Downstairs he found Barry hunched up in an armchair sobbing. 'Barry,' he said softly, 'I'll wake Rosie and I'll ring Mum too, she can take care of Norma until we return home with Gary.'

Barry made eye contact with Ray. 'Will we bring him home?'

'Of course, he's a strong young man, he'll be fine.'

Barry still had this feeling of dread. Gary had been due to come home in a few days and instead he was probably being prepared for surgery. Ray went back to Rosie and shook her gently. 'Rosie,' he whispered.

Rosie turned over, smiled, and wrapped her arms around his neck. 'Again,' she murmured.

'No, Rosie, listen, you need to get dressed, we have to drive to Plymouth. Gary's been mugged and he's in hospital.'

Rosie's eyes snapped open. 'No,' she cried, 'no.' Within minutes she was out of bed and pulling on her clothes. In the en suite, she splashed some water on her face and tugged a comb through her hair. Throwing some clothes into a holdall for herself, Ray, and Raydon, she took a quick look in the mirror and hurried downstairs.

'What happened?' she cried to a tearstained Barry.

'I don't know. All I know is he needs surgery; I've given my consent.'

Ray came downstairs with baby Raydon wrapped in a blanket. 'We need to drop Norma off at Mum's.'

'I'll go and wake her.'

'No need,' said Barry, 'look behind you.'

Norma stood behind Ray looking very agitated. Spotting Rosie's holdall, she cried, 'Are we off on our hols? I'll get my coat, I love holidays, are we going to Great Yarmouth? I love the beach there, it's so lovely, your feet sink into the sand. I'd better pack.'

'I'll get her dressed,' said Rosie. 'Why did I let Gary go with the band? I thought better of Kevin.'

Barry was inconsolable. Gary couldn't die, he couldn't.

Rosie remembered nothing of her drive to the Derriford Hospital, not even when Norma was dropped off at Ada Lynne's house. Her mind had gone blank and the power of speech had left her. Ray had driven them there, realising that Barry was in no state to do so. Raydon slumbered peacefully in his mother's arms. They drove through the night with Ray and Barry conversing, or trying to. Rosie had been struck dumb. On reaching Plymouth, they made their way to the hospital, and Rosie followed Barry and Ray inside in a trance. Barry approached the desk, and the nurse, seeing Rosie's holdall, asked if one of them was being admitted.

Something inside Barry snapped. 'No, you stupid bitch, my son is a patient here, his name is Gary Grayson.'

The nurse took it in her stride; she'd had many confrontations with relations in this situation. Ray attempted to apologise. 'We've driven through the night from Essex,' he said, 'Barry is overwrought. I apologise for his outburst, as he would if he wasn't so worried over his son.' The nurse smiled, told her colleague to take over and asked everyone to follow her.

In Gary's ward, there were four beds. Gary was in the bed nearest the door, and at his bedside sat a young girl. She wore a mini skirt, white top and high heels, her hair was bleached and it resembled candyfloss. On Rosie's arrival, the girl got to her feet, smiled, and said she was going to get a coffee, and did anyone want one. The trio declined her offer and stared at the motionless Gary; tubes were attached to him and his head was bandaged from the surgery. His chest was moving, owing to the fact that he was rigged up to a ventilator. Rosie handed Raydon to Ray and seated herself at Gary's bedside. She took his hand in hers; it was warm. Barry shook his head and seated himself the other side of the bed.

'I'll go and find out where we're sleeping,' said Ray, 'I know that you won't want to leave until you can take him home.'

'Okay,' replied Rosie. She gazed at Barry and sobbed her heart out. 'It's Francine,' she cried, 'she took my first born, then Ed's parents, followed by my father and Ed, and now she wants Gary. She's still working her evil from behind the grave, and she won't rest until she's wiped out my entire family.' Barry said nothing; there was nothing to say.

A few hours later, Barry and Rosie were called into the specialist's room. Rosie was shaking as the surgeon said, 'We've operated on your son and removed the blood clot that was causing the problem, but unfortunately we can't stop the bleeding inside his skull. We've done all the tests and there is no response. You have to prepare yourself for the fact that you may not take him home; he appears to be brain dead.'

'No,' screamed Rosie, 'he can't be, he has his whole life in front of him. Doesn't anyone know what happened?'

'He appears to be the victim of a mugging; the young lady who found him in the car park has been keeping a vigil by his bedside.'

'The blonde girl, I thought she worked here.'

'No, she found him and she's been here since he arrived.'

Rosie got to her feet as the surgeon said, 'If there's no response in the next forty eight hours, we will need to switch off the ventilator.'

'No,' screamed Rosie, 'we need more time, we'll sit with him until he wakes up but first I need to speak to that girl.' She rushed back to Gary's ward and found the girl seated at Gary's bedside. She dragged her to her feet, crying, 'Right, you bitch, I want answers.'

Barry had completely broken down as the surgeon continued. 'We will be switching the ventilator off in a couple of days, as there is no point in keeping it on for longer. I know that you and your wife are hoping for a miracle but as far as we're concerned, he is clinically brain dead. We will continue to do tests on him and, in your case, I will consider extending the forty eight hour deadline to a further twenty four but I assure you it will make no difference. You may want to consider donating his organs to help someone else live.'

'He's not dead yet.'

'I understand how you feel but...'

'Do you?' retorted Barry. 'Has your son been mugged and been on life support?'

'No, but...'

'Then don't give me so much shit; we'll sit by his bed for the next three days and try to bring him back to us. I won't give up and neither will my ex-wife. Oh God, how could this have happened?'

'I'm sorry, really sorry.'

'So am I,' replied Barry, feeling beaten. Gary had to recover or life was pointless. He made eye contact with the doctor once more and then got to his feet and left the room with sobs wracking his body.

Rosie had dragged Candy halfway down the corridor. She pinned her up against the wall yelling, 'Right, what happened, have you got my son's wallet? Did you and a boyfriend mug him and you're sitting by his bedside, afraid that he might wake up and recognise you?'

'No.' Rosie's fingernails were digging into her shoulders.

'Then where were you when this happened?'

'Inside the building with Kevin.'

'You bitch, Kevin was supposed to be looking out for him. Why wasn't he with him? I suppose you were fucking each other senseless while my son was being attacked.'

'We weren't, Mr Lee was there too.'

'So what was it, a threesome?'

'No, you're hurting me, I was in the toilet.'

'God, Kevin's gone down in my estimations, fucking in the toilet, what was wrong with the dressing room?'

'I wasn't with Kevin.'

'You don't fool me, I know what groupies are like, I used to be a performer, they chase band members relentlessly and the guys love being chased. You whore, my son is fighting for his life because of you.'

Candy was in tears, and Rosie's nails were now digging into her flesh. She dropped to her knees and Rosie released her but then began to slap the girl around her face. 'Rosie, stop, where have you been? I've been looking everywhere for you,' cried Ray, running down the corridor with Raydon in his arms. He handed him to a passing nurse and dragged Rosie from Candy who got to her feet and fled. Ray took his distraught wife in his arms. 'Rosie, calm down, I know this is a nightmare, but it's not that girl's fault. Gary was mugged by some evil bastard; come with me and I'll show you where we're sleeping. We can take it in turns to sit with Gary.' Raydon began to cry and Rosie broke free of her husband's embrace and took the child from the nurse. Rosie was back to her dumbstruck mode; she tried to speak but couldn't. In a daze she followed Ray to a nearby room and went inside. Seating herself on a bed, she put her baby to her breast; everything seemed unreal. Her eyes were heavy and, after feeding and changing Raydon, she put him in his carrycot and then laid on the bed. Closing her eyes, she dozed and woke with a start twenty minutes later. In a trance she left the room and headed for Gary's bedside. Ray was keeping a vigil with Barry and got to his feet as Rosie put in an appearance.

'Raydon's asleep,' said Rosie, 'you'd better get some shuteye, Ray, I'll take over.' Ray nodded and left the room.

'Okay,' he said, sadly surveying his traumatised wife.

Rosie sat down and squeezed Gary's hand. 'Mummy's here,' she said softly, and extended her other hand across the bed to hold Barry's. Barry forced a smile; Rosie thought he looked so old and drawn, so different from when she'd first met him and been swept off her feet. She'd been eighteen when the tall, dark, handsome man had entered her life. He'd been twenty years her senior with a devil may care look, and he had dazzled her so much that they'd married in 1964 while she was carrying Ed's baby. The child had been stillborn, but the following year she'd given birth to Gary. He was a special baby, a precious baby, and had grown into a handsome young man who was now lying motionless in intensive care on the cusp of life and death. Barry's eyes were bloodshot; he couldn't believe that his son was dying. What sort of evil being could mug him and leave him to die? He needed sleep but couldn't bring himself to leave Gary's side. Rosie read his thoughts. 'Get some sleep, Barry, I'll come and get you if he wakes up. We both know that he will at some stage, these doctors know nothing.' Reluctantly Barry agreed; she was right, he couldn't keep his eyes open.

Chapter Six

Rosie and Barry continued their vigil at Gary's bedside, but it bore no fruit and Gary remained breathing with the help of the ventilator. Rosie needed someone to blame, and Kevin and Candy were top of her list. She'd been standing outside the hospital taking some air when Kevin showed up. He attempted to console her but Rosie was fuming and kneed him in his groin. 'You were supposed to be taking care of Gary,' she screamed, 'but you were too busy fucking that groupie to go to his aid. No wonder he went outside, he'd hardly want to witness you and her getting it on.'

'You've got it all wrong,' cried Kevin, attempting to straighten up; she'd really knocked the wind out of him. 'I had to speak to Vic, so Gary went outside to open the car up and wait for me.'

'Liar,' screamed Rosie, 'I don't believe that Vic was there unless you were having a threesome.'

Kevin finally managed to get his breath back and stared at Rosie; he could see the pain in her eyes. Rosie dealt him a slap around his face and one of her rings caught his cheek making it bleed. She lashed out a second time smacking him on his mouth and opening up his lip; it was badly split. She continued to rant and rave at him. 'You arsehole, you lying arsehole, excite you, did she, it had to happen at some stage I suppose, you haven't been near a woman since Cathy's death. Everyone thinks you're gay, proving yourself, were you?'

'Stop it,' yelled Kevin, grabbing Rosie by her shoulders.

'Let go of me, you arsehole.'

'Not until you calm down. It was Candy who found Gary.'

'Candy,' screeched Rosie, 'she's well named, her hair's like a stick of candyfloss and what was that line in Lou Reed's *Walk On The Wild Side,* something like she was giving head in the back room and was everybody's darling; it could have been written about her.' Her eyes blazed angrily and Kevin could see the fires of hell in them; she was magnetic even in this state. She was struggling violently to free herself and Kevin could see another knee to his groin was imminent. He was angry now, with her for injuring him, and himself for the lust that was building up inside him. There was only one thing left to do; he brought his lips down on hers passionately. Shocked, Rosie stopped struggling, she could taste the blood from his split lip. She'd been unprepared for this and was even experiencing a guilty pleasure from it. The fight went out of her and she burst into tears.

'It's okay, Rosie,' soothed Kevin. He held her close, murmuring, 'I'm sorry Rosie, I shouldn't have done that, but I didn't know what else to do; I didn't need another knee in my groin.'

Rosie tried to hide her blushes, and pulling away from Kevin she said, 'I'm fine, just leave me alone.'

'But you need to hear me out, Candy was Gary's girlfriend, and the only reason that she was in the building was because she'd gone to the ladies. She was the one who found him in the car park; she was completely traumatised and rushed back to me to tell me to get an ambulance, the poor girl's devastated. She's been sitting by his bed without getting a wink of sleep. They were in love and he'd been planning on bringing her home to meet you.'

'Gary's girlfriend, she can't be, I roughed her up.'

'I know, she rang me last night.'

'Oh God, what have I done. I feel awful and I attacked you too.'

'It's okay, and I'm really sorry that I kissed you.'

'Are you?'

'Yes, I mean no, oh Christ, how can I put this into words, no I'm not, but you're off limits.'

'Let's forget that it happened.'

'Thanks.' Kevin was relieved at her acceptance but wondered if he'd ever forget it.

'I'd better find Candy,' said Rosie, 'I've mega grovelling to do.'

Candy was reading a magazine and was unaware of Rosie's presence until she heard her name being called softly. She looked up and saw Rosie holding two cups of coffee in her hands. For a moment she wondered if the contents were about to be poured over her head and she cringed into the corner of the waiting room. Rosie placed the coffee on the table and held her arms out to the girl who still shrank back.

'Candy, I'm sorry, Kevin's here and he's explained everything, I didn't know that you were with Gary.'

'You're not angry with me?'

'No, it was all my fault, I overreacted; it's just that Gary's been pronounced brain dead and Kevin had promised me that he'd take care of him and I thought that...'

'It's okay, you weren't to know.'

'Rosie.' Ray stood framed in the doorway with Raydon in his arms. 'Your son is hungry; will you please stop running off?'

'I'm coming, this is Candy, she's Gary's girlfriend, not Kevin's; as usual I got the wrong end of the stick.'

'It's okay, shock does funny things to people; you had to hit out at someone and I was closest to hand,' said Candy.

'I hit Kevin too, I split his lip and kneed him in his balls.' Rosie omitted the kiss, but she could still feel his lips upon hers and taste the blood from them. Even in this sad hour, Kevin had ignited passion in her. How disgusting was that, how could she allow such feelings to surface when she should be crying for her son. At that moment she wanted to trade places with Gary, she didn't deserve to live. Raydon started crying and Candy asked if she could hold him, adding that she'd been a nanny for a few weeks previously. 'What happened?' asked Rosie, 'didn't you like the job?'

'I loved it but didn't like what went with it, the husband wanted my duties to extend to other things and I refused him.'

'Sounds like you're well out of it,' said Rosie, placing Raydon in Candy's arms.

'He told his wife that I was coming onto him, so I got the sack, and now, I have no job and no home, nothing in fact. When the band arrived in Plymouth, I followed them around, and that horrible Romany kept chasing me. I hung around with Kevin; he was a gentleman and then Gary arrived and it was love at first sight, we just gelled. He said that he wanted to take me to America, but before that I had to be introduced to you; he said that he loved you more than anyone else in the world. I thought that was so touching, my mum never loved me; she divorced my dad who was a drunk and then she had boyfriend after boyfriend. They always left her eventually and she blamed me, saying that no man wants to take on another man's child. A couple of them abused me, but Mum didn't believe me and said that I was making it up; she said that I was always flaunting myself in front of her boyfriends. One day, she caught her latest boyfriend trying to have sex with me and she threw me out; I was only thirteen.'

'Where did you go?'

'To my gran, but three years later, she died and my mum inherited her house so I was thrown out again.'

'That's inhuman.'

'I got odd jobs, I did anything, cleaning, shop work, anything to earn a crust and then a friend of mine got pregnant. She already had two kids and when her husband walked out on her she offered me board and lodgings to look after her kids. She wanted to go back to work as she had a high paid office job and her nanny had left as she was pregnant herself. So I took over, but a year later, she met someone who had an even higher paid job. He moved in and she became a stay at home mum, so once more, I had nowhere to live. I got a job flipping burgers and rented a room in a shared flat and then I saw this ad for a nanny and bluffed my way into it. I didn't have any qualifications, just my love of children, and you know the rest.' She gazed at Raydon. 'You're gorgeous,' she added, 'I can feed him if you like, is his bottle ready?'

'I breastfeed,' replied Rosie.

'Really, that's unusual in this day and age. Breast milk's the best start that any mother can give her baby.'

'She's loaded with milk, always has been. She's the real deal, an earth mother, look at her dress, the milk's seeping through it now,' laughed Ray.

Candy smiled and handed Raydon back to his mother. 'Well, if you want to express some milk into a jug, I'm sure that the staff would keep it and I could go to the shops and buy a baby's bottle. It would give you a break now and then, you must be exhausted.'

Rosie was taken aback. 'No,' she said, 'I prefer to do it myself, but thanks anyway.'

Candy looked crestfallen. 'Sorry,' she said, 'I'm being too pushy, me and my big mouth.'

'You're not,' replied Rosie. 'It's a nice offer, but what you could do for me is take care of my other son, he won't wake up for me or Barry, maybe he will for you, drink your coffee and then sit with Gary until I've fed and changed Raydon.'

'Can I?'

'Of course, you loved each other, love conquers all.'

Candy's eyes lit up. 'Thanks,' she said, 'thank you so much.'

Rosie picked up her coffee and drained it, then she left the room with Ray saying, 'God, I really screwed up this time, didn't I?'

'We all make mistakes. Your dress is soaked with milk, so tell you what, put Raydon on one breast and I'll suck on the other one.'

'You're an idiot, Ray Lynne, but I love you.'

'And you're a ball breaker.'

'How's that?'

'Well you nearly busted Kevin's.'

'I'll have to apologise.'

'I wouldn't bother, he probably enjoyed it. I don't think his balls have had female contact since Cathy's death.'

'That's awful, Ray, don't laugh at his misfortune.' Rosie followed Ray into their allocated room and put Raydon to her breast. Ray was her everything, but Kevin had released something inside; that kiss was haunting her. After feeding Raydon she returned to her post with Barry, they prayed for a miracle and spoke to him about everything and anything. His baby days, birthdays, Christmases, schooldays, his sister Susie, life in England, sunny days in Los Angeles, sports days, work, Candy, and just about everything they could think of. Talking to him was a necessity; the surgeon had informed them that hearing was the last thing that closes down in a dying person.

Candy was broken-hearted; she'd truly loved Gary and knew that he'd loved her. She didn't know where she was going from here; the band's tour was almost over and Kevin had no interest in her other than as a friend, so she'd probably have to go back to flipping burgers again.

The organ donation squad were once more on their case, and a devastated Barry refused to believe that at some stage he'd have to give his consent to them. Rosie didn't fancy the idea of her son being cut up either, and Ray had no input at all as Gary was nothing to do with him. In the end it was Candy who solved the situation by producing a donor card that Gary carried. Neither Rosie or Barry knew anything about it, but decided that if that was Gary's wish then it needed to be carried out. They continued their vigil but in the end they had to give up, they were defeated and sadly allowed the ventilator to be switched off. They said their goodbyes to him as he was wheeled down to the operating theatre to donate his organs, and then made their way back to their rooms to pack their belongings and Gary's.

Chapter Seven

Two years later

There were many changes in Ray and Rosie's life. Ray was now playing full time with the Z Tones. Kevin had persuaded Vic to bring him on board as Romany was becoming very unreliable and unpredictable. Rosie wasn't exactly happy with the arrangement but seeing that Ray really did want to play with the band, had to back down and swallow hard.

Candy was now a fixture in the Lynne household; she was also Rosie's nanny and the kids loved her. Susie had just turned fifteen and had developed into a real beauty. She was very popular with the boys but she only had eyes for Kevin. She went out regularly with her friend Rachel who lived in Collier Row. Rosie approved of Rachel who was also fifteen and stunning. She was also a sensible girl with jet black hair, a slim figure and a sunny smile. Rachel had a flair for designing dresses and made one for herself and one for Susie for Rosie's fortieth birthday. Susie's was red and Rachel's was black, and they were admired by all at the party.

Raydon was a perfect baby, whilst Bobby was the child from hell; he loved dancing and could dance before he could walk, and he'd bounce around in his playpen holding onto the bars which supported him. Rosie had bought him a baby bouncer which he sat in and pushed his feet off the floor. His little legs never stopped moving, and as soon as he was able to walk he danced even more, driving Ray crazy. Deanne had reached the grand old age of eight, and was every inch her father's child. She was defiant, very temperamental and knew how to get her own way. She was funny too and had everyone in stitches when she talked down to Vic, making him all tied up in knots or exploding with rage. She adored her half brother Eddie, and the two of them were inseparable in the school holidays.

Norma, Rosie's mother, was even more demented; she spoke of her dead husband, and the Rex Cinema which she insisted that she visited everyday, and also said that Ed visited her at night. She took little notice of her grandchildren, apart from Bobby who was the apple of her eye; she'd formed a strong bond with him. Candy had found herself becoming Norma's carer too but she didn't mind, she loved the old lady and listened to her tales of the old days when she was a girl. The only thing that disturbed her was Norma's reference to her night visitor; she slept in the next room to her and often heard her talking to herself.

Sometimes she thought that she heard a second voice but dismissed it as imagination. It didn't help when she told Susie that she thought she'd heard someone playing a guitar and singing. Susie had scared her by saying, 'Oh that's my father, he often visits here.' This really freaked Candy out and she turned to Rosie for reassurance.

'My mother has dementia so she imagines things, and as for Susie, she sees Ed because she wants to.'

'But have you ever seen him?'

'I thought I did once, but at the time I was very tired, it was just after Cathy's funeral. We'd spent a few days with Kevin and had just returned home. I was dozing on the settee and Ray was in the kitchen. I felt a draught on my neck and turned around to see what was causing it. Ed was standing by the window so I got up and walked over to him, we embraced for a while and then he said, 'goodbye Eden's Rose' and vanished. I went back to the settee and dozed until Ray woke me up with a mug of drinking chocolate.'

'So you did see him?'

'I don't know, like I say, I was very tired, I was carrying Raydon at the time, and I could have just dreamt it all.'

'Eden's Rose, I remember that song when it was in the charts.'

'Ed wrote it for me, he will always live on in my heart, but Ray is my husband; he's a good man and more than I deserve really. Oh I'm rattling on, aren't I? Now to get back to what I was saying, my mother is sick and Susie has a very vivid imagination. You have nothing to fear, Ed won't haunt you, I promise.'

Candy smiled but she still felt unsettled.

Ray's bank balance was soaring; he was now in a strong position to provide well for his family and buy them little luxuries. The only fly in the ointment was the touring. When he was away he missed his family so much. Kevin was great company though, he was neither a hell raiser or womaniser which suited Ray down to the ground; he loved the female adulation but had no intention of cheating on his wife.

He'd been thinking about buying a holiday home in the Canary Islands and was going to discuss it with Rosie when he returned home after his tour. After a while his heart began to ache, the separation from Rosie was getting to him. He took solace in the bottle and was soon putting away almost a litre of spirits a night. Kevin tried to restrain him but it was to no avail. Ray's dependence on alcohol was changing his personality. At first he was happy and chatty, switching to silly and stupid, and finally to morose. He told Kevin in no uncertain terms to stay out of his business, so Kevin approached Vic.

'Vic, I'm worried about Ray, he's always pissed and, at night, he drinks himself into oblivion,' said Kevin.

'He's just letting off steam after the show. I'm pleased with him; he doesn't have Romany's attitude but he shares his talent,' replied Vic, wiping his glasses with a filthy handkerchief.

'But he's starting to drink before he goes on stage now.'

'But, it's not affecting his performance, in fact it might be enhancing it.'

'But it could wreck his marriage.'

'Not my problem. The way to solve this is to get Rosie on board; you'd like to sing with her, wouldn't you?'

'Neither Ray nor Rosie would agree.'

'If he's missing her that much, he may have a change of heart.' Vic held his glasses up to the light and added, 'I've decided that if Romany does come back, I'll still keep Ray on board.'

'Does he know that?'

'No, it'll be a nice surprise for him. I'll have a word with Rosie once the tour's over.' Vic replaced his glasses and squinted; they were dirtier than before.

'Rosie won't agree,' said Kevin.

'Just leave it to your Uncle Vic. You'd be great as a vocal duo; you did it with Cathy, and Rosie has a greater vocal range, plus if Ray continues to drink he may become a hardened drinker. It would be good for his image and if he's unconscious at the end of the night, you could get it on with Rosie.'

'Vic, you're disgusting.'

'I've seen the way you look at her; it's like having Cathy back again, isn't it? If you could get your leg over, you would, so would I for that matter.'

'She's happily married.'

'She won't be if he becomes a piss artist. Yes, we need her on board, and you need her under you.'

'That's disgusting too.'

'I've never been interested in anything unless it's underhand, pornographic, illegal, lewd, or disgusting.'

'Rosie's none of those things.'

'I know but she must be good in bed, I knew nothing of her until the memorial concert but I've found out plenty since. Romany's got a big mouth, he tells me all.'

'You're evil.'

'That's right, evil Vic Lee, that's me. Now let's not worry about Ray, he can drink himself into a stupor for all I care. As long as he gives a good performance every night, I'm fine with his drinking. I like a good drink myself; he could be a great drinking buddy. Maybe I could fix him up with a couple of groupies to give him a good time, just imagine what Rosie would do if she found out.'

'She's a good faithful woman, why put her through that?'

'Faithful? Don't make me laugh; have you looked closely at Bobby? He was conceived just before Ed died. Ray never fathered him.'

'Impossible, Ed and Cathy were soul mates, they were devoted to each other.'

'And Ed used to visit the girls, he dipped his wick all right, Bobby's the spitting image of him.'

'You're sick.'

'That's me, sick Vic, come on, Kevin, chill out, I'll have Rosie on board before you can say Jack Robinson. Either Ray will sober up, or Rosie will dump him. What a top vocal duo you could be. Just think about it, Rosie dumps Ray and we dump the rest of the band. They've had their day; you and Rosie could play Vegas, plus all the other venues, top venues, wouldn't that be wonderful?' Kevin said nothing; it was certainly food for thought. Seeing that he'd got Kevin going, Vic dismissed him with a final parting shot. 'Oh and Kevin, just think, Rosie's probably in bed alone at this moment in time. If you play your cards right she could be in yours, great eh?'

Kevin left Vic's room disgusted with him; he was disgusted with himself too. Ray was his best friend, there was no way that he could deceive him but Vic's offer was very tempting; it sounded like heaven. Pushing his thoughts to the back of his mind, he went in search of Ray.

Chapter Eight

On Ray's return, he discussed the idea of a holiday home with Rosie. She thought that it was a good idea as they could escape the English winters if Ray wasn't touring. Three weeks later, the entire family flew over to Lanzarote to view properties. Kevin and Eddie accompanied them as Deanne refused to go if her half brother wasn't included. Finding nothing to suit them, they relocated to Fuerteventura. Rosie liked Correlejo but Ray found it too windy. Norma loved it. 'I always did love Great Yarmouth,' she said, 'but it never used to be this hot.'

'This is the Canary Islands, Nana, it's Spanish,' cried Deanne.

'Oh is it, it used to be called Great Yarmouth. Is there a place where we can get some fish and chips?'

'We'll find you one,' replied Ray. He was indeed a happy man as he was back in the bosom of his family once more.

Their next stop was Tenerife; they viewed many properties in the region of Puerto de la Cruz where the children discovered the delights of Lloro Parque. It was a parrot park but also housed many other animals including performing dolphins and a huge tortoise called Tom. Eddie was fascinated, his pet tortoise was huge but Tom was much larger. 'Why is he so big?' asked Eddie.

'Because he comes from the Galapagos Islands where tortoises are all that size,' replied Kevin.

'Can we go and live there?'

'Afraid not, the islands are for tortoises, not people.'

'If we lived here, could I have a tortoise like that?'

'No, because Wacky would get jealous and so would Daisy, you wouldn't want to upset them, would you, especially now that they're having babies.'

'But the baby tortoises live with Uncle Vic; he's selling them and he's opened up a savings account for me.'

'I didn't know that.'

'He gives some away to the poor people, that's kind of him, isn't it?'

Kevin frowned, kind was not exactly a word that fitted Vic. Eddie's tortoises were producing several clutches of eggs a year, and they were not small clutches. Vic had provided an incubator for the eggs, and Eddie and Deanne had watched a few babies hatch out. It began with the egg chipping, cracks appearing and then a baby tortoise would emerge. Vic was making a fortune; he had opened a savings account for Eddie but little of the profits made their way into it. He repeatedly told Eddie that many of the babies had died, and Eddie, in his innocence, believed him. Kevin had other ideas; Vic was not above fleecing a child.

'I love Daisy and Wacky but it would be great to have a tortoise like Tom,' said Eddie, scrutinizing the huge reptile.

'Well, Ray might buy a home in Tenerife and then you'll be able to visit Tom when you're on holiday.'

Eddie smiled, he loved that idea and prayed that Ray would buy a home in Tenerife and forget going to Gran Canaria which would be their next stop. His prayers were answered as Ray didn't buy in the north of the island, but bought two apartments in the south. It had been a tossup between Paloma Beach and the Costamar, and Rosie couldn't make up her mind so the decision was to buy both. Los Christianos was a beautiful resort, and Ray looked forward to spending some quality time on the island. Paloma Beach was to be their holiday home, and the Costamar rented out. The Costamar was quite old but had a beautiful outlook across the beach and the harbour and, added to that, it was front line so it was impossible to build in front of it. Rosie loved both apartments, and Ray loved his Rosie.

Later that night in their hotel, Ray told Rosie just how much he'd missed her. 'The money's great, the adulation is nice, but nothing compares to being with you,' he murmured. 'I love you more than life, and tonight I want your full concentration because I'm going to make love to you until you scream out to me to stop.'

Rosie smiled and said, 'Less talk, more action.' If that was what Ray wanted, she wasn't about to argue.

The following morning after breakfast, Rosie noted just how lovesick Candy appeared in Kevin's presence. Her sad eyes watched his every move, and Rosie decided to play matchmaker.

'Why don't you tell him how you feel?' she asked.

'Because it's only a short while since Gary died.'

'Gary would want you to move on, and I feel sure that he'd approve of Kevin. You're grieving for Gary, and Kevin's still mourning for Cathy; he needs a nice girl to help him move on.'

'He might reject me.'

'And he might not, so tonight Ray and I will take care of the kids; it's time that you had a night out.'

'He might not want my company.'

'Leave it to me.'

The conversation ended when Susie burst into the room in a very short sundress. 'What do you think?' she said twirling around revealing her bikini bottoms.

'Very nice,' said Rosie.

'Too short,' snapped Ray, 'the Spanish men are very hot-blooded, and that outfit could cause them to burst a few blood vessels; you need to cover up and not flaunt yourself.'

'But everyone else dresses like this.'

'You're not everyone else and you're only fifteen.'

'Mum, what do you think?'

'You look lovely, but Ray is right.'

'It's the eighties, girls dress like this when they're on holiday. I want to go to Playa de las Americas, there's lots of clubs there.'

Kevin entered the room and sauntered over, causing Susie to blush as he stared at her. She stared back with intense longing.

'Hi princess,' he said, 'you look nice, are you going to the beach?'

Susie lowered her eyes. 'I was, but Ray said I should cover up.'

'Ray's right for two reasons. One you might get sunburn and, two, we don't want the Spanish guys chatting you up.'

Susie was crestfallen; it had been Kevin that she'd wanted to impress. She wished that she was older, maybe if she was, he might notice her. Kevin cupped her under her chin and gazed into her eyes. 'Princess, you are a beautiful young girl and one day, you'll meet the right guy and settle down and get married, but until then you need to cover up a bit more.'

'Am I really beautiful, Kevin?' asked Susie, drowning in his eyes.

'You are the most beautiful girl in the world,' replied Kevin.

'Course you are,' said Ray, 'look at your mother.'

'Will you take me to Playa de las Americas one night? I promise that I'll cover up. We could dance the night away.'

'Maybe we'll all go one night.' Kevin was getting very uncomfortable in the trouser department. He was standing right next to Rosie. Vic had been right, if Ray were off the scene, he'd certainly make a move. Guilt washed over him; Ray was his friend and here he was lusting after his wife. 'See you later,' he said, 'I'm off to Lloro Parque again with Eddie and Deanne, Eddie wants to see Tom.'

At that moment, Susie hated her outfit. She'd wanted to impress Kevin and she'd done the opposite. She watched as he walked away; he'd said that she was beautiful so maybe she needed to dress down a bit. She'd seen a dress in a shop window a few days ago which was white and floaty. Walking over to Ray, she said, 'I'm sorry that I upset you. I saw a beautiful dress the other day; can I have it?'

'Does it cover you up?'

'Yes, it's even got a mandarin collar, please can I have it?'

She threw her arms around him and gave him a hug. Ray kissed the top of her head. 'Course you can, baby. We'll have a few hours on the beach, have lunch, come home for a siesta, and then hit the shops when they reopen at four.'

'Thanks Ray, you're the best stepdad in the world. I'll get out of this outfit and change into something more suitable.' Susie was a happy bunny and, singing, she rushed off to get changed.

She got her dress and paraded around in front of everyone in it. It really suited her and made her look older, causing everyone to voice their approval. Susie couldn't wait to see Kevin's reaction, but when he returned he seemed totally disinterested. He was tired, owing to the travelling time between the south and north of the island, and he'd missed dinner too. Eddie and Deanne had had lunch but he'd not bothered, thinking that he'd be back in time for dinner.

He voiced his feelings to Rosie, stating that he was starving. Rosie smiled and said, 'Well there's plenty of good restaurants on the island.'

'I know but I don't fancy eating on my own.'

'Candy must be hungry, she missed dinner too; she'd fallen asleep and I didn't want to wake her.'

Susie seized her chance. 'I'll go with you if Candy doesn't want to go, I didn't eat all of my dinner,' she cried.

Candy emerged from the balcony. 'I'm starving,' she said. She'd deliberately missed dinner after Rosie saying that Kevin would most probably miss the evening meal as both Eddie and Deanne would keep him hanging about. Her ploy had worked and now she was about to spend a hopefully romantic meal with the man of her dreams. 'So am I,' replied Kevin, 'I'll go and clean up and we'll hot foot it to a restaurant.'

A petulant Susie pulled a sulky face. 'Can I come too?'

'Not this time, princess, you should eat your meals; this trip is costing Ray a small fortune, and the least you can do is eat up your food.'

A furious Susie made for her room. She'd wanted Kevin to admire her, not give her a dressing down. Tears were filling her eyes; she was hurting badly until Kevin called her back. 'Love the dress, Susie, you truly are the most beautiful girl in the world. When we all go to Playa de las Americas, I'll keep you on the dance floor all night, and I won't let any young Spanish buck get close to you.'

Susie blushed. 'Really?' she said, perking up.

'Yes, if anyone tries, I'll say, hands off, this is my princess Susie.'

'What's a buck?' queried Deanne, screwing up her face.

'It's a young male,' replied Eddie, pulling a smug face.

'Fuck, fuck, fuck,' cried Bobby, jumping up and down with glee.

'Stop that at once,' snapped Ray.

'Fuck you,' cried Bobby, spinning round and round.

Rosie slapped his legs and was rewarded with a punch to her stomach. Ray had had enough and carted the unrelenting child to the bedroom. Several slaps later, Bobby settled down in floods of tears, screaming, 'Want Nana.'

Norma rushed into the bedroom and took the sobbing child into her arms. 'Nana loves you,' she cried, 'come with me, I bought some nice sweets today, you can have some and then I'll read you a bedtime story.'

Bobby stopped crying and, getting to his feet, he followed Norma to her room. 'Mother,' shouted Rosie, 'he needs punishing, not rewarding.'

Norma turned back. 'You don't understand, Rosie, the poor lamb's lost his father, he needs loving, not slapping,' then she went into her room with Bobby and closed the door.

Ray was incensed. Here was yet another reference to Bobby's true parentage, and in front of Kevin too. He stared at Rosie with anger blazing from his eyes. 'I'm going out, expect me when you see me,' he yelled, then went out slamming the door behind him.

Kevin was alarmed. 'Shall I go after him?' he asked. Ray had never walked out on his wife before.

'No, he just needs to cool down; my mother's illness makes her say things like that now and again, she's confused,' replied Rosie. All eyes were upon her and, scooping up Raydon into her arms, she went into her bedroom.

Deanne shrugged her shoulders saying, 'All I asked was, what's a buck, and we get an all family fight.'

'Aunty Rose is upset, Bobby's very naughty. When I'm naughty, I get punished but Bobby gets sweets,' replied Eddie.

'Yes, but my nana is loop the loop, let's go and play, I bought some skittles yesterday, let's see who can knock the most over.'

'But maybe we should go and see if she's all right.'

'We'll check later, she likes to be on her own when Ray and her argue.'

'But she might...'

'I'll check on her before we leave; you go and play,' said Kevin. Candy was upset. These rows were nothing new, and Ray was responsible for most of Bobby's bad language. At night she would often hear Ray shout, 'That's all you and Ed ever did, fuck, fuck, fuck, and Bobby's the fucking result', and then she'd hear Rosie crying. She could never intervene; after all she was just the hired help. Kevin made his way to the bathroom and splashed some water on his face, then, returning to Candy he said, 'Keep an eye on the kids and I'll go to my room and change. When I come back, I'll check on Rosie and, after that, sweet lady, we'll go and eat.'

Candy complied; she'd agree to anything that he said.

Kevin left the room seething; he hated to see Rosie treated this way. Ray was becoming paranoid, it was ridiculous; if he really believed that Bobby wasn't his and it was driving him mad, why stay in his marriage. He was being a complete bastard. Poor

Rosie was in a no win situation, she loved Ray and Bobby, plus she was trying to cope with Norma's dementia. How could Ray treat her this way? If he had her, he'd be prepared to take on all of her family. Ray needed to stop drinking and put his demons to rest, or it would be only a matter of time before he stepped in and spoke his mind. He wasn't going to stand by and see Rosie belittled; he loved her even if Ray didn't.

Vic's idea of the vocal duo was becoming more attractive as the days went on. If he could hold Rosie in his arms for just one night, he'd die a happy man. His stomach rumbled; he needed to eat, so, rummaging around in his wardrobe, he found an outfit suitable for the evening. Putting on some aftershave and admiring himself in the mirror, he went back to Candy.

Chapter Nine

'You look nice,' said Candy, opening the door to Kevin. She felt her pulse pick up as she stared at his killer body. It wasn't just his fair attractive features that were turning her legs to jelly, it was also the liveliness in his eyes and his very expressive mouth. He was dressed in a blue check shirt which he'd unbuttoned owing to the heat, and stone washed denim jeans.

He would have liked to return the compliment, but couldn't as Candy looked a mess. Her blonde candyfloss hair had been backcombed making it look ten times worse, and her makeup was caked onto her face. The bright red lipstick and peacock blue eye shadow made her look very tarty, and her rouge was comparable to a pantomime dame's. Her dress sense was no better; her short red dress was almost revealing her knickers, and to complete her ensemble she'd put on a pair of white high heels and carried a yellow clutch bag. Kevin brushed past her. 'Kids okay?' he muttered.

'Yes, Bobby's still with Norma, and Deanne and Eddie are knocking down skittles.'

'I'll check on Rosie.' Kevin was already halfway to Rosie's door. Candy was hurt, she'd made such an effort to get herself looking nice and Kevin was only concerned with the kids and Rosie. Still, the night was young and anything could happen.

Kevin opened Rosie's door, the room was in darkness and baby Raydon was slumbering in his cot. Rosie lay on her side with her back turned to Kevin and stirred when the door opened. Kevin sat on the edge of her bed. 'Can I do anything?' he whispered.

Rosie shook her head and sat up. 'I'm getting up in a minute,' she replied, switching on the bedside lamp.

Kevin stared at her tearstained face and held out his arms to her. She melted into his embrace and sobbed into his shoulder. 'There, there,' soothed Kevin as if he were comforting a baby, 'everything's fine. Norma didn't know what she was saying, dementia's an evil illness, and Ray will be back soon once he's cooled down.'

'Will he? Sometimes I think he hates me.'

'He adores you.'

'Does he?' Rosie pulled free. 'You must be starving, so must Candy, don't keep her waiting.'

'I'm not going while you're in this state; I'll wait till Ray comes home.'

'No, go and enjoy yourselves, it's time that Candy had a night off, go and put a spring in her step, she needs some fun.'

'If you're sure.'

'Positive, now go, its bad manners to keep a lady waiting.'

Candy wasn't exactly what Kevin would describe as a lady but she was a sweet girl and a hungry one too. He emerged from Rosie's room saying, 'I just want to say goodbye to the kids.'

'Okay,' replied Candy. At this rate they'd be eating breakfast.

Eddie and Deanne were now playing I Spy and looked up when Kevin appeared. 'Bye you two, I must go, my stomach thinks that my throat's been cut.'

'Why?' asked Deanne.

'Because I'm starving.'

'Then why didn't you say so, grownups are so weird. Are you taking Candy out?'

'Yes, why?'

'Just wondered. Will you sleep with her tonight?'

'Deanne, I heard that,' cried Candy, standing framed in the doorway. 'What gave you that idea?'

'Well I just thought that you might, because if you sleep in Kevin's bed, Eddie won't be able to sleep in his own bed, so he'll have to share mine, I like sleeping with him, we cuddle up together, don't we Eddie?'

Eddie said nothing, he was concentrating on what to spy next. Bobby came bounding into the room. 'Want Mummy,' he said.

'She's in bed,' replied Deanne.

'Want Mummy to dance,' replied Bobby jumping up and down and then landing in the splits.

'She'll dance with you later,' said Deanne, 'she always dances if Ray upsets her, she says dancing releases endorphins.'

Kevin was amazed; that was something that he hadn't known, and he was also dumbfounded by Bobby's very supple body. The child appeared to be a contortionist. He was now lying on his belly with his back arched and touching his head with his feet.

Norma emerged from her room. 'I've got chocolate,' she cried.

'Not hungry,' replied Eddie and Deanne in unison.

'Then I'll eat it myself,' said Norma. 'I'm off to bed.'

Bobby was on his way to Rosie's room. 'Mummy dance,' he cried and opened the door.

'Ray doesn't like it when I sleep with Eddie,' said Deanne.

'That's because you're related,' replied Kevin.

'So?'

'You'll understand when you're older.'

'Everyone says that, I'll be glad when I am older then I'll know what they all mean.'

Kevin laughed, swept Deanne up into his arms and swung her around. 'Don't change, darling, you are one special little girl, and I love you to bits.'

'As much as Susie.'

'Yes.'

'But you have to love one more than the other.'

'No I don't.'

'Then maybe when I grow up, you'll love me more than Susie.'

'We'll have to have this conversation another time. I need to go now or I'll starve to death, see you later, bye.' Finally Kevin and Candy left the building and, as they got into the lift, Kevin questioned Candy about how often Ray and Rosie argued.

Candy felt a bit awkward, and had to be careful what she said. 'Well, they don't argue that often but when they do, it's very volatile. She copes by dancing, saying, as Deanne says, that it releases the endorphins in her body, otherwise known as the happy hormones.'

'Does he hit her?'

'I don't think so, but he's got a vicious tongue. Norma winds him up a lot about Bobby but her gobbledegook means nothing. I love Rosie, she's like a mum to me, and Ray's a good man but lately he's been drinking a lot more and his attitude to Bobby is becoming disturbing. Bobby loves Ray and doesn't understand why Raydon's treated better; still it's none of my business.'

'Are you sure that he doesn't hit her because if he does I'll...'

'You'll what?'

'Nothing, let's get out of here and find somewhere to eat. We could eat here in Los Christianos but Rosie says that Playa de las Americas has some of the best restaurants on the island.'

The lift doors opened and the couple got out. 'We passed a place called Banana Garden today; it's a night club as well,' said Candy.

'With night club prices,' said Kevin. 'I don't want to spend a small fortune, I just want to eat.'

'Of course,' replied Candy, 'but I just thought I'd mention it.' She felt as if he'd had a swipe at her; she wasn't after him having to spend loads of money on her, she just wanted a good time.

They bumped into Ray as they headed for the taxi rank; he was staggering a bit. 'Rosie okay?' he grunted.

'I think so, she was in bed but she's probably dancing with Bobby now because he was going in to see her when we left.'

'Great, you two going out?'

'Yep.'

'Have a good time then, I guess I'll have to endure the Rosie and Bobby floorshow before I go to bed. Norma definitely needs to go into a home but Rosie won't allow it. She loves her mother too much, trouble is, she loves everyone, that's all she does, give love and in return, what do I give her? Shit, that's what I give her, I should be strung up.'

'She loves you, Ray.'

'And I love her; I'd kill anyone that came near her. Christ, I'm beginning to sound like that arsehole Ed Gold; I've got to stop giving her grief or I'll drive her away.'

'Have you been drinking?'

'I've had a few, what's it got to do with you, or are you my father all of a sudden?'

'Kevin,' Candy was tugging on his arm, 'I'm hungry,' she bleated. Her stomach was rumbling badly.

'Yes, go and eat, ignore me as I'm pissed,' and Ray turned on his heel and walked away back to the hotel.

Kevin was warming to Candy; she was very funny and warm. They had an enjoyable evening and, after a nice meal of peppered steak, chips and vegetables, they headed for the Veronicas strip in Playa de las Americas. After perusing several bars, they finished their night up by going dancing. Candy was in seventh heaven; they'd had several slow dances and she'd adored the feel of Kevin's arms around her. Walking out onto the beach, they stared out at the ocean. It was a lovely night, warm and balmy. The Z Tones were virtually unknown in the Canaries; they'd just never taken off over there and Kevin loved the freedom of being able to walk around unrecognised. 'Penny for them,' said Candy, noticing that Kevin had a faraway look in his eyes.

'I was just wondering how Rosie was,' replied Kevin.

'Probably lying in Ray's arms,' said Candy, 'they have a fantastic sex life.'

'How do you know that?'

'My room is a couple of doors away from theirs, and sometimes the noises coming from their room are ear splitting.'

'Really.' Kevin was disturbed, he was beginning to feel jealous of Ray, and his own feelings were getting more intense each day. He smiled and added, 'I worked here in the seventies with Cathy; we were known as Platinum.'

'I remember you both on Top of the Pops.'

'That's right, Vic had great plans for us but then Vic has many plans when it comes to money. When the time was right, he dropped me and got Cathy singing with Ed. That was the end of Platinum.'

The couple had bought a bottle of champagne from the bar and taken a couple of glasses. They sat on a couple of sun loungers and demolished the champagne in record time, after that, they made small talk and gazed around them.

'I reckon Ray's made a good decision buying in Tenerife,' said Kevin, 'I doubt that Gran Canaria would have been able to improve on his purchase.'

'Plus Eddie has Tom.'

'That was the clincher,' laughed Kevin, 'come on, let's find a taxi.'

Back at the hotel, a slightly tipsy Kevin invited Candy in for a coffee. He thanked her for her company, and a starry-eyed Candy leapt at the offer to be alone with him. They drank their coffee out on the balcony and stared out at the deserted swimming pool and various sun loungers, some with towels already on them. 'Germans,' laughed Kevin, 'they do this all the time just to take possession of a sun lounger for sunbathing. Cathy used to find it hilarious.'

'You really loved her, didn't you?'

'With all my heart and soul, but it was Ed that she wanted. She committed suicide after the memorial concert when she knew that I'd be at a party. She'd planned it for weeks; she had terminal cancer and had told nobody. Everyone thought she had gallstones apart from her sister-in-law and she was sworn to secrecy.'

'How awful for you.'

'I found her stone cold on her bed; she'd left me a note, leaving custody of Eddie to me. I do my best for him but sometimes I think that it's not enough. It's a blessing that Rosie came into our lives because now he has a female who cares for him too.'

'But don't you think that you should have someone for yourself?'

'No, whoever I became involved with would always be number two in my life; my heart still belongs to Cathy and always will.'

'Some girls would put up with that, if they loved you enough.'

'It wouldn't be fair; shall I put on some music?'

'Yes please.' Candy was excited, Kevin was baring his soul to her. Another coffee later accompanied by Elton John, Rod Stewart and the Eagles, Candy plucked up the courage to ask Kevin for a dance. He agreed and they smooched for a while. She raised her head and gazed into Kevin's blue eyes, this was her chance and as he bent his head to speak to her, she pulled him in closer and kissed him full on the lips. He was silent as Candy said, 'I wouldn't mind being number two in your affections. I believe that if Gary had lived, we would have been married by now but he's gone and so is Cathy. I've grieved for so long, and Rosie says it takes time to move on and go forward, she says that Gary would want that. Just give me a chance and I'll make you happy. I know that I can do it and I know that I'll be a poor second to Cathy, but I can give you all the love that I possess.'

'You can't live in someone else's shadow.'

'I'll gladly do it, I love you so much, what have you go to lose? If it doesn't work out, I'll understand.'

Kevin was lost for words; he'd been unprepared for this. He looked at the girl before him; she was sweet with her crazy candyfloss hair, petite figure, and soulful brown eyes.

'I can't put you in that position.'

'Okay, so you don't love me, it doesn't matter, I can keep you warm at night. I've got enough love for both of us.'

Kevin pushed her away. 'I can't, Candy.'

Candy's eyes filled with tears. 'I suppose it's because of the way that we met, you probably think that I was a groupie and I've never been one. I've always loved the band and followed them, and when my friend's brother got a job as a roadie; he managed to get me backstage several times. You never noticed me but that awful Romany did, he never gave up and then Gary turned up and my life began to change for the better.'

'I did notice you, you dressed a bit tarty but then most of the girls that came backstage did. They thought it was the best way to get noticed, and believe me it's not. Dress like that and you attract the Romanys of this world who will use you and discard you after one night.'

'Gary didn't discard me.'

'Because he fell for you, it wouldn't have made any difference if you'd been wearing a bin liner. Underneath your tarty appearance, you're a lady and you don't realise it.'

'I could change, I'll cut my hair and take it back to its natural shade. I could get Rosie to give me advice on how to dress. I'll do anything, Kevin, and I'll even let you into a secret, one that I've told nobody else apart from Gary.'

'Secrets are meant to be kept.'

'I want to tell you as long as you don't laugh at me.'

'Of course I won't laugh, let's have a drink.'

'Okay.' Candy sat fidgeting as Kevin poured them out some white rum and pineapple. She perched on the edge of his bed as Kevin offered her her drink and sat down beside her.

'Now I'm all ears,' he said.

Candy blushed and said, 'I was a virgin when I met Gary.'

'Lucky man, I've never had one, I bet Gary was over the moon about it.'

'He was. He said he couldn't believe how lucky he was.'

Seeing how embarrassed Candy was, Kevin tried to make light of the situation. 'So if I had noticed you first and come on to you, I would have netted myself a virgin; it's every man's dream.'

'Really?'

'Yes, every man wants to be first. I remember Ray telling me that he'd first met Rosie when he was eleven and that it had been love at first sight.'

'So why didn't they get together?'

'Because of Ed Gold. He'd known Rosie since she was seven, and from that day forth, she became his possession. Ray stole a kiss from Rosie on his sixteenth birthday, and when Ed discovered them together, he rode off on Ray's motorbike and smashed it up, just to get back at him. He beat him up too and knocked him out cold, some birthday present.'

'God, was he a nutter?'

'Many would say so. Now, you finish your drink off, we've had a great evening and you've been lovely company but if you don't go soon, I might do something that we'll both regret in the morning.'

'Can we dance some more?' Candy was stalling.

'Okay, we'll have two and then you leave, is that a deal?'

'Suppose so, maybe we can go out another time.'

'That would be lovely, but just remember, I'm not into one night stands, and I'm neither Romany nor Ed Gold.'

Defeated, Candy drained her glass and soon found herself in Kevin's arms dancing to 10CC's *I'm Not In Love* followed by The Moody Blues' *Nights In White Satin*.

Candy clung to Kevin, whispering, 'I love you, Kevin, just give me one night; if you don't want me in the morning, I'll understand.'

'I'm not going to use you.'

'I want you to; I've not been with anyone since Gary died.'

She tilted her head back and gazed into his eyes; hers were soft and yielding. Kevin wanted her to leave for her own sake but at the same time was in the same position. He'd not made love to a woman since Cathy's death in January 1983, it was now 1986 and he had needs too. The only time that lust had reared its head had been when he'd been in Rosie's company, so maybe this wouldn't hurt; Candy and he were two lonely souls who had lost a loved one.

'You're sure that you want to do this, Candy, whatever the outcome?'

'Yes, it would make me so happy.'

'I think that you deliberately skipped your evening meal in order to trap me.'

'Are you angry?'

'No, I'm flattered. My father once told me that if a woman sets a trap, there's only one thing to do.'

'What's that?'

'Walk right into it,' laughed Kevin, and pushed the gypsy style top of her dress down.

'Oh,' cried Candy, 'can we turn the lights out?'

'Why?'

'Because my tits are almost non-existent; I'm built more like a boy in that department.'

'Let me see.' Kevin had forced the top right down and Candy's tiny breasts surfaced. 'They're perfect, darling, just like you.'

'You're not disappointed?'

'No, you're a tiny girl, so if you had huge breasts, you'd be top heavy. It's not important, if you want the lights off we'll turn them off but I want to look at you.'

'Leave them on then,' said Candy as Kevin's lips came down on hers; lust was taking over both of them.

Once she was naked, Kevin held her at arm's length. 'You're beautiful,' he cried, 'truly beautiful.' Picking her up, he was amazed how light she was; it was like carrying a child. Putting her down on the bed, he stripped off and covered her in kisses. Candy was in ecstasy, as at last he was about to become hers even if it was only for one night. Kevin took her gently, making her heart sing, and then they fell asleep in each other's arms.

'I love you, Kevin,' murmured Candy as her eyes began to droop.

'You'd better,' replied Kevin, 'and tomorrow you can go shopping with Rosie.'

'Shopping?'

'Yes, if we're to become an item, young lady, I want you to be dressed as befits a lady.'

'An item?'

'That's right, Candy, I told you I'm not into one night stands.' Candy wept tears of joy and then drifted off into a contented sleep.

Chapter Ten

The following morning, Candy woke up feeling refreshed; she kissed Kevin and he awoke. Rolling her over onto her back he made love to her straight away. It was over very quickly and he apologised. 'Bit one sided, wasn't it?' he said. 'I'll make it up to you later.'

'Later? I thought that you were joking last night when you spoke of us being an item.'

'I don't joke about things like that; it is time that I moved on. I'll go and see Rosie a bit later and give her some money to pay for some new clothes for you. I want to see the back of your tarty image; you can visit the hairdressers too and get your tangled mane sorted.'

'What colour do you want me to choose?'

'Your own natural shade.'

'It's mousey.'

'I don't care, natural and classy, that's what I like.'

'Okay.'

'Go and run the shower.'

'I can have one when I get back to my room.'

'You can have one here, I'll get under it with you.'

'But Rosie...'

'Rosie can wait, so can the kids, I'm your priority from now on.'

'You're so masterful.'

'I can be, now go and run that shower.'

Once back in Ray and Rosie's abode, Candy felt all eyes on her. Susie viewed her with suspicion. 'Have you been out all night?' she asked.

Candy blushed and nodded. Deanne looked up from her book. 'I hope you took precautions,' she said, her eyes boring into Candy.

'Deanne,' cried Rosie, 'how do you know about such things?'

'Well, I heard you and Ray talking the other night about you not having any more babies and he said that he was sick of taking precautions.'

Ray choked on his coffee. 'You were supposed to be asleep,' he said.

'Well I wasn't. You said that using a condom was like taking a bath with your mac on.'

'What's a condom?' asked Eddie.

'Dunno,' replied Deanne, 'but I think it stops ladies having babies.'

'What does it look like?'

'I don't know, I'm only eight, ask Ray.' Ray spluttered into his coffee a second time.

'Why do you take a bath with your mac on?' asked Norma.

Ray got to his feet. 'I'm off to see Kevin,' he said.

'You see,' said Deanne. 'Ray is now doing what he always does, saying nothing and leaving everyone guessing.'

'Condom, condom,' shouted Bobby turning head over heels on the rug.

Candy shot Rosie a sympathetic look. 'Come on, kids, the weather's beautiful,' she said. 'Let's go out and give Mummy a break.'

'But I want to see Ray in the bath in his mac,' cried Eddie.

'Forget Ray, I'll buy you a strawberry ice cream,' said Candy.

'Great,' replied Eddie. 'Come on Dee Dee, we can go in the swimming pool.'

'Okay,' said Deanne putting her book down. 'There's no peace in this place, it's just like home.'

'I fancy a paddle,' said Norma. 'I do love Great Yarmouth.'

Susie felt dejected; she'd had a row with Rosie over nothing and stormed off. It was obvious what had happened between Candy and Kevin, and it had destroyed her. She was almost sixteen and beautiful, so why didn't Kevin take her seriously? Candy wasn't even pretty, so how could Kevin want her. She wandered off to the beach alone and sat at the edge of the sea with her feet in the water. Her heart felt as if it were about to burst, life was so unfair. She began to throw pebbles into the sea, wishing that she was aiming them at Candy's skull. Unaware that a predator was watching her, she started screaming 'I hate you' as she launched each stone.

Susie was quite unaware of the stranger's presence until he was right behind her and said, 'Hola senorita, como estas?' Susie looked up; it was the waiter who worked at a nearby bar that her family frequented.

'May I sit beside you?' asked the intruder that had invaded all of Susie's angry thoughts.

She wanted to tell him to go away; she was sunk in her misery. Instead she said, 'It's a free country.'

'And a beautiful one, almost as beautiful as you.'

Susie blushed. 'You're Vidal, aren't you? You wait at our table most times when we visit your bar.'

'Correct. Can I help you? You look so sad and angry.'

'Nobody can.'

'Has someone upset you? If they have I will kill them, it hurts me to see you crying.'

'Why?'

'Because you are a lovely young woman, you need love not tears.' Susie loved flattery, she was suddenly attracted to this dark and handsome young man.

'Lovely? Shame Kevin doesn't think so.'

'How old are you?'

'Nearly sixteen.'

'A beautiful age, this Kevin must be blind.' Vidal was taken aback, he'd thought she was older; that had put a stop to a bit of rumpy pumpy. He wasn't about to fall out with the girl's parents as they tipped him well, plus he had his eye on the girl's mother. Apart from waiting on tables, he was a professional gigolo and brilliant at making the older ladies part with their money. He was a thief too and made a good living from that as well.

'Do you live in Tenerife all the time?' asked Susie, who was now taking an interest in the swarthy gentleman sitting beside her.

'No, I spend a lot of my time in England. My mother lives there; we are travellers, so I have the best of both worlds.'

'Travellers? Are you talking fairgrounds, carousels, waltzers and fortune tellers?'

'I am.'

'What an exciting life you must lead.'

'Sometimes it is and sometimes it isn't. I'm staying here at the moment because I wanted to spend some time with my father who lives in the Torres Del Sol.'

'On the new beach?'

'That is correct, I can take you there if you like.' Vidal was feeding Susie lie after lie. He hadn't seen his mother for over ten years; he didn't know where she was and couldn't care less. As for the traveller story, he'd found that, just like Susie, the girls were fascinated by it and usually fell into bed with him on the promise of travelling with him and the fair on his return to England.

'I'd love to travel, my Uncle Rusty lives in a caravan, he loves it. He says that there is nothing better than the open road,' said Susie.

'And he is right. If you leave me your address, I could look you up next time I am in England.'

'That would be lovely, thank you.'

'My pleasure, would you like to go for a drink?'

'Maybe we could go another time, I'll have to ask my parents.'

'Why? You are almost sixteen. They needn't know, it can be our little secret.'

A thrill ran through Susie. This man was dangerous, she could feel it. She liked dangerous, it was exciting. Vidal took her hand and kissed it. 'Then if you do not want to go for a drink today, maybe you will tomorrow. I will meet you here at four o'clock; we can go for a drink and then go and visit my father.'

'I don't know.'

'Are you a young beautiful woman or a little girl?'

'A young woman, okay, I'll meet you tomorrow but I must go now. I was very disrespectful to my mother earlier and I need to apologise.'

'That is very good, you only have one mother and you should take care of her and not answer back.'

'My mother said that you reminded her of David Essex,' said Susie, getting to her feet, 'I don't remember him.'

'That is indeed a compliment,' replied Vidal, 'he was very handsome when he was younger.' He took Susie's hands in his own and kissed them. 'Until tomorrow then, Susie.'

'I didn't tell you my name, how do you know it?'

'I wait on your table when you come to the bar, and when I see a beautiful woman like yourself, I take the trouble to find out.'

Susie blushed; she wanted to see more of this young handsome Spanish boy. 'See you tomorrow,' she said, 'I really must go now.'

'Okay, guapa.'

'Woppa, am I fat?'

'No, that is a Spanish word, it means very beautiful.' Susie was tingling inside as she left Vidal. She was scared but excited, her dance with the devil had begun. He waited until she was out of sight and then threw several pebbles into the sea. 'Rich stupid bitch,' he said out loud, 'just my type.'

Later that day, she accompanied her mother and Candy to the hairdressers and dress shops. She watched in amazement as

Candy's blonde frizzy hair was taken back to her base colour and cut and styled into a shiny bob. Candy hadn't exactly been at the front of the queue when looks were handed out, and as far as Susie was concerned, she looked plainer than ever. Surely Kevin would ditch her now, but she was wrong. Kevin loved Candy's new look and thanked Rosie for the transformation. Susie was distraught. How could Kevin prefer this flat-chested plain creature to her? She needed to speak to her mother, but would leave it until the following day. Her encounter with Vidal had filled her with excitement, and that night she fell asleep dreaming of him.

The following day, Susie waited until Candy had taken the children and Norma out, and then approached her mother. Rosie was bathing Raydon and looked up as Susie came into the room. 'I thought you'd gone out,' she said.

'No, I needed to speak to you. Are Candy and Kevin an item?'

Rosie poured some shampoo onto Raydon's head and lathered it up. 'I really don't know, Susie, why?'

'Well Candy's so plain, he could do better.'

'Beauty is in the eye of the beholder. Take a look at Barry's new wife, she's plainer than a pikestaff but Barry adores her.'

'Am I ugly?'

'You know you're not; what is all this about?'

'Then why doesn't Kevin...'

'Why doesn't Kevin turn to you instead of Candy?' said Rosie, finishing Susie's sentence. Susie blushed crimson and looked at the floor. Rosie rinsed the shampoo from Raydon's hair and said, 'the reason is that he respects you. He's a decent human being and entitled to go with whom he likes, besides you're only fifteen.'

'I'll be sixteen soon.'

'Yes, but Kevin sees you as a beautiful young lady, one who needs protecting from the evils of this world.'

'How old were you when you dated my father?'

'Fifteen.'

'So why am I different?'

'Because the whole situation is different; your father and I grew up together and we became childhood sweethearts.'

'So how old were you when you first had sex?'

'What kind of question is that to ask your mother?'

'One that demands an honest answer.'

'Oh is it?' Rosie lifted Raydon from the bath and wrapped him in a white fluffy bath towel. 'I'm not sure that I want to give it.'

'Mum, we need to talk, my whole world has collapsed.'

'Okay, I take it that you don't want Ray to overhear our girl talk, do you?'

'No.' Susie was tapping her fingers on the window sill; she wanted to be far away from the hotel, sunbathing with only her mother as her companion.

Rosie began towelling Raydon dry. 'Right,' she said, 'Ray can look after this young man. I'll get Raydon dressed and take him in to Ray, he's still in bed.'

'You've worn him out again, he's even missed breakfast.'

'Is it that obvious?'

'Well you keep me awake sometimes, you're just like a couple of teenagers; here, let me dress Raydon,' and Susie held out her arms to her younger sibling.

Rosie handed Raydon to Susie. 'Be my guest,' she said, 'I'll just go and get his clothes.' She walked to her bedroom and opened the door. Ray was snoring his head off, but stirred as Rosie entered the room. 'Come back to bed,' he grunted.

'No,' replied Rosie, 'today's a bonding day, I'm going out with Susie and you are going to spend a few hours bonding with your son.'

'What time's breakfast?'

'You've missed it.'

'Shit, I'll have to eat out.'

'Good thinking.'

'I'd rather have you for breakfast.'

'You can have me later, but right now, I'm going out with Susie.'

'Why can't we go together?'

'I told you, today's a bonding day, besides, Susie and I need to talk about things that men don't understand.'

'Then you can definitely count me out, that's one conversation that I don't need, girl talk. I can't think of anything worse.'

'I can, boy's talk.'

'Okay, you win, is Raydon dressed?'

'No, he's just come out of the bath and he smells delightful.'

Rosie rummaged around in the chest of drawers and found Raydon's little royal blue dungarees, white socks, and red t-shirt, then picking up the child's sandals from the floor, she made her way back to Susie who was cuddling her little brother and crooning in his ear. The child clapped his hands. He was a picture of happiness; his bright blue eyes sparkled and he chuckled away merrily. Susie stroked his hair which was now dry. 'His hair's such a beautiful colour, it's really blonde,' she said.

'That's what happens when you put two blonde people together, he's a real little cherub,' replied Rosie, putting her son's white ankle socks onto his tiny feet. She handed the rest of his clothes to Susie who set to dressing the happy little chap. Minutes later he was dressed and dispatched to his father who was still in bed.

Ray opened his arms to his son and held him to him. 'How's Daddy's best boy?' he cried. Rosie looked on; they made a charming picture.

'See you later,' she said, closing the bedroom door behind her.

After a leisurely stroll to the beach and a refreshing orange juice, Rosie and Susie sat on a couple of huge rocks and stared out to sea. The Gomera ferry passed by, and several passengers could be seen waving from the deck. Susie swallowed hard and then said, 'Tell me about my father, I miss him so much.'

'What do you want to know?'

'Everything.'

'That would take forever.'

'When did you know that you were in love?'

'We drifted into it, your father talked mine into letting him date me; I was just fifteen.'

'How exciting.'

'Actually I could have done without it. I loved going out with a group of friends, and I didn't want anything too serious.'

'So why did you date him then?'

'Because when your father set his mind to something, he always got his own way, and he could never take no for an answer. We used to sing in my father's band, we were good together.'

'So when did you know that things were getting serious?'

'When he went down on one knee on stage on my sixteenth birthday and presented me with an engagement ring.'

'How romantic.'

'Yes, it was, very romantic. We were going to get married and then he screwed everything up and we split.'

'Why?'

'I found him in bed with my so called best friend. I'd had my suspicions about them for a long time but they always denied it. Ray witnessed it too.'

'What's it got to do with Ray?'

'Jenny was his girlfriend.'

'Poor you, and poor Ray.'

'Ray was devastated. We were all in a band called Golden Red which had been formed by your Uncle Rusty, and that day both Ray and Ed quit. Romany, who was then Roy, took Ray's place, and I carried on working with them as much as possible, but by then I had a full time job with the Doug Trent agency so couldn't always get to gigs.'

'So what happened to you and Dad?'

'I told him that I wanted space, but he wouldn't give it to me. He was on the phone constantly, begging me to forgive him. In the end, he became a pest and, seeing that I wasn't going to cave in, he cleared off with June Maclaine, a singer that we'd known for years. She was doing a five month tour around Europe and she found him work out there.'

'So you lost touch.'

'Not completely, he kept saying that he was coming home but he never did, and it was over a year before we met up again.'

'So what happened next?'

'By then I'd met Barry and we both went with Doug to go talent spotting at a showcase in France. Your father was on it, and as soon as we set eyes on each other, the old feelings rekindled.'

'So did he come back to England with you?'

'No, he had commitments in France.' Rosie wasn't going to mention his involvement with an evil cult which was run by an even more evil high priestess called Francine. Rosie shivered at the memory of it. She'd been drugged, lost her virginity, almost kidnapped, and returned home pregnant. This was something that she would never divulge to her daughter.

She was brought back down to earth by her daughter saying, 'He could have terminated his contract and come back to England with you; did you still keep in touch?'

'To start with he did, and then the phone calls stopped.'

'Why?'

'I don't know, anyway, by then Barry had asked me to marry him and I accepted his proposal.'

'You should have waited for Dad.'

'It was different in those days, I was heavily pregnant and your dad showed no signs of coming home, plus my parents put pressure on me, they wanted the best for me.'

'So what happened when Dad did come home?'

'He was furious and tried to break up my marriage.'

'What year was that?'

'1964.'

'That must have been baby Rex.'

'That's right, he was stillborn; your dad was there at the time. Barry was in Los Angeles sorting Vic out. I haemorrhaged later that night and your dad drove me to the hospital, if it hadn't have been for him, I probably wouldn't be sitting here now.'

'So what happened to Dad when Barry came home?'

'He went back to his parents and then met up with Jenny again, but he soon dropped her once he met Cathy. She was the love of his life.'

'But you must have got back together; I was born in 1970.'

Rosie reached inside her bag and removed some sun cream, and after putting some on she handed the cream to Susie saying, 'Your grandad had a stroke and I was living with Barry, you and Gary in Los Angeles. My mother needed me, and Barry couldn't get away so I flew back without him. I was on the pill but Barry wanted another child so he got the doctors to give me placebos and you were the result. Ed and I met up again and we realised that we were still in love and began making love again. Need I say more?'

'Making love, it sounds so beautiful.'

'It is, but only if you're with the right person.'

'I'm still a bit confused, because I was born in Los Angeles and yet we ended up back in England.'

Rosie sighed. 'After your accident, it was found that Barry couldn't possibly be your father and he kicked us out.'

'Charming.'

'Yes it was, considering that he'd been having an affair with his secretary Iris for God knows how long.'

'I remember Dad coming round one night, and he sort of stayed, and then we used to visit his place at weekends. What happened?'

'Your father had had a breakdown on his American tour, and Cathy had left him. After several spells in mental institutions, he came back to England.'

'But how did you get back together? I still don't understand.'

'Uncle Rusty rang me one night and asked me to give Ed a call as he thought that I might be able to help with his depression. So I called him and that's when he paid us a visit.'

'And he moved in. I think they were probably the happiest days of my life; we were all happy.'

'We were, but you've got a lot of your life left, Susie.'

'I know, but then Dad spoiled it all and went back to Cathy.'

'He had to be true to himself, she was the love of his life, I know that I'm repeating myself, but she was. I think that he'd probably kidded himself that I was, but then he found himself confronted with the real thing.'

'You looked like twins; I couldn't believe it when I first saw her that Christmas at the mansion.'

'Sometimes I think that he was torn between us.'

'I hated him when he left us. You were pregnant with Deanne.'

'You must never hate him, Susie. He always loved you, you know he did.'

'But he made you suffer, and it wasn't fair.'

'Life's not fair, Susie, whoever told you it was?'

'Nobody, but I couldn't have coped, I would have killed myself.'

'You wouldn't and, besides, I had you, and Deanne was in my belly. Ray put me back together again. I have a loving family and that's all I need.'

'Why does being in love hurt so much? I've always thought that Kevin and I were destined to be together.'

'Then if you are, you will be in the future. Kevin and Candy may not last, but until things change you need to get on with your life and enjoy it. Now, come on, let's get some serious sunbathing in, there's no males to ruin it.' Susie watched as her mother spread her beach towel on the sand and lay down on it. She followed suit, giggling. Her mother was right; she was sixteen with her life in front of her. She intended to enjoy it with the help of Vidal.

Chapter Eleven

Back in England, Vic was fuming; he'd been to visit Romany and was appalled at the sight of him. 'Christ, you look bad. What happened to you?'

'I'm just a bit off colour.'

'Off colour, I've seen healthier corpses.'

'Love you too, Vic, what was it you wanted?'

'I want you to do a few guest spots with the band.'

'Get lost, you've got Ray.'

'Yes, but the band's losing gigs and what they are getting is rubbish, you and Ed were the main attraction, Ray and Kevin just don't cut it. Ray's a faithful husband, and Kevin lives in cloud cuckoo land. I need hell raisers as front men; the fans need excitement, not a couple of ninnys. Still, looking at you, I think excitement is the last thing on your agenda, you look as if you've just been dug up, a walking corpse.'

'Ed looks worse. He may have been a hell raiser, but now he's been through the flames of hell and is in an urn.'

'He's been scattered.'

'Scattered?'

'Yes, Kevin scattered his ashes with Cathy's and baby Amara's at Bacton; apparently it was Cathy's last wish.'

'What a prick, that guy is such a nonce, he's nothing like a front man. He should be making patchwork quilts or knitting; how's Cathy's lad coming on?'

'His father won't let me represent him, he called me a devious fat nasty little man, and said that I couldn't be trusted, but I'm not beaten yet. As soon as he's old enough to overrule his father, I shall take him under my wing.'

'Rumour has it that Barry Grayson's got him under his; he's informed the boy's father that you'd be bad for him.'

'What a cheek, I'll fix him, bloody Barry Grayson, he'll eat his words.'

'Rumour also has it that he once dangled you upside down in Los Angeles from his office window that's several floors up.'

'You've been listening to too many rumours, and what's this one about you getting married?'

'That's right; I've decided that Ellen's the one for me.'

'Not for much longer, looking at the state of you. She'll be a widow within hours of your wedding night. I hope you've already consummated your relationship otherwise it might not ever happen.'

'You're sick.'

'Not as sick as you.'

'Have you ever been in love, Vic?'

'No, and neither have you, it's just a silly little phase that you're going through.'

'I'm not, anyway you should think about tying the knot.'

'I don't need to tie anything up; I've been sterile all my life.'

'But think about it, Vic, in some countries, the girls wait on you hand and foot; just think, you'd have a warm bedfellow for the rest of your life. I mean you're getting on and you won't be able to take care of yourself forever.'

'I can have any woman I want.'

'Only because you're rich, but if you had a young wife, she would do anything for you. You wouldn't need to go looking for sex, you'd have it on tap; some of those Thai and Filipino girls are really stunning.'

'You've got a point; I haven't had a holiday for a while.'

'It would do you the world of good.'

Vic was getting tired of this conversation and, lighting up a cigar, he said, 'Enough of this shit, will you guest with the band or not?'

'I'll think about it.'

'Hello, Mr Lee.' Ellen stood framed in the doorway. Vic looked her up and down; she was a looker but not as stunning as some of his conquests. She had long black hair, was tall and slim with kind brown eyes, a full mouth, and a small nose. Even her style of dress surprised Vic; Romany's girls were usually wearing skirts cherry high and low-necked tops. This girl was clad in a polo neck dress that ended below her knees.

'This is my beautiful fiancée, Ellen,' said Romany proudly.

'Hello my dear, how are you, Elaine?'

'It's Ellen.'

'Sorry, Helen, my mistake.'

'It's Ellen,' corrected Ellen once more, 'how are you, Mr Lee?'

'Fine, Aileen, I'm trying to get Romany to join us for a few guest performances; nobody plays *Sabre Dance* like he does.'

'I haven't played it for years.'

'Then start practising, you'll be great, I know you will. I don't suppose you want to buy a couple of baby Sulcata tortoises, do you?'

'No,' replied Romany. 'Eddie's bank balance must be growing.'

'I'm taking care of his interests.'

'Rumour has it that you've hatched many baby tortoises, so if his bank balance isn't healthy, I bet yours is.'

'What is it with all these bloody rumours; loads of babies hatch and don't survive, and many die as in the case of Eddie's.'

Romany shook his head and sat down in his burgundy recliner chair; he reclined in it and then gazed up at Vic. 'I went to our local pet shop the other day because Ellen wanted a puppy like the one on the toilet roll advert on television.'

'Did you get one?' asked Vic, puffing on his cigar.

'No, but in the shop were several vivariums full of baby Sulcata tortoises. I asked if they were home bred and was told that they were, and the supplier was one Victor Lee who lived locally.'

'Coincidence,' spluttered Vic, knowing that Romany was on to him, 'there's obviously another man with the same name breeding them too. Will you cut the crap, I need you to guest with the band, and I've even thought about ditching Kevin and bringing a female vocalist on board, but there's a shortage of good ones.'

'But not a shortage of baby Sulcata tortoises; shame on you Vic. Eddie trusts you; it must have been like taking candy from a baby.'

'Will you shut up. I don't want to talk about tortoises.'

'Didn't think you would. What about Rosie? She's got a great voice.'

'I'm working on it. Her talent is wasted, she should be singing in Las Vegas.'

'Then talk to her, or better still get Ray to speak to her, she'd do anything for him and her kids.'

'I said I'm working on it, but meanwhile, I need you for a few gigs. You look rough but I'm sure that with a bit of makeup, we can make you look human.'

'Okay Vic, but give me a couple of months to get my act together.'

'You can have as many months as you like as long as you agree to perform. At this rate, Z Tones will be doing holiday camps.'

'Never mind, Vic, let's have a drink.'

'That's the best thing you've said all night.'

Later that night, as Vic drove home, his mind was in overdrive. He was pleased that Romany had agreed to be a guest artist with the band, and the remarks about the Thai bride intrigued him. It would be like having a servant, a beautiful one that obeyed his every command and looked good on his arm. It was quite tempting but then he thought about the downside. He would have to keep her, and that didn't appeal to him at all; suddenly the lovely vision became shoddy. He needed to concentrate on the band and get them some good gigs, not fantasise over women. 'Fuck all women,' he said out loud as he speeded up his car. Women were two a penny, he could manipulate each and every one of them, well apart from one who he needed to liven up the band and make them gig again.

'Eden's Rose,' he said over and over again, and then it struck him that there was a way to get her on board even if she didn't join the band. She might not want to help him, but as Romany had said, she'd do anything to please Ray and her kids. Tomorrow he would visit Al Simpkins, and once Ray and Rosie returned from Tenerife with their brood, he would tell them about his idea, his brilliant idea.

As it got closer to four o'clock, Susie began to get very jittery; she wondered if maybe it hadn't been a good idea after all agreeing to meet Vidal. However, she could also feel excitement building up inside her and in the end the excitement won. She realised that he was quite taken with her, and he was very good looking. Telling her parents that she was going shopping, she left the hotel and headed for the same stretch of beach where they'd met the last time. She was a little early and sat on the sand and waited. She didn't hear him approach, and craned her neck around when a voice said, 'Hallo, baby, how are you?'

'Fine,' she replied. 'I had a nice relaxing morning with my mother. We had a long chat, and I feel so much better now.'

Vidal helped her to her feet, and Susie feasted her eyes on him. He was dressed in a white vest which showed his sexy body off to perfection, his jeans were very tight almost to the point of indecency, and on his feet he wore sandals.

'You have a lovely mother,' said Vidal, 'but I think she spoils you.'

'Why do you say that?'

'Because whenever you come to the bar, she buys you the best of everything, no matter what it costs.'

'But she does the same for my brothers and sister.'

'Yes, but they are little children, everyone spoils little children, you are different, you should not take advantage of her good nature; she has brought you up and now it is your turn to repay her. What do you intend to do when you leave school?'

'I don't know.'

'Then you should think about it. You should be looking for work now so that you can help your mother out. Over here we take care of our parents.'

'Ray takes care of her.'

'Why call him Ray, why not Father?'

'He's my stepdad, my father was a famous rock star.'

'Really,' Vidal raised his eyebrows, 'what was his name?'

'Eden Gold.'

Vidal had heard the name before but knew nothing about him. 'Who did he sing with?'

'The Z Tones.'

Vidal was flummoxed. He vaguely remembered the band but wasn't a fan of theirs owing to the fact that the band had never gigged in Tenerife or any other Canary Island. He was not educated in their fame at all but knew that his father had a couple of their albums. 'Oh yes,' he replied, 'your father was a great singer, so you are Eden Gold's beautiful daughter.'

'I am,' said Susie, blushing beetroot red, 'so is Deanne, my little sister.'

'Oh yes, the cheeky one. I do not understand her at times, she seems to have a language of her own, one that she shares with one of the little boys.'

'Oh Eddie, he's my half brother.'

'Another family member; what about the other two little boys?'

'Ray's their father. What did you mean about Deanne's language?'

'Sometimes she say, hobble dee, hobble dee, hobble dee, and then the little boy says, and down into a ditch and then they both burst into laughter.'

'Oh she does that when she's bored; my father taught her that song. He taught it to Eddie too.'

'But what does it mean?'

'Years ago there was a programme on the radio called *Listen with Mother,* and my mother and father used to listen to it. It was a preschool programme. Dad said that the presenters were called George Dixon and Daphne Oxenford, and they did this song about riding horses. I can't remember all of it but I think the ladies used to trit trot, the men gallop and so on, and the last verse was about the old men riding their horses. It used to go, "this is the way the old men ride hobble dee, hobble dee, hobble dee and down into a ditch".'

'So what happened to the old men?'

'They fell off their horses.'

'When was this on the radio?'

'Not sure, Mum and Dad started primary school in 1950, so it had to be before that.'

'You English do some crazy things.'

'So do the Spanish.'

'We do not.'

'You do, you celebrate Christmas on January the sixth, it's crazy, everyone knows that Jesus was born on Christmas Day.'

'Ah, but can you prove it?'

'No, but the bible says so.'

'On January the sixth, the Three Kings ride into town and give out sweets to the children, however now that there are so many English people here owning homes, their customs are now recognised. I used to spend Christmas with my mother in England and then fly back here for January the sixth.'

'Spoilt for choice.'

'You could say that.'

'My mother and stepfather have bought two apartments here.'

'Two?'

'Yes, my mother couldn't make up her mind so Ray bought both.'

'Then he must love her very much.'

'He does.'

'Did they ask you where you were going?'

'No, they were in bed as usual, they're at it all the time. I just tapped on their door and said I was going shopping. They shut the world out when they're together.'

'Love is a beautiful thing, querida, may I kiss you?'

'Well I...'

'You are the most beautiful girl in the world and I have been smitten by you. As soon as I saw you the first time, I knew that you were the one for me.' Vidal gazed into Susie's eyes and drew her close and the kiss that followed was inevitable, the girl was being swept away by this handsome Spaniard. Vidal released the blushing Susie and held her at arm's length. 'Te quiero,' he said.

'What does that mean?'

'It means, I love you. Come, let's visit my father.'

Chapter Twelve

'You're nuts,' cried Al Simpkins, scratching his head and making his hair stand up on end, 'how is making a video of *Eden's Rose* going to help Z Tones' flagging career? The party's over, Vic, you need new blood.'

'Don't call me nuts, you imbecile, new blood is exactly what this video will exist on.'

Al pulled a face, he wanted to get on with his latest porn film, not film a video of an old Ed Gold song. 'So what's so great about this song? We don't even know who the girl was; I suppose she was a groupie.'

'She was not, she's Barry Grayson's ex-wife.'

'Ed wrote about her? Did they have an affair or something?'

'No, they were childhood sweethearts. I want a video that will make people sit up and take notice, something beautiful.'

'Well, how are you going to achieve that?'

'I'll explain if you let me in. This is humiliating, being kept on the doorstep; people will think I'm selling something.'

'You are, a stupid piece of nostalgia.'

'Are you going to let me in or not?'

'I suppose I'll have to, I won't get any peace if I don't.' Al stepped aside and let Vic pass.

The little fat man made himself at home straight away, helping himself to a glass of vodka. Then he flopped down into an armchair and stared at a confused Al.

'I'm aiming for Mother's Day,' said Vic, 'this video could put the Z Tones back on top.'

'No chance, that song is sentimental and sad.'

Vic wasn't listening. 'We'll start with a close-up of Bobby. He's a dead ringer for Ed, I've seen his baby photos, just a few shots and then we'll move onto Deanne and Eddie, followed by Susie and some spotty youth from stage school. Do you get my drift?'

'No, and neither will anyone else.'

Vic still wasn't listening, and continued. 'We'll then move onto Kevin, he still looks quite youthful.'

'I'd say quite feminine.'

'If I want your input, I'll ask for it.'

'Well, he's always been a bit girly. He may be an Ed lookalike but he doesn't possess his masculinity, anyway, I'm the one shooting the film so you will need my input.'

'Shut up and pour me another vodka. We'll follow Kevin up with some footage of Ed in his heyday, and finish with Rosie and her brood.'

'I've never worked with children, they're scary and smart. I'd rather work with animals than kids.'

'Then I'll bring Eddie's two tortoises along instead.'

'Are they relevant to the song?'

'No, you blithering idiot, I was being sarcastic.'

'You're not a nice person when you're being sarcastic.'

'And you're a prize idiot, just think about it, women love sentiment and kids, and they are the ones who will buy this video. Do you remember that Keith West song? It went to number one.'

'*Eden's Rose* has already been at number one, people won't want to buy it again.'

'It wasn't in video format last time, what more can I say?'

'Not a lot, every time you open your mouth, shit comes out.'

'I don't talk shit, I make money. Ed kept his second family well hidden, and if Rosie's identity gets found out, the press will pay a fortune for a story.'

'Which you will sell to them; anyway who's Keith West?'

'He did *Ballad of a Teenage Opera*.'

'Oh, I remember, it went "grocer Jack, grocer Jack, is it true what Mummy says, you won't be back, oh no no".'

Vic got to his feet and swung a punch at Al, but he ducked making Vic sprawl face down on the floor. 'You look like a beached whale,' mocked Al.

'And you look like a poor man's Stan Laurel.'

'What?'

'I said...'

'I heard what you said, you're a nutter, my time's precious, and I've got a new porn film to shoot; it's gonna be a biggie. Plus I'm hungry, as I missed lunch and dinner. Would you like an omelette?'

'No I wouldn't, you and your bloody late night fry-ups.'

'At least I can cook.'

'So can I.'

'Then why do you employ a housekeeper?'

'It's good for my image.'

'Really, I've seen your housekeeper, she looks like Nora Batty from *The Last of the Summer Wine*.'

'She has excellent references; she used to work at the Queen's residence in Sandringham.'

'The only queen she's worked for is probably a drag queen. You should get married, you've got plenty of cash, and could most probably net a young woman. I don't suppose that it would be a match made in heaven but she'd have to be good to you to share your lifestyle.'

Vic hauled himself to his feet. 'What's the matter with everyone? You're the second person to say that.'

'Well it makes sense. It would be cost effective too, as she'd do everything for you.'

'Mrs Monk does everything I ask.'

'But does she keep your bed warm?'

'Of course not, I can have any woman I want.'

'But a wife would be cheaper.'

'So why aren't you married?'

'Because I can look after myself, and several of my porn stars are happy to oblige for a starring role; anyway what does this Rosie bird look like?'

'Cathy's twin sister.'

'I didn't know she had one.'

'She hasn't. Do you know that if you had more than one brain cell, you'd be dangerous.'

'I'm not listening to you any more, I'm hungry.'

Al left the room and headed for the kitchen with Vic following in his wake. Vic looked on as Al removed a couple of eggs from his fridge. 'If you keep eating those fry-ups, you'll get like a house end,' he grunted.

Al was lost for words; everyone called him Al Stan Laurel Simpkins because he was as thin as a rake. He stared at Vic and then said, 'You should try wearing a black wig, painting on a moustache and putting on a bowler hat, you'd be a dead ringer for Oliver Hardy, your gut gets bigger every day.'

'I'll fix you,' snapped Vic and, opening the fridge, took out a box of eggs and tipped them onto the parquet floor. He stood with his hands on his hips muttering, 'now what are you going to do about that, there's your omelette.'

Furious, Al picked up his frying pan and began to chase Vic around the kitchen.

'It was an accident,' cried Vic, 'I'd changed my mind, I'd decided to have an omelette after all and I dropped the box, I've got weak wrists, they give out at any time.'

'Your head is about to give out.'

'No, no, Al, we're buddies, I was just messing around, let's have a drink, I'll clean the mess up, I don't know what comes over me at times, I'm like a man possessed.' Vic was out of condition; his little fat legs were giving up on him. The telephone rang, giving Vic his chance for a quick exit but he didn't look where he was going and skidded on the broken eggs. He almost did the splits, making him collapse in agony.

Al picked up Vic's car keys and jangled them. 'You can't drive without these, you dummy, no wonder everyone calls you thick, sick Vic prick,' laughed Al.

Vic struggled to his feet; his abductor muscles were killing him. Al towered above him with the frying pan raised. Vic was scared and stuttered, 'Let's settle this civilly, go and put your feet up and I'll clean this mess up and cook your omelette for you.'

Al lowered the frying pan. 'You can peel the potatoes,' he said, 'I fancy some chips to go with the omelette. You need to learn how to cook if you're not going to get married.'

'I don't peel potatoes, I'm an impresario,' snapped Vic, snatching his keys from Al's hand, 'haven't you got any oven chips?'

'I don't like them, get peeling.'

'I won't.'

'You will.'

'I won't.' Vic picked up another frying pan and raised it trying to look menacing.

'What's this,' cried Al 'frying pans at dawn.'

'Don't you threaten me.'

Vic stepped backwards into some more slimy egg, he skidded, then slipped and banged his head on the corner of a unit, knocking himself clean out. Al stepped over him. 'Now who's the imbecile?' he said out loud, staring down at the unconscious Vic. He was starving hungry, and added, 'And now for something completely different, omelette and chips. I'm going to enjoy this.'

Chapter Thirteen

When Susie left Vidal, she was buzzing, he'd been a real gent and his father was very polite to her too. He knew a lot about Eden Gold and had a few of his albums. He even had a copy of *Eden's Rose* which delighted Susie. 'My father wrote it about my mother,' she said, her cheeks flushed with happiness. Senor Martinez viewed the pretty little teenager who was very talkative. By the time that she'd left, Susie had spilled the beans about Ed and Rosie, plus other family secrets. 'I used to hate Cathy,' she said. 'But my mother said that Cathy was my father's soulmate and he had to be true to himself.'

'So your mother lost out to this Cathy?'

'Yes, but Mum used to say that Deanne and me were all that she needed. She was pregnant with Deanne when he left, and when he used to visit us it was as if nothing had changed. It was the look that passed between him and my mother, like a sort of chemistry.'

'She is an amazing woman,' said Vidal. 'I notice how she takes control of everything and everyone when she is in the restaurant.'

'Ray lets her; he always says that she knows best.'

Susie gabbled on until it was time to leave. She was introduced to a girl called Luisa who Susie recognised from the restaurant. Vidal said that she was his half sister and once more he was lying. She was in fact his long suffering girlfriend but she kept up the pretence with Vidal and his father. All three had the stench of money up their nostrils, and Susie was the pawn in their game. 'So when do you return to England?' asked Luisa.

'In ten days' time, but my mother and stepfather will be returning in three months' time to take over the two properties that they've bought.'

'Will you be coming with them?'

'I don't think so.'

'That is a pity; still I suppose that you will return at some time.'

'Of course, I would love to live here.'

'Then you must marry a Spanish boy and then you can.'

Susie blushed and looked at her watch. 'I must go,' she said. 'Thank you for having me.'

'My pleasure,' said Senor Martinez, kissing Susie's hand.

Susie left with Vidal and he walked her back to her hotel. 'Are you in the bar tonight?' she asked.

'No, tonight I work at a bar in Playa de las Americas, why, do you want to see me again?'

'Yes.'

'Then I will see you at the bar tomorrow night if you can talk your mother into dropping by. I shall look forward to it.'

'But I'm free tomorrow during the day.'

'But I am not, baby, see you tomorrow night.' He kissed Susie gently and then left her with her hormones raging. Confused, she walked inside the hotel feeling reckless.

Vidal walked along Los Cristianos' main beach, then he passed the harbour and walked onto the new beach. The Torres Del Sol was in sight and he knew that Luisa would be in bed waiting for him. Susie was clearly interested in him but he was more interested in her mother. He'd made a fortune out of pleasuring the older ladies, and Rosie was a challenge. She was the one with the money, and Ray seemed to be doing well for himself. The way to Rosie was through Susie, and already a plan was hatching in his mind. He entered the Torres Del Sol and got into the lift. Life was getting better by the second; it had taken him thirty years to get to this golden situation where he could elevate his status and become part of a wealthy family, and he was going to milk it for all that it was worth.

When Vic regained consciousness, he wondered where he was. He was flat out with his head in some gooey mess and after several attempts to get to his feet he succeeded, only to skid once more and land on his backside. Now his trousers were a gooey mess. 'What the fuck?' he exclaimed.

'Oh, back in the land of the living, are we?' shouted Al from the lounge.

'Never mind that, come and help me up.'

'You created the mess, you can stay in it.'

'You bastard.' Vic's memory was returning. 'I suppose you've had your omelette?' he yelled.

'Yes, it was lovely, yours is on the floor. Come and watch this film, it's a good one.'

'I can't sit down in this state,' snapped Vic, hauling himself to his feet with a superhuman effort.

'Then go upstairs and take a shower, you can borrow one of my dressing gowns, this film is ace.'

Cursing, Vic went upstairs and fifteen minutes later returned wearing Al's dressing gown. It gaped everywhere owing to his bulk. 'It fits where it touches,' said Vic. 'And my suit's ruined.'

'I'm sure that Mrs Monk will take care of it.'

'What am I going to tell her? It stinks of egg.'

'Shouldn't think she'll take any notice. I remember the time that you went home covered in puke and you've done worse. No one would sit next to you after the last fiasco.'

'I had an upset stomach.'

'You upset a lot of people too; your insides must have been rotten that night.'

'Enough of that, I can't do this gown up.'

'Well if you weren't so fat, you'd be able to; you need a wife to keep you in shape.'

'Will you button it, who's in this film?'

'Not telling you.'

'Right, you plank, I'll read it off the sleeve.'

Picking the sleeve up, Vic attempted to read the credits and the cast. 'Starring Nick Hand and Fussy Fenfect.'

'It's Rock Hard and Pussy Perfect, you don't know your R's from your N's, your eyesight is appalling. I've noticed lately that your secretary reads everything out loud to you, and all you do is sign documents. You could be signing your life away. You need to get a wife; she'd sort out all of your washing, clean the house, be your personal secretary, and give you a good seeing to at night. Think of the money you'd save, you could get rid of your secretary and Mrs Monk.'

'She'd need feeding and clothing.'

'Two can live as cheaply as one, and you could always get her clothes from Oxfam. I got a smashing suit from there last week.'

'Who's the little Asian girl on this film? She's got great tits, and her mouth looks first class.'

'Anna, she's a Thai girl, very westernised, bit of a nightmare really but great on film.'

'I'll say, she's a horny bitch, she could keep my bed warm.'

'And she'd nag you to death.'

'Beautiful girl though.'

Al stared at Vic, the gaping dressing gown hid nothing and it was visible that he had a hard on. 'She's got a sister who still lives in Thailand. I've got a photo somewhere; she's sweet and very innocent and works on her parents' farm. Anna used to until she spread her wings and came to England. Her sister is very shy and knows nothing of men. You could break her in, Vic, she's a virgin. Perfect wife material and she wants nothing more than to please the man of her dreams. She believes that one day her prince will come riding to her on a white charger and carry her off to a life of happiness.'

'What's her name?'

'Lop.'

'What sort of name is that? That's what you do to branches.'

'It's a Thai name and probably means something beautiful, just think how good it would sound, Lop Lee.'

'Reminds me of Leapy Lee singing *Little Arrows*.'

'I think it's got a ring to it.'

'Well, I'm not thinking of giving anyone a ring apart from Ray and Rosie when they return from Tenerife.'

'Oh, we're back to *Eden's Rose* again. Tell you what, Vic, pour yourself another dink, watch this film, and later we'll discuss the possibility of making your video.'

'Later on, we'll be pissed.'

'Who knows, but if you can get Ray and Rosie to agree to your master plan, I'll consider it.'

'Great,' replied Vic, knowing that if Al was pissed, he'd agree to anything. Unfortunately, much later, they were both spark out, and all that Vic got was a full English the following morning.

Deanne was very confused and bored; she liked the sun and the holiday atmosphere but was now fed up with it. Susie kept disappearing on a regular basis, all Eddie spoke about was Tom, Bobby never stopped dancing, making her feel dizzy, and her parents were always wrapped up in each other. Norma was doing her head in too; Bobby was the apple of her eye and she turned a blind one to his bad behaviour. The child was fine when he was dancing, but as soon as he stopped, he would turn into a little monster. If Deanne tried to intervene, Bobby would bite or kick her, he did the same to Eddie too. One day he'd been play fighting with his younger brother and smacked him in his face, making Raydon scream. Rosie had intervened and got a kick in her shins for her efforts. He loved making his mother cry; it was his way of getting her full attention. Candy chastised him, so did Kevin, but it was to no avail and the only one that he responded to was Norma who spoilt him more and more each day. Ray punished him, but the child responded by taking it out on Raydon who was too small to defend himself efficiently. It was as if Bobby had to have an audience when he misbehaved because if he didn't receive the attention that he craved, he would disappear with Norma and be as good as gold. He hated being ignored, and found that the only way to get Rosie's undivided attention was to ask her to help him with a particular dance step that he was attempting to master. That was a good ploy and Bobby soon latched on to it.

Deanne realised that her family was dysfunctional, and wished that she'd been Eddie's full sister instead of half. Apart from her mother, the entire Lynne family were nuts, especially Nanny Ada who made a spectacle of herself at family gatherings. Ray's brothers were all short of a full shilling, Roland being the favourite sibling, Tim continuing to change his girlfriends like he changed his underpants, Martin being scared of his own shadow, and then there was Ray himself, a complete nutter who now drank too much, making him even more of a nutter. Her own siblings were no better; Susie was a silly secretive vain girl, Raydon too good to be true and, as for Bobby, words could not describe him. Norma had moments when she seemed quite normal, but most of the time she drifted into her own little world. Gary had been a lovely half brother, and Deanne had looked up to him but now he was dead and life had to go on.

She could still remember her biological father. She'd loved him so much, and many times had prayed for Cathy to die so that he would return to Rosie, making them one big happy family. She consoled herself that she had her mother who adored her. She wanted to be just like her when she grew up, and then they could go out and do things that mothers and daughters did. The only other family member that Deanne had warmed to was Grandad

Alf who was a kindly but strict man and fun to be with; he had Deanne's full respect. Deanne felt that she needed to snap out of things that depressed her and become more positive. She had a mother and stepfather who loved her, which was more than a lot of children had, and she'd never gone without anything. She was fortunate in many ways and she also had the option of the open road in the school holidays with her Uncle Rusty and his family. Eddie often stayed with them, and she was always invited along too. Life wasn't too bad, and she had to rise above things that annoyed her.

Positivity, that was the answer, things could only get better.

That night, things did exactly that. The entire family had been perusing the bars and were getting thirsty. Susie wanted to go to their usual bar, but Ray had heard that there was a very good comedian at another bar which was a little bit further on along the promenade. Bobby was dancing along it and didn't want to go into the bar. He threw a massive tantrum and ended up outside the bar face down on the ground screaming and cursing. Ray and Rosie left him and seated themselves near the door where they could keep an eye on the screaming child. After a few minutes, Del Brown the comedian took to the stage and soon had everyone falling about with his jokes. Most of them went over Deanne and Eddie's heads until he announced that he was going to do his speciality which involved him and a condom. The two children stared at each other, wondering if a bath and a mac might be part of this special trick. They were shocked when Del stretched the condom over his head almost covering his entire face. 'That's dangerous,' said Eddie.

'He must be nuts,' replied Deanne. 'I can't see how that would stop ladies having babies.'

Candy was dumbstruck. Kevin was speechless too and suggested that they left. 'The content of this act is not suitable for children,' he said. 'And there's loads of them here.'

'Chill out,' said Ray. 'He's very funny, isn't he Rosie?'

'Well I...'

Her sentence had been cut short as Bobby bounded into the room and ran up to the stage. He stared up at Del who had now removed the condom from his head and shouted, 'Want one.'

Del stared at the child. 'When you're older,' he quipped.

'Want balloon.'

'Oh, you want a balloon; I thought you wanted my special one for a moment, what colour do you want?'

'Blue.'

'Okay, I'll make you a magic one. What's your name?'

'Bobby.'

'Well, you go back to your mum and you can watch me make a dog.' Bobby hurried over to his mother and clambered up onto her lap. His eyes were focussed on the stage and the funny fat man who was making everyone laugh. Several balloons were twisted together and soon took the formation of a dog. A big grin spread across Bobby's face and he got down from Rosie's lap and went back to the stage. People applauded as Bobby was handed the dog.

'Is that okay?' asked Del.

'Yes, can I have one for Raydon?'

'Who's Raydon?'

'My little brother.'

Rosie was gobsmacked. Bobby never bothered giving Raydon anything; he usually took things away from him. Del twisted up some more balloons, this time into the shape of a teddy bear. Bobby took it and hurried over to Raydon who sat on Ray's lap. 'This is for you,' said Bobby, handing Raydon the teddy. Then he reached up and planted a smacker on Raydon's cheek. Not finished, Bobby walked back to the stage.

'What now?' said Del. 'I've got to sing.'

'I can dance, I can sing.'

'Oh, what can you sing?'

'*Mama Mia*, I can dance to it.'

'Well I was going to do that later, but I suppose I could do it now. Do you want to perform with me?'

'What's perform?'

'Sing and dance with me, although you'll have to do all the dancing, I'm past all that. Do you want Bobby to perform, ladies and gents?'

'Yes,' yelled the crowd.

'Okay, they want you to perform, take it away Bobby.'

The music began and Bobby sang his heart out; he was in his element singing along with Del. He did a dance routine too to a delighted crowd and they cheered when he'd finished. Del handed him a small guitar and told Bobby to go home and practise with it. 'Daddy plays the guitar,' said Bobby. 'So does Kevin.'

'Wonderful, there'll be no shortage of teachers then, take another bow and take this bag of sweets too, that should keep you quiet for a while.'

'Thanks,' replied Bobby, then he bowed and ran back to his parents. His family were overawed especially when Bobby gave the sweets to Eddie and Deanne. He was like a different child. Looking up at his mother he said, 'Love you, Mummy' and clambered back onto Rosie's lap, then he snuggled up to her. Rosie smiled at Ray. She was happy, and if Rosie was happy, so was Ray.

A little later they passed Vidal's bar. Susie said that she wanted to speak to her new friend Luisa and added that she was thirsty. Rosie and Ray seated themselves, but Candy and Kevin said that they were tired and offered to take the children back to the hotel. Raydon was falling asleep, and Bobby wanted to go home to practise on his new guitar. Rosie agreed, so Candy took Raydon from Rosie's arms and he cuddled up to her. Kevin and Candy made for the hotel, with Bobby dancing along in front on them. Rosie caught Vidal's eye and he sauntered over. Deanne nudged Eddie. 'I don't like him,' she said.

'Neither do I,' replied Eddie.

'Ah, my good amigos,' exclaimed Vidal. 'What can I get you?'

Rosie gave him the drinks order and watched as he walked away. She was uneasy as Susie was watching him like a hawk. 'Where's your friend, Susie?' asked Ray.

'Probably in the kitchen, I guess that she'll be out soon. Vidal will tell her that we are here.'

'Well, if she's not out by the time we've finished our drinks, we'll be going home and you'll have to see her tomorrow.'

'She'll be out soon,' replied Susie. 'She's probably busy cooking.'

She fiddled with her hair and it wasn't missed by her mother. Susie always fiddled with her hair when she was nervous. Rosie made eye contact with her daughter who immediately dropped her eyes and opened her bag as if looking for something. 'Okay, Susie?' asked Rosie.

'Fine, just a bit tired.' Susie's heart was racing; just the mere sight of Vidal had filled her with desire.

Vidal was in the kitchen making a phone call; his plan was about to take off. He gave the person on the other end of the line a full description of Rosie, plus where she was sitting. Then after replacing the receiver he began to make up Rosie's drink order. Once he'd delivered the drinks to the table, he became his usual charming self and laughed and joked with the family. One round of drinks later, the family made to leave, but Luisa emerged with a second round on the house which Ray happily accepted.

Vidal was getting impatient; he'd expected his partner in crime to have arrived by now and was therefore relieved when he saw him walking toward the bar. The man strolled past so that he could get a good look at Rosie, and then continued on his way toward the harbour. Vidal turned his attention to Ray and asked if he was enjoying his stay in Tenerife. Ray replied that he was and told Vidal about his two properties in Los Cristianos. There ensued a pleasant conversation and nobody took any notice of the figure that had passed them previously.

Susie by now was in the kitchen conversing with Luisa, she had to make things look good in front of her parents. The figure crossed behind Rosie as if he was about to enter the bar and then he struck. Snatching Rosie's bag, he ran down a dark alleyway that was adjacent to the bar. Rosie screamed, and Ray was on his feet in an instant. Vidal was faster and chased after the assailant. Luisa suddenly came running out of the kitchen; she was in on the act and rushed to Rosie's side.

'What happened?' she cried. 'I heard screaming.'

Norma was lost for words for a few minutes and then she yelled, 'That dirty dago's snatched my daughter's handbag.'

Ray had gone in search of Vidal but the alley was pitch black owing to the fact that the surrounding bar was closed and in darkness. He couldn't see a thing and, feeling beaten, wandered back to Rosie who was sobbing her heart out. Luisa had her arm around Rosie's shoulders and was wailing. 'Oh my God, what you must think of us, you come on holiday to enjoy yourselves and then some bastard does this. I am so ashamed to think that one of my countrymen could do such a thing. I am so sorry, maybe Vidal has caught up with him.'

'Dirty dagos,' said Norma over and over again.

Ray took Rosie into his arms. 'It's okay Rosie, don't worry, everything will be okay.'

Susie had been in the toilet when she'd heard her mother scream. She rushed out with her knickers at half mast and pulled them up as she ran through the bar. Deanne and Eddie were traumatised and ran into Susie's embrace. 'What happened?' she cried.

'A man stole your mother's bag,' cried Luisa, 'and Vidal ran after him. I hope that he has caught up with this evil person.'

Vidal had indeed caught up with his accomplice; they'd raced to a nearby bar and made their way to the gents. Vidal took 2,000 pesetas from his pocket and handed it to his friend Carlos. Carlos in turn handed Rosie's bag over. 'Good work,' said Vidal. 'Now hit me and make it look good.'

Carlos hesitated. 'Are you sure about this?'

'Yes, I need to look as if I've been in a fight.'

'Okay amigo,' and Carlos hit Vidal square on his jaw.

'Again.'

Carlos punched once more, this time splitting Vidal's lip. Blood pumped out and Vidal smudged some of it around the base of his nose making it look as if it had been bleeding. He let the blood run down his shirt and then gazed into the mirror. Satisfied, he turned to Carlos. 'Okay, now vamos.'

Carlos didn't need telling twice and left the bar like a greyhound; he was happy and now 2,000 pesetas richer, and all he'd had to do was steal a handbag. Vidal waited for a few minutes and then half walked, half staggered back to his bar. The scene that met his eyes was what he'd expected. Rosie was being comforted by Ray, Susie was comforting her younger sibling Deanne and half brother Eddie, and the old lady was shouting about filthy dagos and wanting to let the tortoises chew every dago's bollocks off. He didn't quite get the gist of Norma's rantings, but realised that she was very angry. He staggered over to Rosie and placed her bag on the table.

'He no do that again,' he said. 'I hit him real good.'

Rosie looked up and saw the battered waiter. 'Oh my God, are you okay?' she asked.

'I am fine, Senora, he is in a worse state than I, but he got away. He, how you say, kneed me in my privates.'

Ray released Rosie from his embrace and shook Vidal's hand. 'How can we repay you?' he asked.

'I want nothing, Senor, you are a nice family, and I am just glad that I got the bag back. Would you all like another drink?'

'I want to go home, Mummy,' cried Deanne. 'So does Eddie.'

'Okay, darling, we'll go, thank you for your offer, Vidal, but I'd like to go home too.' Rosie opened up her bag and took her purse out. She checked the contents and smiled. 'All there,' she added. Ray took out his wallet and handed Vidal 5,000 pesetas.

Vidal refused at first, but Ray insisted and the crafty Spaniard took the money and gave Ray a hug. He got a hug from Rosie too. 'Thank you so much,' she said. Vidal could feel his pulse quicken, this woman was such a lovely armful.

'The pleasure was mine,' he replied. 'You are my friends.' She was turning him on big time. She was the one with the big bucks, and she also had two other big things, which he could feel pressing into him. He released her reluctantly and watched as she walked away with her family. Susie followed on behind and blew Vidal a kiss. He winked at her, saying, 'Buenas noches, Senorita.'

'Buenas noches,' Susie replied. Her stomach was turning cartwheels.

'Susie, hurry up,' cried Rosie.

'Coming,' replied Susie and quickened her pace.

After they were out of sight, Vidal turned to Luisa. 'I am now in their good books and 5,000 pesetas richer,' he said.

'Was it worth it? Your lip is split and swollen.'

'Then you can give me your undivided attention tonight. It's late, let's lock up, there are no customers about. Things are looking up, Luisa. Very soon, we will be rich and I will give you everything that money can buy.' He laughed out loud and began to lock up.

That night back at the hotel, both adult males missed out on their conjugal rights. Deanne insisted on sleeping between her parents, and Eddie slept in Kevin's room. Candy wandered off to the room that she'd originally shared with Norma. Eddie had to come first; the child was very upset and scared.

Susie gained satisfaction from knowing that Candy and Kevin were split up for the night. Vidal excited her but her heart still cried out to Kevin. She recalled her mother's words. 'If you are meant to be together, you will be one day.' Those words had gladdened her heart, and she fell asleep dreaming of herself being held in Kevin's arms.

Chapter Fourteen

Bobby appeared to have turned a corner; his mood was still good and he excelled himself the following night in the hotel. A flamenco group were performing there, and Bobby was transfixed by the male dancer. He was billed as the successor of the great Antonio and, as the evening progressed, members of the group invited members of the audience to join them. Bobby was straight up onto the stage and grasped a pretty dancer's hand. When the dance was over, everyone returned to their seats apart from Bobby, who wanted to dance with the male dancer. He refused to leave the stage and stared the lead dancer out.

The old man smiled and began to stamp his feet in time to the music. Bobby followed suit and copied the dancer's movements. He was having a field day, and was a real extrovert. Faster and faster went the maestro, and faster and faster went Bobby. Rosie and Ray were stunned. It was obvious what was wrong with their son; he was a born performer and lost himself in his dancing. Any anger evaporated and was channelled into the rhythm of the dance; he was spinning and stamping, enjoying every second that he was on stage.

'There's your dancer, mother,' cried Rosie.

Norma pursed her lips. 'You were a brilliant dancer,' she replied. 'You could have been the next Margot Fonteyn but you threw your life away on Ed Gold. He ruined you and your career, talent like yours should have been cherished, not discarded. The only good thing I can say about Ed is that his son is very talented; he obviously shares your gift.'

'Yes mother, Eddie is very talented, but then so was Cathy.'

'Don't mock me, Rosie, I meant Bobby, and you know it.'

'Bobby gets his talent from myself and Ray.'

Norma grunted as Ray leaned over and kissed Rosie on her lips. She was getting nowhere, so as soon as the maestro had finished dancing with Bobby, she shouted over to him. 'I saw Antonio do the zapateado, do you do it?'

'Si Senora, and I will do it especially for you.'

'Thank you. Come here, Bobby. Watch the next dance carefully. If you practise hard enough, you will be able to do it one day.'

Bobby sat down on the floor cross legged and fixed his eyes on the man on stage who was giving his all. It was a virtuoso performance of the famed dance. Bobby loved the showmanship that was before him. In this very moment, he knew exactly what he wanted to do; his destiny was to be on stage and get the adulation of many.

In Playa de las Americas, Susie was the centre of attraction and basked in the limelight. She'd persuaded Kevin and Candy to take her to the bar where Vidal occasionally worked and found herself surrounded by many males. Kevin kept them at bay; he'd promised Rosie and Ray that he would. Susie smiled over at Vidal who was behind the bar mixing cocktails. She'd been seeing him on a regular basis over the last few days and, so far, he'd behaved like a true gentleman. Susie didn't realise that he was grooming her; he'd so far given her a ring, a bracelet, and a necklace which appeared to be the real deal. Rosie had questioned her about all three golden objects, and Susie had replied that a gypsy lady had been selling them on the beach and that she just couldn't resist them. Rosie wondered if they were stolen, as there were so many pick pockets around.

She wasn't wrong; Vidal and Luisa were expert thieves. They also had in tow a couple of ragamuffin children who were paid a few pesetas to help out. Holiday makers took pity on the little waifs, but their pity was wasted. As soon as they got up close to the children and offered them help, watches, wallets, rings, and cameras disappeared in the blink of an eyelid. Vidal's finest moves were on girls or women. He would chat them up and stroke their faces and hair, telling them how beautiful they were and that he hated Spanish women.

'They are all crazy,' he would say. 'Look at my sister, she is loco too. Do you know, I have never made love to a Spanish girl, it would be a waste of time.' Luisa would smile, pretending that she didn't speak English. Then she would wander off after gaining many spoils from the girl's handbag while Vidal distracted her. As she left, Vidal would cry 'Vamos estupido,' and then he would turn his attention back to his latest victim making her fall prey to his charms. A few hours later the girl would find herself minus a purse and several other valuables, including her earrings if she wore any. The scheming waiter, Luisa, and the two bedraggled children worked as a team and made a good living out of it.

Susie was on cloud nine. Girls always flocked around her Spanish boyfriend, but she knew that it was her that he wanted to marry. He excited her, and she wondered when he would actually make love to her. It was obvious that Kevin was now in love with Candy, so there was no point in hanging on for him. She needed to move on and make a life for herself with Vidal. The thought of actually having to go to work horrified her. She'd been spoilt and indulged all her life, and the thought of being married to the handsome Spaniard was a much better prospect. They could split their time between Tenerife and England. Her future looked rosy.

Vidal was an expert at mixing cocktails; he excelled at it, and he watched as Candy, Kevin, and Susie walked over to him. Putting on his most dazzling smile, he said, 'And what can I do for you?'

'I'd like a Pina Colada,' said Candy.

'And I'd like Sex on the Beach,' added Kevin.

'So would I,' quipped Vidal, 'but unfortunately I am working.'

The trio laughed at his attempted joke, as it seemed polite to do so. Vidal mixed Susie a non-alcoholic cocktail, telling her that it was a special one for a very special young lady. Susie accepted it and was about to follow Candy and Kevin to their table when Vidal called her back. The music was deafening and she couldn't hear what he was saying so she leaned across the bar to listen. Vidal seized his chance and planted a smacker on her lips. Pleasantly surprised, Susie backed away and blushed, then she went in search of Candy and Kevin. The couple only had eyes for each other and Susie was beginning to feel like a gooseberry. The trio stayed for another hour or so, and then Kevin suggested that they should leave. He made his way to the gents and then it happened, a power cut; they were regular things on the island.

Susie and Candy remained seated and awaited Kevin's return. Suddenly Susie felt a hand in hers; she knew who it was and allowed herself to be led away. Vidal led her outside the building and pressed her up against the wall.

Veronicas was pitch black, a contrast to its usual Blackpool illuminations look. Vidal's lips came down on Susie's, taking her breath away. Every hormone in her body reared up and responded with a passion that she didn't know she possessed. Vidal stroked her face and told her that she was the only one for him and that he wanted to spend the rest of his life with her. He ran his hands over her body, making Susie groan with pleasure. He guided her hand to his crotch, and she could feel the hardness between his legs. 'Do you see what you do to me?' he said huskily. 'You are driving me crazy.' Susie felt as if she was about to pass out when his hand made itself felt by rubbing her over her knickers. Then his hand was beneath the fabric and began to stroke her between her legs. Susie could feel his penis straining against his jeans; they were both hot for each other.

'You like that, querida?'

'It's wonderful,' cried Susie, thinking that she was about to faint.

'Good,' replied Vidal. 'Let's go back before we are missed. I will meet you tomorrow in our usual place at four o'clock.'

'Oh,' cried Susie. 'I thought that we...'

'You thought that we would make love on the beach. That would be wonderful, but you would be missed and we don't want anyone to know our secret until the time is right.'

'What do you mean?'

'I mean that the time will be right when I ask your father for your hand in marriage.'

'What?'

'Come on, querida, your friends will be waiting.'

Susie allowed herself to be led back inside the building; her dream was becoming a reality. Vidal returned behind the bar, and Susie to Candy. The bar staff were lighting candles and placing them on tables. Candy was frantic. 'Where did you go?'

'Outside, I felt sick and needed air; it's not so dark outside, the moonlight's reflecting on the water.'

'Well, thank God you're back, I was having kittens.'

Kevin stumbled over to their table. 'We might as well leave,' he said. 'The power cut could last for ages. If you two take an arm each, we can stroll along the beach in the moonlight.' Susie didn't care where they went; she was floating on air and couldn't wait to see Vidal again.

The following day, the Lynne family, plus Norma, Kevin, Candy, and Eddie decided to go to Lloro Parque at Eddie's insistence. He just wouldn't shut up about Tom the tortoise. Susie feigned sickness and stayed behind. She knew exactly how long she could spend with Vidal as Rosie had said that they were going shopping in Puerto de la Cruz once they'd left the animal park. She almost had the whole day. She met Vidal at four, and they made their way to the Torres Del Sol on the new beach. Susie was a bit scared as she knew that her relationship was about to move up a notch. She tried to make conversation as they passed Los

Cristianos harbour on the way. 'This is so lovely,' she said. 'I love all the boats; I've never been on the 'Jolly Roger' before, it looks like fun.'

'It is, querida, everyone gets drunk and there is music and dancing. Sometimes people have to walk the plank; the food is wonderful and the water warm.'

'I can't swim.'

'Then I will have to teach you one day.'

'I'm going home in a couple of days, but I don't want to leave.'

'And I don't want you to leave but you will be holidaying again now that your parents have two apartments here, and I will visit you the next time I am in England.'

'England. It seems ages since I set foot in it, we've been away for almost eight weeks.'

'That long?'

'Yes, we spent time in Lanzarote and Fuerteventura too, and we were going to view Gran Canaria next, but then my mother fell in love with Paloma Beach and the Costamar, so Gran Canaria is now not an issue.'

'Then I am indeed fortunate that your mother chose this island, otherwise you and I would never have met.'

Susie smiled and looked over her shoulder; people were now disembarking from the 'Jolly Roger'. She felt Vidal squeeze her hand and turned her attention back to him. They strolled along the new beach and went to the Torres Del Sol. Once inside the building, Vidal took Susie into his arms. 'I have never been in love before,' he said. 'I have had many girlfriends but never one like you; you're in my heart and soul.'

'You're my first boyfriend.'

'And the last, I hope.'

Susie didn't answer as the lift doors opened. It wasn't long before the couple were outside Vidal's front door. He inserted his key into the front door and opened it. Stepping back to let Susie enter, he whispered, 'Te quiero.'

Susie shivered with anticipation, and was filled with desire. Vidal's father was seated in an armchair watching the television; he nodded to Susie. 'Buenas tardes,' he said.

'Buenas tardes,' replied Susie.

'Ha, you're speaking Espanole,' laughed Senor Martinez.

Vidal rattled off something in Spanish to his father, who nodded. Getting to his feet, he muttered 'Mucho trabajo.'

'What did he say?' asked Susie as Senor Martinez left the room.

'He says that he has much work to do,' replied Vidal.

'At this time of day?'

'Yes, and Luisa has been working since eight this morning, she works as a cleaner in the morning and cooks in the bar in the evenings; sometimes she doesn't finish until the early hours of the next day.'

'What long hours.'

'She needs the money, so what else can she do, everyone here works long hours. I too have worked this morning, and tonight I shall be back in Playa de las Americas working as a cocktail waiter.'

'I couldn't do it.'

'You would if you had to. Would you like a drink?'

'Lemonade, please.'

'Okay, one lemonade coming up.'

Susie seated herself on a battered armchair and gazed around the room. All the seating furniture had seen better days, and the television appeared very dated. On one wall was a huge fan depicting Spanish dancers, and on the opposite one was a massive poster of a bullfight. A display cabinet adorned the corner of the room and was full of ornaments and photos. Obviously the family were not financially secure but the place felt homely.

Vidal returned to the room with Susie's lemonade in one hand, and a bottle of San Miguel in the other. 'Come, we will go to my room,' he said. Susie got to her feet and followed him as if on auto pilot. Once inside his bedroom, Susie sat on a chair which was beside the bed. Vidal seated himself on it and swigged down a bottle of San Miguel. Now Susie was getting apprehensive; she wanted to leave, uncertain of what was coming next.

After placing his bottle of San Miguel on the bedside table, Vidal took the glass of lemonade from Susie's hand and placed it on the floor. He gazed into the frightened girl's eyes. 'Are you scared, querida?'

'A bit.'

'Then don't be, I'm not about to pop your cherry.'

'Oh.' Susie couldn't hide her disappointment.

'No, baby, I just want to pleasure you, now come and lay down beside me and we'll cuddle.'

Susie obeyed and Vidal pulled her close. They kissed and then he began to stroke her face, once more pouring out undying love to her. His hands caressed her body, sending thrills through her, and then his hand slipped under her blouse and groped her breasts. 'Beautiful,' he cried. 'You have breasts like Aphrodite.' Unbuttoning her blouse, he then undid her bra and exposed her lovely pert breasts. 'They are better than Aphrodite's,' he added, and then suckled on one nipple. Susie felt as if she'd gone to heaven, and knew that she had when his hands hiked up her skirt and moved over her thighs. His digits stroked her skilfully, making the girl sigh; she'd never felt this good. Everything was out of this world; sensations lifted her higher and higher until everything was obliterated in a screaming moment. She was jettisoned out into space, and she clung to Vidal, clawing at his back with her fingernails, crying out and then, just as suddenly, she fell to earth and became like a rag doll. Vidal stared at the glassy eyed girl beside him.

'Was it good, baby?'

Susie nodded, wondering what was coming next; he'd said that her cherry would remain intact so maybe it was all over. If it was, it didn't matter, she felt like the cat that got the cream. Vidal was getting bored, he liked receiving not giving, however he had to persevere with Susie and slid down her body.

'Did I do something wrong?'

'No, querida, you were fine but I want to taste you and feel that musk and honey run into my mouth, so just lay back and enjoy it.'

He removed her knickers and then began to give her oral pleasure. Susie lay back and closed her eyes; this was something else. The sensations this time were more intense and as she reached her climax, she cried out, 'I love you, Vidal.'

'I love you too, baby,' murmured Vidal after he'd felt the girl's body relax once more. Actually he was bored stiff and awaiting a phone call from Luisa; he needed rescuing. He stared at Susie who lay on her back all glassy eyed again. The phone finally rang and Vidal got to his feet; saying, 'I wonder who that can be?'

'Get rid of them,' replied Susie. 'I need to do something for you; you've made me feel wonderful.'

'Don't worry about it; it is enough just to hold you in my arms.'

He left the room and answered the phone. Minutes later he was back saying, 'I have to leave, I am wanted at the restaurant, a waiter has had to go home unwell.' The last thing that he wanted was a young inexperienced girl tugging on his manhood. It would have been fine if he could have just fucked her but he couldn't for two reasons. One he needed to gain Ray and Rosie's trust and, two, Susie was underage. If he knocked her up now, it could spoil his plans and he wasn't about to do that. The alternative was a condom, but he'd never worn one in his life and that wasn't going to change either. Susie did up her blouse and put her knickers back on, then sadly she walked through to the lounge.

'Can we meet up tomorrow?' she asked.

'I am working all day tomorrow, but I am finishing early and will be at the fair tomorrow night. Try to persuade your parents to take the children there, and we can slip off somewhere.'

'But if my parents are there, we won't be able to...'

'We will, baby, your parents will be busy with the children. Now, write down your name and address on the pad by the phone so that I can contact you once you are back in England.'

'Can't you fit me in at all tomorrow through the day?'

'No, I have to work, I will see you tomorrow night at the fair. I will have a special surprise for you too.'

'I love surprises.'

'That is good, don't look so sad. When we are married, I will work even harder so that I can give you the best of everything; all you will have to do is keep me happy and give me sons.'

Susie giggled; she was getting swept along by everything. 'Sounds heavenly,' she said, writing her address and phone number on the pad. Her body was tingling, she felt so alive, and her heart still belonged to Kevin but Vidal was cushioning the pain. She also felt grown up now.

'Susie, hurry up, I am needed urgently.'

'Okay.' At this moment in time she'd agree to anything that he asked of her.

When they reached the restaurant, Vidal asked her if she'd mind carrying on the rest of her journey without him. 'Not at all,' replied Susie. 'See you tomorrow night at the fair.'

Vidal pecked her on her cheek and went inside the restaurant.

'How did it go?' asked Luisa.

Vidal screwed up his face. 'Okay I guess, she's mine for the taking.'

'Did you have sex?'

'No, I gave her oral pleasure; I shall take her once she reaches the age of consent.'

'And you expect her parents to stand back and allow this?'

'My darling Luisa, I have her exactly where I want her, all starry eyed. Her parents are returning here in three months' time without her, and it is then that I will make my move by flying to England and moving in with her. The English have a saying "When the cat's away, the mice will play", and I will play hard, very hard.'

'You are a genius, at first I thought it was the mother that you wanted.'

'It was but her husband guards her well, so I will have to settle for having her as a mother-in-law, but if the opportunity arises, I will take it. When I first set eyes on her, I thought, my God that could do me some good, and when I discovered just how rich she was, I realised that she would be more than good.'

'I seem to recall that she put you down.'

'Yes, I spoke my thoughts out loud and she didn't take it too well.'

'It was quite funny; I remember clearing a table next to theirs when you upset her.'

'I didn't intend to, but none of her party could decide what they wanted to eat apart from her, and in the end she said, "Do you want to start on me while the others make their minds up?" I replied that I would love to, and she snapped back at me angrily, "I beg your pardon, how dare you, I'm married, and I'll thank you to keep your lewd thoughts to yourself." We made eye contact and I swear that I could see the flames of hellfire reflected in them. I apologised and said it was a joke but she wasn't impressed and told me to have some respect for her and her family. I kept my head down for the rest of their order.'

'And I noticed how you bolted into the toilet straight away after giving me their order; you were in there longer than usual too.'

'You read me like a book, I couldn't help it, I had to relieve myself; never before have I been turned on so much.'

Luisa threw back her head and laughed. 'Many of your regulars are now on the island; it is a blessing that your little English girl is going home soon.'

'I love you, Luisa,' said Vidal taking her in his arms. 'All these women mean nothing to me; we are a team and tonight we will be the A team.'

'How?'

'Do you remember Senora Driver?'

'The English lady with a face like a horse?'

'That's the one, tonight I am taking her out. She is staying in Las Floritas in Playa de las Americas, and she has exquisite taste in gold.'

'I have noticed, she is covered in it.'

'Well tonight, I shall persuade her to leave most of it in the apartment, telling her that it is not safe to go out at night wearing it. Naturally, she will lock the patio doors as she is on the ground floor. However, as soon as we are outside the building, I shall tell her that I have forgotten something. She will return to reception and I will return to the apartment. Once I am back in the apartment, I shall unlock the patio doors and you will be able to gain access. Take whatever you want. You have an eye for gold, and she has so much that I doubt she will miss it. When we return from our date, I will give her a night of passion. She will notice nothing until morning, maybe not until later in the day, and then she will think that she's mislaid it or the cleaners have stolen it. After you've taken the gold, lock the patio doors and leave by the front door, and that way it will look as if they've been locked all night.'

'You are a super genius.'

'And you are my one and only love. When I am making love to the ugly lump of lard, I will be thinking of you.'

'So I'm fat and ugly?'

'No, my darling, I shall be dreaming of the day when you and I can shut the rest of the world out.'

'And what about Susie?'

'Oh yes, simple Susie, I need an engagement ring for her, so see what you can find for me amongst Senora Driver's possessions. The bigger the stone the better, I want it to look impressive.'

'I will do my best.'

'Tomorrow, I will give her oral pleasure again and it will cost her a fortune.'

'You are going to steal from her?'

'No, I shall tell her that my grandmother is at death's door and needs an operation to save her life.'

'Both of your grandmothers are dead.'

'I know, but simple Susie doesn't know that; she is soft hearted and besotted with me, and by the time I have finished with her she will be begging to pay for the operation.'

'Can she afford it?'

'The whole family is filthy rich, and it is a shame that people should have so much. I will marry into that family and live like a lord. Soon you will be able to afford anything that you want, and I will shower you with gifts once I can afford to.'

'All I need is you.'

'It is just as well, Luisa, I've told you before that if you ever leave me or cheat with someone else, I shall kill you.' A chill ran through Luisa; she knew that he meant it.

Chapter Fifteen

At Lloro Parque, Eddie was conversing with Tom's keeper, and rattled on about his tortoises in England and his breeding programme. 'Geochelone sulcata,' said Tom's keeper. 'We have none here, Tom is our only tortoise and he's a different breed. We hope to get him a couple of girlfriends in the near future and begin our own breeding programme.'

'Daisy has lots of eggs, but most of the babies die; she usually lays about twenty eggs.'

'Then you must be doing something wrong.'

'Oh,' piped up Deanne. 'We don't hatch them, Uncle Vic does.'

'Why don't you do it?'

'Uncle Vic said that we were too young to do it. He said that if we didn't do it properly, the babies would die.'

'Well it doesn't sound like he's doing it properly. How does Uncle Vic keep them once they've hatched?'

'In a large vivarium. Uncle Vic says that maybe there's something wrong with Daisy and that we should get another girlfriend for Wacky.'

'How many clutches does Daisy lay a year?'

'Usually three.'

'That's a lot of eggs. I think that the only problem here is Uncle Vic. Buy an incubator and tell him that you want to take over the programme yourself. How old are you, Eddie?'

'Nine.'

'I think that Uncle Vic's too old to look after the babies. I told Eddie that he should do it himself but men never listen,' said Deanne.

'But, Deanne, Uncle Vic bought Daisy.'

'Yes, for you, so the eggs belong to you too.'

'But Uncle Vic won't like it.'

'Tough,' snapped Deanne. 'My mummy would do it for you; she doesn't go to work.'

'I think that it's a good idea,' replied the keeper.

'And I think that Uncle Vic's a crook. I can't think why my dad worked for him,' said Deanne.

Kevin laughed. 'He made him a star,' he quipped.

Deanne stood with her hands on her hips and replied, 'Then when he became rich, he should have left him. Barry was a much better bet. Vic is a horrible man; he's creepy, and he doesn't like me much because I speak my mind even though I'm not double figures yet.'

The keeper smiled. 'Couldn't your mummy and daddy help you, Eddie, or aren't they keen on tortoises?'

'Our daddy's dead,' said Deanne before Eddie could open his mouth.

'Oh, I'm sorry about that.'

'My mummy's dead too,' said Eddie.

'Then how can she do the breeding programme? I thought you said that she didn't go to work and could do it.'

'We've got different mothers, and Gary's dead too.'

'Who's Gary?'

'My half brother. My mummy was married to Barry and lived in Los Angeles, then Gary came over and died when he was mugged.'

The keeper was getting unsettled. There seemed to be an awful lot of deaths in this family, plus a deceased father who had fathered both of these children that were standing before him. He decided to change the subject, thinking that maybe if he stuck around much longer with the family he might die too.

'Are you enjoying your holidays?' he asked.

'Yes,' replied Deanne. 'My daddy has bought two apartments in Los Cristianos, but I can't wait to get home and start this breeding programme.'

'I'd do it too,' said Kevin. 'But I tour a lot, so it's not possible.'

'Well, Eddie needs to take over and put Mummy in charge. He's stupid if he doesn't. Uncle Vic's ripping him off; those babies couldn't have all died.'

'They don't all die, some live,' replied Eddie. 'Uncle Vic wouldn't rip me off.'

'He would, he's nasty.'

'Listen to your sister,' said the keeper. 'You'll be able to take full charge of live babies and watch them hatch.'

'That would be lovely,' said Candy. 'I'd help out too.'

'Settled then,' laughed the keeper. 'I'm sure that you'll be a great success. Next time that you're on holiday, come and see me, I'd love to hear how you're getting on. I must go now as I have to catch a few terrapins that keep getting out.'

Eddie laughed, but inside he felt scared. Uncle Vic was a formidable man and he believed that he wouldn't give up the breeding programme easily. The whole episode ended as Rosie, Ray, Bobby, Raydon, and Norma came into view. Bobby was excited. 'I sat in a dinghy and the dolphins pulled me around in it; some of them were jumping beside me too and following the dinghy. I had to give them a kiss, it was great. Can we go and see the sea lions now?'

'Don't you want to see the parrots on bikes and scooters?'

'Yes, but Raydon likes the seals and sea lions best.'

'Okay, sea lions first, and parrots next.' Ray was happy. Bobby had become a changed child since grabbing the limelight at the bar on the night of his tantrum. He'd come out of himself and been very absorbed in learning to play the guitar; his gifts were coming to the fore. Norma was delighted, as at last she had a family member who actually wanted to dance and entertain.

If Susie was gullible, her younger sister certainly was not. She was a bright child and missed nothing. On the final night at the funfair, she espied something that really put Vidal's street cred in doubt. Susie had spotted Vidal straight away and awaited her chance to spend some time with him.

After the children had had their fill of candyfloss, plus rides and side stalls, Rosie decided to go back to the hotel with Ray, Norma, and her two youngest children. 'It's going to be a long day tomorrow,' she said. 'Our flight is at midday and I need to start packing now.'

Kevin and Candy had already packed and decided to stay on and dance to the Salsa band. Eagle-eyed Deanne spotted someone talking to Vidal whom she recognised, and curiosity was getting the better of her.

She asked her mother if she could remain behind, as she'd like to stay and dance for a little while. Eddie didn't like dancing but he didn't want to go back to the hotel either; time was running out and he didn't know when he'd be returning to this pleasant island with its lovely weather. He decided to suffer the dancing and, after Ray and Rosie had left, Deanne beckoned him over. 'Come over here,' she cried.

'Why?'

'Because I want to get a closer look at someone.'

'Why?'

'Don't ask so many questions, just do as I say.'

Eddie frowned; he always gave in to Deanne and wandered over to the hot dog stall where Deanne was standing.

'See him?'

'Who?'

'The man who's talking to Vidal.'

'Yes, they're sharing a joke.'

'Open your eyes, dummy, don't you recognise him?'

'Yes, you just said it's Vidal.'

'Not him, you idiot, the other man.'

'No, oh yes I do, that's the man who stole Aunty Rose's bag. I thought that Vidal had beaten him up and now they're laughing like old friends.'

'They probably are friends. I never liked Vidal, he used to undress my mum with his eyes.'

'How can you undress someone with your eyes?'

'Oh why are boys so stupid? Let's go and tell Kevin that Vidal's taking the piss out of my mum. Nobody does that while I'm around.'

Eddie and Deanne hurried over to Kevin and relayed the news. 'Where are they?' asked Kevin looking in the direction where Deanne was pointing.

'Over there behind the hot dog stall; oh, they've gone.'

'Deanne, are you sure? Candy and I were not with you on the night that Rosie's bag was snatched.'

'Positive, maybe he's gone back to the bar.'

'Well we'll call in on our way home; this needs sorting out.'

'It was the man,' said Eddie. 'I recognised him too.'

'Maybe we should leave now then,' said Kevin.

'We can't, Susie's missing,' replied Deanne.

'Okay, we'll wait for her, any ideas where she might be?'

'She could be anywhere, she's probably with Luisa.'

'Who's she?'

'Vidal's sister. Susie's been seeing a lot of her lately.'

'Do you want a hot dog or something?'

'I'd like some of that tortilla stuff, it's nice, and I'd like a coke too, please.'

'Let's grab some seats then. Have you no idea at all where Susie might be?'

'Maybe she's gone to Establo, I don't suppose she'll be long.'

'Establo, is that the bar with a little dance floor down a side street?' asked Candy.

'That's the one; there's always someone standing outside handing out tickets. Mum thinks they get paid for it. Probably washers, I reckon.'

Candy burst into laughter. Deanne was such a funny child, she never held back. 'Wouldn't you like a job like that Dee Dee?' she asked. 'You could lay in the sun all day and hand out tickets at night.'

'No thanks, when I leave school I want a proper job, one that pays loads of money; I don't mind working hard.'

'I'm sure you don't. We'll give Susie half an hour, and if she's not back by then, we'll visit Establo; she can't be far.'

Susie wasn't far away; she was sitting on the beach consoling Vidal who was crying crocodile tears. 'I love my grandmother so much, and she will die without this operation. What am I going to do? I spent my last pay check on your engagement ring, so I have no money.'

Susie held him in her arms and stroked the back of his head. 'I have £3,500 in my savings account. Would that be enough? I could lend it to you.'

'I cannot accept it, baby, it would not be fair.'

'But if we're getting married, surely what's mine is yours.'

'I suppose so, but no I cannot allow it.'

'Vidal, I love you, please accept the money. How much do you need?'

'About two thousand pounds, it is a lot of money.'

'I want you to take it. When did you find out about the operation?'

'Tonight, I did not really want to come out, but I wanted to give you your engagement ring and see you before you left the island.'

'How thoughtful. I love you so much.'

'I shall pay you back every penny.'

'There's no rush, I come from a very privileged background.'

Vidal grinned. That was the only reason that he was with her. He kissed her passionately. 'Come on,' he said.

'Where are we going?'

'Establo.'

'I can't stay long; I've left the others at the fair.'

'I will not keep you long.'

Vidal pulled Susie to her feet and kissed her passionately once more, then they left the beach and headed for Establo. Once inside the club, Vidal headed for the toilet with Susie in tow. After locking the toilet door he sank to his knees, pulled Susie's knickers down and proceeded to give her oral pleasure. The toilet stank, but Susie was oblivious to it as her boyfriend took her to paradise. She screamed at the point of orgasm and, once it was over, Vidal seemed in a hurry to leave. 'Come,' he said. 'You need to go.'

A satisfied Susie pulled her knickers up and unlocked the toilet door. Outside was a very attractive blonde with a Northern accent. 'I wouldn't mind a piece of whatever you had,' she quipped. 'It would do me the power of good.' Vidal winked as he passed her, and made a mental note to return the following night. If the girl was there, he'd certainly grant her request and more, with Susie back in England.

As they returned to the fairground, they discussed the financial arrangements for the operation. Vidal was very happy; his simple Susie had performed exactly as he knew she would, all for lies, a stolen ring, and a blow job. Luisa was waiting for them and escorted Susie back to Kevin after she'd shared one last lingering embrace with Vidal. They'd been practically locked together, and when they separated, Susie could hardly get her breath. After promising to ring Susie the following night, Vidal made his way back to Establo; he was on a mission and hoping that the little blonde Northern beauty would still be there. Why wait until tomorrow, Susie had served her purpose for now. He would keep in touch with her and as soon as her parents returned to Tenerife he would board a flight for England.

Susie made her return with Luisa; it looked better that way. Candy and Kevin could now relax but Deanne was uptight. 'Where have you been, you selfish cow?' she yelled.

'I bumped into Luisa and we went for an ice cream, then we sat down and ate it on the beach so that we could look across the harbour. Anyway, what's it got to do with you?' replied Susie.

'I'll tell you what it's got to do with me. We're flying tomorrow, and Eddie and I are tired, plus Kevin and Candy were worried about you.'

'I'm not a child.'

'Better act like a grown up then.'

'How dare you.'

Luisa stepped between the two warring sisters. 'Dee, calm down, your sister is safe, and soon you will be asleep in your bed. You have a long day tomorrow. I shall miss you all so much, and I hope that you will miss me also.'

'I want to go home to England. Can we go, Kevin?'

'Of course, do you want a piggy back, Deanne?'

'No, I want a flying angel.'

'Your wish is my command,' replied Kevin and lifted the child onto his shoulders.

'Bye Luisa,' cried Susie. 'Keep in touch.'

'I will,' replied Luisa who then turned and made her way over to the hot dog stall. Susie fingered the ring on her finger; it was a real beauty. How she loved Vidal, and her future looked so rosy. How wonderful it was to be almost sixteen.

Chapter Sixteen

In England, Vic was feeling anything but wonderful. His eyesight was really a problem now, and he was sat behind his desk while his secretary reeled off bookings and acts that needed paying. 'Bakerlite have a contract to fulfil in Finland, and you haven't paid them for two months.'

Vic puffed on his cigar. 'I've given them plenty of work, and they're always pissed or stoned. If the venue refuses to pay me, how am I supposed to pay them? Fred Baker looks like he ate all the pies, and as for Fanny Lite, there's nothing light about her; if she fell on you, she'd kill you.'

'Spangles are splitting up.'

'Best thing that could happen, they don't stop fighting. The drummer knocked me out last time that I intervened.'

'But you still owe them money.'

'Okay, pay them.'

'Mad Mick and the Looneys are doing well in Spain, and their contract's been extended. The Silver Streaks are taking off too.'

'Thank God for that.'

'Dave and the Druids are leaving and signing with Barry Grayson.'

'Do I care?'

'And the Mighty Marbles are owed a month's pay; the lead singer says that if you don't pay them after their next gig, they're going to ram the mic up your arse.'

'Pay them.'

'Oh and Sammy Silver called.'

'Christ, is he still performing? Surely he's not still trying to be a teeny bop idol. He was fine in the seventies but its 1986 now. He looked just like Donny Osmond, but I hate to think what he looks like now. What did he want?'

'Don't know, he said he'll call later.'

'Tell him I'm out, the last thing that I need is a clapped out seventies pop star.'

'Z Tones have been going since the sixties; even Romany is showing his age now. Why did you replace him with Ray Lynne?'

'He became unreliable and, anyway, Ray has something I want.'

'What?'

'His wife.'

'What?'

'Oh I don't mean it that way, but Rosie has a great vocal range and she'd look good with Kevin. They could both play Vegas; it would be 'Platinum' all over again.'

'Poor Cathy.'

'Yes, poor Cathy, now where do you want me to sign?'

His secretary passed the documents to him and indicated where she wanted his signature. Vic signed, then reached for his cheque book. His eyes were really hurting now. 'I'm going home,' he said. 'Take care of everything, dear.'

'I will, Vic, after you've signed the cheques.'

Vic said nothing, his eyes were smarting badly. After signing the cheques, he left the office and, once he'd driven home, he called the doctor. Whatever was wrong with him was getting worse. His sight was getting bad, and at night he could see coloured haloes around lights; sometimes the pain was severe. It wasn't just in his eye, it was around it too and, at moments like that, he could hardly see out of one of his eyes. Vic's descent into blindness was marching on.

Susie loved her engagement ring, and couldn't wait to see her Spanish boyfriend again. She guessed that he was about twenty-three, but he was in fact going into his thirty-first year on the planet. She couldn't sleep and was now upset about her imminent return to England. From now on, she would have to satisfy herself with his phone calls and letters until her parents left again for Tenerife, then Vidal would join her and they would live as a couple. She was so happy, and lived for the day when she would be with him again.

Deanne had relayed her suspicions to her mother. Rosie was horrified. 'Are you sure?' she cried.

'Yes Mummy, and Eddie saw him too.'

'I'm going to see him now.'

'No point in going to the bar,' said Kevin. 'We called in and were told that he finished early today, and it's his day off tomorrow.'

'Was Susie's friend Luisa there?'

'No, and it's her day off tomorrow too. Deanne and Eddie saw Vidal laughing and joking with someone, but it was dark and to be honest, there must be many guys that look like the handbag snatcher.'

'But Deanne's usually right.'

'It was him, Mummy,' cried Deanne.

'But, Deanne, Vidal got my bag back and there was no money missing.'

'Did he, I don't trust him?'

Rosie gave her daughter a hug. 'Thank you for telling me, Ray and I will have to sort things out next time that we're on the island.'

'He'll only lie, so will his sister.'

'Well I think that you need to go to bed, you too, Eddie.'

'Okay, goodnight, Mummy.'

'Goodnight, darling.'

Eddie looked crestfallen. 'We did see him, Aunty Rose.'

'I know, I believe you but now it's time for bed.'

Eddie threw his arms around her. 'Goodnight, Aunty Rose.'

'God, it's like the Walton's,' said Ray coming out of the bathroom. He ruffled Eddie's hair as he passed him, then he poured himself and Rosie a drink and took it out onto the balcony. This was going to be the last time that he'd be able to make love to his wife in Tenerife for a long time. After a long drink, Ray took Rosie's hand. 'Bedtime, Mrs Lynne,' he said. 'Or do you want sex on the beach?'

'I'll settle for the bed,' laughed Rosie. She smiled at her husband and then allowed him to take her to bed.

'I don't believe that Luisa is Vidal's sister,' said Deanne to Eddie, the children cuddled up together like spoons.

'Why do you say that?' asked Eddie.

'Because one night in the bar, I went to the toilet and on the way back I got lost and ended up in the kitchen. They were both in there and he wasn't behaving like her brother.'

'What do you mean?'

'He had his tongue down her throat and his hand up her skirt.'

'Wow, but why would he do that?'

'Because if you get touched down there, it's nice.'

'Is it?'

'Yes, I do it all the time.'

'Why?'

'I just told you, it's nice, but brothers and sisters don't do it.'

'Why not?'

'I'm not sure but I know that Ray doesn't like us sleeping together in case something happens.'

'Like what?'

'I suppose in case we make each other feel nice.'

'But surely that's good.'

'No, because we're related.'

'I don't care.'

'Neither do I, but until I find out what the problem is, we can't do it. I suppose we'd better get some sleep, I hate flying, goodnight.'

'Goodnight,' replied Eddie. He didn't really care about Deanne's desire to make herself feel nice, or Vidal putting his hand up his sister's skirt; all he knew was that he wouldn't be seeing Tom for a very long time and he was heartbroken.

The following morning, everyone left for the airport. Susie was quiet and hardly spoke a word; she even refused her meal on the aeroplane. When it had taken off, she'd gazed down at the landscape, wondering where her future husband was and if he was missing her. He was in fact cuddled up to Luisa after a night of passion with the Northern lady. The girl had told him that she had come to Tenerife to work at Island Village as a rep. Vidal had listened to her but had no interest in what she was doing; once the sex was over, she was history and he'd returned to Luisa who was waiting for him with open arms.

Back home, Susie went to her room, stripped off, and gazed at her reflection. She decided that she didn't look too bad. She was five foot two with eyes of blue and long golden blonde hair that almost reached her waist. She felt that her legs were her best feature, as she was attractive rather than beautiful.

Her friends were always trying to get her to change her appearance. They told her to put coloured streaks in her hair, lose weight, and dress older. Susie listened but never took their advice. She was a size twelve and proud of her figure, not wanting to lose any part of it, plus her rich golden blonde hair was almost auburn in places. There was no need to put streaks in it, as her natural shade was one which many girls would have died for. Susie put a lot of the remarks down to jealousy; her friends dyed their hair, apart from Rachel whose hair had a glossy sheen to it. Susie was going to stay natural and if her friends didn't like it, that was their problem.

She posed in front of the mirror for a while and pouted, trying to look sexy. In the end she gave up and put on her jeans and a baggy top. Deciding to make her way downstairs, she fingered her ring once more and went in search of her family.

When she found them, they were discussing the possibility of Rosie taking over the tortoise breeding programme. Susie smiled to herself; tortoises were the last thing on her mind.

Vic was throwing a surprise party for the Z Tones, but to his dismay found that it clashed with Susie's sixteenth, meaning that neither Ray nor Kevin would attend. Vic wrung his hands; the only members that attended were the ones that he didn't want, even Romany had forsaken him for Susie's party.

'Can't believe it,' said Al. 'Don't your friends like you?'

'I don't know,' replied Vic sadly. 'Most sixteen-year-olds wouldn't want their parents to be present at their party, and as for Romany, he doesn't even like Ray or Kevin. Says a lot for what he thinks of me, doesn't it?'

'Never mind, I'm here, and we'll have a ball.'

'What you mean is, we'll get pissed; there's more to life than that.'

'Is there?'

The telephone rang and Vic answered it. It was his doctor bearing bad tidings; he had the results of Vic's tests. 'I was right, Vic,' he said. 'It is glaucoma. We'll do our best to control it, but you have to face the fact that at some stage you'll need help.'

'Why, what's happening to me?'

'Well, when you mentioned the coloured haloes around lights and the pain, it sent alarm bells off in my head. You told me that it was only one eye that was affected but that both were painful. You need drops for your eyes, and tablets to bring the pressure down; you may also need surgery. The iris is pushed to the back of the cornea and aqueous humour builds up causing a rapid increase in pressure.'

'It's no good telling me in your lingo. I don't understand all that mumbo jumbo, so put it into English, I'm not a doctor.'

'Okay, there's a strong possibility that you'll lose your sight, and you will definitely be partially sighted sooner rather than later.'

'I already am.'

'Well, I'll get you the best treatment possible, but there are some things that money can't buy, so maybe you should consider moving in a full time carer or even getting married.'

'Thanks a million,' snapped Vic. Now the bloody doctor was telling him to get wed. What was wrong with people? First Romany, then Al Simpkins, and now the doctor. He gazed around the room and viewed his guests, all six of them; this was going to be some party.

Susie's party was going with a swing, and she was surrounded by people. Barry had turned up; he still viewed her as his daughter even though he knew that she wasn't. He'd raised her for five years and treasured those memories. Vidal had rung every night since Susie's return, although he always got Luisa to make the call so that Ray and Rosie didn't get suspicious. After making sure that it was Susie that she was speaking to, Luisa would hand the phone to Vidal so that he could declare his love for the girl. He'd pocketed the money sent by Susie for the so-called operation, and he and Luisa had had a whale of a time spending it.

Rosie had remarked that Susie and Luisa must have formed a very strong bond, saying that the girl must be spending a fortune on phone calls. Susie had smiled and agreed, her secret was safe for now. Vidal's main interest was about Ray and Rosie's return to Tenerife. He couldn't wait to deflower the girl, and hopefully knock her up. 'They're returning at the beginning of December,' said Susie, 'and staying for three weeks because they want to return home for Christmas.'

'Wonderful,' replied Vidal. 'I will be able to give you your present early, I can't wait to see you again, I miss you so much.'

'I miss you too; it will be wonderful to see you again.'

'Susie,' cried Deanne. 'You've got to blow out the candles on the cake, we're waiting.'

'In a minute,' snapped Susie.

'No, you go baby,' replied Vidal. 'Enjoy your party, I will call you tomorrow.' He was glad that Deanne had intervened.

'Okay, speak tomorrow.' Vidal didn't answer, he'd already hung up.

Later that night, Vic decided to look in on Susie and take her a gift; he felt that any party was better than his own. He sent his guests home, telling them that he didn't feel well and, once they'd left, he headed for Havering Atte Bower. He needed cheering up; the news of his glaucoma, plus a call from Sammy Silver inviting him to another party, had put the kiss of death on his own. Armed with plenty of booze and his cheque book, he felt much better as he headed for Essex.

Chapter Seventeen

It was Deanne who let Vic in. 'Hello, Uncle Vic, what are you doing here?'

'I've a gift for the birthday girl.'

'You'd better come in then. Ray's had a lot to drink, but Mum's sober.'

Once inside the lounge, Vic surveyed the scene. He'd smartened himself up and had put on his best suit that stunk of moth balls. He couldn't see Rosie, but then he couldn't see much at all. There were many people on the dance floor, with Bobby centre stage moving around like John Travolta.

It was Candy who noticed Vic first, and nudged Kevin. 'Vic's here,' she said.

'Shit, I thought that he was throwing his own party. I wonder what bad news he's got?'

'It might not be bad news.'

'Where Vic's concerned, it's always bad.'

Susie was dancing with Steven, Cathy's oldest son, and they were dancing real close until Susie spotted Vic. It was obvious that he had something for her or he wouldn't be here, so leaving Steven alone on the dance floor, she headed Vic's way. Steven was unhappy. He liked Susie; he was sixteen too, and a genius on lead guitar. Seeing Barry standing alone in a corner, Steven made his way over to him; he needed to discuss work badly. Barry mentioned several venues that he had lined up for him but he could see that the boy wasn't really listening; his eyes were fixed on Susie who was conversing with Vic.

'Looks great, doesn't she?' said Barry.

'Yes and she knows it, she never notices me. I've asked her out but she's always busy, so I guess that she's aiming higher than me.'

'Hope not,' replied Barry. 'Her mother was a high flyer and look what happened? I worshipped her, but her heart belonged to Ed.'

'So did my mother's, still I can't blame her for leaving Dad, he was a lazy sod. If he'd gone to work, my mother would never have been on the road, so she'd never have met Ed.'

'Ed was a charmer; he had faults but the women loved him.'

'I know but my mother never wanted to work, she wanted to stay at home with us. Dad made her go, he's a bad lot. Recently he had a mega row with Ingrid, they were making such a racket. Ingrid was yelling, "You never wanted kids, you want sex but it's always the woman that has to use birth control", and then Dad screamed back, "I love all of my kids, it destroyed me when Sandy died, if Cathy had been at home, Sandy may have never had her accident", then Ingrid shouted, "How could she be at home when she was touring the country while you sat on your lazy arse". Dad was furious and really lost it, shouting, "Cathy was worth ten of you."

'I got scared and Michael woke up; he was terrified and so were my two younger stepbrothers. I tried to soothe them but they wouldn't settle so I went downstairs to get Ingrid. Dad had Ingrid by her throat up against the wall, and I tried to separate them. Ingrid broke free and rushed upstairs, and Dad glared at me shouting, "Piss off upstairs, you bloody kids have ruined my life, so has your lousy mother. She should have done what I told her to do."

'I stared him out and said, "My mother was a good woman, she loved us, you never did." Dad then retorted that my mother was a whore and that he never wanted me or Michael. I couldn't

145

believe what he was saying but he made things ten times worse when he cried, "I told her to abort both of you but she wouldn't. If I'd had my way, neither you nor Michael would be here, it would have been just your mother, me, and Sandy." It was too much for me and I rushed upstairs in tears. I never told Michael what he'd said but from that day on, I hated him.'

Barry was shocked by Steven's revelation. How could a father say such things to his son? It was unbelievable. He gave Steven a hug, saying, 'I wish that I could help, but unfortunately, without your father's consent, my hands are tied. I know that it's hard for you but life flashes over and very soon you'll be free of your father; you're very talented and a future star. As soon as you leave school I will get you a contract and take over sole management of you. I know that your father will agree because he loves money. Vic Lee wanted sole management, and your father refused, not only that, he told Vic what he thought of him.'

'What did he say?'

'Can't repeat it, but it wasn't pretty.'

Steven laughed. 'Will I work abroad too?'

'You bet, and a lot of your work will be in Los Angeles, so you'll be able to stay with me and my wife and kids.'

'Really?'

'Yep, now go and ask Susie to dance; she's caught up with Vic and keeps shooting me desperate glances.'

'She won't want to.'

'She will, go and rescue her in her hour of need, faint heart never won fair lady, I should know.'

'Okay, thanks Barry.'

'Don't thank me, go and get her.'

'Okay,' and smiling, Steven made his way over to Susie who happily accepted his invitation to dance. With Susie in his arms, Steven gazed across to Barry who was giving him the thumbs up. He was right, life did flash over but at this moment in time, he wanted it to stand still; Susie was a lovely armful.

Vic was feeling his age and focusing on Bobby on the dance floor; the child was excelling himself. Norma sidled over. 'Great dancer, isn't he, Uncle Jim?'

'I'm not Uncle Jim, and, yes, the boy is brilliant, takes after his mother, I suppose.'

'And his father, Bobby has a good voice too.'

'I wouldn't say that Ray has a good voice, it's okay but not good.'

'Ray's not his father.'

'Then who is?'

'Are you crazy? I thought that I was the nutter, it's Ed Gold.'

'But Ed was married to Cathy around the time of Bobby's conception.'

'You can take it from me, Ed visited the girls and Rosie just before he died, and he stayed the night.'

'Where was Ray?'

'Away working.'

'Why did he stay the night?'

'Rosie said that Deanne was upset and wanted him to stay.'

'But that doesn't prove that Rosie slept with Ed.'

'Those two have been joined at the hip since they were kids plus I got up through the night and I could hear noises coming from Rosie's room.'

'Noises?'

'Don't act stupid, Uncle Jim.'

'Maybe Rosie was having a nightmare.'

'Then Ed must have been having the same one, he was making noises too; they were going at it hammer and tongs all night.'

'What?'

'They were fucking, Uncle Jim, what did you think they were doing, praying? I wouldn't be surprised if they were at it in the afternoon too. They could never keep their hands off each other.'

'Were they making noises in the afternoon?'

'How would I know, I go to day centre, but when I came home, he was still here.'

'But it doesn't prove that he's Bobby's father.'

'Are you blind as well as stupid? You must have seen photos of Ed when he was a baby. Rosie told me that when she'd gone to Cathy's funeral she'd seen a shrine in the mansion that Cathy had dedicated to Ed, and that some of them were baby photos.'

Vic was taken aback. The old girl was quite lucid about certain things; he was loving this and wanted to hear more but he didn't get the chance. Rosie was heading their way, making Norma clam up. Vic stared at Rosie's undulating gait. She looked fabulous, just like Cathy's twin but more voluptuous. She was wearing a little black dress which clung to her body, accentuating every contour. Her breasts were almost escaping from her low cut neckline, and her hemline was short, showing her gorgeous legs off to perfection. Vic could feel himself hardening, and hoped that he could disguise it. He needed to talk to her about *Eden's Rose,* but at the moment, all he could think about was giving her a good seeing to. Her long blonde hair spilled around her shoulders and she was giving him a dazzling smile. 'Hello, Vic, would you like a drink?' she said. 'And how about you, mother, would you like one?'

'No thanks, I'm going to bed,' said Norma, realising that she'd said too much. 'Look at Bobby, he's a real little star, I'll just go and say goodnight to him.' She got to her feet and wandered off, leaving Vic and Rosie staring at each other.

'Well?' said Rosie.

'Well, wh... what?' stuttered Vic, his mouth had gone dry.

'Would you like a drink?'

'No, just a chat.'

'Okay.' Rosie seated herself beside Vic and crossed her legs making her dress ride up. Vic was now tongue-tied and couldn't speak; he was staring at her stocking tops. 'Well come on, Vic, fire away, what brings you here?'

'Susie's party, I didn't realise that hers had clashed with mine.'

'Surely you didn't walk out on your guests?'

'I left Al Simpkins in charge, I couldn't miss Susie's party. I gave her a cheque for five hundred pounds, I hope it's enough.'

'More than enough.'

Vic's eyes were locked onto Rosie's heaving bosom. She was driving him nuts; the woman was sex on legs. He recalled Norma's words and imagined that Rosie was red hot in bed. He'd sampled the delights of Cathy's body when he was making her a star, getting her into drugs which made her more than a willing partner. Then he'd got her back with Ed and they'd married. He'd made a fortune out of both of them and was furious when Cathy had given birth to Eddie, followed by miscarriages until she'd given birth to Amara. Her career was over, and the final blow had come when Ed had opted out of the band and was replaced by Kevin. Three months after Ed's death, baby Amara had followed him, leaving Cathy engulfed in grief. Her loss was Vic's gain or so he thought, believing that Cathy would return to working with the band, but, stricken with terminal cancer, she'd committed suicide.

'Vic.' Rosie was snapping her fingers in front of his face. 'You wanted a chat.'

'Oh yes, I want to release *Eden's Rose*, but this time with a video.'

'So what's that got to do with me?'

'Well, you are *Eden's Rose*, aren't you?'

'How on earth did you find that out?'

'Ed told me.'

'He would never have told you; was it Romany?'

'Can I change my mind about that drink, my mouth is rather dry. I'd like a whiskey.'

'Okay, wait till I get my hands on Romany.'

Rosie got to her feet and walked away. Vic noted her sexy walk and his jaw dropped. He recalled the times when Ed and Cathy had stayed at his home and he'd viewed them through his two-way mirror. He would have loved to see Ed and Rosie in action, it would have been magic. Ed and Cathy were electric, but Ed and Rosie would have probably blown every fuse in the house. His seedy thoughts had made his body react, and he'd had an accident in his pants. Not only was he losing his eyesight, he'd now lost the power to control his own ejaculation. Sickened by the thought that he'd have to sit in sticky pants for the rest of the night, he sighed and turned his attention back to the dance floor where Bobby was giving a rendition of the Beatles' *Hey Jude*, and getting his audience to join in.

So this was Ed Gold's son; he was multi-talented that's for sure. Eddie showed no interest in show business at all, preferring anything to do with animals. Bobby was the real deal; his father's talent lived on in him. Here was yet another gifted soul to watch, encourage, and exploit.

Chapter Eighteen

Rosie was a happy bunny. Susie's party was going well and everyone seemed to be enjoying themselves. She hadn't expected Vic to turn up but she knew as long as his glass was filled on a regular basis with some kind of spirit, he'd be no problem. Ada Lynne had turned up wearing a too tight black satin skirt and a leopard print top. She was a large woman who dressed a little oddly at times; Rosie had noticed people sniggering at the larger than life lady. Alf, her husband, adored her so, as far as Rosie was concerned, Ada needed to change nothing about herself. She had a wonderful personality, and Rosie felt that she couldn't have wished for a better mother-in-law. Her makeup was always caked on thickly and her choice of bright red lipstick did nothing for her thin lips, but when she smiled, she lit up the room. Her big brown eyes always sparkled with fun and she had the knack of making everyone happy. At the moment, she was seated in a corner with a crowd around her listening to Ray's jokes.

Ray was quite a comedian when he was inebriated and Vic decided to wander over and join in with whatever was going on. His sticky pants were making walking very difficult, he was almost limping and of course this did not go unnoticed by Deanne. She was, as far as Vic was concerned, a mouthy little madam who needed taking down a peg or two; already she was pointing at him and giggling. Vic was glad that he'd never had kids, as these days it seemed as if all they did was make fun of the older generation. He went beetroot red as Eddie was now laughing at him too. Ray spotted Vic heading his way. 'Vic,' he cried. 'Come and join us, we were just reminiscing about the old days when we were in our prime; haven't you got a drink?'

'Rosie's getting me one,' replied Vic, seating himself on an easy chair. 'I've forgotten what it's like to be in my prime, it seems yonks ago.'

'Now now Vic, you're only as old as the woman you feel. How's Lucy Lastic? I gather that you were an item not long ago.'

'She's in New York working; she was all right but she was a handful and wanted marriage.'

'Well, what's wrong with that? It's a great institution, and I couldn't wish for a better wife.'

'I'm staying single.'

'Okay, your choice, did I ever tell you about the bonfire party at the Chase in Dagenham?'

'No,' replied Vic.

'Oh no,' groaned Martin, Ray's older brother. 'Not again.'

Ray was centre stage, a position that he loved, and his slim body showed no signs of a middle age spread. He was in his prime even now with his sparkling blue eyes, fair hair, and pale complexion. Vic knew the fans loved him, but that he'd never cheat on Rosie; their marriage was rock solid. Martin was a much plumper version of Ray but you could see that they were brothers. Martin obviously didn't work out as often as Ray but he looked pretty good. In fact, everyone looked good to Vic these days except himself, and even Al Simpkins looked better. Despite Martin's protests, Ray began his reverie that Vic hadn't heard.

'Mr Lee might not want to hear this,' protested Ada.

'He does, don't you, Vic?'

Vic nodded, he needed a laugh. Suddenly he caught the stench of urine and realised that Ada had been laughing for far too long as she'd obviously wet herself. The smell was making him feel sick, but he could hardly move as it would be too obvious; he was kicking himself that he'd sat next to her. Rosie was heading his way with a glass of whiskey in her hand. On reaching him she said, 'I wondered where you'd gone. Is Ray boring you with his jokes?'

'I may be many things, but boring I am not. Deanne came over a bit earlier and she said that you'd whip my arse if I drank any more. I said that that was okay as long as you wore your bondage gear,' replied Ray with a wicked glint in his eye.

'Ray, pack it in,' cried Rosie.

Eddie and Deanne wandered over, and Deanne fixed Ray with an icy stare. 'Are you still drinking?' she said. 'I told you what Mum will do, she'll whip your...'

'Deanne, what sort of language is that?' cried Rosie.

'You didn't let me finish, did she Eddie, so how did you know what I was going to say?'

'I've already been told. Now why don't you go and join Bobby on the dance floor; Susie's still dancing too.'

'Yes, with Steven. They're dancing real close; I suppose he wants to get into her knickers.'

'Deanne, what's got into you?'

'Oh don't make such a fuss, Rosie, she's only a little girl. Look, do you want to hear my bonfire story or not?'

'Will it take long, you can be a bit long-winded at times,' said Ada, wriggling around in her seat.

'No, but it'll embarrass Martin and Tim for that matter.'

'Well hurry up, I want to dance.'

'Is everyone sitting comfortably?'

'Yes, get on with it.'

'Right, then I'll begin. In 1961, myself, Tim, Martin, and assorted girlfriends visited Dagenham. Sadie, Tim's posh date, was a groom at the stables, hence the invite.'

'Ray, get on with it.'

'Can I have my drink?' said Vic, wondering when Rosie was going to hand it over.

'Oh yes, sorry, Vic, I didn't realise that I was still holding it,' said Rosie, handing over the whiskey to Vic.

Ray continued. 'When we arrived, the owner of the stables was trying to attach a guy to a chair at the top of the bonfire; he was having no luck, so Tim volunteered to fix it for him. He was showing off to his girlfriend, and he'd really gone for it that night, new jacket and trousers, not to mention his flash shoes. He'd also bought some fireworks and coloured matches and stuffed them into his jacket pockets.'

'Will you get to the point?'

'I am, some bright spark must have put a lighted firework into his pocket as he was about to climb to the top of the bonfire. He managed to reach the guy after several attempts and was about to anchor the guy to the chair when smoke started coming out of his pocket. The next thing that happened was that the smoke turned to sparks and he made it to the bottom of the bonfire in record time. He threw his jacket onto the ground where it moved along the ground by itself. Tim was shouting "Dad will kill me," making everyone laugh.'

'And I would have done if I'd known about it,' snapped Alf Lynne. 'Tim borrowed the money from me for that jacket and it took him months to pay it back. He told me the jacket had been stolen, so the truth's coming out now; do carry on, Ray.'

'Well, Martin and I both found it funny; the jacket was ruined and it stank of smoke.'

'I did not find it funny,' cried Martin. 'It was me that put the jacket out and when I turned round, you'd gone.'

'Too true, I said to my girlfriend, "Let's get out of here," and we did. I took her to another field and gave her one.'

'Animal,' snapped Martin.

'Well we were young and in love. About thirty minutes later, Tim turned up and asked me if I was making some fireworks of my own and I told him to piss off. He refused, saying that it was a free country and that he wasn't going anywhere. Sadie was boring him, she wasn't bothered about his jacket, and all she cared about was her stiletto heels, evidently she'd broken one. What a twat, going to a bonfire party in the middle of a field in heels, and her a groom too. Tim always got the wrong women; he was a womaniser, every girl loved him.'

'Is this going anywhere, Ray?' asked Ada. 'I need the loo.' Vic was horrified and hoped that she'd go now, but she showed no signs of moving.

'So,' continued Ray, 'we decided to go back to the bonfire, and we linked arms and danced along like that film *The Wizard of Oz* until Tim put his foot into a hole and landed in a pile of horse shit; now his trousers were ruined too. He stank; anyway, this is where the fun starts.'

'Thank God,' cried Ada, wriggling around in her seat even more.

Deanne was lapping this all up. 'What happened next, Ray?' she asked.

'Well, back at the bonfire, we noticed that Martin seemed to be doing a sort of war dance around it. His girlfriend Anita was mortified and screamed that someone had tied a jumping cracker to him and she told me to go to his aid. I replied that he was doing fine on his own and that I didn't realise that he could dance. She slapped me, screaming that he could burn to death. I laughed, but someone who nearly did was a guy called Bill, who was fixing the guy when someone lit the fire. I wondered if he was about to end his life like Joan of Arc. The flames shot upwards and with a cry of "Geronimo", he jumped down, landing on Martin who had just completed another circuit. I helped them both up, realising that Martin had to be the unluckiest guy on the planet. Anita told me to remove the jumping cracker and I refused, telling her that the firework might still have life in it and that I didn't want my head blown off. Anita slapped me again, saying, "You're a coward, Ray Lynne", and I answered, "Yes mam, that's me." It was a hoot. Neither she nor Martin spoke to me for the rest of the night, I don't know why.'

Ada's mouth was set in a firm line. 'And what about Tim?'

'Sadie dumped him and he borrowed a pair of jeans from the owner's son and threw both his jacket and jeans onto the bonfire.'

'Is this true, Tim?' asked Alf.

'Yes, but what was I supposed to do? I couldn't drive home with my trousers covered in horse shit.'

'No, but you could have brought them home in a carrier bag, and maybe the jacket could have been fixed. What an idiot you were Tim, and I thought that you were the sensible son in my family.'

'No,' laughed Ray. 'That's Roland; look he's on the floor doing the 'Birdie Dance' with Gloria.'

'Have you any more revelations, Ray?' said Ada, yawning. 'Because you're sending me to sleep and I didn't find your story funny; you were just taking the proverbial out of your brothers.'

'No,' said Ray. 'I'm bored now; I fancy a smooch with Rosie once the music slows down.'

'Good idea,' replied Ada, getting to her feet. 'Would you like a dance, Mr Lee?'

'Er no, my back's playing up.' The thought of doing the 'Birdie Dance' with an incontinent Ada Lynne was too much.

'Oh well, I'll have to dance with my husband, come on Alf.'

Alf got to his feet; he couldn't believe Ray's revelation of the bonfire night. It happened in 1961; it was late 1986 now and he'd only just found out about it. He stared at his brood: moody Roland, lanky Tim, reticent Martin, and fiery Ray; they were like clones. What a handful his kids had been whilst growing up, and what a brilliant mother Ada had been. He smiled, he didn't regret a thing. Kevin watched as Ray took Rosie out onto the floor as the band slowed the tempo down. Deanne and Eddie were giggling again.

'Everything okay?' he asked, bending down to their level.

They nodded, and then Deanne said, 'Hobble dee, hobble dee, hobble dee,' and Eddie added, 'And down into a ditch.'

'I guess that means you're bored,' said Kevin.

'A bit,' replied Deanne. 'But I think that granny Lynne has had an accident, her dress is wet where she's been sitting down.'

'Maybe someone spilt something on the chair,' said Eddie. 'And she's sat in it.'

Vic was relieved that Ada had gone; she'd taken the stench of urine with her. Deanne was now fixing her eyes on him. 'I think that Ada's pissed herself; sometimes older ladies do if they cough, sneeze or laugh. My nana wears pads and, talking of pissed, look at Ray, Mum's holding him up, he's had far too much. There'll be a massive row tonight when everyone's gone home. Nobody will get any sleep because after they've rowed, they'll make up again and that's even noisier.'

Eddie wandered over to Candy who had just returned from fixing her makeup. He had a question to ask and needed an answer. 'Candy, can I ask you something?' he asked.

'Anything.'

'Well, Ray said that he took his girlfriend to another field and gave her one, do you think that it was a rocket?'

Candy gave him a hug and kissed the top of his head. 'It must have been,' she replied. 'Just stay as sweet as you are, babe.'

'Thanks Candy, I've got to get ready to sing with Bobby, Deanne, and Raydon. I don't really want to do it, but I suppose I have to as it is for Susie; we're singing *Hello Goodbye* by The Beatles. Raydon keeps getting his hellos and goodbyes wrong.'

'Well he is only three.'

'Bobby's only four but he never gets anything wrong, he's better than Deanne and me.'

'Well I'm sure that you'll be great. I don't like performing either but I'm joining Rosie, Romany, and Kevin on stage just after you. Ray's supposed to be performing too but at the moment he's having trouble just standing up. You run along now and get changed, Deanne's calling you.'

'Okay, thanks Candy,' and Eddie ran off to join his half sister.

Chapter Nineteen

Susie's cabaret was quite unexpected; first the guests were entertained by the Sweetles aka Eddie, Deanne, Bobby, and Raydon singing *Yellow Submarine* and *Hello Goodbye,* followed by a band that nobody had heard of called Streetwise Shack. The latter was made up of Candy, Kevin, Ray, Romany, Rosie, and a couple of late arrivals consisting of Mick Fraser the original front man with the Shelltones which later became Z Tones, and his drummer, plus Gerry the keyboard player of both groups. The whole thing was made to look as if it was an impromptu performance, but the whole line up had been practising for weeks to make it perfect for Susie's party. The Sweetles had captivated everyone, but both Eddie and Deanne looked bored sick, and neither could raise a smile.

Bobby delighted the audience, and Raydon had everyone in stitches with his goodbyes and hellos all over the place. The children had been decked out in 'Sergeant Pepper' outfits and looked charming, but as Deanne left the stage she could be heard saying that she couldn't wait to get out of the embarrassing outfit.

Vic was intrigued as Streetwise Shack was announced; he'd never heard of them and wondered if they might be interested in signing up with him until the group bounded out and onto the stage. Then he realised that they were just a tribute act covering Fleetwood Mac songs. A nervous Candy took her place alongside Gerry at the keyboard, she'd pulled out all the stops in an attempt to look like Christine McVie; she knew that she'd never be able to match her voice but she was about to give it her best shot. Romany had donned a wig to imitate Lindsey Buckingham, and actually looked quite good, Ellen had always loved Lindsey and had fantasised over him many times, but she'd given Romany his orders; he had to keep the curly wig on in bed that night. Ray looked nothing like John McVie, as his wig kept slipping off, so it was fortunate that the line up had included a second bass player in the shape of Mick Fraser. He'd really gone for it and looked like the real thing. Ronnie, the drummer actually resembled Mick Fleetwood so it had taken no effort at all to prepare for his role. Vic was puzzled; the whole ensemble were unrecognisable to him until Rosie glided out dressed as Stevie Nicks in a gypsy style dress alongside Kevin who was also playing the part of Lindsey Buckingham. Both Kevin and Romany had beards that were driving them crazy, as the adhesive had obviously produced some kind of allergy. Ray's beard was hanging off; he really looked a sight especially with the wig that he was now wearing back to front.

The band went into their first number, *The Chain*, after which Kevin introduced the band stating that tonight they had two Lindsey Buckinghams and two John McVies, adding that his band was great value for money. Then they launched into *Go Your Own Way*, followed by a very shaky rendition of *Think about Me*, delivered by an even shakier Candy. Kevin had given her a huge build up, so she was well received, but as she moved back behind the keyboard, she promised herself that this was her first and final attempt at singing.

Landslide was the next up and featured Kevin on acoustic guitar and Rosie on vocals. Rosie had watched Stevie's performance before as she'd performed this particular number and followed it as identically as possible. Everyone loved it, especially Vic, making him even more determined to get Rosie and Kevin together. Ray wasn't impressed as after the song had ended, Kevin gave Rosie a hug and then kissed her hand. The wig was now slipping even more and his beard had completely fallen off, he needed another drink and couldn't wait for this set to be over.

He watched as Rosie delivered *Rhiannon,* followed by *Gypsy,* and was angered because, when Rosie announced the latter, she said that she was dedicating it to Kevin in memory of Cathy. Ray threw the wig to the ground, staggered over to Rosie, and then fell off the stage. Alf and Ada rushed to his aid and sat him down on a chair by the side of the stage. 'Bloody fool,' muttered Alf.

'I'm ashamed of you, Ray,' cried Ada. 'How could you get so pissed on Susie's birthday? You're making a spectacle of our family.'

Vic thought that that was a classic considering that about an hour previously, Ada had gone out into the garden and pissed on the lawn in front of him and several others. The words pot and kettle came to mind. On stage, Rosie was singing her heart out, and Romany was complementing her on lead guitar. Tears were streaming from Kevin's eyes, as that song brought back so many memories of his time with Cathy. Rosie's rendition was perfect, and as soon as the song was over, Kevin took her into his arms crying, 'Thank you, Rosie, thank you so much.'

Ray's blood pressure was rising; that was the second time that Kevin had embraced his wife. Getting to his feet, he staggered toward the stage. 'Now, Ray, don't do anything silly,' cried Alf.

'What the fuck's wrong with you, the set's not over yet, we've got another song to do,' snapped Ray. 'What did you think I was going to do, are you nuts or something?' He took his place back on stage and wandered up to the microphone. 'Tonight is a special night,' he slurred. 'Today my eldest daughter Susie celebrated her sixteenth birthday, and I'd like everyone in the room to sing happy birthday to her. Come up here on stage, darling, and let everyone see you.'

Alf sighed with relief. He knew his son only too well and had thought that Ray had been about to knock Kevin's lights out. He watched as Susie went up onto the stage; she was a real little stunner. He joined in with the rest of the throng as they serenaded the girl with the tune of *Happy Birthday*. Susie was delighted; she loved being the centre of attraction. As she left the stage, Kevin shouted out, 'I want the next dance after I've removed my face fungus.'

'Get a load of him,' cried Ray. 'His girlfriend is on the keyboard, he's just been all over my wife, and now he wants to dance with my daughter. I don't know about face fungus, I think we should rename you Bluebeard. Right, that's enough from me, we'd like to finish on this number… Christ, I can't remember what it is… what is it, Mick?'

'*Don't stop*,' cried Mick.

'Well I've got to stop talking and get this set finished.'

'Ray,' murmured Rosie into the microphone. 'That's the set title of the song.'

'What?'

'*Don't stop.*'

'But I just said that I...'

'Ray, shut up, this next song is called *Don't Stop*. Take it away boys.'

Bewildered, Ray joined in the number and soon everyone was rocking along. Susie had had a great time; she'd been given loads of money, perfume, designer dresses, chocolates, and niceties. She watched the action on stage and focussed on Kevin, who had asked for the next dance. She couldn't wait, and confided in her best friend Rachel about her feelings for him.

'But I thought that you were in love with a Spanish boy?' said Rachel.

'I am, but if I thought Kevin wanted me, I'd say adios to Vidal.'

'You're so fickle.'

'I know but I'm only sixteen,' giggled Susie.

The band had now left the stage, and the band that had been booked for the duration of the party were resuming their places.

About fifteen minutes later, Kevin reappeared and led Susie out onto the dance floor. They had a couple of smooch dances together, with Susie almost fainting with pleasure. She was so in love with Kevin, but her feelings were not returned.

Vic was crashed out on a sofa, oblivious to everything and anyone. Susie had said goodbye to Steven and had accepted a couple of dates from him. She thought that it wasn't a bad idea, she could date Steven for a while until Vidal turned up and then she would marry him and be a good wife until Kevin wised up and realised that she was his soul mate. It was wonderful to be sixteen and have your life stretching out in front of you even if it did mean trifling with people's emotions. She was in love with love, but not everyone would allow themselves to be played with, especially her Spanish boyfriend.

Later, when everyone had either gone home or gone to bed, Kevin and Barry helped Ray up the stairs to bed. Rosie followed and undressed him as he was in no state to do it himself. She covered him up with the duvet and then went into the en suite to prepare herself for bed. Minutes later, she heard the television come on and realised that Ray must have woken up. Once she was ready for bed, she got in the covers, took the remote control from him and switched off the television. She was just about to switch off the bedside lamp, when Ray snatched the remote control from her hand and switched the television back on again.

'Ray,' cried Rosie. 'It's half past two in the morning, let's get some sleep.'

'So now you're telling me when I can watch television.'

'No, but...'

'Don't but me Rosie, there are two of us in this marriage, and I've got as many rights as you,' replied Ray, his face contorted with rage.

'But I'm tired, Ray.'

'Ahh, so Rosie's tired. Do you expect me to bow down to

you? I want to watch this film, so if you don't want to watch it, you can fuck off.'

'Fine.' Rosie had never seen Ray like this before. 'I'll sleep with Susie.'

'No you fucking won't, your place is with me; we'll watch this together and then you can give me your point of view.'

'But I don't want to watch it, I'm tired.'

'Shut the fuck up.'

Rosie leapt out of bed, tears were stinging her eyes. 'You don't even like this film, you said it was crap; we both hated it.'

'Well, I've changed my mind, now come back to bed.' Ray attempted to get out of bed and grab her but he crashed to the ground. Rosie headed for the en suite, she wanted to wash her tears away and get away from the man that she now didn't recognise. Once inside the en suite, she gazed into the mirror and ran the taps, however, she was soon aware of Ray's presence; he'd crawled after her and was heaving himself up with the aid of the bath. 'I need a drink,' he cried.

'You've had enough, you're drunk.'

'I want a glass of water.'

Ray crashed to the floor once more, this time falling against the bath panel, making it cave in. Rosie dragged him to his feet and took a glass tumbler from a cabinet. Filling it with water, she said, 'Here's your glass of water.'

'Not big enough.'

Rosie tipped the water down the sink. 'Fine,' she cried, and was about to leave him slumped against the wash basin when Ray picked up a toilet roll which had been standing on top of the low level cistern. She couldn't believe her eyes as Ray turned on the taps and tried to fill it with water. Time and time again, he poured water into it and raised it to his lips not understanding why there was no water in the item that he was holding. Turning the taps off, he staggered from the room and collapsed across the bed. Distraught, Rosie helped him to bed, turned the television off, reached over and switched off the bedside lamp, and then got into bed and snuggled up to him. It had been a lovely party, but Ray had ruined everything with his drunken antics. Exhausted, Rosie closed her eyes and soon drifted off to sleep, promising herself that she'd have this out with Ray in the morning.

About an hour later, Rosie awoke and could hear crashing noises coming from the kitchen. She wondered if she had burglars, and was about to wake Ray when she realised that he wasn't beside her. Throwing on her negligee, she hurried downstairs and into her kitchen.

Ray was taking trays from the oven and dropping them on the floor. He looked up when he saw Rosie framed in the doorway. 'Hi Rosie,' he said. 'I wanted to surprise you.'

'Well, you've certainly done that, what are you doing?'

'Making dinner for us.'

'But it's quarter to four.'

'I know, I'm cooking a roast dinner, it should be ready by six.'

Rosie opened the curtains. 'Look, it's still dark, it's a quarter to four in the morning, not evening, we've had dinner, and plenty of party food too.'

'So I've had dinner.'

'Yes.'

'Did I have dessert?'

'Yes, and plenty of alcohol.'

'Oh well, I'll just have some of this.' He took a jug of grapefruit segments from the fridge and placed it on the work surface. Rosie took a small bowl from an overhead cabinet and was about to take the jug from Ray when she looked over and saw him pouring some of the contents over the work surface.

'Ray.'

'What?'

'What are you doing?'

Rosie snatched the jug from his hands, and an angry Ray screeched, 'I want to drink this, why are you stopping me?' He snatched the jug back and put it to his lips, making the segments run down his chin and onto the floor.

'Ray,' Rosie screamed with frustration.

'What's the matter, Rosie? All I want is a drink.'

'You're spilling it onto the floor.'

'I'm not, someone else has done that.'

Rosie put her head into her hands and rested her elbows on the work surface. 'Then who did it?'

'I don't know, maybe it was Kevin.'

'But I just saw you do it.'

'I did not,' and Ray threw the empty jug across the floor making it shatter. Rosie felt helpless; she'd seen him drunk before but never like this, he seemed to be in denial and on another planet. She didn't even know how he'd got downstairs; he'd been spark out when she'd fallen asleep. Maybe he'd fallen downstairs, although he looked okay but then she'd heard that drunks feel no pain when they injure themselves. Sighing, she took out a dustpan and brush from the cupboard and cleared the broken glass up, then she washed down the surface with disinfectant. It was one sticky mess and covered with grapefruit segments. Deciding to leave him to it, she finished clearing up, washed her hands then left the room. He'd either come back to bed or crash onto one of the sofas in the lounge. As she ascended the stairs, she met Kevin and Barry on the way down.

'Everything okay?' asked Kevin. 'We heard a lot of noise and thought that maybe someone had broken in.'

'Everything's fine, Ray's disorientated; he's had too much to drink.'

'But we heard shouting, are you sure that you're okay?'

'I'm fine, Ray will be fine when he sobers up, I'm off to bed, goodnight.'

Both men wished her goodnight and watched the sad retreating figure. As soon as she was out of ear shot, Kevin snapped, 'His drinking is getting out of hand, you should see him on tour, he's like a man possessed and doesn't listen to anybody. Rosie doesn't deserve this, we're back on tour in two weeks' time, he can only get worse.'

'I'm surprised that Rosie's suffering all this, normally she wouldn't.'

'That's because he usually only drinks on tour, this is an isolated incident and that's the way that she'll view it. It was a party, there was plenty of booze on tap and he got drunk. Anyway, I'm going to have a word with him once he sobers up.'

'I wouldn't advise it, Rosie might not like it.'

'I'm not having her treated this way.'

'Got a soft spot for her, have we?'

'She's married.'

'And if she wasn't?'

'Let's change the subject. Christ, what was that?'

Vic's screams were echoing around the lounge. 'Get away from me,' he repeated over and over again.

Barry and Kevin wandered into the lounge where a terrified Vic was sprawled on the sofa. Ray was towering over him stark naked. Vic had been asleep when he'd been rudely awoken by Ray shaking him and asking him to play snooker. To top it all, Ray had a huge hard on which was inches away from Vic's face. Both Barry and Kevin found this highly amusing and laughed out loud, making Vic turn the air blue. Ray was bewildered. 'What's wrong with everyone? All I wanted was a game of snooker. Come on, there's four of us, surely one of you wants to play.'

'We all need our beds, we're tired,' said Barry.

'You're getting old, and so's Vic. Come on Kevin; I'm game, aren't you?'

'I couldn't lift a snooker cue, let alone play with one, I'm far too tired.'

'Then we won't use cues.'

'You can't play snooker without cues.'

'We could use our willies, Romany does.'

Barry and Kevin were in hysterics. The thought of Romany using his penis as a cue defied belief.

'Leave it out,' laughed Barry.

'It's true,' said Vic, getting to his feet. 'I've seen him do it, he asked me to join in.'

'Why didn't you then, couldn't you reach?'

'Very funny, look, is there a spare bedroom in this house with a lock on the door where I can get away from this maniac? I nearly had a heart attack when Ray woke me up.'

'You can share my room,' laughed Barry. 'It's next door to Ray and Rosie's.'

'Rosie,' cried Ray. 'Where's my beautiful Rosie?'

'In bed, where you should be.'

Ray grinned. 'Sorry guys, snooker's off, I want Rosie.' Then he half walked, half staggered toward the stairs.

Kevin followed him. 'Better help him up to bed,' he said. 'I don't think that Rosie will thank me if Ray breaks his neck.'

'Rosie, Rosie, Rosie,' laughed Barry. 'Come on, Vic, let's have one more drink and then we'll hit the sack.'

Vic agreed; he never turned a free drink down.

The following morning, Ray could not understand why Rosie was angry with him; he recalled nothing of the night before. When she revealed his drunken behaviour, he denied it and turned to Barry and Kevin for support, but they backed Rosie up and when they divulged the offer of a snooker game using his willy, he snapped, 'That's Romany's style, not mine; you're all ganging up on me.' He stormed off into the garden where Eddie was playing with a football.

'Can I play?' asked Ray.

Eddie nodded; Kevin rarely played football with him. After about fifteen minutes, Ray was out of breath. 'I'm not as fit as I used to be,' he laughed.

Eddie took his chance; he needed Ray to answer a couple of

things that were driving him nuts. 'Ray, when you were young, did you go to many bonfire parties?'

'A few, why?'

'Well, last night, you told everyone that you took your girlfriend to one at the Chase.'

'Oh yes, that was a good one, I was about sixteen at the time.'

'It was funny, and one of your brothers fell in horse poo.'

'That's right.'

'And your other brother had a jumping cracker tied to him.'

'Yep, that was funny too, well it's not really, it's stupid, still he didn't get hurt.'

'You said you gave your girlfriend one, was it a rocket?'

'What?'

'You said that you took your girlfriend to another field and gave her one. I thought that it had to be a rocket that you gave her.'

'Oh yes, so I did, you're right, it was a big rocket that exploded into lots of lovely colours.'

'I thought so; do you know what Deanne said yesterday?'

'She says lots of things; she's never lost for words.'

Eddie frowned. 'Susie and Steven were dancing last night, and they were dancing to a slow song close together.'

'And?'

'Deanne said that Steven probably wanted to get into Susie's knickers. What did she mean, did Steven want to wear them? I wear pants.'

Ray cleared his throat, and was lost for words. 'It's just a silly saying,' he said. 'It just means that he likes her.'

'I like Deanne, but I don't want to wear her knickers.'

Ray could feel a headache coming on. 'Of course you don't, oh look, here comes Deanne now, maybe she'd like a game of football. I'll leave you both to it.'

'Okay, Ray, was it a really big beautiful rocket?'

Ray grinned, his mind switching back to his youth in 1961. 'It certainly was,' he replied. 'Really big, really beautiful, and very explosive.'

'What are you talking about?' asked Deanne as Ray passed her.

'Nothing,' replied Ray. 'It's just boys' talk.'

'Boring,' said Deanne. 'Hobble dee, hobble dee, hobble dee...'

'And down into a ditch,' laughed Eddie.

Ray smiled and made his way back into the house; if Rosie had been right about his drunken antics then he had some serious grovelling to do. Making his way back into the kitchen, he found Barry about to leave and Vic seated at the kitchen table leering at Rosie who was cooking him a fry up. Ray noted the lusty expression on Vic's face. 'Put your eyes back into their sockets, Vic,' he said.

'What, oh I was miles away; you had a good night, you were on top form.'

'Cut the crap, Vic, I just caught you out having a lewd fantasy. I can read you like a book; you can dream about it but it will never happen.'

'I have no idea what you're talking about; I'm a bit hung over this morning.'

'I bet you are.'

'I'm off, Rosie, thanks for inviting me to Susie's party,' said Barry, picking up his suitcase.

'Can't you stay a bit longer?'

'Sorry, no can do, I've enjoyed the last forty eight hours and you were great as Stevie Nicks, you've still got what it takes, Rosie.'

'Thanks Barry, you'll have to come and see us again. Have you seen Susie this morning?'

'No, I stuck my head round her door but she was sound asleep and I didn't want to wake her. I really must go, the cab's outside.'

Barry shared a final hug with Rosie, then left her; sadly she turned her attention back to Vic's breakfast. Ray crept up behind her and encircled her waist with his arms. 'Hurry up with that breakfast,' he said. 'You need to go back to bed, and so do I.'

'But Vic wants to discuss making a video of *Eden's Rose*. He thinks that it could be a nice release for Mothers Day, don't you, Vic?'

'It will be a smash, especially with the kids taking part,' said Vic.

'Well that can wait; right now I want *Eden's Rose* to myself for a few hours, here, hand me that toast, I'll butter it,' replied Ray.

Rosie handed over the plate of toast and, within minutes, Vic had his breakfast set before him. 'Thank you, Rosaleen,' he said, watching as Ray took Rosie's hand and led her away.

Vic smiled. Things were working out fine; Ray's drinking was getting worse and it would be only a matter of time before Rosie would tire of it and throw him out, then Kevin could make his move and a new double act would grace every top venue on the planet. He began to wolf his breakfast down, his jacket was still upstairs and he needed to leave. If he hurried he might just catch Ray and Rosie in the throes of ecstasy. He cleared his plate in seconds and then hurried upstairs. Once inside his room, he gazed out of the window. Deanne and Eddie were kicking a football around, and they made a charming scene.

However, the sounds in the next room were more interesting; they were very vocal and were turning him on. So, lying on the bed, he unzipped his trousers, put his hand inside his crusty underpants and began to pleasure himself.

Chapter Twenty

Susie and Steven met up a week later. Steven fancied the cinema but Susie wanted to go horse riding and she won on the toss of a coin. They both liked horse riding so Steven wasn't too bothered that he'd lost his trip to the cinema. They had an awful lot in common and later over a meal at a beef burger chain they discussed their dreams, hopes and fears. Susie thought that it was a laugh that both Steven's mother and hers had shared Ed's bed. 'Isn't it strange that my father dicked both our mothers,' she giggled.

'Well, he married mine too; Eddie's my half brother as well.'

'And mine, but what I found even stranger was that both our mothers looked like twins.'

'Suppose it was really,' said Steven. 'My real father has never loved anyone but himself, he wanted both me and Michael aborted. My mum went to work while he sat on his arse; he was a bully to everyone.'

'That's dreadful, I spent a charmed childhood in Los Angeles in the days when I believed that I was Barry's daughter, and if it hadn't been for my accident when I needed blood, I'd still be there today. You're going to Los Angeles next year, aren't you? Barry told, me it's a great place, lovely weather and friendly people. It will really open your eyes.'

'What I've never found out was why Ed and my mum split up and how he got back with your mother.'

'I think your mum left him because of his paranoia and drug

taking; he just turned up one night and never went home, he was very ill when he arrived. I'd only met him once before at his mansion when he held that party, and Mum looked after you, Michael, and Sandy. I remember you then; you tried to play the piano.'

'I was rubbish then and still am, but I play the guitar well.'

'More than well; Barry says that you're the best, he likens you to Hendrix.'

'Really, I didn't know that. Vic says I'm above average but that he could make me a star if I worked hard enough. I'm playing next week in Ilford; would you like to come along?'

'Love to; I won't tell Deanne though otherwise she'll want to come too.'

'I don't mind.'

'I do, no it'll just be me and the audience.'

'So Ed was Deanne's father too.'

'Yep, on the night that he turned up, he stayed the night. I didn't really understand what was going on. I thought he'd be sleeping in one of the spare rooms, but later that night I heard Mum making noises that she used to make when she was with Barry. She's very vocal my mother, so was Ed that night; he kept saying he loved her, over and over again. I was only five at the time so I wasn't really sure what was going on. The next morning, he took me to school and was waiting for me at the gates later when school was out. After that, he was either at our house or we were at his; we were just one happy family. He was very fickle though because Deanne was in Mum's belly when he returned to your mother. When he left, I was angry, I couldn't make out why he'd left us when he'd told us that he loved us so much. Mum said that Cathy was his soul mate and that he had to follow his heart. She's got a big heart, my mum; she loves everyone.'

'You're lucky to have her; I wish that my mum was still alive. Will you really come and see me play?'

'I just said so, didn't I?'

'That's great.'

'I'll make myself really beautiful for you.'

'You are beautiful.'

'Thank you, kind sir.' Susie was finding Steven fun to be with; he was also very intelligent and quite silly at times.

In return, Steven found his date also fun to be with but a bit scatty at times. Susie drained her milkshake. 'What shall we do now?'

'Whatever you want, I'm happy if you are.' Steven finished his milkshake and pushed his light brown hair from his face, his brown eyes sparkled as he said, 'Thanks for coming out with me.'

'I've really enjoyed our date, we must do it again.'

'Really?' Steven could not believe his luck, he got to his feet and stretched, making Susie admire his lithe frame. He was quite a catch and on the brink of a successful music career.

'I'll ring Ray and get him to pick us up; you can come home with me and listen to some of my music.'

'I can't stay too long, because if I stay out too late, Dad will go nuts and take it out on Michael.'

'Yes you can, I'll get Ray to ring your dad and tell him where you are, and that he'll drop you off later at your door. Mum's making spaghetti Bolognese tonight, do you like it?'

'Love it.'

'Great, I'll ring Ray now. He's like my own personal chauffer; he's a great stepdad. What music do you like? I love Prince.'

'He's great, but I love all music.'

'So does Mum, but Ray loves Rod Stewart. He knows all his songs off by heart, and he's always serenading Mum with them.'

'I like the Kinks too, they did some great stuff.'

'Mum's got everything that they ever recorded.'

'Wow, what about Led Zeppelin? Does she have any of their stuff?'

'Yep, she had a crush on Jimmy Page.'

'You must have some fantastic stuff.'
'We have, come on, let's find a call box.'

The following week, Steven was a bag of nerves. He wasn't worried about the gig itself, it was Susie that he wanted to impress. He was one of the support acts, bottom of the bill in fact. Vic was nervous too. He'd put the whole gig together, and the nauseous Sammy Silver was topping it. Vic had avoided him for as long as he could, but he owed Sammy's agent a favour so had had to book him. Sammy greeted him like an old friend; his teeth were dazzling white, his hair dyed jet black to cover up his grey areas, and he'd just had a face lift. Vic shuddered. Sammy was still dressing like Donny Osmond, and looked as if he belonged in a freak show. There was also a duo from America. Vic thought that they were quite good, but they dressed like hillbillies. He had faith in Steven; Barry had loaned him for this gig and had made sure that Vic paid him up front.

Susie arrived, looking like a page three girl, her top was scarcely there and the same went for her skirt. Ray had driven both her and Steven to the gig, and had expected to take Steven's father too but Tony Peterson greeted him with the news that there was a great football match on the box and that he could see his son play anytime. Ray was disgusted, but hid his feelings and concentrated on driving Steven and Susie to Ilford. At the gig, Ray fastened his eye on Vic who was smoking a cigar and strutting around like a peacock, telling Sammy's agent just how wonderful Sammy was. 'I remember him from the seventies,' he said. 'He was a real pro; the girls went crazy over him.'

'They still do,' snapped Morgan Kane, Sammy's agent. 'He has a great following.'

Al Simpkins sniggered, as far as he was concerned, Sammy was a has been. He'd been booked to take photos but so far he hadn't found anyone worth taking photos of. He took a few of Steven, at least he was up and coming, he took a few of Susie too, now that girl certainly had star potential. 'Who's she?' he asked Vic.

'Rosie's daughter, her name's Susie.'

'Who's Rosie?'

'Eden's Rose.'

'You just said she was Susie.'

'You bloody fool,. Ray and Rosie are married and this is Rosie's daughter.'

'I didn't know that Ray had a daughter.'

'He hasn't.'

'But you just said...'

'Oh for God's sake, the whole thing's beyond you. Take some more photos of Steven and Susie.'

'Okay, got great legs, hasn't she? Great tits too. Do you think...?'

'No, I don't, now don't stand there gawping, you haven't taken any shots of Silver yet.'

'Do I have to?'

'Yes, you imbecile, he's the headliner, get snapping.'

Steven played a brilliant set that night and was very well received. As soon as he was finished, Susie made her way back to the dressing room to wait for him. After fifteen minutes had elapsed, she decided to go back to the wings to watch him; obviously he'd had to do an encore. Suddenly the door opened and in strode the American duo. The older man eyed a startled Susie up and down and grinned. 'Hi honey, my name's Luke, you look as if you could do with a drink.'

Susie ignored him; all of a sudden she was feeling vulnerable. She attempted to get to her feet but was prevented as the other man knelt before her and placed his hand on her knee. 'I'm Hank,' he said. 'You're a real cutie, aren't you; are you waiting for Sammy?'

'Well, she's waiting for someone,' said Luke. 'Look at that rock on her finger; it's expensive by the look of it.'

Susie removed Hank's hand from her knee. 'My fiancé gave it to me,' she stuttered.

Luke laughed. 'That Sammy's a sly old fox; you can't be any more than sixteen.'

Susie attempted to get to her feet but her legs refused to hold her up and she sat down again shaking, feeling as if she was about to faint. Hank replaced his hand on her knee and let his fingers do the walking. Luke was now standing behind her trying to get his hands down the front of her top.

'Stop it,' cried Susie. 'Leave me alone.'

'You don't mean that, honey; why don't you admit that you're waiting for Sammy.'

'We could give you a much better time than him. He's an old man, plus we work as a double act, maximum satisfaction guaranteed with us. A girl with your looks should aim high, we're loaded and going places.'

'I suppose that's why you're one of the support acts,' snapped Susie, feeling as if she were in the grip of an octopus. As she removed Hank's hands which were creeping over her thighs, Luke's hands delved beneath her top and began to fondle her breasts.

'Bit stand offish, aren't we,' said Luke. 'Keeping ourselves for the golden oldie, I suppose.'

'I'm here with Steven Peterson,' cried Susie.

Luke threw back his head and laughed. 'Him,' he scoffed, 'he's a kid and a born loser, you need to aim higher, why don't you listen to us?'

At that moment, Ray and Steven entered the room. 'Why didn't you stay for the encore?' asked a hurt Steven.

'Didn't realise that you were doing another one, you'd already done one,' replied Susie.

'Right, we're on, it's show time,' said Luke. Then as an afterthought he added, 'If you're ever in the States, look us up, baby, here's my number,' and he produced a card from his pocket and offered it to Susie.

An angry Ray swung Luke around by his shoulder and said,

'If she's in the States, she'll be with Steven. He's her fiancé and I'm her stepdad, dig?'

'Okay buddy, cool it, I didn't know that she was engaged, she's real cute.'

'Yeah,' snapped Ray. 'So go and perform and then take yourself and your Yankee slang back to the States, your act is mediocre and when Steven hits the States, you'll be busking and picking up dog ends.'

'Now watch it,' said Hank, 'or I might have to bring you down to your own size. If this kid is her fiancé, he'd better watch out and stick close because a girl like that is really something. The kid's status is nothing and never will be.'

'How dare you,' cried Susie and slapped Hank around the face. 'Steven's been likened to Hendrix, and my stepfather is Ray Lynne, lead guitarist with the Z Tones.'

'Well time will tell, and as for the Z Tones, they're a Mickey Mouse band, washed up sixties rejects,' sneered Hank.

Susie dealt up another slap. 'You bastard, my father was the lead singer for years.'

'They were shite and so was Ed Gold, come on Luke we need to get on stage, or we won't get paid,' said Hank, holding his face. Susie's ring had cut him.

'Prick teasing bitch,' cried Luke.

'What did you say?' shouted Ray.

'I called her a prick teasing bitch.'

Ray slung a punch, yelling, 'No one calls my daughter a prick teasing bitch.'

He caught Luke off guard and soon both men were trading punches. Unfortunately, Vic chose that moment to come in and soon found himself in the thick of the fight. Ray threw a punch that was intended for Luke, and Vic found himself on the floor, out for the count.

Al Simpkins came rushing in. 'Vic, Vic, the audience are getting restless, you need to get the next act on.' There was no reply and

177

Al noticed the seriousness of the scene before him. 'Is he pissed?' he asked.

'No, I slugged him, I didn't intend to but my target side stepped.'

'Then who's going to announce the next act?'

'You are.'

'I can't do it, I just take photos.'

'Oh shit, then I'll have to do it; I'll plug Z Tones at the same time. What's your names, boys?'

'The Cody Brothers,' said Luke and Hank in unison.

'Not related to Bill Cody and the pony express, are you?'

'No,' snapped Luke. Suddenly all the fight had gone out of him. All he wanted to do was get on stage, get paid and leave.

'Okay,' said Ray brushing himself down and straightening his tie. 'Here I go.'

'You okay?' asked Steven putting his arm around Susie.

'I'm fine, just a little shook up that's all. Ray knows how to handle himself, doesn't he?'

'Yes, shame the same can't be said of Vic.' Vic lay on the floor oblivious to everything, sleeping like a baby.

On stage, Ray addressed the audience. 'Ladies, gents and others. I've been asked to introduce the next act; Vic Lee thought it was a good idea. There are some of you who know me, some who don't know me, and others who couldn't care less if they know me or not.' There were cries of, 'We love you, Ray' which bought a smile to Ray's face. He continued, 'I play lead guitar with a fabulous band called Z Tones which is fronted by Kevin Howard; he can't get here tonight as he's washing his hair.' That was greeted by laughter and several girls chanting 'We want Kevin' over and over again. Ray waited for the crowd to quieten down and then added, 'We will be embarking on a short tour next week and, wait for it girls, we have a guest artist appearing for a few gigs by the name of Romany.' There were even louder chants and screams at the mention of Romany's name, one girl even fainted and had to be hauled up onto the stage. The Cody Brothers were getting very impatient as Ray continued to witter on about the Z Tones.

Finally he said, 'Anyway, I won't bore you any more, I'll leave that to the next bunch, only joking, these guys have supported Sammy Silver on several of his tours and they're great pals of mine so let's have a big hand for The Cody Brothers.' He left the stage as the brothers strode out to loud applause; they couldn't wait to get this gig over.

Ray walked back into the dressing room where Vic was now beginning to come round. Susie threw her arms around Ray. 'My hero,' she cried. Ray grinned; he'd quite enjoyed the punch up and the sight of a groggy Vic sitting up made him feel even better.

'What happened,' groaned Vic. 'I think my jaw's broken.'

'Ray was fighting and you got in the way,' said Al.

'Why were you fighting?' asked Vic, fixing his eyes on Ray.

'One of those American pillocks called Susie a prick teasing bitch, nobody does that.'

For a moment, Vic was silent and then he erupted, 'You fucking idiot, Ray, you're getting as bad as Ed used to be. Every time something goes wrong, you're there. You scared the shit out of me at Susie's party. I was sound asleep on a sofa and you woke me up by shaking me. It's dangerous to do that to a sleeping person.'

'Sorry.'

'Sorry, you should be more than sorry; you were stark bollock naked with a massive hard on. What a wakeup call, then you said that you wanted to play snooker.'

'My friend plays snooker in the nude,' piped up Al.

'It wasn't the snooker that was the problem, it is was what he wanted to use as cues.'

Susie and Steven couldn't conceal their laughter, making Vic frown. He stared at Steven saying, 'Good show tonight, Steven, you were very good which is more than can be said for that lot on stage; what a racket. You can go now if you like.'

'Thanks, Vic,' replied Steven, and taking Susie's hand they left the room.

Ray was about to pick up Steven's guitar and leave when Vic said, 'One of the Cody Brothers has a cut face, did you do that?'

'No,' replied Ray. 'He insulted Ed, so Susie retaliated and whacked him, cutting his face with her ring.'

'She's a force to be reckoned with.'

'She certainly is, see you next week, Vic.'

As Ray left, Vic rubbed his jaw. 'You know, Al, I think we could make a hell raiser out of Ray yet, all he needs is a bit of encouragement,' he said. His mind was in overdrive; Ray loved plenty of alcohol so he would make sure he had plenty on the ensuing tour.

On the drive home, after dropping Steven off, Susie began to laugh at Vic's misfortune. 'You really slugged him,' she cried.

'About time someone did, that fight really got my adrenalin going, it was just like the old days.'

'Did you used to fight a lot then?'

'Oh yes, your father and I were always scrapping; he knocked me out cold on my sixteenth birthday.'

'Why?'

'He thought I was coming on to your mother. I was a bit drunk at the time, so was he, and he smashed my motor bike up that night too. Oh the folly of youth.'

'Dad was a nutter at times.'

'He certainly was. Another time we had a punch up in the dressing room, and he roughed Romany up that night too.'

'Why?'

'This time it was my fault. I'd had one too many and I blabbed to Romany about certain things that your father had told me about him and your mother. It was a domino effect. Rosie found out about the gossip and went ballistic at Ed, then he in turn beat me up. When we went back on stage, we were like the walking wounded. Your mother was on form that night, she whacked me and did the same to Ed; she actually knocked one of his teeth out.'

'Show business is exciting, isn't it?'

Ray sighed. 'It has its moments. I long for the old days; everything seemed to be right then. Don't waste your youth, Susie, it passes very quickly.'

'Barry says that.'

'And Barry's right.'

'How old were you when you met Mum?'

'Eleven, she was a beautiful young girl, and dazzled me that much that I tripped up and spilt my drink all over her. I had no chance with her; she was joined at the hip with your father, anyway, I'm going to shut up as I'm waffling on. Steven played a blinder tonight, didn't he?'

'Yes, he's had a rough life. I know that Cathy loved him, but I don't like his dad. I wish that you were my real dad, Ray.'

'So do I, Susie.'

'Do you think that Steven likes me?'

'Steven is besotted with you.'

'Really?'

'Yes, he's a nice guy; Barry will point him in the right direction, unlike Vic.'

'Nobody likes Vic.'

'Well he has one friend, good old Al Simpkins.'

'Only one?'

'Yes, Vic's a creep but he's my boss, so I have to stick with him, but to get back to Steven, why not give him a chance; you could do a lot worse.'

'Maybe,' replied Susie. 'Maybe.'

'Oh well, nearly home. Are you still going on that ride next week?'

'I wanted to but my friend Jessica has pulled out and I don't know if I want to ride on my own.'

'Then invite Steven.'

'Do you think he'd come?'

'Princess, he'd do anything for you.'

'Okay, I'll ask him.' Susie smiled to herself; she had Steven as an admirer, Vidal as a fiancé, and the two guys at the gig had scared but excited her. She loved excitement and danger, and never did boring, and as far as she was concerned, never would.

Chapter Twenty-One

The following week, Ray and Kevin left for their tour with a very agitated Vic Lee. Rosie had dropped the bombshell about taking over the tortoise breeding programme, and Vic was not a happy bunny. 'I've always done it for Eddie,' snapped Vic.

'I know but you're getting older and your eyesight is not good. You've got enough to do running your agency, and this will take the pressure off you,' replied Rosie.

'But...'

'No buts, Vic, Eddie has asked me to do it and I've agreed.'

'But you know nothing about the care of hatchlings.'

'Neither did you until you read up on it, and I shall do the same. Susie's left school, Deanne's in school, and Bobby starts very soon. That leaves me and Raydon, so I'm sure I'll cope.'

'But you have to care for Norma.'

'Norma goes to the day centre, and Candy still works for me as a nanny; she helps with Norma too.'

'Well I suppose if that's what Eddie wants, you'd better do it.'

Vic was fuming; his little money making scheme was vanishing before his eyes. 'I'll drop the incubators and vivariums off after the tour. Better still, you can come to dinner and pick them up yourselves. I must admit that I'm not as fit as I used to be,' he added.

'Fine, I'll look forward to it.'

Vic leered; he was looking forward to it too. After dinner he would ply both Ray and Rosie with drink, making Ray incapable of driving, then he'd offer them a bed for the night and view them through his two-way mirror. This was worth giving up the breeding programme for.

A few days later, Steven and Susie made their way to Dagenham and saddled a couple of horses at the riding school. Susie's horse Goldie had blown himself out, trying to convince her that his belly really was that size and stopping her from tightening the girth. He didn't fool her though and she slapped his tummy twice making him expel the extra air. His middle had shrunk quite a lot and enabled the girth to be tightened. Goldie turned his head around and stared at Susie with a doleful expression. He was a beautiful horse, a golden palomino with a white star on his forehead and four white socks. He pawed the ground impatiently and snorted. 'There,' said Susie. 'You want to get going and yet you delay us by blowing your belly out.'

Goldie snorted again and, after adjusting the stirrups on the saddle, Susie mounted him. The owner of the riding school issued last minute instructions. 'We will be riding in double file. Havering atte Bower is quite a long ride from here, but as long as you stay calm, so will your horses.'

'I didn't know that we were going there,' said Susie. 'I was told that it was a mystery ride.'

'It was but now that we're all together, you need to know where you're going.'

'But why there? I live in Havering atte Bower.'

'Because we are assembling at the village green where the Vicar is going to bless the horses.'

'We'll be on the road for ages.'

'Are you nervous of the traffic?'

'A bit, I think it scares the horses too.'

'Then why come on the ride?'

'My friend booked it then dropped out, so I brought my boy-friend.' Susie indicated Steven who was mounting a bay gelding.

'Well make sure that your boyfriend rides on the outside of you.'

'I will, but I'd much rather be cantering around the field.'

'Probably your mount would too, but keep your chin up, you'll be fine.'

'Wish I had your confidence,' replied Susie, fiddling with Goldie's mane, then, digging her heels in Goldie's sides, she rode over to join Steven.

When they reached the village green, the Vicar came out and blessed the horses. Susie thought that it was quite quaint and was now pleased that she'd come on the ride. Steven enjoyed it too and chatted incessantly to Susie on the ride to and from Dagenham; he was great company. To Susie he was like a breath of fresh air, just what she needed, as she was beginning to wonder if she'd made a mistake by encouraging Vidal.

Steven made another date with her and, once they were back in Dagenham, they caught a bus and headed for McDonalds, followed by a trip around Debenhams. 'Are we going back to my place?' asked Susie.

'I'd love to,' replied Steven. He'd go anywhere she asked.

Back at Susie's home, they listened to the latest sounds, and a nervous Steven handed Susie a small paper bag. 'This is for you,' he said. Susie took the contents of the bag out; it was a very pretty silver bangle.

'I love it,' she cried, throwing her arms around Steven. 'I really like you, Steven, you're special, we're best friends now, aren't we?'

Steven nodded; he was in seventh heaven as Susie leaned over and kissed him on his cheek. She fastened the bangle onto her wrist, and was elated. Steven really did have feelings for her, so if it folded with Vidal, she had Steven on ice. 'Come on,' she said. 'Let's show Mum. We're having roast tonight; you will have some, won't you?'

'Well, I have to get back because my father...'

'Oh sod your father, you can go home in a cab. Mum will pay.'

Steven hesitated. 'But I can't expect your mum to do that.'

'Course you can. If I ask for anything, she coughs up every time, so does Ray. Oh I do love my bangle.'

Susie threw her arms around him once more, this time kissing him on his lips. Steven was nicely shocked; things were moving up a notch, and he was definitely staying for dinner now in the hope that Susie might kiss him again. She'd referred to him several times on the ride as her boyfriend, so maybe he really was. 'I'd love to stay for dinner,' he said, blushing beetroot red.

'Come on then, let's tell Mum and then I can show her this lovely bangle.'

Romany was all loved up; he adored Ellen and had fallen for her on the first night he'd met her. She'd hooked him by being anything but easy. When he spoke to her, she said 'Hello' and then walked straight past him. Annoyed, he'd told Vic to give her his phone number, which she accepted, put it into her handbag and then walked away, totally ignoring Romany's lustful gaze. Vic then approached her saying that Romany wanted to fix up a dinner date. She laughed and then handed him her phone number, saying, 'Tell him to phone me himself, I'm not that desperate.'

Romany was furious, he wasn't used to being treated this way but realised that if he did want to go out with her, he'd have to make the call. He rang her and she accepted his offer gracefully, but insisted that it was she who chose the restaurant. Once more, Romany agreed, and at the plush expensive eatery, they chatted about show business until she got up and said she had to leave as she had to get up early the next day. 'I'll take you home,' said Romany, hoping that he might get an invite for coffee, plus other delights.

Ellen shook her head. 'Tim will take me home, that's him at the bar.'

'Who's Tim?'

'My boyfriend, we share a flat, thank you for the meal.'

'But I was hoping to see you again.'

'I'll check my diary and see if I can fit you in. I might be free one night next week, but I'm very busy.'

'Fit me in, do you realise who you're talking to?'

'Yes, the lead guitarist with the Z Tones.'

Romany was furious; how dare she speak to him like that. He watched as she left with Tim, promising himself that he'd have no more to do with her, but a week later she did fit him in and they went on several dates after that. He wanted Ellen badly, but realised that she was no pushover and that he'd have to behave like a true gentleman if he wanted to bed her. She changed her boyfriends on a regular basis; Romany had met his match. He still fucked other women but his emotions were all over the place. Two months on from their first date, Ellen showed no sign of giving up her lifestyle. He still hadn't been inside her flat or received a kiss. Just when he thought that it would never happen, she relented and Romany crossed the threshold of her flat, making him believe that he was home and dry. She made coffee, saying, 'Don't make yourself too comfortable, I'm expecting a phone call later, Mike's coming round.'

'Who's Mike?'

'My new boyfriend.'

'And when am I going to find myself in that category; it's nearly four months since we met, and I'm not used to my girls having boyfriends.'

'One, I am not one of your girls, and two, I probably never will be; you've got a reputation and are probably riddled with disease. As a friend I like you, but as a lover I don't want you.'

'But this could be the best sex you've ever had, you're nuts.'

'On the contrary, you're the one who's nuts, I bet you've never had a steady girlfriend.'

'Who needs a book when there's a whole library out there?'

'Better go then, I've had many boyfriends but at least I have them one at a time, not multiples like you.'

'Concentrate on me, I'm the best.'

'Says who?'

'Every girl that I've fucked; give up your boyfriends.'

'Okay, give up fucking other women; I'm not going to be another notch on your bedpost.'

'Then if we're not going to fuck, I'm off.'

'Fine, nice knowing you.'

Romany got to his feet and crushed Ellen to him; he was rewarded with a knee to his groin. Doubling up in agony, he screeched, 'I wish I'd never set eyes on you.'

'The feeling's mutual. I demand respect, so if you want me, it'll be on my terms.'

'Fuck you,' yelled Romany. He straightened himself up and left, slamming the door as he went; he wasn't about to waste any more time on this one. However, the following morning, he rang and apologised, telling her that he was prepared to play it her way.

'Good,' replied Ellen. 'Come over and we'll discuss things. I like you but I'm not prepared to be treated like a piece of meat.'

Romany was relieved, telling her that he'd come over after his gig that night, and Ellen replied that if he could get her a backstage pass, she'd come and see him play so that they could leave and spend the night together. That was music to Romany's ears; he was finally home dry, or so he thought.

Things didn't exactly work out in the manner that he'd expected. After discussing their future together, Ellen stated that he could either sleep on the sofa or share her bed. 'You can sleep with me, but you'll have to keep your clothes on, and there'll be no funny business even if you have a condom,' she said.

Romany agreed to remain fully clothed, thinking that once he finally got his leg over, he'd dump her, and then it suddenly dawned on him that he didn't want to discard her; he'd finally found someone who he wanted to spend his life with, sex or no sex. He followed Ellen to her room, and once in bed, snuggled up to her. They shared a kiss and then he fell asleep. The feelings that were sweeping over him were new, he'd never felt this way before; he was in love and he still hadn't touched her. In the next few months, he'd wooed and won her with flowers, champagne, expensive holidays and gifts; he was even wearing condoms and went to the clinic to have himself checked out. Miraculously, he was clean, and groupies were gone forever. Six months later, Ellen moved into his palatial mansion, making Romany the happiest man in the world. Now he knew how Ed had felt about Rosie and Cathy.

And then things changed, Rick had work for him in Los Angeles, and Ellen couldn't go owing to the fact that her father had just died and, as an only child, she was needed to support her mother in her hour of need. Romany was lost; he and Ellen had been inseparable, and he didn't know how he was going to cope without her. He told her that he would turn the work down, but Ellen told him to go, saying that her mother was suicidal and that she'd probably have to go home for a while anyway. Reluctantly, Romany left for Los Angeles and found that for over two weeks he couldn't function properly. Then Rick stepped in and, pretty soon, Romany was back on drugs and partying hard. The brothers had always shared girls, and once more the old Romany re-surfaced and condoms were forgotten.

On his return to England, he was riddled with guilt and made straight for the clinic, he'd been lucky, or so he thought, as there appeared to be no sign of any transmitted diseases. He was tested for Aids too and was declared negative, but told to return at a later date as sometimes it can become positive after two or three months. Romany had no intention of returning, the word negative at this moment in time was sufficient for him, and then, out of the blue, he caught a dose of what seemed like glandular fever. He explained it away as drinking out of a glass from an infected person. He was still using condoms anyway, so felt that Ellen was not at risk at all. Blindly in love with him, Ellen accepted his explanation, believing that his cheating days were over.

One who was not fooled was Rosie. She'd been horrified by his appearance when they'd been rehearsing for Susie's birthday surprise; he'd lost weight and had hollow cheeks. He was ill, and there was no doubt about it.

Therefore, when she was invited to his birthday party, she accepted the invitation happily, wanting to get to the bottom of this. Ray was on tour, and Candy was in charge of the children and Norma, so Rosie went merrily on her way to visit the former stud.

At the party, Rosie stared across the room at Romany and Ellen; they were such a loved up couple. Ellen was glowing but by the side of her, Romany looked like death warmed up. The house was filled with druggies, hangers on, would be stars, and gate crashers. As the night wore on, the liquor flowed, coke was snorted, and everyone got merry. Romany gave his famous rendition of *Sabre Dance* and bathed in the limelight. In another week, he'd be meeting up with the Z Tones as a guest artist and wasn't exactly looking forward to it. Vic's rule of no wives and girlfriends on tour still remained, and if Romany wanted to do the gigs, he had to take note of the rules. Later when the music slowed down, he asked Rosie to dance and, once she was in his arms, muttered, 'Ray's a lucky sod, so was Ed; are you staying overnight?'

'Are you propositioning me?'

Romany pressed his body up against her. 'No, I love Ellen, I couldn't cheat on her, not even with you; we go back a long way, don't we?'

'1956 to be precise. Yes, I'll stay, might as well, Ray's away and Candy's taking care of things at home.'

'Where did the years go?'

'God knows. Are you okay? You're burning up.'

'It's you, you're turning me on, can't you feel it?'

'Yes I can, either that or you've got a gun in your pocket, you look tired.'

'Too many late nights, I'm fine.' Rosie gazed into his eyes; all she could see was a very sick man.

Later that night, she tossed and turned in bed. Romany was sick, very sick. Had he got cancer or something even worse? He and Ellen were almost joined at the hip, so it was unlikely that he was cheating on her. They'd been together now for almost two years and were never apart. And then she remembered his trip to Los Angeles without Ellen; he'd been staying with his brother at that time and had stayed for a month. Could something have happened there?

She looked at the clock on the bedside cabinet, it was half past two. She needed some shuteye, and it was no use dwelling on Romany. Ellen may be her friend but her problems were her affair. She focussed her thoughts onto Ray and wondered what he was up to; he was away a lot these days and she missed him terribly, how she ached to be in his arms.

The following morning, Ellen awoke her and asked her to come to her room. 'Don't say a word,' she said. 'I want to see Romany's face when he wakes up and sees us either side of him, it'll be such a laugh.'

Rosie complied, but somehow she didn't think that the sleeping man would appreciate Ellen's little joke. Once Ellen and Rosie were in bed, Ellen began to caress Romany. He half opened one eye, murmuring, 'Love you, baby, it was a great night, wasn't it?'

'It was great for me, how about you, Rosie?'

'Rosie.' Romany's eyes snapped open and he turned to his right beholding Rosie propped up on one elbow gazing at him. 'What are you doing in my bed, Rosie?' cried Romany.

'What do you think?' laughed Ellen. 'She had a great night too; you really rose to the occasion.'

'But I don't remember it,' replied Romany.

'Too much to drink, but you performed magnificently. I'm going downstairs to make some coffee, see you later,' and with that, Ellen got out of bed and left the room giggling.

Romany was horrified, and this was the reaction that Rosie had expected. She held Romany's stare as his dark eyes flashed beneath his long fringed lashes and over her scantily dressed body. Suddenly he burst into tears crying, 'Rosie, tell me that we didn't, I'm begging you, I need to know.'

'Am I that repulsive?'

'No, you're still as gorgeous as ever.'

'It's never bothered you before having two women in your bed.'

'But I wouldn't have touched you for fear of...'

'Fear of what?'

'I don't know, since I visited Rick, I've never felt well. I went to a few parties with him and we...'

'You screwed around without condoms.'

'Well, when I'm with Rick, things are different, he knows a lot of beautiful women, and it was just like the old days but it won't happen again. I love Ellen.'

'Sounds like a case of closing the stable door after the horse has bolted.'

'What do you mean?'

'Well let's put it this way, have you been tested for sexually transmitted diseases?'

'I got it done as soon as I came home.'

'Was an Aids test included?'

'I had one done and it came up negative; they said to go back two or three months later because it could become positive but I never went back.'

'Maybe you should.'

'I haven't got Aids.'

'Really, then why does it bother you so much that you might have screwed me. Look, you've got a massive hard on, it's playing tents with your duvet. I won't tell Ray or Ellen if you don't; shall I get on top of you?' Rosie licked her lips provocatively knowing that he wouldn't touch her; he was sick but in denial.

'I'd love to but we can't.' Romany was in agony.

Rosie threw the covers from him crying, 'What a waste, that's one big stiffy.'

'Rosie, don't tempt me.'

'Why not, I hardly see Ray these days since he took your place, and I have needs too. Why don't you take his place inside me?'

'I can't.'

Rosie got out of bed and stood before him allowing the straps of her chemise to fall down. Romany swallowed hard as she exposed her breasts. She fondled them and then bent her head and took one nipple into her mouth.

'Rosie, stop it, this is more than flesh and blood can stand, I can't cheat on Ellen.'

'You just admitted that you did in Los Angeles,' replied Rosie, removing her nipple from her mouth.

'It was a mistake, I love Ellen.'

'Then you'll have to confess all to her, you're sick.'

'I'm not.'

'You are. What do you think women talk about when their men aren't present?'

'I don't know.'

'They talk about their partners. Ellen's worried about you, she's spoken about your colds and bronchitis, plus your outbreaks of herpes. She also says that you suffer from a condition called candidiasis, a fungal infection, and you're running a fever too; I felt it last night when we were dancing.'

'That was because you were turning me on.'

'Rubbish, I'm surprised that Ellen hasn't clocked on to what's wrong with you.'

'I'm not sick; tell me, did we have sex?'

'No we didn't, it was Ellen's idea of a joke, she wanted to see your reaction when you woke up with both of us.'

'Thank God.'

'So you're not sick?'

'No, how many times do I have to tell you?'

'Great, let's have a quickie.' Rosie was advancing on him and got back into bed.

Romany had broken out in a cold sweat, Rosie was driving him crazy. She was now leaning over him as if she were about to straddle him. 'No, Rosie,' implored Romany. 'Don't, please don't.' He wanted to force her onto his throbbing manhood, lust was taking over. Rosie however had no intention of performing the sex act, she just wanted him to admit that he was sick and in need of help. She ran her tongue over her lips once more; it became all too much for Romany and he ejaculated all over himself.

'Oh dear,' cried Rosie. 'What a waste. Oh well, I think I'll get dressed and go home.' She rose from the bed and made for the door.

'Rosie, please don't tell Ellen.'

'I won't, but you're sick and so will she be in time, seek medical help, Romany. If you really love her, you will confess all.'

'I've been using condoms when we've had sex.'

'Well at least that's something, thanks for the party, it was great.' Rosie left the room, leaving Romany to collect his thoughts and change his sheets. He was finally getting his comeuppance after his hell raising days as a womaniser, and had given himself a death sentence. 'Live by the sword, die by the sword,' she said out loud. She didn't want to spend another minute in this house.

Chapter Twenty-Two

It was almost countdown time for Ray and Rosie's return to Tenerife. They were only taking Raydon and Bobby with them, as both Susie and Deanne didn't want to go. Deanne threw a strop, saying that if Eddie wasn't going, she wasn't. So the decision was taken to allow her to stay with Kevin and Eddie at their house. Susie had a different agenda; she wanted the home empty so that Vidal could visit her. 'Nana's getting older and she doesn't really travel that well these days. Four hours is a long time in an aeroplane, so if I stay at home, she can still attend the day centre too. It will be nice for us to spend some time together, we can visit her own home at weekends, she'd like that.' Susie wasn't lost for words. Rosie wasn't sure; it was unusual for Susie to consider someone else.

'I hoped that we could all go as a family,' she said. 'First Deanne opts out, and now you.'

'But it would be better for Nana, it's not just the four hours in the sky, there's the drive to Gatwick which takes about an hour and then we have to check in two hours before the flight takes off, and what about flight delays, I really think that it's too much for her.'

'Susie's got a point,' said Ray. 'And then Candy could stay with Kevin, Eddie, and Deanne, so that would keep her happy. We can manage with Bobby and Raydon; there's no need for her to accompany us. She'll need eyes in the back of her head managing Deanne, she's becoming quite a handful and she's mouthy with it.'

'Okay Susie, if you don't mind keeping Norma company, its fine by me,' said Rosie. 'But are you sure that you'll be okay?'

'Mum, I'm sixteen; I'm all grown up now.'

'Of course you are, I just worry about you that's all.'

'I know, maybe we can have another family holiday sometime next year, it'll be Christmas in a few weeks,' said Susie.

'Relax Rosie, maybe Steven will come over and keep Susie company too.' Ray was delighted; the thought of just him, Rosie, and the two boys in the sun was a wonderful idea.

'I've got to stop this mother hen act,' said Rosie. 'Before I know it, you'll be married and I'll be a grandma.'

Susie smiled, thinking sooner than you think; she couldn't wait to feel Vidal's arms around her again. She had under a week to wait, it would be bliss. She'd be the lady of the house and would do anything that she wanted.

At the weekend, Ray and Rosie visited Vic to pick up the vivariums and incubators for the tortoise breeding programme. Vic still felt sore about handing it over to Rosie, but realised that if he wanted her for his video of *Eden's Rose*, he had to give a little. He was encouraging Ray's drinking whilst on tour, and he intended to do the same tonight too, plus spike Rosie's drinks with sedatives. Excitement was building up in him; the two way mirror would be in use tonight. Hearing their car drive up outside, he surveyed himself in the hall mirror and then went to the front door to welcome his guests.

A couple of hours later, both Ray and Rosie were feeling rather strange. Rosie could hardly keep her eyes open, and Ray surveyed his wife anxiously. She'd only had two drinks but looked almost comatose. 'What are your apartments like, Ray?' said Vic. 'I've only been to Tenerife once. I stayed in the north of the island, and the weather was fantastic, here have another drink.' Vic was proffering the whiskey bottle. Ray accepted, he never turned down drink these days.

'Thanks Vic, I will have another one. Both of the apartments are close to the beach, in fact one of them is front line; we're letting that one out. Maybe you could visit us some time.'

Vic stared at Rosie; she was almost out of it. 'It's good of Rosie to take over the tortoise breeding programme; my eyes are not what they used to be, I'm getting old now.'

'Vic, you're as old as the woman that you feel.'

Vic laughed; Rosie had now closed her eyes. 'She's out for the count,' he said. 'It's too late to be moving incubators and vivariums now, better do it in the morning in the cold light of day, plus I need to find the books to help Rosie with the programme. They were on the table yesterday; I suppose Mrs Monk must have moved them. I'll ask her where they are when she comes in in the morning. How about we get Rosie up to bed? Then we can have a bit more to drink and talk about only things that men talk about.'

'That's very kind of you to put us up.'

'I think that if Rosie sleeps now, she'll wake up by the time that you get up the wooden hill. I reckon that she'll be raring to go.'

'Sounds good to me, let's get her upstairs now.' Ray put his arm around Rosie. 'Bedtime, Mrs Lynne,' he said.

Rosie opened her eyes. 'Oh Ray, I feel so tired, and so sick too,' and with that, she threw up and then apologised profusely.

'Don't apologise, dear.' Vic was triumphant, and after helping Ray to get Rosie upstairs, he went back down again to clear up the puke.

Upstairs, Ray helped Rosie into bed, and she lay there feeling as if she were on a merry go round. Ray gave her a cuddle and then went back downstairs to where Vic was waiting with the bottle of whiskey poised to refill his glass. There was a faint smell of Dettol in the air where Vic had cleared the sick that Rosie had thrown up. 'Nice room, Vic, thanks,' said Ray.

'Think nothing of it, Ed and Cathy slept in it many times; it's always been a guest room. Have a refill.'

'I haven't finished the last one yet.'

'Well, get it down you, we've got all night. I know that you like a wee dram or two and as you're not driving you might as well enjoy yourself.'

Ray wasn't going to refuse; the booze was free and he intended to indulge. Vic lit a cigar, then leaned back in his chair and surveyed the inebriated man. 'I believe that you are equalling Romany,' he said.

'Don't think so,' replied Ray. 'I don't think anyone comes close to him.'

Vic puffed on his cigar. 'You should have more faith in yourself, Romany's had his day and he's going into meltdown. I must admit I think he's ill. He's talking about getting married, but that's no image for a hell raiser, that's if he's got any hell left in him, he looks very poorly.'

'Rosie's worried about him too.'

'Maybe he has cancer.'

'Rosie thinks that it's far worse.'

'Worse than cancer, is that possible?'

'Some cancers can be cured; what Rosie thinks he's got is incurable.'

'So what is it?'

'Think about it, Vic, he's screwed around for years, it's much more than clap. I watched him when he joined us on tour, *Sabre Dance* was brilliant but several times in other numbers, his hand missed the strings on his guitar and he didn't seem to notice.'

'Maybe it's motor neurone disease or multiple sclerosis.'

'Maybe, but whatever it is, I don't think he'll beat it.'

'So tell me, what does Rosie think he has?'

'The plague, Vic.'

'That died out years ago.'

'Not that plague, I'm talking about the new plague.'

'What?' Vic dropped his cigar onto the carpet in shock.

'I'm talking Aids, he's got all the symptoms. Rosie, Candy, and Ellen are friends, and Ellen believes that he's just run down and anaemic, but Rosie's looked up all the symptoms in her medical dictionary and he's got the lot, even his emaciated appearance matches her findings.'

'But Rosie's not a doctor.'

'I know, but then ask yourself this, why is he wearing condoms?'

'Romany has never worn them.'

'He does now.'

Vic picked up his cigar from where he'd dropped it. Romany was invincible, he couldn't die. 'But I thought that he was all loved up with his fiancée. Could she be a carrier?'

'She worships the ground that's coming to him, she's faithful.'

'Then how?'

'Apparently he went to Los Angeles quite a while ago to gig with his brother and things got a little out of hand.'

'Rick, Christ he's riddled with everything, but how do you know that he cheated?'

'He told Rosie. Did you know that he had his first sexual experience with his aunt when he was nine years old?'

'Yes.'

'I was fifteen when I seduced my first girlfriend. Did I ever tell you about that threesome that Ed and I had with June Maclaine?'

'No, but knowing that woman, nothing surprises me. She initiated Mick Fraser when he was seventeen; that woman must have an inside like old boots, she's in her sixties now and still at it.'

'Well she certainly knows her way around a man's body; Ed and I were only sixteen at the time. She was brilliant; we did things that I never knew existed, my eyes were opened that night.'

'So were June's legs I should think.'

'And everything else.'

Vic laughed out loud. 'That's my boy,' he said getting to his feet and slapping Ray on his back. 'A little crudity never hurt anyone; Ed was first class at it. Eddie worries me though. There's no sign of his father in him, and all he's interested in is reading books about tortoises. His father must be turning in his grave.'

'Kids are all different, look at Bobby, he was the child from hell. One night in Tenerife, he was throwing a tantrum and then next minute he was on stage performing to an audience as if he was born to do it. Susie's beautiful and a born tease, but hasn't a clue what she wants to do with her life and, as for Deanne, she is her father's daughter and doesn't understand the word no. Eddie's henpecked already and she's not double figures yet.'

Vic laughed. 'That little Madam will lead someone up the garden path one day. Ed must be more than proud of her; she's him all over again.'

'Sometimes, I think she's a boy in knickers.'

'And Raydon?'

'Raydon's just Raydon. He's got a very happy disposition, but then so did Bobby at one time, now all he wants to do is dance; he never stops, he wears me out just watching him, but at present Raydon is the perfect child.'

'Kids, who'd have 'em?'

'Me, I love them, you can't beat being part of a happy family especially if you've got a wife like I have.'

'I'll take your word for it.'

Ray cast his eyes around the room and viewed Vic's display cabinet which was full of classic cars. 'You've got a great collection of cars in your cabinet, Vic,' he said.

Vic puffed his chest out. 'I've got the best collection around,' he said. 'Nobody can equal mine, I've been collecting since the sixties and I've paid an arm and a leg for some items that are really rare.'

Ray took a closer look and then burst into laughter.

'What's funny?'

'It's just these two little lorries that you've got standing on top of the cabinet, one's red and the other is yellow.'

'So?' Vic sank back into his armchair.

'Well, when I was in my teens, my mum took me to London; she'd got some tickets for the radio show 'Take your Pick' with Michael Miles. It was held in Rodmarten Mews and one of the audience had to pay a forfeit. She had to say red lorry, yellow lorry as fast as she could. It was hilarious, but not as funny as another forfeit in which the contestant had to say 'I'll chew, chew, chew till my jaws drop off'. It was really funny, Vic, but very noisy, and in the end the lady was going so fast that her jaws had turned into drawers. I loved it, the contestants had to choose keys to open boxes and Michael Miles tried to bid for them, the noise was deafening. I was sitting beside my Mum and she's not exactly a shrinking violet, she was giving me a headache. When we left the show, the man on the door was handing out headache pills. What a gas.'

'Suppose it was, I remember the show well; Al Simpkins went on it and won a key. Michael Miles bid him a hundred quid for it but Al was determined to open the box so he refused the money, then when he opened the box there was a tin of dog food in it.'

Ray was cracking up. 'That guy never has any luck, does he?'

'No, but he makes fantastic porn films, would you like to watch his latest epic?'

'Why not, I'd love to, Ed and Rosie made a few home movies of their own.'

'Really, Ed was a dark and devious character, have you seen them?'

'Yep, Rosie and I have no secrets, she was a real star in them, did everything with a smile on her face.'

'Didn't it put you off watching them together?'

'Nope, Ed was behind the camera most of the time and anyway I'd seen it for real a couple of times. Ed's parents had a summer house, and he and Rosie were always sneaking off down there. I remember one night when Rosie's mother was on the warpath, I saw something that I didn't expect to see. I'd gone to warn them that Norma was looking for Rosie and I caught them in a really horny position.'

'What was that?'

'She was giving him a blow job, what a turn on that was. Apparently Rosie had been doing it to Ed since she was fifteen.'

'Fifteen,' Vic gloated, so Romany had been right.

'Yep, apparently the first time she'd done it, it had been in broad daylight in Bedfords Park.'

Vic grinned; the booze was loosening Ray's tongue. He poured Ray another drink saying, 'Did you have many girlfriends?'

'No, my first love was Jenny; I took her virginity when she was still fifteen. We were in love, or so I thought.'

'Do go on, Ray.'

'No, I'm boring you.'

'No you're not; sometimes it's better to get things off your chest.'

'Well, its water under the bridge. Jenny was Rosie's best friend but unfortunately whatever Rosie had, Jenny wanted and usually got it, that was if I could afford it. However, neither Rosie nor I realised that it also extended to boyfriends, although Rosie had had her suspicions for some time. Jenny put it on a plate and Ed being a man took it. I was blind to the whole thing; I never thought that she'd cheat on me, how wrong was I.

That night before the bust up occurred, which included all of us, Jenny was acting a bit strange and cold toward me. I shared a flat with several others, and Ed was one of them. We'd all played a blinding gig that night, and Ed had driven Rosie home. When he returned to the flat, he was buzzing, telling us that Rosie was finally going to consummate their relationship the following day which was his eighteenth birthday. Rosie had held him off since their relationship began. She was quite happy to give him as many blow jobs as he wanted, and sixty nines, but penetration was off limits; she wanted the works, big white wedding dress, big reception, expensive honeymoon, a fairytale extravaganza, I guess. But the night before his birthday, she'd moved the goalpost in his favour, telling him that she would give him her virginity as an extra gift. He was so happy and on a high, but Jenny was very quiet when she heard the news. I didn't realise that their affair had just ceased and, as the saying goes, "hell hath no fury like a woman scorned". Anyway we all got pissed, and the following morning had massive hangovers. I somehow made my way to work, and Jenny, who had stayed with me overnight, stayed home.

Then she made the fateful phone call to Rosie which sealed everyone's fate. Rosie had a job interview that morning, and Jenny knew exactly what time she would be arriving to spend her day of passion with her beloved, so the scheming minx put her plan into action. Ed had accepted a lift from me that morning, wanting to pick up a white satin creation from an underwear shop close to us, and he said that as Rosie had a key to the flat he was going back to bed once he'd made his purchase. He was so full of love for Rosie, and said that the satin creation was the least he could do for her as she was about to surrender her most precious gift to him.'

'So he could be romantic.'

'With Rosie he always was, he really loved her, Vic.'

'Carry on, you can't stop now.'

'I soldiered on at work that morning until my boss sent me home, telling me that I was worse than useless. As I pulled into our street, I spotted Rosie walking toward our flat with a large bag and a birthday cake. I stopped and gave her a lift to the front door and, once we were inside the flat, Rosie headed to the toilet and emerged minutes later clad in red and black undies, black negligee, fishnets and high heels; she looked fantastic. She was on a high; she'd just secured a job at the Doug Trent Agency.'

'My cousin, I had no love for him.'

'We were unaware that Jenny had heard us come in and despatched herself to Ed's room where he was still half comatose. Rosie kissed me on my cheek and said, 'Wish me luck' as we made our way along the corridor. She had the birthday cake on a plate and I had taken two glasses from the cupboard and a bottle of chilled champagne from the fridge. As we opened his door, he was still asleep or appeared to be, and then his eyes flickered open and he beheld this vision of loveliness framed in the doorway.

We both cried 'Happy birthday' and then we saw it, a hump beneath the bedclothes. There was a sound of spluttering and then my Jenny surfaced. She fixed Rosie with a mocking stare and then she saw me and her expression turned to fear. I was supposed to be at work. Jenny taunted Rosie, "Do you like my new negligee Rosie? Ed loves me in white." Rosie was stunned, this negligee was the one that Ed had promised to buy her and now it was on the back of her so called best friend. Ed retaliated and pushed Jenny out of his bed saying that he'd bought it for Rosie that very morning and hung it on his wardrobe door. My emotions were all over the place. I wanted to kill Ed; he'd known how much I'd loved Jenny, and then I looked at the girl beside me who had dropped the birthday cake onto the floor in shock. In that moment I realised that the real viper was the girl that I'd worshipped and she'd betrayed me. Jenny's plan had backfired as Ed screamed that he'd never ever wanted her and that he didn't even like her. She begged me to forgive her, saying that Ed didn't want her, and I replied that neither did I; she'd played with fire and got burned.'

'So what happened next?' Vic was loving this.

'Ed pleaded with Rosie to stay but she dressed and left with me. I quit the band that day, so did Ed. He'd been caught out, and for the first time had been innocent. I never saw him again after that day apart from on television when you made him a star. He did well for himself, but he lost the love of his life.'

'And Rosie?'

'I didn't see her again until 1964; she was heavily pregnant with Ed's child. I'd just got a job in Brighton as a doorman at a hotel, and who should I see but Rosie on the arm of an older man.'

'Pregnant, I thought that she'd split with Ed.'

'She had but she'd been to France with Doug and Barry, and Ed was on the bill on some showcase, somehow he got his leg over and made her pregnant. I believe that Barry was in hospital at the time with a stroke. Rosie's spoken of the occult and other things, plus Ed's involvement with a high priestess.'

Vic grinned; that was just Ed's style. 'So what happened in Brighton?'

'We got it on, she slipped away a few times and I thought that I'd died and gone to heaven.'

'Didn't Barry have any idea?'

'He must have done because Rosie said that he brought it up on their wedding night.'

'Men bring lots of things up on their wedding night, what did he say?'

'Rosie didn't say much, other than the fact that she'd wanted more sex and he told her to go to France and find Ed or go to Brighton and see if the young doorman would oblige.'

'Charming, its anger that turns Barry on, always has been.'

'Yes but it's a bit hard on a nineteen-year-old girl on her wedding night.'

'Suppose so, so you got it on in Brighton?'

'Yep, and I asked her to move in with me but she wouldn't, she still loved Ed. I guess she always will; she married Barry because he dazzled her, and her parents put pressure on her.'

'So she had a baby in 1964.'

'It was stillborn; Ed was there when Rosie gave birth. Barry was in Los Angeles working with you.'

'He took over,' snapped Vic recalling the incident when Barry had dangled him upside down by his ankles over the balcony. 'I told him that he should be at home with his wife.' Vic was happy, Ray had revealed plenty. Obviously Ed had darted in and out of Rosie's life, Barry or no Barry. How Vic admired him; the boy done good.

One porn film later, and a line of coke, found Ray on his way upstairs. 'Thanks for letting us stay, Vic. I hope Rosie's feeling better, I'm ready to rock and roll.'

'She'll be fine, I didn't give her much.'

'What, you gave her something?'

'No, I mean I only gave her two drinks,' blustered Vic. He'd almost let the cat out of the bag.

'Oh, that's okay then, goodnight, see you in the morning.'

'Goodnight, Ray,' and with that, Vic switched off the lights and followed Ray upstairs. Once inside his room, he seated himself in front of his two way mirror and waited.

Chapter Twenty-Three

The next morning, a bleary eyed Vic made his way down to the kitchen and made some coffee. His head was spinning round from the scene the night before. Although Rosie had been asleep, she'd awoken at her husband's kiss and straight away slid down his body and pleasured him. The following hours had been the most erotic that Vic had ever witnessed. He'd believed Cathy to be out of this world, but Rosie had surpassed her. Knowing how virile Ed had been had filled Vic with sadness, how he would have loved to have seen the couple together. Then he recalled Ray's remarks about Ed and Rosie's home movies and wondered if he could lay his hands on them; there had to be a way and he was determined to find it. He made breakfast and then took it up to his guests. Tapping on the door he called, 'Are you decent?'

It was Rosie's voice that answered, 'Yes, you can come in.'

Vic opened the door and set the breakfast tray on the bedside table. Rosie shook Ray. 'Wake up, sleepy head, Vic's made us some breakfast.' There was a grunt from Ray, followed by the sound of breaking wind, and then he surfaced. He stretched and then surveyed the breakfast tray.

'Thanks Vic, that looks real great, I've got a real banger of a headache, guess I had too much last night.'

'You had a bit.'

'No, that was when I came to bed.'

'Ray, stop it, don't be so crude,' cried Rosie.

'That's okay,' replied Vic, leering at Rosie's cleavage. 'There's nothing wrong with a bit of crudity or nudity. I'll leave you two to your breakfast and I'll sort out those Sulcata books.' The doorbell rang, and an angry Vic staggered downstairs. 'Who the fuck's that?' he muttered. 'It can't be Mrs Monk, she's got a key.' Opening the front door, he was confronted by Al Simpkins who was beaming all over his face. He was dressed in bright yellow, making Vic flinch, and on his head he wore a red beret. The colours were making Vic feel sick. 'What do you look like?' he said. 'A Swan Vesta match is what you look like and, more to the point, what do you want?'

Al was unfazed and pushed past Vic. 'Was she any good?' he asked.

'Shh, they're still here,' whispered Vic.

'Oh, is that their red Merc?'

'No, it's my wife's.'

'You haven't got a wife.'

'I know that, you idiot.'

'Oh, you're being sarcastic again.'

'Well, whose car did you think it was?'

'I came to get a blow by blow account of last night.'

'Well, it was certainly that, I don't know where her energy comes from. She knocks your porn stars into a cocked hat; she does just about everything.'

'Bet your wrist aches this morning.'

'How dare you, get out.'

'Hit a nerve, have I?'

'No, actually as you're here, you can help me move the incubators and vivariums out onto the driveway.'

'Why, aren't you doing it any more? I thought you were making a small fortune out of it.'

'Eddie wants Rosie to take over.'

'Oh, okay, seeing as it is for Eddie, I'll help you. Have you unplugged everything?'

'Of course I have, Daisy hasn't laid any eggs for ages.'

'Probably shut up shop, she's probably found out about your money making schemes. That's it, she's gone on strike.'

'You do talk some shit at times; how would a tortoise know what I'm doing? Once the female lays the eggs, she buries them and then abandons them.'

'Shame your mother didn't do that to you.'

'Al, are you going to help me or not?'

'Yes, lead on Macduff.'

About twenty minutes later, both men were exhausted, and the equipment was on the drive. Vic could hardly get his breath, and making his way into the kitchen, said, 'Do you want some coffee?'

'Yes please. I reckon that Rosie's got wind of your dishonesty, you should be ashamed of yourself taking advantage of a child.'

'I did not, most of the babies died.' Vic boiled the kettle.

'That's why the pet shops are full of them.'

'Keep your voice down, you thicko.'

A scream echoed through the house, making Vic knock over the kettle. 'Well, someone isn't keeping theirs down,' laughed Al.

Vic had scalded his right hand with the water that had poured out of the kettle that now lay on its side. 'Fucking kettle,' he yelled.

'Well, I'm always telling you that you don't need to boil the kettle when you're making coffee,' laughed Al. 'Run your hand under the cold tap.'

A confused Vic ran his hand under the tap and then yelped, he'd turned the hot one on by mistake and now his injury was far worse. Al stared in disbelief. 'I said cold tap.'

'Stop laughing at my mishaps, I'll have to go upstairs and see if my guests are all right.'

'Liar, you want to see if he's giving her one; well you won't be able to give yourself one off the wrist because you've just scalded your wanking hand.'

'Shut up, make yourself useful and make some coffee. I'll be down as soon as I've checked on my guests.' Vic sped upstairs and charged into his room. He stared through his mirror and watched the couple who were whipped up into a sexual frenzy. Vic's blood pressure shot up along with something else. This was well worth losing the breeding programme for.

A few days later, Rosie and Ray were packing for their trip to Tenerife. Susie was excited and, as soon as her parents had left, she called Vidal. His suitcase was packed already and he made for Tenerife Sur Airport. His response, when he turned up at Susie's home, was one of sheer elation. Her home looked like a dream from the outside. He paid the cab driver and then pressed the buzzer on the gates. An excited Susie cried, 'Who is it?'

'It is I, querida, open the gates and let me in.'

Minutes later, Susie had activated the gates and run out onto the drive. She found herself almost being crushed in Vidal's arms. He swung her around. 'I have missed you so much, my darling,' he cried. Once more he was lying; the only person that he was missing was Luisa. Susie broke free of his embrace and watched as he picked up his suitcase and brushed past her. 'I'd like a shower,' he said, 'and then maybe you could fix me something to eat.'

Susie was taken aback; she'd expected him to be all over her but, smiling, she said, 'Of course, the bathroom's upstairs, follow me.' Vidal followed Susie and gazed around the place, it was really something. Once inside the bathroom he admired the ambience, gold taps, walk in shower, soft fluffy towels, carpet that your feet sank into, it was perfect, this was the life; he'd give his right arm to move in here. Susie wanted for nothing and she'd said that she had a wad of cash coming to her on her eighteenth birthday. She was sixteen now, so he could stick around for another couple of years, maybe even longer. He ran the shower and stepped into it, allowing the water to cascade over his body.

Downstairs, Susie was panicking, searching for something to cook. She'd expected Vidal to wine and dine her, but guessed that he was probably tired out from the flight. She felt a little scared as things would obviously hot up after dinner; that's what she was waiting for, so a little bit of cooking wouldn't hurt her.

Someone who was a little worried was Rosie; she was wondering if Susie would be able to cope. She knew that Deanne would be fine and, as for Norma, she had no grip of where she was, so as long as she was fed and watered, she'd be fine. It wasn't only that that was bothering her, Ray had gone bareback at Vic's home, and they'd coupled several times on their stop over. She tried to kid herself that at forty one, it was unlikely that she'd get pregnant and voiced her fears to Ray who said not to worry as he was going to book himself in for a vasectomy on his return to the UK, and that he was sick of using condoms. Rosie had tried just about every form of contraception possible. First the pill, which had given her a deep vein thrombosis, so that had to be stopped. After Raydon's birth, she'd been fitted with a coil, but it had given her so much pain that it had to be removed. A different one was fitted, followed by a third, but after many infections and agonising pain, that also had to be discontinued, making Ray revert to condoms. He didn't want any more kids, as Susie and Deanne were Ed's, and he honestly believed that Bobby was too. Telling Rosie to stop worrying, he gave her a kiss and told her to concentrate on more pressing things like signing documents and meeting the mayor who would be welcoming them to Tenerife once the apartments had become theirs. Rosie sighed; she was a born worrier, and she'd never change but she was in the sun, on a lounger and sipping a Pina Colada through a straw with her husband by her side. She needed to relax, but still her thoughts returned to Susie; something wasn't right.

Back in England, Vidal had got his feet firmly under the table.

He'd charmed Norma, and Susie had explained his presence as the new gardener. Norma had been confused and said, 'My garden needs doing, I haven't been to my home in months.'

'Then I will take you there this weekend,' said Vidal, 'and you can tell me what you want done.' He wanted to view her property too.

'Thank you,' replied Norma. 'You remind me of someone that I met in Great Yarmouth, he was a dago, and your skin is very tanned too.'

'I come from Tenerife, Senora.'

'Tenerife, I've never hear of it; we went to Great Yarmouth by aeroplane, have you been there?'

'Indeed I have, my father is Spanish and my mother English.'

'You must be all mixed up then. I don't like the Spanish, they kill bulls, and I love animals.'

'I hate bullfighting too, it should be banned,' Vidal winked at Susie.

'You're not a bad chap, are you, can you plant me some pansies?'

'I will plant whatever you want.'

'Good, I'm going to bed now. I'm going to the Rex Cinema tomorrow to see *Boy on a Dolphin*; Sophia Loren's in it, my husband likes her; I don't know where he is tonight.'

'She's confused,' said Susie as Vidal shot her an enquiring look.

'What is this Rex Cinema?' asked Vidal as Norma left the room.

'Oh, it's not there any more, it's Tesco's now.'

'It is sad when the mind goes. You look beautiful tonight, your dress is lovely, in fact everything about you is beautiful. I like your hair like that; what do you call it, a horse's tail?' Vidal touched the clip on Susie's ponytail and her hair tumbled down.

'Oh,' she cried. 'It took me ages to get it right, I wanted to look special for you.'

Vidal seemed mesmerised by Susie's hair, he took a handful of it in his hand saying, 'Your hair is such a beautiful colour.'

'Thank you,' replied Susie. 'But I need to fix it again.'

She tried to extricate her hair from his grip but as their hands contacted, Susie felt an electric charge rush through her. Vidal's arm snaked around her waist and he murmured, 'I have missed you so much, querida.' Then his lips came down upon hers and Susie was lost. He didn't just use his lips, he used his tongue too. Susie's mouth was spilling over with saliva and so was Vidal's. Then the arm around her waist moved downward, pushing her toward him. Susie could feel him getting harder by the second, and by now she was choking on their saliva and needed to come up for air. Finally he let her go and said, 'I think that it is time for us to go to bed too.'

'Oh but I thought that we could watch some television and have a drink.' Susie was getting very scared.

'Afterward, my darling, now show me the way to your room.' Trembling, Susie smiled and together they ascended the stairs.

'Welcome to Tenerife,' the mayor's voice boomed out around the room; he shook Ray's hand and then Rosie's. Raydon was reading a picture book and he flicked one page over after another. Bobby was fascinated by a poster of two Spanish dancers which adorned the wall. The mayor noticed his interest. 'You like Spanish dancing, boy?'

'Si Senor,' replied Bobby with a mischievous grin on his face.

'And you are speaking in Espanole?'

'Si Senor, I like to dance and speak Spanish.'

'Would you dance for me?'

'Si Senor' and Bobby began to stamp his feet with gusto.

'What is this dancing called?'

'The Zapateado, Senor.'

The mayor was impressed. 'You must practise very hard, and one day you could be as great as Antonio. Have you heard of him?'

Bobby nodded and continued to dance until Rosie stopped him. 'We need to go, Bobby, the mayor is a very busy man, and we need to go to our apartments.'

'Can I dance on the terrace?'

'Yes, now come along, if you hurry, I'll buy you an ice cream.'

'Helados,' giggled Bobby. 'Quatro helados.'

'Very good,' laughed the mayor. 'Adios.'

Rosie and Ray said goodbye and then left with their two sons. Ray was on cloud nine, he was now the proud owner of two apartments in Tenerife. He had everything, four lovely kids, two holiday homes, a palatial home in England and, last but not least, the jewel in his crown, his beautiful wife Rosie; his cup was overflowing with happiness.

Susie's deflowering was not as she'd imagined it. In her dreams, she'd been on a beach with the waves crashing against the shore, the moon would be bright reflecting off the water and the man in her arms would take her to paradise. In fact it happened in her own bed with Norma in the next room, muttering away to herself and singing *My Old Man's a Dustman*.

Susie found it hard to concentrate; she was not exactly being swept along in a tide of passion. Vidal had gone through all the preliminaries with her, bringing her to orgasm, but just as she was relaxing in the afterglow, he'd mounted her and attempted penetration. Susie was not enjoying this, neither was Vidal, every time he thrust, the girl tensed up making it impossible. Finally, he broke through her maidenhead and thrust away as if his life depended on it. Susie was in agony, and relieved when he collapsed across her; the pain had been intense. She hadn't realised that it would be so painful. Vidal rolled off her saying, 'Did you enjoy that?'

'Yes,' lied Susie, hoping that he wouldn't want a repeat performance straight away. Her luck was in as he turned his back on her and fell asleep. Susie cuddled up to him but couldn't sleep as his loud snoring kept her awake. Hearing Norma go downstairs, she decided to join her. In the kitchen, Norma was sorting through the cupboard and muttering to herself. Susie wandered over. 'Did you want something, Nana?' she said.

'Oh, it's you; I've just been speaking to your father.'

'Really?' Susie was used to Norma's revelations about her spiritual contact with Ed.

'Yes, he's very angry with you, he says that you're a stupid vain creature and that you've let him and your mother down; he wants the gardener out of the house too.'

'But, Nana.' Susie gazed at her grandmother; she had her long pink nightdress on which was far too big for her, and her blue terry towelling dressing gown on inside out. Her face was plastered in moisturiser and her hair in pipe cleaners. Susie also noted that she was only wearing one slipper, and that that was on the wrong foot. Norma banged her fist on the work surface in temper.

'Don't Nana me, you know what your father's temper is like, you'll regret it if you don't take note of what he says.'

'I can't send him away, I didn't employ him.'

'Well, you've been warned, anyway where is the gardener, he said he'd plant some pansies for me. I want some rose bushes put in too, and some wallflowers and daffs would be nice.'

'Nana, it's the middle of the night.'

'Oh, is it, I'd better go back to bed then, I'll just take a few of these up,' and Norma gathered together several chocolate bars and stuffed them into her dressing gown pocket. Susie watched as Norma left the room, her grandmother's words were disturbing her. She felt as if she was being watched; someone was behind her, but she was too scared to look over her shoulder. After switching the lights off, she hurried up the stairs and, once on the landing, ran to her room. Vidal was still snoring and, getting back into bed, Susie snuggled up to him.

Rosie and Ray wandered around the Costamar apartment; it did need updating but neither of them wanted to spend too much money on the place as it was going to be let. It had a prime position in Los Cristianos and looked right across the sea and the harbour. In the end, they put in a new cooker, fridge, and double bed, as the rest of the furniture was okay. As for the Paloma Beach apartment, Ray bought everything new; this was the apartment that they would use solely for themselves and he wanted the best of everything. He put in top-of-the-range furniture and added more security. Rosie stared around the apartment; she loved the place, and wished that she could relocate there, but Ray wanted to continue to work and support his family, so her dream had to be shelved.

On the terrace, Bobby was dancing his socks off. He'd recently done a couple of television commercials and there were many more in the pipeline. The child was multi-talented; he was no longer the child from hell, but he became moody when he stood still for too long. Raydon loved painting and looking at picture books. He was very quiet and well behaved, and he never had tantrums which amazed Alf and Ada as Ray had always been a bit of a problem child. Ada had said that, as a small child, Ray had always thrown tantrums, and as he'd grown older he developed into a real nutter, causing most of the rows in the family. Ray thought that it was probably a good thing that his son was so placid; the child was only three, so God only knew what could be in store as Raydon got older.

He was enjoying his time in Tenerife, but he'd be glad when they were back in England so that he could get his vasectomy done. He was using condoms again, and hated them, knowing that there was a slim risk that Rosie could get pregnant and that was something that he didn't want. He looked forward to the day when all the kids had flown the nest, leaving him and Rosie to be together. His forty second birthday was looming and, as Raydon was only three, the Derby and Joan years seemed eons away. He turned and watched his wife who was romping with her young sons; they made a charming picture. What a fantastic life he had. It was silly to wish your life away; time was precious, and the years passed quickly enough.

Chapter Twenty-four

'This is my house,' cried Norma to Vidal. Her eyes were twinkling with merriment; she didn't get to see her home very often. It was up for sale and, apart from Rosie and Ray checking on it now and again, it was unlived in. The estate agent held a set of keys for the property, but so far there had been no takers. Many people wanted it, but wanted the price dropped and Rosie was having none of it.

'It backs onto Raphael Park, its unique, and how many houses back onto a lake. Until we get the full asking price, we'll hang onto it.' The estate agent tried to convince her that everyone was dropping their prices, but Rosie replied that if it didn't sell within a certain time, she'd probably sell her own house and move into Lake Rise herself. Beaten, the estate agent backed off.

Vidal loved the property. Ray and Rosie were obviously loaded, and when the old girl died, they'd fall in for this house too. Norma couldn't wait to show him the garden and the lake where various water birds lived. Vidal had no morals, but his one redeeming feature was that he loved animals and put them above humans. He walked through to the garden and drew in his breath. There were two beautiful white swans swimming on the lake, plus geese, ducks, and moorhens. 'This is fantastic, Susie,' he cried. 'What a view, and how wonderful to be surrounded by nature.'

Norma tugged on his arm. 'I'll show you where I want my flowers and bushes put,' she said.

'Of course, Senora, but please give me a moment to digest all of this.'

'All right,' said Norma, making her way to the shed. 'I've got some garden seats in the shed; have you got the key, Susie?'

'No, I'll go and get it.'

Vidal loved this place more than the other house. It was smaller but it had this wonderful garden and lake. How he wished that he could get up in the morning and walk out into this paradise. Susie returned with the key and unlocked the shed door. Norma bustled inside and retrieved a folding garden chair; she had a huge smile on her face.

'Here, let me,' said Vidal, taking the chair from her. He unfolded it and then seated Norma on it.

'You're a good boy,' she said and patted his arm. Vidal smiled and then took another two chairs from the shed. Susie had made a pile of sandwiches before she'd left her home, and brought some tea bags, milk, and sugar with them too.

'I'll make some tea,' she said, and headed back to the house.

'I'll give you a hand,' replied Vidal, and followed in her wake. Once inside the house, he came up behind Susie and rubbed himself up against her. 'Hallo, baby, I need you.'

'Oh but we can't, Nana's out there and...'

'She's fine; I can't help it if I find you irresistible, can I?'

'But the estate agent might turn up.'

'Don't deny me, baby, you're my fiancée and it's up to you to pleasure me.'

'But I'm sore, really sore.'

'Do you like it when I go down on you?'

'I love it.'

'Well, it's not a one way trip, baby.'

'What do you mean?'

'I mean that if you love me, you'll return the favour.'

'But, I've never done it before and...'

'There's always a first time.'

Vidal unzipped his trousers and released his throbbing manhood. Susie was horrified as he pushed her onto her knees, grabbed her head with both hands, then forced his penis into her mouth. Scared, Susie tried to accommodate him and felt herself gagging; this was horrible and seemed to go on forever. Suddenly he spurted his sperm into her mouth, making her want to vomit. Now what was she supposed to do, spit it out or what? 'Swallow it,' ordered Vidal, releasing the girl's head from his grasp. Susie complied, but this was disgusting; how could people do it? Vidal zipped his trousers up, took the two plates of piled sandwiches from the worktop, and then walked back out into the garden. Susie felt tears stinging her eyes, but regained her composure and made the tea. She opened a box of iced cakes and put them onto a plate. They were Norma's favourites, and after putting the mugs of tea onto a tray alongside the cakes, she wandered back outside into the garden.

'About time,' snapped Norma. 'I was dying of thirst.' Susie sighed and placed the tray onto a garden table. She listened as Norma rattled on about plants and bushes; she had Vidal's full attention and Susie was beginning to feel like a gooseberry, her lovely dream was fading, and she wanted to be loved and pampered, not used and abused. Smiling, she offered Norma an iced cake and joined in the conversation. Staring across the lake, she saw a man staring at her. It looked like him, no it couldn't be, but he pointed an accusing finger at Susie, making her go cold inside. Turning to Norma, she said, 'That man looks just like Dad.'

'What man?'

Susie was about to point him out when she realised that he'd gone. 'Oh nothing, Nana, I was mistaken, anyway he's gone.'

'You're such a daydreamer, Susie,' replied Norma, stuffing the cake into her mouth. 'Give me another cake, I'll have a yellow one this time.'

In the next few days, Vidal became Norma's golden boy. He regularly took her to her home, telling Susie that her grandmother

219

needed to be placated. 'To have lived here all those years with her husband is paramount to her. The house must hold many memories for her, and it is wrong that she doesn't visit more often. In Spain, we look after our old people; in England, you seem to discard them as soon as their usefulness wears out. Maybe when we get married, we could live here with your grandmother, and you could care for her whilst I'm at work; her roots are here.' Susie thought that it was a wonderful idea, and how thoughtful Vidal was, but then she didn't understand his motives.

In his eyes, Norma had dementia and she could conveniently fall into the lake in the middle of the night while he was tucked up in bed with Susie. Then, when all the grieving was over, Susie would probably inherit the house and, if they were married, half would belong to him. Susie was happy now; when he'd arrived, she thought that maybe she'd made a mistake. He'd been like an animal when he'd first made love to her, and now that she was no longer sore, she welcomed his passion. Vidal hadn't asked for a blow job again, realising that he'd made a silly mistake that could drive her away. She obviously didn't like it, so he had to calm himself down and concentrate on getting her pregnant; he wanted the good life and couldn't wait to get a wedding ring on her finger.

'Where is your brother?' Rosie's voice cut the air.

Luisa spun round; she'd been caught off guard and had been day dreaming when Rosie had arrived. 'He is in England visiting his mother; she is very sick,' she stuttered.

'Well I'm sorry to hear that; when is he due back?'

'I do not know, Senora.'

'Shame, I wanted to speak to him about something.'

Luisa was now sweating buckets; had Susie confessed all? She offered Rosie a drink, but Rosie declined it, saying, 'Do you recall the night that my bag was snatched?'

'Si Senora, it was a terrible thing to happen.'

'Was the bag snatcher a friend of your brother?'

'No, we had never seen him before that night.'

'My younger daughter says that she saw the two of them laughing together at the fun fair.'

'She is mistaken, I never saw him.'

'But you wouldn't, would you, because you were out with Susie that night, or has she been lying to me?'

'No Senora, I was with Susie most of the night, but earlier I was with Vidal and I never saw this man.'

'Are you sure?'

'If we had seen him that night, Vidal would have killed him, we love your family.'

'I find it strange that you are not in England visiting your mother if she's that sick.'

Luisa was squirming; her body language was giving her away. 'We do not share the same mother.'

'Oh, so you're only half brother and sister.'

'Si Senora, are you sure that you don't want a drink?'

'No, I just wanted a word with Vidal, I'll be back later with the rest of my family, and we would love paella. Can you arrange it?'

'Si Senora, what time do you wish to eat?'

'About eight. I must go, see you later,' and Rosie walked away, leaving a dumbstruck Luisa staring after her. She hurried inside the restaurant and rang Vidal. It was Susie who picked up the receiver and listened. 'Susie, it is Luisa, I need to speak to my brother.'

'Oh, okay, is everything all right?'

'Yes, but I need to speak to Vidal urgently.'

'Okay, Vidal, it's for you, it's Luisa.'

Vidal rushed to the phone and listened for a while, then he began to speak very rapidly in Spanish. When he replaced the receiver he was silent and Susie asked him if things were okay. He nodded and then broke down sobbing. 'You remember my grandmother?'

'Yes, the one that had the operation?'

'She has died. I will not be able to stay and talk to your parents as the date of the funeral is the same as their return.'

'Oh, I wanted us both to talk to them about us.'

Vidal was now howling. 'I cannot go, you are the best thing that has ever happened to me. I must stay here; Luisa and my father will have to cope.'

Susie clung to him. 'Don't be silly, you must go to the funeral, we can tell my parents another time, and maybe you can come back in a few weeks' time.'

'How lucky I am to have you, my darling, your kindness knows no bounds.'

'Well, we've still got another week together.'

'Yes, my darling, and we will live every moment as if it is our last.'

'I must give you some money for flowers; can you put my name on the card?'

'Of course, now let's go to bed, I need to show you just how much I love you.'

'I can't wait to be your wife.' Susie was now in love with her Spanish lover, and she wanted him so much. Vidal looked into her eyes; he didn't love her, but she was going to make a wonderful meal ticket.

'Oh baby, I love you so much,' he cried and, sweeping her up into his arms, he carried her upstairs to her room.

Chapter Twenty-five

Susie had told all her friends that she was going to Tenerife with her parents, as she didn't want them intruding on her and Vidal. Therefore, her best friend Rachel was surprised to bump into her in Debenhams restaurant. Vidal cast his eyes over her and her cousin. Rachel was attractive but her cousin left a lot to be desired, and he wouldn't touch her with anyone else's dick, let alone his. Susie made the introductions, and Vidal kissed both girls' hands, murmuring 'Enchante'. Rachel was nobody's fool but her cousin bathed in the compliments that Vidal showered on her.

'Won't you join us, girls?' asked Vidal.

Rachel eyed the sleaze ball up and down, she couldn't believe that this was the man that Susie had enthused over; she hated him on sight. You could see that he couldn't be trusted, plus he was much older than Susie had said.

'We were just about to get a coffee,' said Rachel, staring at the nasty creature that was undressing her with his eyes.

'Then I will get it,' replied Vidal. 'Maybe one of you ladies could accompany me; they have some lovely desserts here.'

'I will,' cried Lucy, and followed Vidal to the counter.

Rachel sat down facing Susie, and her eyes flashed angrily. 'He's too old for you and he's shifty. I thought you were in Tenerife.'

'He's not too old and you're jealous.'

'Of that, what are your parents thinking of, letting you loose with him while they're away?'

'They don't know.'

'What, they don't know that he's here, or don't know about your relationship?'

'Both.'

'Susie, you're crazy; have you slept together?'

'Yes, we're in love.'

'I hope he used something.'

'Doesn't need to, we're getting married.'

'But your parents might not give you permission.'

'Then we'll run away together.'

'But you're only sixteen.'

'I don't care.'

'You've lost the plot. I saw Steven the other day, and he thinks you're away too. He's bought you a couple of Prince albums, and paid a fortune for both of them.'

'He's a nice guy.'

'Yes he is. When is lover boy going home?'

'In a couple of days, his nan's just died.'

'I thought you paid for her to have an operation?'

'I did.'

'Did you ever meet her?'

'No.'

'Then how do you know that she ever existed? He's taking you for a ride, and when he leaves, you may never see him again. He's had his leg over; he's got no reason to come back.'

'Don't say such horrid things; why can't you just be happy for me?'

'I care about you and I don't want to see you get hurt.'

'I won't get hurt, we're in love.'

'Then grant me one favour, when lover boy leaves, ring Steven, he's really into you; don't keep him on a string, he deserves better than that.'

'Okay.'

'Promise?'

'Yes, oh look, Vidal's got us all a piece of lemon meringue pie, I love it.'

'Then you can have mine because as soon as I've drunk my coffee, I'm out of here. I love you dearly, Susie, but I don't trust Vidal any further than I can throw him.'

Vidal and Lucy sauntered back to the table with four coffees plus desserts. Placing a portion of lemon meringue in front of Rachel, he said, 'A beautiful dessert for a beautiful lady.'

'No thanks, I'll just have the coffee.'

'But a beautiful girl like you needs to keep her strength up.'

'I hate meringue.'

'Then let me get you something else.'

'I just said that I'd have the coffee, I don't do dessert.'

'Are you afraid of putting on weight; you could do with putting a bit on. What dress size are you?'

'None of your business.'

'Why so secretive, a man likes a woman with curves, he likes to have something to hold on to.'

'Susie's not exactly voluptuous.'

'Rachel, stop it,' cried Susie.

'Then tell him to stop it; my personal life is nothing to do with him. He's damn rude and nosey.'

'I apologise, Senorita, I did not mean to pry.'

'Will you be a bridesmaid, Rachel?' asked Susie trying to change the subject.

'I doubt it,' replied Rachel.

'I will,' cried Lucy.

Vidal stared at the podgy girl before him; the thought of her in a pink satin creation was making him feel nauseous.

'Please, Rachel.'

'I'll think about it, but I don't think your mother will let you marry him, you're too young.'

'When you're in love, age doesn't matter,' said Vidal.

'Well it wouldn't in your case; you must be twice Susie's age.'

'Rachel, you're the one being personal now,' cried Susie.

'Sorry but I can't help the way that I feel, I can't hold back.'

'It's okay Susie, Rachel doesn't know me, she is only being protective towards you; if she knew me, she would think differently, isn't that right, Rachel?'

Rachel didn't want any more bad feeling and muttered, 'I guess so.'

'There, everyone is happy, I leave for Tenerife in forty eight hours, so maybe on my last night, we could all meet up.'

'Lovely,' cried Lucy.

'We're going out,' snapped Rachel.

'We could cancel.'

'No we can't, come on drink your coffee, Mum's making dinner, and we don't want to keep her waiting.'

'But I haven't eaten my dessert.'

'Take it with you, I've a Tupperware box in my bag; it's empty now that we've had our picnic in the park.'

'Which park did you go to?' asked Susie.

'Raphael Park, it's so lovely there,' replied Rachel.

'I agree,' said Vidal. 'Only a few days ago, we took Susie's grandmother to visit her home, and she has a beautiful view from her garden. I suggested that, once we're married, we could move in there and take her with us. Her memories are there, and she would be much happier.'

'How thoughtful of you,' quipped Rachel. Susie gazed at her friend; she could see that she was being very sarcastic.

'I'd love one of those houses,' said Lucy, swigging down her coffee. 'But us poorer mortals can only gaze at them from the other side of the lake.'

Rachel removed the Tupperware box from her bag and put Lucy's dessert into it. Getting to her feet she said, 'Call me in a couple of days, Susie. Nice to have met you, Vidal. I'm sure that our paths will cross at some time in the future, but we really must go, come on Lucy.'

Susie was upset. It was obvious that her best friend didn't approve of her fiancé and, deciding that it was jealousy, hugged both of her friends, said goodbye, and then turned her attention back to Vidal.

He left on Friday morning and Susie was heartbroken. Rachel's words about Vidal never coming back haunted her. On that score, he had everything mapped out; he'd hooked her and hoped that she was now pregnant. If she was, he would do the decent thing and marry her. He could suffer all of her stupidity, and loved the thought of maybe moving into Norma's house with Susie as her carer. Later, Norma could have an accident, leaving her home to Susie and putting him in line for a half share of the property. Then there would be children; he was determined to keep his bride barefoot and in the kitchen. Maybe at some stage she might die in childbirth or even better have a tragic accident, leaving him and Luisa to sail off into the sunset.

He smiled as the cab drew up outside the house. Susie had given him money for flowers for his so called grandmother's funeral, and had decided, at Vidal's suggestion, to open up a joint bank account in Tenerife. It made sense to Susie, and it made it easier to access funds whilst on holiday over there. Money hadn't been a problem for Vidal whilst he'd stayed with Susie as she'd paid for everything. Crying crocodile tears, he clung to her, telling her that he couldn't live without her, and then he left without so much as a backward glance. He wanted to get back to Luisa.

Ray and Rosie returned in the early hours of Saturday morning, tanned, relaxed, and happy to be home. Susie heard them come in, but put her head under the duvet, feigning sleep. She couldn't face her parents straightaway; she was feeling guilty and needed time. She missed Vidal and wondered what he was doing. The reality was not pretty, he was in bed with Luisa, laughing and joking about how gullible Susie was. He relayed all to Luisa who was more than happy that Susie was deflowered and possibly pregnant. 'Soon it will be our turn to live a privileged life,' said Vidal. 'Just give me time and you'll have everything that your heart desires.' Luisa smiled and kissed him, and then drifted off into a contented sleep.

The following morning, Norma rattled on about Ed again. 'He's very angry, Rosie, and he's glad that the gardener's gone.'

Rosie placed Norma's egg and bacon in front of her and frowned. 'Gardener, what gardener?' she said.

'The one that was here when you were away. Susie said that you'd employed him; he was going to do my garden for me.' Norma picked up her knife and fork and began to tuck into her breakfast.

Ray stumbled downstairs looking like death warmed up. 'I feel like shit,' he said. 'I need a fry up.'

'You look like shit,' replied Rosie. 'Is Susie up yet? I need to ask her a few questions.'

'Yes, she's up, I heard the shower running, but as for the boys, they're still spark out.'

Rosie put the kettle on. She knew that her mother was confused but she'd had her own suspicions about Susie having a guest. When she'd opened the laundry basket to put their holiday clothes in it, she'd found it almost full up. That didn't surprise her as Susie never did her own washing, and some of the clothes were Norma's too, which also was expected, but nestling between the clothes was a pair of black boxer shorts. Reaching up into the cupboard and removing a jar of coffee, Rosie said, 'Since when have you been buying boxer shorts, Ray?'

'I haven't, I don't like them, I like my balls supported.'

'You don't have to be crude, I asked a simple question.'

'And I answered it; what are you going on about?'

'I found a pair of black boxer shorts in the washing basket.'

'Maybe Steven stayed over.'

'They're the gardener's,' said Norma, cutting into her egg and making the yolk run out.

'What gardener?'

'Your guess is as good as mine,' replied Rosie, making the coffee.

'He's going to do my garden but I don't know when, as Ed says he's left,' said Norma, mopping up the yolk with a piece of bread.

Susie skipped into the room. 'Mum, Dad, when did you get back, did you have a good time?'

'Lovely,' replied Rosie. 'Did you?'

'Yes, we had fun, didn't we, Nana?'

'Yes, where's the gardener?'

Susie was flustered. 'When we were at Nana's house, the people next door had a gardener and Nana asked if he would do her garden.'

'Did I? I can't remember.' Norma shrugged her shoulders and continued with her breakfast.

Rosie stared at her daughter; she looked different, more knowing. 'Did anyone stay over?' Rosie wanted to get to the bottom of this.

'No.' Susie was blushing to her boots.

Ray was getting pissed off. 'Cut the crap,' he snapped. 'I'm more interested to know if you went for that job at the florists.'

'No, I was sick, I think that maybe I might apply for a job in a care home, I enjoyed looking after Nana. What have you brought me back?'

'I'll show you later, I haven't unpacked everything yet, and Ray hasn't had his breakfast. Do you want some?'

'No I don't, you've only been back five minutes and you've given me the third degree, plus you've been nagging me about getting a job,' and with that Susie stormed off; she couldn't wait to leave home.

Rosie stared after the retreating figure. Susie's body language was worse than Luisa's; something was up and, given time, she'd find out what it was. Norma got up and left the table. 'I wish that gardener would come back, he seemed such a nice chap, I think I'll go and read, I do love Catherine Cookson, her books are so full of the ups and downs of life; she tells it as it is. Thank you for my breakfast, Rosie, it's so nice to have you home.'

'It's nice to be home,' replied Rosie. 'Now what do you want for breakfast, Ray?'

'The works, then I'll ring Kevin and arrange to pick Deanne up.'

On Monday, Norma returned to her day centre and, when she returned that evening, she was full of the day's events. She'd had her hair done, and Rosie admired it, telling her mother how lovely she looked. Ray let out a wolf whistle. 'I bet all the boys were after you today, Norma.'

'Don't talk rubbish, Bob's the only man for me. Is he home yet?'

'Mum, Dad died years ago.'

'Did he, nobody told me.' Norma dissolved into tears adding, 'I'm scared Rosie, I'm just a silly old fool. I won some pansies today in a raffle; do you think the gardener might plant them for me? He was very helpful while you were away; he had a strange name too.'

'Did he come here every day?'

'No, he stayed here.'

Rosie went cold. Was Norma rambling or not, somehow she didn't think that she was. She gave her mother a hug, saying, 'You're not a silly old fool, and your hair looks great, anyone would think that Vidal Sassoon had done it.'

Norma pulled free. 'That was his name; does he do hair as well as gardens?'

Rosie laughed. 'Vidal Sassoon is a fabulous hairdresser, Mum.'

'But he said that he'd do my garden. Susie called him Vidal; he comes from Great Yarmouth, you know the place where we went on the aeroplane.'

Rosie's heart was beating nineteen to the dozen. Surely Susie wouldn't use her grandmother as an excuse to stay at home and entertain someone while Ray and herself were away.

'We went to Tenerife, Mum.'

'Oh did we, the gardener used to work at that place that we ate at. I knew I'd seen him before, he got your bag back for you when that dago stole it.'

To Ray, Norma was rambling on but to Rosie, everything was falling into place; tomorrow she would visit Norma's home and look for clues.

The following day, Rosie made her way over to Lake Rise and let herself in. The 'For Sale' notice was still standing; obviously there were still no takers. Once inside the house, she played detective. Norma's bed had been slept in or used. The covers and sheets were rumpled but that meant nothing as Norma may have had a nap on one of her visits. Closer inspection revealed that there were stains on the sheets and, to Rosie's trained eye; it was painfully obvious what they were. She was disgusted and made her way to the kitchen. In the sink were tea plates and cups filled with cold water. This was just Susie's style, she never washed up. Rosie opened the plastic waste bin; inside were about a dozen empty lager cans and she knew that her daughter didn't drink lager. Susie hadn't exactly covered her tracks well; she must have had other thoughts on her mind. Routing through the bin, she found more clues, and this clinched her suspicions, there were empty cigarette packets right at the bottom, Spanish ones. The lounge was practically untouched apart from Norma's chair which had the usual plumped up cushions adorning it.

She rang the estate agent and asked if there had been any viewings, and was informed that the last one had been two months previously. Replacing the receiver, she felt anger building up inside her; her treacherous empty headed daughter had allowed someone into her grandmother's house and abused it. The thought of her coupling in Norma's bed infuriated her; had the girl no shame? She remembered her feelings when she was sixteen. Yes she'd been consumed with lust at times, but she would never have stooped this low. It was evil to allow Norma to visit her home on the understanding that it was for her own good when all of the time, Susie had been visiting just to make use of the place herself. Rosie's head was spinning. Why had Susie felt the need to use Lake Rise anyway? She had a perfectly good bed at home which she could use while her grandmother was at the day centre. Were the stains on the bed that of mutual masturbation, or had her daughter gone all the way? Was it Vidal, or was Norma confused, and it had been Steven all the time. Maybe Vidal wasn't in the frame at all. Luisa had stated that he was visiting his sick mother in England, so he may have visited Susie, and it could have been at a time when Norma was at home. Was it pre-arranged and, if it was, why take advantage of a demented old lady under the guise of kindness? Had the name Vidal just triggered something off in Norma's head when she couldn't recall the so-called gardener's name, if he existed at all? Rosie's mind was in turmoil. She was going mad, this was too much to take in. Her lovely daughter had turned into a devious minx. One thing was certain, someone had helped Susie to put those stains onto the sheets.

Tomorrow she would accompany her daughter to the doctor and get her on the pill. She couldn't control her daughter's sexual behaviour but she could prevent her from getting pregnant. There was only one way to find out if Vidal was the culprit, she'd take her family to Tenerife for a holiday. It would be a last minute surprise, and she'd include Eddie and Candy too. Ray and Kevin were due to tour in the New Year so the timing would be perfect.

Chapter Twenty-Six

The following morning, Rosie woke Susie, telling her that she needed to do some Christmas shopping and wanted her to go along for the ride. 'We can have a day out, just the two of us,' she said. 'Deanne's still at Kevin's home, driving everyone nuts, and she's coming home tonight so we might as well get all the Christmas presents sorted out today.'

Susie thought that it was a good idea for a few reasons; one, she could tell her mother what she wanted for Christmas, two, they'd probably have a nice lunch out and, three, she wouldn't have her younger sibling snapping at her heels. These days, Deanne was a pain in the arse to her. Rosie hadn't mentioned the doctor, so Susie was somewhat surprised when she found herself being ushered into the surgery. She was even more surprised when she realised why she was there. Rosie took full control, telling the doctor that, although she didn't think her daughter was sexually active, it would only be a matter of time before she was, plus her periods were irregular. Mother, daughter, and doctor conversed for about ten minutes, and then Susie left with a prescription in her hand.

She felt a little bit concerned. Did her mother know her guilty secret, or was she just thinking of her welfare? Whatever it was, she'd been given a lease to enjoy sex without getting pregnant, which was wonderful. Already she was missing the sex she'd enjoyed with Vidal, and she knew that Steven was besotted with her. He'd do nicely until she was reunited with Vidal once more. Smiling at her mother, she said, 'Can we go to Debenhams? They've got some lovely new clothes there.'

'Of course,' replied Rosie. 'And then maybe we could look in on your grandmother's home. It might need cleaning, as I haven't done it for a while.'

'Oh no.' Susie was shaking; she couldn't recall what state she'd left the place in. 'I'll sort it; Nana wasn't too well on our last visit so things got left a bit untidy. I'll get Rachel to come and help me; she's a whiz kid at cleaning. I think I'll ring Steven later too, as I haven't seen any of my friends since you left. I wanted to concentrate on Nana.'

'So what did you do with yourself when she was at the day centre?'

'I looked for work, took long walks, and did a bit of Christmas shopping. I quite liked my own company; you can please yourself when you're on your own. I'm thinking of going to college to study photography.'

'I thought you wanted to do care work.'

'I did, but I think that maybe photography might be better.'

'Then you should have a chat with Steven's younger brother Michael.'

'He's just a kid.'

'Fourteen to be precise, almost fifteen. I've seen some of his photos, and they're very good.'

'Good thinking, Mum. What shall I get Nana for Christmas? It's almost here.'

'How about some new sheets?'

'What?' Susie dropped her handbag in shock and almost fell over. Rosie noted the guilt that was all over Susie's face.

'Susie, what's wrong? You know that your grandmother likes flannelette sheets, and you could buy her a couple of blankets too, she hates duvets. Look, there's some pretty pink ones over there.'

Rosie indicated a pile of blankets in the bedding department. Susie picked up her bag and regained her composure. 'I just felt a bit dizzy, but I'm fine now. Will those pills really help my periods?'

'Yes, now how about some lunch and then we'll hit the shops big time?'

Susie was beaming. 'Great,' she said, 'come on, Mum, let's go and eat.'

Rosie gazed at her daughter; she was as guilty as sin and crafty too, but she wouldn't outsmart her. Once they'd returned to Tenerife, she'd set a trap, one that Vidal would walk into, and then she would confront the scheming couple and make them own up to their disgusting treatment of Norma.

That night Susie rang Steven. He asked her how her trip to Tenerife had gone and she answered that she didn't want to discuss Tenerife; she wanted to talk about their relationship. Steven was overjoyed, and later they met up in Romford and had a fish and chip meal. Susie was all over Steven, telling him just how much she had missed him. Steven couldn't believe his luck when she kissed him and said, 'Tell your dad that you won't be home tonight and, if it's a problem, I'll get Ray to ring; nobody argues with Ray. You can sleep in the room next to mine and, once everyone's asleep, you can come into my bed.'

'Do you know what you're saying?'

'Of course I do, I've decided that we need to get closer. I got the pill this morning, so surely that tells you how serious I am.'

'But it doesn't work straight away.'

'That's okay, you can use a rubber, or two or three.'

'I can't believe it, you've sprung this on me so fast, I can't take it in.'

'Well if you don't want me...'

'Of course I want you.' Steven picked up a carrier bag that he'd brought with him. Handing it to Susie, he said, 'I got these two Prince albums; they're very rare and special, just like you.'

'Thanks,' replied Susie, opening the bag up and removing the two albums. She stared at them for a couple of minutes and then said, 'Come on, eat up, and then we can go home.'

Christmas 1986 arrived, and in the Lynne household there was great merriment. Vic spent Christmas with Al Simpkins and argued most of the time. Rosie sent both of them an invite for her New Year's Eve party, which was a kindly gesture as she couldn't stand either of them, but she had the festive spirit and wanted everyone to share it. They both attended and got blind drunk after several arguments, but they were happy and glad that they'd accepted the invitation. The New Year chimed in, and 1986 became 1987, leaving everyone wondering what the New Year held for them.

In January, Ray celebrated his forty second birthday, and a week later went into hospital to have his vasectomy, saying that it was his birthday present to himself. For a whole week after the procedure, Ray was in agony. His testicles swelled right up and he couldn't walk, and at one time he wondered if he'd be fit enough for the forthcoming tour, but the following week the pain began to subside and he began to pursue Rosie. 'You'll still need to use condoms,' said Rosie. 'It's not safe yet.'

'Give me a break, I've been cut and the sperm can't get through; you won't get pregnant, there'll be no more rubbers.'

'But supposing that you're wrong, you're supposed to have three tests before you're announced all clear. The doctors wouldn't have told you to take precautions for nothing.'

'Rosie, if my name was Ed, you would not be arguing with me. My operation wasn't exactly a walk in the park. I did it all for you.'

Rosie sighed. She was being silly, she was almost forty two, and of course she wouldn't get pregnant. Ray was right, he had done this for her. Smiling she took his hand and followed him upstairs as he said, 'Come on Mrs Lynne, I've missed you.'

Ten days later, Ray and Kevin left for their tour, and Rosie confided in Candy about their trip to Tenerife. Nobody else knew where they were going, it was one big mystery. Susie was glad to be going away, wherever it was; Steven was getting far too clingy. Once inside the airport, Rosie revealed their destination and the children jumped up and down with glee. 'I can see Tom again,' cried Eddie.

'We can go to the water park,' shouted Deanne.

'I can do more Spanish dancing,' screeched Bobby.

Raydon said nothing, he just looked up at his mother and smiled, he was happy wherever he was. Norma was spinning round and round. 'I love Great Yarmouth,' she cried. 'I can have a paddle and buy some rock.'

Only Susie remained unmoved; part of her was happy knowing that she would see Vidal again, and part of her wasn't. She felt sure that her mother was up to something; she'd been far too secretive. She found a call box and rang Vidal but there was no answer. Six calls later, there was still no answer, so she gave up, deciding that she would go in search of him as soon as she was in the apartment.

Arriving at Reina Sofia airport, passports were flashed, baggage was reclaimed, and very soon the family were heading for their apartment. Once they were installed in Paloma Beach, a happy Candy made tea while Rosie checked the place thoroughly.

'I'm going out,' said Susie.

Rosie thrust Susie's case at her. 'Not until you've unpacked, and then you can help me to make the beds.'

'We can do that later.'

'No we can't.'

'But...'

'Susie, this holiday is not all about you, you're an adult now, Candy and I are on holiday too, so you'll have to muck in.' In a huff, Susie dragged her case to her bedroom, cursing her mother under her breath; she wanted to see Vidal right now. Rosie on the other hand was pleased with Susie's reaction; she could see that her daughter was rattled and knew why.

About two hours later, everyone was sat in their usual restaurant. He was absent, but a phone call from Luisa brought him to the restaurant poste haste. 'My family,' he cried. 'How happy I am to see you.'

Rosie made eye contact with him and he dropped his eyes. Luisa was gushing all over everyone and offering them free drinks. 'We'll pay our own way,' said Rosie, trying to catch Vidal's eye once more. Vidal suddenly noticed Ray and Kevin's absence, and asked where they were. 'Touring,' replied Rosie. 'So I decided to treat my family to a break, the weather in England is not that wonderful at this time of year.'

'Then I hope that you will enjoy yourselves in Tenerife this time,' said Vidal.

'I did last time until my bag was snatched,' replied Rosie.

'And your friend did it,' snapped Deanne, fixing her eyes accusingly on Vidal.

'Deanne,' cried Susie. 'What a terrible thing to say; Vidal got Mum's bag back.'

'That's right, after his friend had stolen it.'

'You are mistaken, little one,' cooed Vidal.

'I'm not, and Eddie knows it too. We were at the fair, and you were having a laugh with the bag snatcher.'

Luisa disappeared into the kitchen, and a guilty looking Vidal attempted to explain, saying, 'The little one is correct, she is very observant, but the man was laughing at me, not with me.'

'You were laughing too,' said Deanne sipping her orange juice through a straw.

'I was laughing in his face; he called me a chicken and I took him round the back of the hot dog van and beat shit out of him.'

'Charming,' said Rosie.

'I apologise for my language, Senora, but I find the whole thing embarrassing.'

'Not surprised, Luisa said you never saw him that night.'

'Luisa was not with me all night; she was out with your charming daughter.'

'Whatever,' said Deanne. 'Hobble dee, hobble dee, hobble dee...'

'And down into a ditch,' cried Eddie.

Susie, Vidal, and Luisa were unsettled and Rosie was very proud of Deanne for sticking to her story and exposing Vidal as a liar. He had just scored another own goal. Rosie stared at the quaking waiter before her; he didn't seem so cocksure now. The looks that were passing between Vidal and Susie were not missed by Rosie; something was going on. Ordering lunch, she basked in the sunshine and drank her Pina Colada. Candy was embarrassed, but she was on holiday and wasn't going to let this revelation spoil things.

After lunch, Rosie went inside the bar and paid the bill. 'It is on the house, Senora,' said Vidal, staring at Rosie's ample cleavage.

'And I say it is not,' replied Rosie, handing over the money. 'You won't win, I'm used to getting my own way with men and you are no exception; oh and this is for Luisa. Susie asked me to give it to you.' Rosie handed him an envelope which Vidal accepted.

'Where is Susie?'

'I sent her on ahead with the rest of my group. Raydon's had a slight accident; I suppose it's all the excitement. We might be back later. Adios.'

'Adios, Senora, it is lovely to see you again.'

'Likewise.'

Vidal watched as Rosie walked away; she was poetry in motion. With trembling fingers, he opened the envelope and took out the letter. Susie hadn't signed it but she wrote that she had missed him and wanted to meet him later at the Costamar. She added that she would leave the door open and couldn't wait to feel his arms around her once more. Vidal was perplexed; why hadn't she signed it? Deciding not to dwell on it, he made several excuses to the boss and left.

Ray and Kevin were hating their tour; nobody had told them that Sammy Silver was headlining. Vic was pissed off, he'd been told that Sammy was too sick to tour, and now suddenly he'd made a miraculous recovery. The Z Tones were now toppled from the top of the bill and were supporting Sammy. Not only did they have to suffer Sammy, they had to suffer his sickly sweet plastic girlfriend. She was a real pain as she'd taken a real shine to Kevin. 'If soppy bollocks can bring his girlfriend along, why can't we bring our wives and girlfriends with us?' raged Ray.

'I'm not Sammy's manager, he plays by a different set of rules,' replied Vic.

Ray kicked over a table, shouting, 'Then maybe we'd be better off working for him.'

'Ray, calm down, I'm throwing a party on our final night, and the wives and girlfriends will be more than welcome there.'

'Why only then? My Rosie's so pissed off about it that she's fucked off to Tenerife with the family.'

'Then maybe, Ray, you could talk her into joining the band and fronting it with Kevin, that way you'd see her every day and wouldn't be suffering with night starvation.'

'Piss off.' Ray was fuming.

'Plastic Kerry Sunshine's heading our way,' laughed Vic. 'She's game.'

'Sammy should keep her on a leash.'

'Are you calling her a bitch?'

'Yes, a bitch on heat. I bet if you got married, you'd bring your wife on tour, Vic.'

'I'm not getting married; now, how about a brandy to steady your nerves?'

'Might as well, there's nothing else on offer.'

'There's always Kerry.'

'I wouldn't touch her with yours, let alone mine.'

'So, Kerry or brandy?'

'No contest, I'll have the brandy.'

Back in Tenerife, Susie was anxious; after helping her mother with the children, she left the apartment and headed for the bar restaurant. Vidal wasn't there, neither was Luisa. Despondently, she made her way to the Torres Del Sol, but there was no reply when she rang the doorbell. Sadly she walked away and made her way back to Paloma Beach. Vidal was in, but he had no intention of answering the door, he was in bed with Luisa and not looking forward to the night ahead. Susie had stated in her letter that she'd be there about seven thirty, so he was going to arrive about seven forty five, 'treat 'em mean and keep 'em keen' was his motto.

Susie mooched around the apartment, wondering where Vidal was; she was in a real sulk. Candy tried to cheer her up by suggesting a shopping trip the following day, but the girl would not be placated. Then she recalled that occasionally Vidal worked at a bar in Playa de las Americas. The trouble was, she couldn't recall which bar it was, and asked Candy. Candy was flummoxed, there were so many bars there, she had no idea where it was. Susie's sulk got worse, and she was now wishing that she was back at home with Steven. This was some holiday, so deciding to have a very early night, she stormed off into her bedroom and slammed the door, vowing to go in search of her Spanish lover the next day.

Chapter Twenty-Seven

Vidal arrived at the Costamar at approximately seven forty five. He knew exactly which apartment it was, as Susie had pointed it out to him shortly after her parents had decided to buy it. He pushed the door open and wandered inside. The lighting was dim and, closing the door behind him, he stared around the room. On a table was a bottle of champagne on ice alongside two glasses. The apartment was very quiet but he guessed that Susie was planning some surprise for him. He uncorked the bottle and poured out two glasses of the fizzing concoction.

'Susie, my darling, I have missed you so much, every night I dream of our time together in England. I cannot forget the first time that we made love; it was exquisite and so beautiful. I cannot wait to hold you in my arms once more,' he cried. There was no answer and so picking up the two glasses of champagne, he headed for the bedroom, thinking that Susie was in there. The moonlight was streaming in the window, illuminating the room. Placing the glasses on a bedside table, he switched on the light. The bed was empty so he returned to the lounge.

'Susie, baby, why are you playing games? Come to me and I will make mad passionate love to you.' Suddenly he realised that the door leading to the terrace was open and that there was a figure sitting out there. 'Susie, baby, come inside, my heart is bursting with love for you,' cried Vidal, suddenly feeling very uneasy.

The figure got to its feet and replied, 'Well, I will come inside, but you won't be making mad passionate love to me.'

Vidal froze, it wasn't Susie at all, it was Rosie. 'Senora, I am so sorry, I thought...'

'You thought that my daughter would be waiting for you.'

'She said in her letter to meet me here. I guess that she was playing a joke.'

'Joke's over, I wrote that letter. You'd better sit down, I don't bite. You owe me an explanation.'

'Senora, I am so sorry, my mouth has run away with me, it was the ramblings of a man that is in love.'

'So you are in love with my daughter?'

'Very much. Can I get you a drink? My mouth is very dry.'

'Yes, I will partake since I bought it.'

'I will get it; I left it in the bedroom.'

'Well hurry up then, or I'll get it myself, or shall we go in together?'

'What?'

'Just another joke.'

Vidal was shaking; this woman did strange things to him. He retrieved the glasses of champagne and after offering Rosie a glass, sat down opposite her. She was sprawled on a sofa looking frighteningly beautiful. Vidal took this image in, the long blonde hair, big green eyes, full lips and a slender neck. Her bosom heaved and her breasts looked in danger of falling out of her short dress. Her body was curvy and her shapely legs tapered down to very slim ankles. She was the mistress of seduction and she knew it. Taking the glass that Vidal was offering her, she licked her lips seductively. Making eye contact, she said, 'You'd better come clean. I heard an awful lot while I was sitting out on the terrace.'

'I do not know if I can.'

'Then if you don't, I will ring Susie, rip my dress and tell her that you tried to rape me.'

'You would do that?'

'Yes, I need to know everything.'

Vidal swallowed hard. 'It is like this, when you first came to Tenerife, I fell in love with her, I did nothing at first, but one day I saw her on the beach and she was crying. She said that she'd been rejected by someone called Kevin and that her heart was broken. She looked so lonely and so sad, so I tried to cheer her up. I swear that that was all I intended to do. We met up the following day and I took her to meet my father. Susie loved his apartment and it seemed to take her mind off Kevin for a while. Then we met up several days after that.'

'So she lied to me; she said that she was meeting Luisa.'

'Sometimes she did meet Luisa; I work a lot of the time.'

'Did you take advantage of her?'

'No, Senora, the first time that we made love was at your home.'

'I only ask, because in my country it is called corrupting a minor and I could have done you for it. She was still only fifteen when we arrived here.'

'I swear that the first time was in her bed in England.'

'She was sixteen then; did you use protection?'

'She would not let me; I used the how you call it, the withdrawal method.'

'Not exactly safe, it can fail. However it worked this time, so she's not pregnant. How do you see your future?'

'I would love to marry her with your permission.'

'And become a wealthy man.'

'Senora, how can you say such things? I am a hard working man, and over here the man works and the woman stays at home with the babies.'

'Have you discussed this with Susie?'

'I have, and she looks forward to the day when we can marry.'

'My mother thinks that you're the gardener.'

'What a wonderful woman she is, she was so happy to be visiting her home.'

'I suppose she was, but I'm disgusted that you used her bed.'

Vidal hung his head. 'I know that it was wrong, but when you are in love, things happen. Norma fell asleep in her chair and Susie suggested that we have a nap too.'

'Little minx, lying to me was bad enough, but having sex in her grandmother's bed is ten times worse, plus leaving empty Spanish cigarette boxes and empty lager cans in the rubbish bin is just stupid.'

'Your mother has a lovely home. I love nature, and I would never see any of God's creatures harmed. The water birds are beautiful. We went to Bedfords Park too and saw the deer; they are magnificent, and Susie showed me the tortoise set up.'

'Yes, I've taken the programme over from a shady character; he was ripping young Eddie off.'

'He took advantage of a child?'

'Yes, but then so did you, you're no spring chicken.'

'What is this spring chicken?'

'It's a saying; it means that you're getting on a bit.'

'Love knows no boundaries.'

'But you don't exactly cover your tracks well, do you?'

'What do you mean?'

'Spanish cigarettes, empty lager cans, plus these.' Rosie opened a drawer from a cupboard that stood beside her. Removing a plastic bag from it, she threw it at Vidal who attempted to catch it but missed, making it land on his feet. He picked up the bag and looked inside as Rosie said, 'These are not my husband's, he wears pants.'

'Madre mia, I forgot these; what a fool I am.'

'There was stacks of washing up in the sink, plus a sheet covered in semen at my mother's house. Did you want to get caught?'

'No Senora, I had planned to stay and greet you on your return, but Luisa phoned me and told me that my grandmother had died, so I had to return to the funeral.'

'Really, Luisa told me that you were in England visiting your sick mother; there's a lot of illness in your family, isn't there?'

'My mother was very sick; she drinks too much, and her liver is damaged but she continues to drink.'

'My husband drinks too much. It's just as well that he's not here or he would have knocked you into next week and, as for her true deceased father, he would have killed you.'

'You appear to be a strong passionate woman and yet you have not raised your hand to me.'

'I've had time to reflect on this situation. I can't stand liars, they destroy me, plus my daughter has hurt me badly, but in some ways your situation reminds me of my own youth. My mother stood in my way when I wanted to marry Susie's father. I should have stood up to her and, if I had, things would have been so different. I wanted to be a teenage bride, and in the end I was, but to the wrong man. My parents approved of Barry; he was rich and powerful, but my heart belonged to Ed. I have few regrets in my life but that is one of them. I obeyed my mother and ruined my own life. Still it's water under the bridge, and we're not talking about me.'

'That is sad, Senora, you are a lovely woman, and any man would be proud to call you his own.'

'You included?'

'Of course, it is only my love for Susie that holds me back.'

Rosie was up to her old tricks. 'Really, I won't tell her if you don't. Do you want to have sex with me?'

The temptress was emerging and for good reason. If Vidal made a move on her, he was history. Still sprawled on the sofa, she began to move her body seductively making her short dress ride up. Vidal was in agony. If he made a move, his impending rich status was gone, and he couldn't risk it.

'Come over here.'

'No, or I will do something that I will regret later, I love Susie.'

'Then I'll come to you.' Rosie got to her feet and wandered over to the shaking waiter. She leaned over him, pushing her breasts into his face; how he longed to touch them. Rosie was in her element; she wanted this guy out of her daughter's life.

'What's wrong, are you scared?'

'No, Senora, but I cannot do this.'

'Do you want me to undress you?'

'No.' His hard on was visible.

'But you are pleased to see me, aren't you? I'll strip off if you want me to.'

'Senora, please don't tempt me.'

'Why not, you love sex, don't you? You even made lewd remarks to me on our first encounter.'

'I love Susie.'

Rosie stood up, then perched herself on his lap. She could feel his penis straining his jeans; she wriggled around on his lap. 'Doesn't that feel good?'

'Yes, but I can't.'

'Let me unzip your jeans; there's a monster trying to get out.'

'Senora, I'm begging you, please stop. I would love to satisfy you, but I love your daughter.'

'So you're turning me down?'

'Yes, I have to, I cannot betray Susie.'

'Good.'

'What?'

'You have satisfied me. It was never going to happen, but I had to test you out. Now let's have another drink and then you can call Susie.'

'Call Susie?'

'Yes, I want to speak to her in front of you. Don't worry, I won't mention what happened.'

Vidal mopped his brow. The woman was hot just like he'd imagined. That was close; pouring Rosie another drink, he dialled Paloma Beach.

The apartments were practically adjacent and a confused Susie made her way to the Costamar telling Candy that she was going out. Once inside the Costamar, Susie was stunned to see her mother and Vidal drinking champagne. On her arrival, her mother got to her feet and dealt her a slap around her face. Holding her face, Susie cried, 'What was that for?'

'For lying to me and using your grandmother's home for your own sexual gratification. I can forgive you most things, Susie, but never that.'

'But we're in love.'

'I know that, but your actions were disgusting. As far as I'm concerned, you're having a fling and it seems paramount to you as Vidal's your first love.'

'Kevin was.'

'But nothing happened between you and Kevin. Now I want to get back to the rest of my family, but before I leave, I'm giving you these.' She handed a bunch of keys to Susie, adding, 'This apartment is vacant for the next two weeks so you can both stay here. The only thing that I ask of you, is that you pop back now and again to visit your siblings and, if you want to, you can still eat with us at night. As for getting married, you can if you're still an item in eighteen months' time. My own mother stood in my way, but I won't stand in yours. You can make your own mistakes, but if you lie to me again, young lady, you will find yourself out on the streets penniless, do you understand me?'

'Yes Mum.'

'Then say thank you to your mother,' ordered Vidal.

'What, for slapping me and giving me a lecture?'

'Your mother is only looking out for you; most mothers would not be so tolerant, so give her a hug. You should show her more respect.'

Susie obeyed. 'Thanks, Mum,' she said, giving her a hug.

Vidal winked, saying, 'Thanks, Mum.'

Laughing, Rosie left the apartment; she wasn't happy about the relationship but knew that if she tried to stop it, it would draw the couple closer. Her mind drifted back to Ed. Nothing had ever separated them completely, not parents, affairs or marriages, and how she ached to have his arms around her now. 'I love you, Ed,' she said out loud and, as she walked into Paloma Beach, thought that she felt a kiss on her cheek. Imagination she thought, or maybe I'm just tired.

Once Rosie had left, Vidal lost no time in getting Susie into bed, but to her dismay he started to lecture her on her stupidity, immediately after their love making. 'Why did you forget to change the sheets?'

'I don't know, I just did.'

'Then in future, don't forget things; I left my boxer shorts for you to wash. Why didn't you do them, you even left the washing up in your grandmother's sink; don't you do anything, have you a job lined up yet?'

'The boxer shorts were your responsibility, and you were quite happy to share Nana's bed; as for the washing up, why didn't you do it?'

'You are so lazy that you didn't even empty the rubbish bin; your mother found the empty cigarette boxes and empty lager cans.'

'Why is this all my responsibility?'

'Because anything concerning the home is, it is a man's place to work, and the woman's to keep the home in order.'

'So why do I need a job?'

'Because you can't expect your parents to keep you forever.'

'But I thought that we were getting married.'

'We are, your mother has agreed that she will give us her blessing if we're still together in eighteen months; she is a good mother. How many mothers would have let us use this apartment after they'd been deceived?'

'I think this is have-a-go-at-Susie-night. I took most of your clothes to the launderette, it was only one pair of boxers.'

'It was those that your mother found. You could have hand washed them the night before and then put them in my case. I hate having to lecture you like this, but at times you behave like a spoilt brat; you even stopped your friends visiting us while I was there.'

'I wanted you all to myself.'

'You cannot own people. It is love that keeps us together, not possessiveness, and when you go home, you will get a job and start saving for our marriage.'

'Oh, Ray will pay for our wedding.'

'Have you listened to a word that I've said?'

'Yes, I'm sorry, Vidal, I will try harder.'

'I'm all wound up.'

'I'm sorry, let me unwind you.' Susie slid down his body and took him in her mouth. She hated what she was about to do, but if it pleased him that was all that mattered. She was glad that she was on the pill now; a pregnancy was the last thing she needed.

Chapter Twenty-Eight

The fortnight sped over. Eddie got to see Tom, Deanne visited the water park, and Candy and Rosie lapped up the sun. Norma had plenty of paddles, ice cream, and rock, and Bobby continued to dance, even doing a solo one night at the Princessa Dacil. Raydon enjoyed everything, and Susie had her Spanish lover. Her absence was explained by Rosie as to needing her own space, plus sharing the accommodation with Luisa. Everyone accepted this, apart from Deanne who stated, 'I bet that waiter's there; he's probably bonking both of them. I call him Tiddle.' Rosie threw up her hands in horror; nothing got past her youngest daughter. When they ate out, Norma repeatedly asked Vidal when he was going to do her garden, and he replied that he would do it on his return to England.

'Oh, aren't we in England? I thought that this was Great Yarmouth; we used to travel by train, now it's by aeroplane. I would have loved to have been an air hostess when I was young.'

'And you would have been the best ever,' replied Vidal.

'You're a nice man. Did Rosie sack you? You haven't visited us lately.'

'No, Senora, my grandmother died and I had to come home for the funeral.'

'Oh, that's sad. Did you buy me any rock at the market today, Rosie?'

'Yes, Mum.'

'Oh I do love Great Yarmouth,' replied Norma, and with that she picked up her glass of lemonade and drained it.

Ray and Kevin's tour was becoming even more of a nightmare. Kerry seemed to be trying to go through the card of musicians. Sammy viewed Kevin with suspicion, but appeared to be oblivious to other males who Kerry pursued with relish. The entire Z Tones had knocked her back, even their sex crazed drummer who stated, 'I might be hard, but I'm not that hard up. If I wanted someone like you, I'd get a blow up doll.'

A frustrated Kerry refused to give up, and things came to a head at a gathering held by Sammy's press agent. Kerry and Sammy had a nasty argument and things turned sour. She ran to Kevin's side, crying out to Sammy, 'This is a real man who knows how to treat a woman; you are a pompous overrated seventies reject.'

The press had a field day and, before long, flash bulbs were popping nonstop. Sammy threw his drink over Kevin, accusing him of stealing his girlfriend. Kerry sponged Kevin down, which was caught on camera. Upset, Kevin walked away and left the party, but unfortunately Kerry followed him to his hotel. He told Kerry to go back to Sammy, adding that he had a girlfriend whom he adored and he wasn't about to cheat on her. Kerry began to cry and, taking pity on her, Kevin bought her a drink. One drink followed another and, before too long, Kevin was inebriated; he rarely drank and it was taking its toll on him. He staggered up to his room and collapsed onto his bed, remembering nothing until the next morning when he woke up beside a naked Kerry Sunshine.

He shook the sleeping girl, and she moaned and went back to sleep again. Kevin tried to collect his thoughts, 'who was she?' his brain was going around in circles and someone was knocking on the door, or on his head. Whatever it was, it wasn't very pleasant. The knocking became more agitated, and Kevin decided that it was the door. He was about to tell whoever it was to come in when the door burst open and Vic charged in like a bull in a china shop. He hurled a tirade of abuse at Kevin, plus two newspapers.

'Get that cunt out of here,' he bellowed. 'But before you do, get some answers out of her. The stupid bitch has spun a pack of lies to the press. She must have done it last night.' Kevin was bewildered as Vic picked up the newspapers and thrust them under Kevin's nose. 'Read it,' screeched Vic.

Bleary eyed, Kevin read the bold print 'Kevin Howard and His Secret Lover'. Underneath the caption in smaller print it said 'Sammy's Fury as He and Kerry Split. It Was Love at First Sight, Says Kerry. Kevin is splitting from His Girlfriend'. Kevin groaned and read the other newspaper. 'Sammy Out in the Cold, Kevin Swept Me off My Feet, We'll marry As Soon As Possible'. Kevin stared at the photos; one of Kerry giving him a kiss, he recalled that one, she'd kissed everyone when she'd greeted them at the party. As far as he was concerned that was just a show business kiss. The other photo showed him minus his shirt which had been soaked after Sammy had doused him in a temper. The photographer had caught Kerry in the act of sponging Kevin down. He turned to the girl who now had her eyes open and was smiling up at him. 'Why?' he asked. 'I told you I had a girlfriend.'

'Leave her to me,' snapped Vic. 'I'll get it out of her. Ring Candy now or you might be minus a girlfriend when she reads the papers.'

Feeling rather shaky, Kevin dressed and then went downstairs to use the phone. Candy sounded pleased to hear from him; obviously she hadn't seen the papers. 'Hi darling, how are you?' cried Candy. 'How was last night's gig? Our papers haven't arrived so I haven't been able to read any reviews.'

'Candy, listen to me, it's better that you hear this from me, before you read the press.'

Candy's heart jolted; she was nobody's fool and knew that both Kevin and Ray played around these days. Rosie knew it too but both women accepted it, having never caught their men out. This was the wonderful world of rock and roll. Trying to keep calm, she sank down into an easy chair and said, 'Was the gig bad, or was it something more serious?'

'The gig was fine, but everything fell apart at the party. Some silly girl has spouted a load of lies about me to the press.'

'A groupie?'

'No, she's Sammy Silver's girlfriend and, contrary to what the press says, she's nothing to me.'

There was silence and, for a second, Kevin thought that Candy had hung up. 'Don't hang up on me, baby,' cried Kevin.

'I haven't,' replied Candy. 'I'll ring you later at your hotel, I've got the number.'

'Candy, I'm innocent.'

There was no reply, Candy had already hung up. When Kevin returned to his room, he found Vic on the bed with a tape recorder, and Al sitting on a chair with a Polaroid camera. 'Make her talk, Kevin,' said Vic, seating himself on the bed.

Kevin turned to Kerry. 'Why, lady, why?'

'I love you, that's why; I have done since I first set eyes on you.'

Memories were now flooding back to Kevin from the night before. He'd gone back to his hotel, Kerry had followed him, he'd bought her a drink and had several himself which was completely out of character for him. The booze had hit him and he'd staggered up to his room. Once he'd half collapsed into his room, he'd fully collapsed across the bed and that was it. Now he'd recalled that there was more. Kerry had followed him into his room and had begun shaking him. Thoroughly pissed off by this woman's declaration of love, he'd allowed her to give him head. He threw back his head and laughed.

'You kept on bleating about wanting to sleep with me, so I let you suck me off just to shut you up. It was pretty good from what I remember, but then you've probably had more dicks in your mouth than you've had hot dinners. We never had sex and I doubt that even Vic or Al would fuck you either. Vic flinched at the last remark; he was glad that he hadn't switched the recorder on yet.'

'We made love,' screeched Kerry.

'No chance, a blow job's one thing, but having sex is quite another. It's your word against mine, and Vic here can make things pretty nasty for you if you don't do as he says and own up to the press that you lied.'

Ray breezed into the room clutching a newspaper. 'You sly old fox, Kevin. I've just read about you and Kerry; you kept that quiet.'

'Nothing happened.'

Ray stared at Kerry. 'My youngest daughter has a doll that looks just like you, except the doll is better looking. Mind you, you've got a good mouth, even if your lips are plumped up with silicone.'

'Try it out, Ray,' laughed Vic. 'I won't tell Rosie.'

Ray laughed. 'Why not, I've been celibate for too long.'

Al's eyes lit up. 'Wait a minute; I need to get the right angle.'

'Whoa, I ain't going on camera,' said Ray. 'Forget it.'

'It'll only be the bottom half of you, it's Kerry's face that we're concentrating on.'

'I won't do it,' screeched Kerry.

'Oh yes you will,' replied Vic. 'This is Al Simpkins, porn film maker extraordinaire, he's the best, and he'll make you look like a whore.'

'I won't, and you can't make me.'

'Take note, pretty lady, when Vic Lee says jump, you reply "how high?" or one day you might not wake up so pretty. Are you ready, Al?'

'Ready, Vic.'

'Okay, Ray, we're ready to roll.'

Ray unzipped his fly, pulled down his underpants and forced Kerry on her knees. He'd been sick of her following him around trying to seduce him; now the tables were turned and she was getting her just desserts. 'Suck,' he ordered, forcing his penis into her mouth. Kerry knew that she was trapped. If Sammy ever saw these shots, he'd never look at her again.

Romany walked in. 'Can anybody play?' he asked.

'Be my guest,' replied Vic. 'This bitch needs teaching a lesson.'

Romany walked behind Kerry and caressed her breasts and when Ray began to climax, he pushed the girl's head further onto Ray, making her take him deeper into her mouth. Immediately after climaxing, Ray zipped himself up, let out a loud fart, walked over to Kevin's bed, and collapsed on it. He'd been drinking all night and couldn't even remember how he got back to the hotel, but now he was home and Kerry had rounded off everything perfectly. As Kevin left the room, he cast a backward glance. The scene wasn't a pretty one; both Vic and Romany were mauling the girl. As the photos developed, Al waved them under Kerry's nose. 'Sammy will love these,' he crowed.

Vic switched the cassette recorder on and then returned to the petrified Kerry. 'Let's have some sound effects,' he said. 'Are you going to fuck her, Romany?'

'No chance, but I wouldn't mind a bit of what Ray's just had.'

Kevin felt sick to his stomach as Kerry screamed out to him to help her. He had no sympathy for this sad little figure; she'd pestered everyone for sex and now she was getting it.

Candy was distraught when she finally saw the headlines. Rosie wasn't very happy either knowing that if goody two shoes Kevin could cheat, so could Ray. She gave Candy a hug. 'It's just bad publicity,' she said. 'Kevin loves you, you know that.'

'Do I? She's a beautiful girl.'

'She's just like a Barbie doll. Men play with them, but they never marry them, and anyway it's the final night of the tour tomorrow. We're invited to the after show party so you'll be able to have this out with Kevin.'

'Maybe I should stay home and look after the kids.'

'No, Ada's looking after them. She'll be round first thing in the morning, and a party will do you good.'

'I don't know.'

'I do, now dry your eyes and we'll go shopping for a beautiful dress for you. You'll knock Kevin's eyes out by the time that I've finished with you.'

'But supposing that the press is right?'

'If they are, I'll knock both of Kevin's eyes out literally, and his teeth.' Candy laughed; Rosie could always lift her spirits.

The following evening, the two women arrived at their hotel and got ready for the party. A sad Kevin had sunk into a deep depression; his final performance had been very lack lustre that night. Rosie and Candy had deliberately arrived late; neither one of them wanted to see the show. They wanted their men on tenterhooks. At first, Candy hadn't been too sure that it was a good idea. Kevin would be wondering where she was, but as Rosie said, 'If we're banned from the tour, why should we turn up for the final show? We'll go straight to the hotel, and later the party, so sod Vic and the Z Tones.'

In the end, Candy agreed. If they weren't there to support their men, it was Vic's fault, and anyway she was now angry with Kevin. The press might have exaggerated things, but there was no smoke without fire.

Kevin was in his room; he didn't want to join in with the after show party. He flopped onto his bed, wondering if Candy had finished with him. She hadn't turned up at his final show, so maybe it was all over. He wanted to end it all if that was the case. For years he'd believed that he'd never get over Cathy, and then into his life had come this diminutive little girl who had taught him how to love again. Now because of some stupid creature, which was all that he could call Kerry, he'd probably lost his lovely girlfriend. Ray came into the room. 'No sign of the girls yet; maybe the car's broken down.'

'Maybe.' Kevin just wanted to disappear into a corner and die.

'Oh for fuck's sake, Kevin, snap out of it, we all have indiscretions on the road.'

'We never used to, what happened?'

'We gave into temptation, everyone does it.'

'Do they?'

'Yes, after all, what we do isn't exactly cheating.'

'Isn't it?'

'No, a blow job's not cheating, you're just being pleasured and coming down from the adrenalin that pumps through you night after night on the stage. I've never cheated on Rosie. I let the girls give me blow jobs, why shouldn't I? It's on offer, so I take it.'

'But our women don't do it. We're supposed to love them, not cheat on them.'

'For the last time, Kevin, a blow job is not cheating.'

'So, if Rosie did it, that would be all right?'

'The hell it would, I'd kill the bloke that did it and give her a beating.'

'You'd beat her?'

'Too true I would, I'd teach her to cheat on me.'

'So it's different for a woman to receive a blow job; that's a bit unfair, isn't it?'

'No, men and women are different; it's been the same since time began.'

'But it's not right, it's still cheating, we shouldn't do it, Ray.'

'Then don't do it. I'm going downstairs to find out what room the girls have been allocated.'

'You just said that there was no sign of them.'

'Well there wasn't when I came up here, but just think, in a few hours' time you'll be cuddled up to Candy, and I'll be in another room with my beautiful Rosie.'

'If they turn up.'

'Oh for Christ's sake, Kevin, I was okay when I came upstairs, but now you've made me feel depressed. I'll leave you to it, but you need to get yourself together because the way that you're acting is enough to put any woman off. Candy deserves better; she's the one that had to read all of that shit, she's the one that should be falling apart, not you. If you carry on like this, even the likes of poxy Kerry Sunshine won't want you.'

'Leave me alone, Ray.'

'I will, I'm going downstairs to have a drink and a laugh. If I stay with you, I'll want to slit my wrists. If you want Candy, fight for her. If she's here now, I'll send her up, you two have got some serious talking to do.' Ray left the room and slammed the door. He passed Kerry on the stairs.

'Hi, Ray,' she cooed.

'Fuck off,' replied Ray and went downstairs.

Kerry wanted to apologise to Kevin. She realised that she'd caused a fracas and that he didn't want her. She doubted that Sammy would want her any more if he saw the photos that Al had taken. She tapped on the door, and Kevin told her to come in, thinking that Candy had arrived. He had his head buried in the pillow, not knowing what to say. Kerry perched on the edge of the bed and stroked his arm. 'I'm so sorry,' she murmured. 'But you can't help who you fall in love with.'

'What?' Kevin rolled over onto his back. 'Get out. Haven't you done enough damage? My girlfriend could be here at any minute, and she's not going to be amused if she finds you here, so go back to Sammy.'

'He won't want me once he sees those photos.'

'Your problem.'

'I just wanted to apologise.'

'Right, apology accepted, now get out.'

'Don't send me away, please, Kevin.'

'Are you going to leave, or have I got to throw you out?'

'Please, Kevin, let me stay.'

'Just go; let's forget that anything ever happened.'

'But I can't, I really do love you.'

'Right, that's it, I'm going to freshen up and then I'm going downstairs.'

'If that's the way you want it, I'll go, but I may kill myself.'

'That's up to you.'

'But I love you.'

'You don't, and I love Candy, now get out, I need to shower,' and with that Kevin hauled the girl to the door and threw her out, then he proceeded to run a shower.

'I am so pleased to see you,' cried Vic, throwing his arms around Candy. 'I think Kevin's resting, he was very tired at the gig tonight, wasn't himself. I'm pretty sure that you will cheer him up.'

'Are you sure about that?'

'Positive.'

'Not what the newspapers say. Apparently he's planning to marry someone called Kerry Sunshine, and I was under the impression that he was splitting with me.'

'Rubbish, she's just a stupid girl who took a shine to Kevin and spouted a load of shit to the reporters.'

'So he's not interested in her?'

'Nobody's interested in her, even Sammy's dumped her.'

'Really?'

'Yes, now go upstairs; he'll be pleased to see you.'

'Okay, Vic, thanks.'

'And where's Ray?' said Rosie, prodding Vic.

'Oh, hello, Rosie, need you ask?'

'No, not really, propping the bar up, I guess.'

'Got it in one.' Vic watched as Candy ascended the stairs, and Rosie went in search of her husband. The nightmare was over, or so he thought.

Candy could hear two voices as she approached Kevin's room, one male, one female; she recognised Kevin's, but not the female's.

'You've got it all wrong,' yelled Kevin. 'Just go.'

'How can you tell me to go when you know I love you?'

'I keep telling you, I love Candy.' Candy was happy, the press had got it wrong, Kevin had just told the girl that he wasn't interested.

'Please, Kevin.'

'Kerry, that night, I was drunk and you made yourself available. If you hadn't put it on a plate whilst I was inebriated, nothing would have happened.'

Candy's heart raced, so something had happened, her fears were now confirmed. Kerry was sobbing as if her heart would break and then there was silence, a long one. The door was slightly open and Candy pushed it a little wider. Kevin was holding Kerry in his arms, soothing her, then she sank to her knees and removed Kevin's bath towel. Candy couldn't believe it, and what made matters worse was that, as the girl began to pleasure Kevin, he encouraged her by pushing on her head increasing his pleasure. He stroked her head muttering, 'That's so good, baby, really good.'

Candy could restrain herself no longer, she pushed the door open wide and darted across the floor. Yanking a handful of Kerry's hair, she knocked her to the floor, punched Kevin on his jaw and left. 'You lousy two timing bastard,' she screamed.

Kerry got to her feet and cowered in the corner. Throwing on a pair of jeans and a loose fitting shirt, Kevin attempted to leave the room, but Kerry rushed to his side. 'Oh darling, did she hurt you?' she cried.

'Get out of my way.' Kevin threw Kerry to the floor.

'But I'm better than your girlfriend, she's plain.'

'She's a lady, unlike the majority of scrubbers that follow bands around; you wouldn't understand that, would you? Now when I come back, I want you gone; you said that you might kill yourself, but if I lose Candy through you, I'll save you the job.' Kevin charged down the stairs and collided with Vic.

'What's up?' cried Vic. 'Why are you holding your jaw?'

'Candy slugged me; she caught me in a compromising position with Kerry.'

Vic downed his whiskey in one gulp. 'You idiot, I thought we'd dealt with that cunt. Oh well, I suppose we'd better present Mr Silver with some snapshots.'

'Forget it, Vic, if Candy forgives me, it'll be a miracle.'

'She's over there at the bar talking to Ray and Rosie, go and get her.'

Ashamed, Kevin wandered over to Candy. 'Can I have a word, please?'

'You can have as many as you want and then I'm leaving.'

'Fine, but hear me out first.'

'Okay, we'll go outside.'

The couple walked outside the building, and Kevin pointed to his car. 'In here,' he said, 'it's more private.'

'Okay,' replied Candy, and waited while Kevin opened the door for her. Kevin was lost for words and then blurted out, 'It was an isolated incident; if you'd been with me, it would never have happened.'

'So it's my fault?'

'No, the whole thing is just a girl's vivid imagination and, as usual, the press lapped it up.'

'I know what I saw; how could you lie to me on the phone?'

'I didn't want to hurt you.'

'Too late, you already have. I know that I'll never live up to Cathy, and I've settled for second place, but I didn't think that you'd cheat.'

'Let's go for a drive and I'll try to explain.'

Candy shrugged her shoulders. 'Okay,' she said.

Vic watched them drive away, and noticed Kerry sitting in a corner. Walking over to her, he leered and said, 'See, you stupid bitch, you wasted your time, didn't you?'

'Can I have those photos? I want to try and make it up with Sammy.'

'Al Simpkins has them, along with some great sound effects; I think he wants to present them to Sammy personally as a last night of the tour gift. I think that Sammy's seen the light; he won't want you, but I'm on my own, and we could get real cosy tonight.'

Kerry's expression was one of real fear as she said, 'No, Vic, I don't want to.'

'You don't get the choice, one word from me and Al will deliver those photographs before you've had a chance to beg Sammy's forgiveness.'

'Okay, but can you get me some stuff?'

'No problem, my dear,' replied Vic, grinning lecherously. 'I can get you whatever you want; will coke suffice?'

Kerry nodded; never before had she felt such a fool, and so wretched.

Chapter Twenty-Nine

Kevin had driven to a desolate spot and sat staring into space, saying nothing. Candy broke the silence saying, 'You brought me here to explain, so let's start.'

Kevin put his arm around her shoulders. 'There are no excuses, but what you don't understand is that when I come off stage, I'm supercharged, I need to unwind and release all of my pent up emotions. I have to fight off all the attention of groupies and starlets, and sometimes it's just too much. I'm only human, and a man too.'

'Meaning that it's okay for you to cheat?'

'No it's wrong; you're the only one that matters to me. I don't recall a lot of my drunken night; I recall the party and Kerry being all over me. I shrugged her off several times, but flash bulbs were popping and we got snapped at all the wrong times. Kerry and Sammy had a fierce argument and he poured his drink all over me, and of course the press had to get a shot of Kerry sponging me down. I was pissed off and left, but Kerry followed me back to my hotel. I bought her a drink and I don't remember much after that. The one thing that I do know though, is that we didn't have sex. I'm not a drinker as you know, but when I do, I always get brewers droop.'

'But something happened.'

'Yes, she gave me a blow job.'

'Even though you had brewers droop?'

'You are making this so hard for me, I'm trying to explain.'

'Brewers droop and making things hard in the same context is not making sense.'

'Look, if you want I'll quit the band, we can get married and I'll work as a soloist.'

'Do you know what you just said?'

'Yes, I'll quit the band.'

'No not that, the other bit.'

'Oh, get married; I thought you knew that we'd get married at some stage. I'd rather it was sooner than later.'

'So you cheat on me and then ask me to marry you.'

'But it's not like that, this has only ever happened twice since we've been together.' Kevin wasn't about to own up to his other indiscretions, there was no need, he was never going to cheat again. 'How many times do you think that Ed cheated on Cathy?'

'I don't know and I don't care, you're not Ed and I'm not Cathy, I just live in her shadow.'

'Not any more, you're the one that I want to grow old and grey with. Will you marry me, Candy?'

'I'll think about it.'

'I bought you an engagement ring a few days ago; I wanted to announce my engagement in front of everyone at the party tonight.'

'So where is it?'

'Here.' Kevin took a small red box from his pocket and presented it to Candy. With trembling fingers, Candy opened it and gasped at the ring. It was a real beauty; she stared at Kevin and saw the way that he looked at her. She could see that he was terrified of rejection. 'Please say yes, Candy,' begged Kevin.

'Will you promise me that you'll never cheat again?'

'Of course, I've learnt my lesson.'

'Yes, Kevin, I'll marry you, but if you ever step out of line, we're finished.' Kevin mopped his brow, the nightmare was over.

'Will you go down on one knee; Rosie told me that Ed did?'

'With pleasure.'

Candy giggled and they both got out of the car. There was a full moon shining on Kevin as he went down onto one knee and said, 'Candice Ryan, will you do me the honour of becoming my wife?'

'Yes,' cried Candy, 'yes.' She felt as if her heart were about to burst with happiness.

Kevin slipped the ring onto her finger and said, 'Let's get back and tell the others, I can't wait to see their faces.'

'Neither can I,' replied Candy, despite her awful findings earlier, her long time dream had come true.

Back at the party, Vic was fuming and frothing at the mouth. Kerry had slipped away and back into Sammy Silver's affections. The couple looked the picture of happiness. Al had the photos and cassette in his possession, and Vic couldn't find him. He approached Romany who was all loved up with Ellen. 'Can I have a word?' he asked.

'Fire away.'

'No, in private.'

'Okay.' Romany kissed Ellen. 'Won't be long,' he said.

'Where's Al?'

'I don't know, why?'

'I need to find him.'

'I haven't seen him in hours; he's probably pissed and sleeping it off somewhere.'

'Stupid bastard, I need those photos.'

'What photos?' replied Romany, staring blankly.

'The photos of us and that whore.'

Romany yawned. 'Forget it, Vic,' he said glancing over at Sammy and Kerry, 'the main thing is that she's off our backs, and Kevin has probably made it up with Candy.'

'But I don't want that bitch getting back with Silver and getting off so lightly; we went to a lot of trouble to get those photos.'

'And we enjoyed doing them, leave it Vic.' Romany waved his hand disinterestedly and then walked away.

'The only thing that confuses me is that you said that Kerry came into your room and you thought that she was me,' said Candy as their car pulled up outside the hotel.

'That's right,' replied Kevin, 'and when I realised that she wasn't, I threw her out and ran a shower, wanting to get myself looking good for you.'

'Then how did she get back into your room?'

'I really don't know, I guess I hadn't locked the door; you don't exactly expect someone to return once you've thrown them out.'

'But when I caught you two out, you were shouting at her first and then you were holding her and soothing her.'

'She was distressed, rejection is not a nice thing. I was soothing her, hoping that she'd leave.'

'And you let her remove your bath towel and begin to give you a blow job.'

'Look, at that moment in time, I was all over the place, you hadn't turned up for the gig and for a while I wondered if you were coming at all, you've never missed a final concert before. I couldn't see the harm in it, after all if you had finished with me, my life was over.'

'So you wanted to go out with a bang.'

'Candy, I can't believe that you just said that.'

'Okay, no more questions, but if you cheat again, you might find yourself unable to do it again because I'll cut your bollocks off.'

'Ouch, give me a kiss and then let's get inside.'

'Okay,' and Candy collapsed in a fit of giggles.

They almost fell over Al Simpkins as they walked in the door, he was sound asleep. Kevin spotted an envelope laying by the side of him and guessed what it was. Picking it up, he put it into his own pocket and excused himself to Candy, saying that he needed the gents. Once inside the cubicle, he opened the envelope. The contents revealed several shots of Kerry in very explicit positions. There was even one of Ray's legs as Kerry performed oral sex on him. Kevin took that one out and kept it just in case Kerry and Sammy had another bust up and she revealed all. Putting the rest of the photos and cassette back into the envelope, Kevin went in search of Kerry and met her coming upstairs. He gave her the package. 'This is yours; sorry that I looked at the contents but I found it by the side of Al Simpkins and wanted to check that it was what I thought it was.'

Kerry blushed. 'How can I thank you?' she said.

'You don't need to, destroy it and stick with Sammy; he's okay.'

Kerry kissed him on his cheek and carried on going upstairs before Kevin could say goodbye. He made his way downstairs and found Candy showing her ring to Rosie and Ray. Taking her hand, he said, 'Come on, I want to make this public.'

Vic had finally found Al, still asleep and blocking the doorway. Vic hauled a startled Al to his feet. 'The photos, I want the photos,' cried Vic.

Al fumbled in his pockets and laughed. 'I've lost 'em,' he slurred. 'Maybe someone's found 'em and sent 'em to the *News Of The World*; you could be front page tomorrow, Vic.'

Vic went blood red and spluttered. His plan had failed. He was now sick of the entertainment world, and could trust nobody. He could hear Kevin announcing his engagement on the microphone. Al fell to the floor once more and stared at Vic with a silly happy expression. As Vic helped Al to his feet, he cried, 'I've made a decision, put me in touch with that Lop girl, I'm getting married.'

'Lop Lee, Lop Lee,' cackled Al. He spun around laughing then fell over and hit his head, knocking himself out. His head was bleeding badly, so Vic accompanied Al to the A & E department of the nearest hospital. This was some ending to the tour. Instead of spending a night with Kerry, he had to settle for a whole night in A & E.

A month later, *Eden's Rose* was filmed after many arguments and wrangling. Susie was quite happy to be in front of the camera;

she loved posing, particularly when she was informed that some of her part in the video would involve Kevin. She was playing the part of a sixteen-year-old Rosie. Deanne hated playing the part of her mother, and Eddie also hated playing the part of his father at a young age. Toward the end of the film was a still of her favourite photo when she'd had a day out at London Zoo and was riding the pony Mr Ed. 'I don't mind my photo being shown, but why I have to caper around pretending to be my mother, I don't know.'

'It's for Dad,' retorted Susie, 'this is being done in his memory.'

'I thought it was about Mum, she was *Eden's Rose*.'

'But it was Dad's song...'

'Written about Mum. This is a stupid idea. Bobby's terrorising that little girl that Vic got from the stage school, and keeps telling her that she's got to dance; he's had her in tears twice.'

Kevin performed to the best of his ability; he knew that it was just another one of Vic's money making schemes. Nobody gleaned any satisfaction from this video, especially Rosie. Vic wanted her naked lying under piles of red rose petals. Rosie refused point blank. It was then suggested that she could wear a g string. Once more she refused. 'I thought that this video was aimed at Mother's Day,' cried Rosie. 'Your idea is hardly relevant.'

'You have to move with the times; how about you wear a strapless bikini?'

'No.'

'How about an off-the-shoulder dress? If we use more rose petals it will still have the same effect.'

'Yes, the effect that I'm naked,' snapped Rosie.

'Would make great shots,' said Al, 'and the posters would look great.'

Ray frowned; he'd been watching the whole thing. 'Rosie agreed to do this in Ed's memory. She didn't agree to doing a nude model shoot; it'll appeal to the wrong audience. Mothers are supposed to be sweet loving caring women, not glamour models.'

'But part of this song makes references to the Garden of Eden.'

Rosie was losing patience. So far her long suffering children had performed just as Vic had asked, and done their best. The video had gone well and was quite appealing, but any nude, or shots that gave the impression of nudity, were out. Deanne stood with her hands on her hips and glared at Vic. 'You just want to see my Mum's tits and fanny,' she said.

'Not at all Dee Dee, it's just that I thought it would be a good idea, it's like getting back to nature.'

'Don't call me Dee Dee, only my friends call me that.'

'I am your friend.'

'No you're not; you're a dirty old pervert.'

Rosie laughed; once more Deanne had put Vic in his place. 'Let's take five,' she said, 'and Ray and I will see if we can come up with something tasteful.'

Vic agreed, obviously his ploy to get Rosie to take her kit off had failed. After a break, Ray and Rosie offered a solution. 'The rose petal idea is a good one; you have a lot of green in this video so the brilliant red petals make a striking contrast. Ray and I believe that a red dress would also look good. I would be prepared to sit on the grass in a red dress surrounded by rose petals, could you even mock up a backdrop of them?' said Rosie.

'What sort of dress?'

'A short one, that way, although you wouldn't be getting a nude effect, I could sit in a position where you would get a glimpse of thigh. It would be much more tasteful.'

'Sounds good,' replied Al, 'you've got good legs, and Ed loved girls with good legs; I'm a tit man myself.'

'Al, shut it,' Vic was getting pissed off.

'Well, Rosie's right, so is Ray, mothers are women to be respected, not exploited,' replied Al.

'You've changed your tune; a minute ago you wanted her naked.'

Ray scratched his head. 'Actually, when she's walking through the supposed Garden of Eden, she is dressed in a floaty white dress that is off the shoulder, so you could do a close up of her head and shoulders; I've got no problem with that.'

'The Garden of Eden,' said Rosie, 'the last time that I saw anything like that was in France, and in that garden lived a huge snake that was used for rituals.'

'Now there's an idea,' said Al, 'there was a serpent in the Garden of Eden.'

'We want the mothers to love the video, not shrink back in fear you, idiot,' snapped Vic.

'But lots of people are photographed with snakes draped around their shoulders; Alice Cooper and Michael Jackson did it.'

'And Rosaleen Lynne won't do it,' replied Rosie.

'I think that's enough for today,' said Vic, 'we've done all of the kids' shots so I won't need them for tomorrow, but I'll still need Susie and Kevin and, of course, you, Rosie.'

'Fine, see you tomorrow, Vic; where's Bobby Ray?'

'Dunno, he was here a minute ago.'

Rosie went in search of Bobby and found him pestering the young girl from the stage school. 'Bobby, leave Charlotte alone, she doesn't want to dance. It's time to go home, say goodbye to her.'

Bobby threw his arms around the little girl and gave her a slobbery kiss. Charlotte screamed. Pleased with himself, Bobby spun round and round and then grabbed the child again. 'Bobby, stop it.' Rosie was aghast, he was now kissing the child on her lips and wouldn't let go of her. Pulling the children apart, Rosie dragged Bobby back inside, wondering why the little girl hadn't got a chaperone. She asked Al who replied that she was his grandchild.

'I thought that she came from a stage school.'

'She does, but she's still my granddaughter.'

'Surprised that you could produce a grandchild as pretty as that.' said Vic. 'Your daughter wasn't exactly at the front of the queue when looks were given out.'

'At least I can have kids.'

The argument began to get more heated, so Rosie and her brood left the warring males to it.

The following day, Rosie brought her red dress with her, and Susie filmed her romantic shots with Kevin. At one point, they shared a kiss, making Susie feel quite faint. At the end of the day, Vic was satisfied with the footage, and all that was left was to leave it with Al to finish it off. Al had made the decision that, when the publicity photos came out, he was going to use the shot of Rosie sitting surrounded by Rose petals, but he was going to remove the colour from her.

'What do you mean?' asked Rosie.

'Well,' replied Al, 'just think about it, the rose petals are bright red and I'm going to put in a stronger contrast by having your photo in sepia; that'll make people sit up and notice. A lot of women have only black and white or sepia photos of themselves when they were young; colour photography wasn't around then. So your photo is ageless and timeless, and the older women will love that. Most of them are grandmothers or great grandmothers now; it will take them back to their youth.'

'Clever old you.'

'There's nothing clever about him, he's an idiot,' snapped Vic.

'Ignore him, if you could just let me take some more photos of you in the red dress, I'll send you the proofs when they're ready, so you'll see the finished article before everyone else. I'm going to take the photos in black and white and then put a sepia wash onto them. Once I've added the backdrop, they'll look great.'

'Nothing you do is great.' Vic hated Al getting any praise.

'Do you want me to phone Lop?'

'Lop, Lop, Lop,' chuckled Bobby jumping up and down.

'Oh, go and take your photos. Would you like a drink, Ray?' Vic was embarrassed now. He hadn't expected Al to mention Lop, and he didn't want anyone knowing about her until he'd met her.

'I would love a drink,' replied Ray, watching Rosie as she walked off.

One drink later, and more photos taken of Rosie, the family left and made for home. A couple of days later, the proofs arrived. Al had been right; the contrast between the bright red and the sepia colour gave the photos a look not seen before on a poster. Rosie showed them to Ray and he enthused over them. 'You look fantastic, Rosie,' he said. 'I'm so proud to have you as my wife; I could never love anyone as much as I love you.' Rosie kissed him, hoping that he'd still love her after she'd delivered her news. She'd been to the doctor that morning as she'd missed a couple of periods and done a pregnancy test with a home kit. The kit had shown positive, and she thought that it must be wrong but a second test had shown the same result, so the doctor was the only option.

'These kits are usually accurate,' said the doctor, smiling at Rosie and wiping his glasses. He'd known Rosie from birth and had seen her through all of her childhood illnesses and pregnancies.

'But Ray's had a vasectomy.'

'Did he get the all clear?'

'He never went back for tests, said he didn't need to.'

'Sometimes a little bit of sperm gets through and stores itself up. It can be active; he should have taken precautions until he got the green light.'

'But what am I going to do, I'm almost forty two?'

'Your age is not a problem but if you want a termination, we can arrange it; you didn't knowingly go into this pregnancy.'

'But that's murder.'

'Speak to your husband; you need a joint decision.'

Later that night, Rosie waited until everyone was in bed and then broke the news to Ray. He was silent, then grunted and took to the bottle. As the night wore on, he got very verbally aggressive, and when Rosie asked him to stop drinking and listen to her, he snapped, 'There's nothing to talk about, obviously you've been screwing around. Who is it this time? Ed's out of the frame.'

'It's yours.'

'Impossible, I've had the snip.'

'But the doctor says...'

'Fuck the doctor, you've cheated on me, how far on are you?'

'About two months.'

'I had the snip around that time; I guess you got it on in Tenerife.'

'I haven't cheated.'

'Get rid of it, if you want me to stay.'

'But it's your baby.'

'It's not.'

'Ray, please, go and see the doctor, he'll explain.'

'Get rid of it, I'm already raising three of Ed's kids.'

'Bobby's yours.'

'The hell he is, you can see Ed staring back at you. I've never loved anyone like I've loved you, and you do this to me; how could you?'

'Ray, I love you.' Rosie tried to hug him.

'Get away from me,' sobbed Ray, 'don't touch me.'

Rosie's sadness was now giving way to anger. 'Right, I won't, I'm going to bed.'

'Great, maybe in the morning, you'll wake up and it'll go down the toilet, now clear off and leave me alone.'

Rosie didn't need to be told twice and went to bed. Ray's drinking was getting out of hand and he wasn't rational. She wanted to close her eyes and make everything go away. Getting under the covers of her bed, she cried herself to sleep.

The following month was purgatory for Rosie. Ray would not be swayed; it was him or the baby he said and, reluctantly, Rosie went back to her doctor and booked herself in for an abortion. It was an awful decision. Rosie loved children, and to her she was committing murder, but if it was a choice between Ray and her baby, Ray had to come first. She didn't tell anyone else apart from Candy who in turn told Kevin. He asked if Rosie wanted the termination and, when Candy replied that she didn't, Kevin saw red. He turned up at the Lynne residence and rounded on a drunken Ray who told him to keep his nose out. Kevin told Ray that he was an idiot, and that his cousin had had the same op and had had to go back for tests. 'You're ignorant, Ray, if you don't realise that sperm occasionally stores itself up; you should have been taking precautions until you'd got the all clear.'

'Are you and Rosie in cahoots together, or is it your kid and you don't want her to abort it? I'm not going to be taken for a fool again; I'm not raising Kevin mark two. I've seen the way that you look at her; Cathy's double isn't she, nothing would surprise me.'

'I'm getting married in the near future, and I resent your comments. Rosie loves you, she's incapable of cheating.'

'So what about Bobby?'

'He's your son.'

'He's not, he's Ed Gold reincarnated, that's it, isn't it? I've just realised what this is all about. Rosie and Ed created Bobby, so that Ed's soul would live on; he was into the occult, you know.'

'You're talking shit.'

Ray attempted to stand up and then collapsed back down into his armchair. 'That's it,' he slurred. 'Rosie's waiting for Bobby to grow up so that he can fuck her and carry on his sick twisted name.'

'You're the sick twisted one, and what you've just said is disgusting.'

Rosie had heard everything; Ray was shouting loud enough. She crept up on her drunken husband who had now managed to stand up, and spun him round. Ray dropped his drink and screamed, 'You bitch, I've fallen in now, you want Ed's soul to live on, that's why you made Bobby. You never wanted me, it was always Ed and still is.'

Rosie was shaking and crying, and couldn't understand why Ray was behaving this way. She'd agreed to the abortion, so what more could she do? Ray was staggering around the room, bumping into things. Candy took Rosie into her arms. 'It's the drink, Rosie, Ray's had too much,' she said.

Ada Lynne entered the room with her husband Alf, and Bobby and Raydon. 'What's going on Ray?' shouted Ada. 'I was out in the conservatory when I heard you shouting; I should think the whole street can hear you.'

Bobby ran up to Ray. 'Are you all right, Daddy?' he cried.

Ray fell flat on his face and then dragged himself to his knees. 'Come here, Bobby,' snapped Ray. Bobby obeyed, wanting to help, and found himself being grabbed by his shoulders. 'Do you think I don't know who you are, you don't fool me,' slurred Ray.

Rosie snatched Bobby from her husband, then she picked him up and rushed upstairs murmuring, 'It's okay, Bobby, Daddy's not well, he doesn't know what he's saying; come on, let's go and find Nana.'

Alf dragged Ray to his feet. 'You disgusting drunk,' he yelled. 'I'm ashamed to call you my son.'

Ray continued to rave. 'Rosie's pregnant, and Kevin's the father.'

'Pack it in, Ray, you need to address your drinking problem. Rosie's upset, and Bobby's probably traumatised. How dare you.'

'I dare because this is my house.'

'It's my mummy's house,' piped up Deanne, wandering into the room with Eddie. 'She had this house before she married you. Barry left it to her when they divorced, and your name's not even on the deeds.'

Ray was lost for words; Deanne beat him every time. The little girl stood with her hands on her hips and added, 'Some father you are, Mum's upstairs trying to calm Bobby down, and Raydon's looking terrified.'

Ray looked around; he'd forgotten that Raydon was in the room, and stared at his son who looked shell shocked. His bottom lip was trembling and he clung to Ada's hand as if his life depended on it. Ray got to his feet and opened his arms to his son. 'Raydon, come here, Daddy's not well, give me a hug.'

'Leave him alone,' cried Alf. 'Ada, take him upstairs.'

'He's my son,' yelled Ray, swaying all over the place.

'And he's my grandson, and he shouldn't have to witness this; you are disgusting.'

'Raydon, I said come here,' ordered Ray.

Ada swept Raydon up into her arms, as the child was now sobbing. Soothing him, she took him upstairs; she too was disgusted with Ray.

'How dare you,' screeched Ray, fuming.

'Shut up, Ray,' replied Alf, his blood pressure rising.

'You can't tell me to shut up.'

'You're right, you're too pissed,' and with that, Alf landed a punch on Ray's jaw, knocking him out cold. 'Would you like to help me take Ray to my car, Kevin?' asked Alf, surveying his son who lay in a heap on the floor. 'I'm taking him home for a few days; tell Ada that I want her to stay with Rosie until Ray's fit to return.'

'Okay,' replied Kevin, and helped to scoop the now out of it Ray up and transport him to Alf's car. Candy looked on. Ray had been out of order but his words had struck home. Many times when she and Kevin had been making love, he'd called out Cathy's name at the critical point. She knew that she'd always be second best to Cathy, but Ray had a point. Rosie and Cathy were mirror images of each other, so did Kevin desire Rosie; he was always protective toward her, but surely she could trust him. This was too much, her head was spinning.

She felt a tug on her hand. 'Eddie and I would like to go to Romford tomorrow; would you take us?'

'Of course I will.'

Deanne laughed. 'Eddie and I were playing Totopoly when everything kicked off.'

'Totopoly, don't you mean Monopoly?'

'No, it's similar but it's horse racing, not properties; you can join in if you like, Kevin can too.'

'Okay, let's wait for Kevin and then we can ask him; he's just putting Ray into Alf's car.'

'Our Dad would have put his lights out, wouldn't he, Eddie?'

Eddie nodded; he liked his Aunty Rose and hated it when Ray shouted at her. Kevin returned and agreed to play the board game, so with a tired Candy he followed the children upstairs. 'You can play with Eddie,' said Deanne to Kevin. 'Candy and I will own Walroy Stables, and you and Eddie can have Stevendon Stables.'

'Fine,' replied Kevin, who hadn't a clue what Deanne was talking about.

Chapter Thirty

Rosie was relieved to see that she had an empty pillow beside her. Ada informed her that Alf had taken Ray home to try to sort him out. 'Good,' said Rosie, 'we both need a bit of space.'

'Is there anything I can do, Rosie? I'll do what I can, you know that.'

'Nobody can help me, Ada, I'm pregnant and Ray wants me to have an abortion. He's told me that if I don't, he'll leave me.'

'But, Rosie, surely you don't want an abortion?'

'No, but I can't lose Ray. I love him, he's my everything.'

'Maybe Alf can talk him round.'

'Too late for that, the abortion's booked, and after the way that he behaved toward Bobby last night, I don't think I want anything of his inside me. He's blinkered and, if I have the baby, he'll never believe that it's his. What sort of a situation is that to bring a baby into? I've made my decision, or rather he made it for me last night.'

'Oh, Rosie, I'm so sorry.' Ada clutched Rosie to her ample bosom.

Just then the telephone rang. Rosie picked up the receiver and listened to the voice on the other end of the line. 'Mrs Lynne, we've had a cancellation for tomorrow; would you like to take it?'

'Yes, better to get it over and done with; what time do you need me?'

'Eleven o'clock tomorrow morning.'

'Thank you, I'll be there.'

'Good news?' asked Ada as Rosie replaced the receiver.

'The best, I can have the op tomorrow morning instead of waiting till Friday; can you stay here for a few more days?'

'Of course I can, I love helping out with the children.'

'Thanks, Candy usually manages with a bit of my input. She's such a lovely girl, Kevin's so lucky.'

Ada smiled. Right now she felt that Ray was the lucky one, as many women would have thrown him out after the previous night's events. 'Let's sort out the things that you need for your stay in hospital,' she said. From where she was standing, Rosie appeared to be very strong but Ada knew that, inside, her daughter-in-law's heart was breaking.

Back at Heaton Avenue in Harold Hill, Alf was berating his son. 'You idiot, your wife is pure gold, you've really blown it this time.'

'Yeah, definitely gold, Eden fucking Gold's ex-girlfriend.'

'That's in the past. What's bugging you? If Rosie's pregnant, why aren't you happy? When I married your mother, we had nothing apart from each other, and that was enough. We had to scrimp and save to raise you and your brothers. You and Rosie aren't short of money, and you've got a nanny, so you should be ecstatic.'

'The baby's not mine, neither is Bobby.'

'Rubbish, have you heard yourself?'

'The baby in her belly could be anyone's, but Kevin's the number one suspect and as for Bobby, he's Ed's.'

'When you were younger, people used to mistake you and Ed for brothers.'

'So?'

'So obviously your children will look similar. What colour are Bobby's eyes?'

'Blue.'

'So are yours, what colour is his hair?'

'Fairish.'

'Just like yours. When I see him pouting and showing off, it's like looking at you when you were his age and as for his nose, Ed had a big nose, Bobby hasn't. Wise up Ray, he's yours and so is this one that Rosie's carrying.'

'Can't be, I had the vasectomy.'

'Tim had one, but he took precautions until he'd got the all clear. Did you go back for tests?'

'No, I'd been cut, that was enough.'

'But it's not, until you get the all clear, you're not safe.'

'Here we go, Rosie and Kevin said that.'

'So why didn't you listen to Rosie? I'm going to book an appointment for you at your doctor's surgery for tomorrow morning.'

'I'm not going to the doctor's.'

'Why, because you're scared that he'll back up Rosie's theory?'

'I'm afraid of nothing.'

'Then you'll come with me to speak to the doctor, and maybe a test could be arranged to prove that Bobby is your son.'

'I don't want a test; Rosie's booked in for an abortion on Friday. We can put it all behind us after that.'

'Have you thought about what you're putting her through?'

'What about me?'

'What about you? You've got the perfect wife and you're driving her away. God only knows what you're putting her through. Address your drink problem, cancel the abortion, and grovel; many men would love to be in your place.'

'I'm not grovelling to anyone.'

'Fine, be stubborn, but will you accompany me to the doctor's, or are you chicken?'

'Don't call me chicken, I'll come to the stupid doctor's with you if you shut up. Have you any spirits in the house?'

'No, can't you see it's destroying you and making you paranoid? Wise up, grow up, and be thankful for what you've got.'

'How did I get here, I don't remember?'

'I brought you home in my car. Ada's staying with Rosie for a few days.'

'So I can't even drive to the off license. Can I use your car?'

'No. But if you're that desperate, you could walk.'

'Fuck that, I haven't walked anywhere for years.'

'Then you'll have to go without.'

'Okay,' snapped Ray. 'I'll go stone cold sober just to prove to you that I can do it. I'll chill here for a couple of days and then go home. I suppose I owe it to Rosie to drive her to the hospital for the abortion.'

'You owe it to Rosie to cancel the abortion.'

'Whatever, how about a full English? I'll cook.'

'You cook?' Alf couldn't control his laughter and watched as his son walked to the kitchen to prepare breakfast.

The following morning, Rosie underwent her abortion, and Ray went to the doctor's with Alf. Alf outlined the situation, and the doctor repeated almost word for word what Rosie had said. 'You are very blinkered, Ray, and very foolish. If you didn't return for tests, how could you believe that you were in the clear? Surely you don't want to abort your own child? It could destroy your wife; don't you realise that your actions are almost criminal? You should be clear by now, but I'm arranging for you to be tested anyway. We need to make sure that you are sterile or the same thing could happen again.'

Ray hung his head in shame; he was sober and feeling very guilty. He left the surgery with Alf. 'Take me home,' he cried, tears streaming down his face. 'I need to apologise to Rosie and cancel the abortion.'

'That's my boy,' said Alf, 'now let's stop off at the florists and surprise Rosie with some beautiful red roses and some serious grovelling.'

'Thanks, Dad.'

'For what?'

'For making me see sense. All I can see now in my mind is Rosie crying and pleading with me to let her keep the baby, and Bobby and Raydon's terrified little faces. I've been a bastard, and I'll never touch a drop of booze again. You're right, I do need help.'

'My pleasure,' replied Alf.

'Hey,' said Ray as they drove away in search of a florist, 'this time, we might have a girl, just think about it, my little girl. I'd better clean my act up; you can have fun with a son but you've got to be a father to a girl. Wow, what a blast.' Alf smiled and said nothing; maybe at last his son had grown up.

When Ray and Alf arrived at the Lynne household, they were greeted by Ada. 'Where's Rosie?' cried Ray. He was loaded with bouquets and his face was flushed with happiness.

'In hospital, there was a cancellation and Rosie took it; she knew that you didn't want the baby. She must have had the abortion by now.'

'No,' screamed Ray, 'no.'

'What's up with you, Ray? She's done what you asked of her. She knew that you were going to leave if she didn't go through with the termination. I went with her when she was admitted; she was heartbroken at the thought of what she was about to go through.'

'No, no, no.' Ray was now feeling even more guilty. 'She can't have had it done. I don't believe it.'

'Well she has, what's the matter with you? You've got your own way as usual.' Ada stared at Alf, wondering what was wrong and needing answers.

'Ray's changed his mind,' said Alf sadly.

Ada whacked her son around his head. 'You bloody fool, Ray, have you any idea what you've put that poor girl through?'

'Yes and I'm ashamed of myself. Come on Dad, we might not be too late, let's go to the hospital.'

'Easier to ring,' replied Ada, 'you'll find out straight away.'

Ray rang the hospital and was told that Rosie had had her operation and that she was sleeping. They added that she'd been sterilized too at her own request. 'Was she okay before the operation?' asked Ray.

'She was crying on her way to theatre, and we asked her if she wanted to reconsider having the operation, but she replied that it had to be done and that it was for the best,' replied the nurse.

'Thank you,' replied Ray who, after replacing the receiver, burst into tears. Alf and Ada both gave him accusing stares; they had no pity for their son. Ray had always been a hot head at times, a real nutter. Rosie was a good girl, and Ray had manipulated her, knowing that she loved him and would never let him go.

'I've been a complete bastard, killed my own child, and trampled on my wife's feelings; I'm a total shit.'

'Yes, Ray, that is an adequate description; even Ed Gold would never have made her do what you did.' Ada was furious, her thin lips were set in a firm line, the pulse in her temple was visibly throbbing, and the veins in her neck were standing out. Pushing her hair out of her eyes, she said, 'Rosie may forgive you, but I can't.'

'Come on, Ray, tidy yourself up and we'll go and see Rosie; she needs you,' said Alf, 'she's been through a lot.'

'If I were her I'd never speak to you again,' replied Ada. 'Most women would have thrown you out.'

'I'm sorry, Mum.'

'Forget it,' snapped Ada and left the room, slamming the door as she went.

'Ray, chop chop,' said Alf.

'Okay, Dad,' replied Ray and after tidying himself up, he left with his father and they headed for the hospital.

Rosie appeared to have recovered from her operation; she was consumed with guilt, but to the outside world she seemed okay. Ray kept to his word and stayed sober, concentrating on keeping his wife and children happy.

Eden's Rose came out at just the right time, and by Mother's Day it was number one. Vic and Al had pulled it off, but Rosie felt that its popularity was mainly down to Al's filming of the children. It had been filmed partly in the studio, and partly in woods and parks. Little Charlotte made daisy chains, picked bluebells, and played hide and seek with Bobby. They looked like two sweet little children that loved each other's company. This made Rosie laugh as she recalled the day at the studio when Bobby had made Charlotte cry several times, demanding that she must dance. The little girl was a real beauty with her golden ringlets, green eyes, ivory skin, dimples, and sweet full lips. Bobby was a natural in front of the camera; he did as he was told but threw in a couple of head over heels too for good measure. His cheeky grin and sparkling eyes added to his boyish behaviour and captivated everyone.

Deanne and Eddie were the schoolboy and schoolgirl sequence; neither wanted to participate in the video but they did their best and pulled off the section well.

Susie was the teenage Rosie, and Kevin the teenage Ed. Kevin had always looked younger than his years which was just as well as he was now in his thirties. Susie loved her part and watched the video over and over again just to watch the kiss that she shared with Kevin.

Throughout the video there were many clips of Rosie walking through the mocked up Garden of Eden set in her white, floaty, off the shoulder dress with a red rose in her hand. Vic had even found some footage of 'Golden Red', the sixties band that Ed and Rosie had fronted. Ray was chuffed; he was in that band too and caught sight of himself a couple of times. 'This is a great video,' he said as the family sat watching it, 'look at that guitarist standing on Rosie's right; he's good, isn't he?'

'Who is it?' asked Deanne.

'Well it's me of course.'

'You didn't have much of a neck in those days, did you? I've seen some of Mummy's old photos when granddad used to keep ducks and geese.'

'So?'

'Well I think that the ducks had better necks than you.' There was silence and then everyone started laughing. Ray joined in; Deanne never failed to make him laugh.

As the video neared its end, there were many old photos that were flashed up onto the screen; there was even one of Norma, Rosie, and Ed taken at the seaside on a day out.

'I remember that photo being taken,' said Rosie, 'it was taken at Southend, and Ed and I were about eight at the time.'

'Wow, look at Granny Norma,' said Ray, 'you were a looker in those days, weren't you Norma?'

'Is that me? Well I never,' said Norma, tucking into a bag of crisps.

The video ended with the shot that Al had done for the posters. However there was one change to the original shot, Al had added a photograph of Ed, making it look as if he was standing behind Rosie. He had run it past both Ray and Rosie first, saying that he could remove it if it caused any upset.

'Is it on the poster too?' asked Rosie.

'No, it's only you on the poster but I thought that it would be a nice ending to the video. After all, it's his voice that's singing, and it's been written about you so I thought that a shot of both of you in the Garden of Eden would be nice,' replied Al.

'I'm okay with it, and I think that the kids would like it; what do you think, Ray?'

'If you're happy with it, Rosie, so am I. Al's right, it is Ed's song, he should be in the picture.' Ray resented the whole thing but he wasn't going to upset Rosie; he'd upset her enough.

Al had even run off still photos of everyone taking part in the video, and they were given away with the single. Vic knew how to play the public. The mothers loved the content, fans that still bought everything that Ed had ever written loved it, and quite a few males loved the shots of Rosie. The close-ups of the off-the-shoulder dress did give the appearance of nudity, and the shot of her sitting amongst the red petals revealed lashings of thigh. It was some package: the single, free photos, free poster, and a rose that was given away with the first two hundred copies. Vic was a happy man. 'You're at number one again, Rosie,' he laughed.

'I've never been at number one before,' Rosie replied.

'Yes you have, cast your mind back to the sixties when the Z Tones were the Shelltones.'

'Oh you mean the *Humping Jumping* song? I wasn't in it.'

'No, but you choreographed it, and it stayed at number one for six weeks; the kids loved it.'

'It was the animals that they loved. Ricky the rabbit, Freddie the frog, Kanga the kangaroo, and Charlie the cricket, and last but not least Humphrey the camel. I was working for Doug Trent at that time, and most of the animals were people in costumes, but Humphrey was real enough; Mick used to come on stage riding him.'

'Poor Doug,' replied Vic. 'I miss him so much.' Actually Vic hated his cousin and had been more than happy when Doug had died in a car crash.

Al was deep in thought. 'Was Ed's name Edward?'

'No.'

'Was it Edmund?'

'No.'

'Well, what was it then?'

'Eden,' cried Vic and Rosie in unison.

'Oh.' Al went silent and then cried, 'that's it, isn't it? It's not just the Garden of Eden, he's Eden and you are Rose; you were his rose.'

'My God,' cried Vic. 'I've told you before, if you had more than one brain cell, you'd be dangerous, you're quite frightening at times.'

'You wouldn't be at number one without me.'

'It was my idea.'

'But my photos, posters, and video are what people are buying.'

'Actually,' said Rosie, 'I think that maybe Ed's voice might have had something to do with it. Bye, guys, I've got to go.'

'Bye, Rosie, now to get back to what I was saying...' Vic was beginning to raise his voice. Rosie needed to escape before there were casualties.

The year sped over; Bobby celebrated his fifth birthday, Raydon his fourth, Eddie and Deanne their tenth, and Susie, her seventeenth. Rosie did a few interviews for various radio stations, following the success of the video, and Ray stayed sober. It was a year to reflect on the highs and lows. The abortion had been an all time low for Rosie, but the video had lifted her spirits slightly, and the fact that Ray was still sober, had put her on an all time high. In October, the country was hit with storms and gale force winds. Many people were hit by falling debris. On one occasion, Ray and Rosie had been returning from a lunch when they found their path blocked by a large fallen tree. It had brought the traffic to a standstill along Havering Road. The storms eventually blew themselves out, but many people were left counting the cost.

A year later, Ray walked down the aisle with Susie on his arm and gave her away to the lecherous Vidal. Neither Ray nor Rosie were happy about it, but Rosie told her husband that as the couple were still loved up, she intended to keep her word and let them marry. Steven was heartbroken, realising that he'd been used; he stayed away from the wedding, unable to watch the girl of his dreams walk down the aisle and be given to another man. It was a lavish wedding. Vidal was in seventh heaven; finally he was in the bosom of a very rich family.

The wedding gifts were expensive. Rosie had decided to buy the couple a house. Ray thought that she'd lost the plot until she explained that a friend of hers lived in a small turning in Collier Row called Walton Road. 'My friend was a council tenant,' she said, 'and she bought it from the council. A bit later it was found to have problems as the steel rods running through the concrete slabs were eroding. Anyone that bought them had a choice: sell back to the council or re-brick the house up. My friend is now able to sell; she's no longer obliged to sell to the council as she's sat tight for three years. She wants £16,000 for a quick sale. It would be a good start for Susie and Vidal.' Ray agreed that there weren't many houses around that you could buy for that price.

Susie was delighted until she found out where it was. 'I hoped that we'd be living with you, the house is plenty big enough.'

'No, Susie, you and Vidal are an item now; you both have to stand on your own two feet. It will be the same for Deanne, Bobby, and Raydon when they get married.'

'So what about Nana's house? We could take her with us and look after her, it hasn't sold yet.'

'It's rented out. The rent money is Nana's income; it is still her home and when someone does put an offer in for the place, it will be sold.'

Vidal was peeved; he'd thought the same as Susie, but still, the house had been bought outright so there was no mortgage to pay, or rent, and it was still an asset. 'Your mother is right, Susie, it will be our own little love nest.'

He was choking on his own words; he'd dreamed of living in Havering atte Bower in the big house, or in Lake Rise in Norma's home. He choked some more when Ray added, 'You need your own space, plus you can keep house while Vidal goes to work.'

Vidal now realised that it might take a bit longer to live the sweet life. 'Be grateful, Susie, it is very kind of your parents to buy us our first home, it is a beautiful gesture.' Susie went into a sulk until Vidal added, 'We will be splitting our time between England and Tenerife. We will have the best of both worlds.'

Susie smiled. He was right, and anyway the house would belong to her and she could furnish it to her taste. She felt sure that her parents would furnish it to her heart's desire, so maybe things would be all right after all. Ray said that he would get the place re-bricked which would add value to the property. 'Thanks, Mum, thanks, Ray, it's a lovely present, I was being silly. Can we view it tomorrow?'

'View it, you can move into it if you want,' said Ray, dangling the keys in front of the couple, 'it's been bought outright so do what you like with it.'

Vidal smiled; he was now a home owner. He had one foot on the property ladder already. His father rented his apartment; none of his family could afford to buy their own home, so he was on his way.

The following day, Susie, Vidal, Ray, and Rosie visited the house. Walton Road was a cul-de-sac that was situated just behind Hamlet Road. The turning also led into Frinton Road which ran into Lodge Lane. On one side of the road was a row of houses that backed onto the fields which were part of the farm land there. Susie's house was on the opposite side of the road and backed onto other houses. She was quite happy about that as those houses were the ones in Hamlet Road, and as that was a private sector, it wasn't quite the same as backing onto council tenants. She wasn't exactly impressed by the location, as her road had once been owned by the council and had been rented out by council tenants, so now it was a mixture of private property and council property.

The front garden was tidy but small. Several children were playing on the large green which was in the middle of the banjo. The red Merc caught their attention and they stopped playing football and wandered over. Vidal put the key in the lock and opened the front door, then he swept Susie up into his arms and carried her across the threshold. Rosie was delighted, and applauded, but Ray was more concerned about the car, as many children were now clustered around it. Once inside the house, Susie saw the place in a different light; it was well decorated with a hall that led to both the kitchen and the lounge. The lounge was very small, but the kitchen was massive. 'You could turn this house into a kitchen diner,' said Rosie, 'it's almost as big as ours.'

Susie sniffed. 'But the lounge is so small,' she replied.

Ray looked out of the window, fixing his eyes on the Merc. 'Why not knock the dividing wall through?' he said, 'You don't have to have a hallway. I could get someone in to do it.'

'Good idea,' said Vidal, 'let's look at the bedrooms.'

Upstairs was a small bathroom, plus two bedrooms. The front bedroom was huge and the back one a good size. 'It's perfect,' said Vidal, thinking that he could invite Luisa over and put her up in the spare room. He looked out into the back garden; it was approximately seventy feet long and had a large shed.

'So, do you like it, Susie?' Ray was growing impatient.

'Yes but I would rather have lived with you. Vidal and I could have slept in my room; it was big enough.'

'Susie, we're married now, it is time for you to grow up and take responsibility for yourself, not rely on your parents. We can furnish this lovely house to our own taste,' cried Vidal, kissing Susie on her cheek.

'Furniture costs money,' said a pouting Susie.

'And the bank of Ray and Rosie will fund it,' said Ray, deciding to go downstairs and open the front door. From the front bedroom window, he could see one of the children outside trying to open the car door.

Susie was now seeing things a little bit differently now. 'Can I have anything I want?'

'Anything.'

'Can we go and look at some furniture now? I know exactly what I want.'

'Of course.' Ray just wanted to get going and away from the turning; the Merc was at risk of being damaged. At Ray's last comment, Susie sprang into action and left the house like a shot from a gun with Vidal at her heels.

Rosie turned to Ray. 'I think that this is going to end up as a very expensive wedding present,' she said.

'Well, at least she's off our hands now,' replied Ray, 'come on, let's go furniture hunting.'

They spent the whole afternoon viewing furniture and, of course, Susie chose the most expensive that she could find. She was getting swept along with everything now and chose a top-of-the-range cooker, fridge freezer, tumble dryer, dining table and six chairs in mahogany, plus a burgundy leather three piece suite, and wall units. The bedroom furniture was very grand, and a trip to Curry's ended with a huge television, video, and music system. The icing on the cake was when Ray handed her an envelope. Susie opened it and found two tickets for a fortnight in Cyprus in a four star hotel. Susie was overwhelmed; she now had her own home, top of the range furnishings, and a holiday in Cyprus. Her cup was overflowing with happiness.

Chapter Thirty-One

One year later

1989 was a year of weddings. Vic was about to marry Lop; he'd been captivated with her on his first trip to Thailand and decided that she was the one for him. She was submissive, beautiful, intelligent, and unspoilt. Kevin had set a wedding date for the following year, and plans were being set in motion for it. Candy was a sweet soul and helped everyone, she'd become close friends with Ellen, and even discussed the possibility of a double wedding with her and Romany.

Romany's health was getting worse, much worse. He had bad night sweats, a dose of pneumonia, and had vaccines pumped into his blood stream. Normally a strong, healthy man, he took this badly. Recovering from pneumonia, he developed hepatitis, followed by a dose of pleurisy. He hallucinated on a regular basis, developed another case of glandular fever, and his platelets fell as a side effect of one of his drugs. His kidneys were damaged due to AZT drug; all in all, he was in a sorry state. He'd told Ellen that he had motor neurone disease, and she knew that it was deadly and that it would be only a matter of time before she became his full time carer.

She looked forward to her wedding day; she was so in love with him. His illness did occasionally go into remission, and as soon as that happened, Romany stopped taking his drugs which was the worst thing he could do. He was careless about his appearance and didn't exercise, because every time he did, he tore calf muscles. Romany was now reduced to a skeletal wreck, and was broken. The couple were making plans for their wedding day when Ellen dropped the bombshell; she wanted a baby, throwing Romany into panic. 'But Ellen, I'm dying, and neither of us knows how long I've got. I won't be around to help you raise the baby.'

'You've got years yet.'

'The baby might inherit motor neurone disease.' Romany was concerned that if he stopped using condoms, there was a very strong chance that Ellen would be infected.

'I'll make us an appointment for the doctor, and then we can discuss the risks,' replied Ellen, giving Romany a hug.

'Make an appointment, but I want to go alone.'

'Oh.' Ellen was hurt; why didn't he want her with him? 'If that's what you want, but it would have been nice to have gone together.'

'I want to go alone. I'll tell you what the doctor says.'

Ellen knew that it was no use arguing so she decided that while she was booking an appointment for Romany, she'd make one for herself for a few days later, to make sure that she was in good enough shape to get pregnant. A baby would be a wonderful reminder of Romany once he'd left the mortal coil.

Candy was so excited about her wedding. She'd chosen her bridesmaids, drawn up a guest list, and was seeking a very special wedding dress. Kevin was looking forward to it, but had given free rein to Candy to arrange whatever she wanted. When Ellen revealed her plans to Candy about having a baby, Candy was shocked. Romany was very ill, and it would be left to Ellen to raise the child alone. She knew nothing about motor neurone disease but knew that Romany was dying. Candy happily went along with Ellen to the doctor's surgery, believing that her friend would need her support if the doctor tried to dissuade her. Ellen had taken Romany's explanation about the possibility of a baby contracting the disease with a pinch of salt; she needed to hear this for herself.

Ellen and Candy sat in the doctor's waiting room, chattering away about their weddings. Ellen had now decided that a double wedding was a great idea; it would be a grand affair and she just couldn't wait to make her dream reality. Her name was called and she got to her feet and went into the doctor's consulting room.

'What can I do for you, Miss Linden? I hear that congratulations are in order. I hope that you are prepared for all the work that is in front of you.'

'I'd walk through fire for my fiancé,' replied Ellen.

'He is deteriorating rapidly.'

'I know, that's because when he feels better, he stops taking his medication.'

'Suicide, I believe that you are here for a medical.'

'I am, I want a baby and I need to know that I'm well enough to carry one.'

'Is Mr Fowler happy about this? Because if he is, I'm surprised.'

'No, he doesn't want me to get pregnant. He feels that raising a child without a father is not a good idea. He's thinking of me, he's thoughtful like that.'

'Go behind the screens and take your clothes off.' Dr Lloyd summoned a female nurse and very soon the medical began.

In the waiting room, Candy flicked through the magazines. Several celebrities had got married and their photos adorned the pages. As far as Candy was concerned, her wedding would outstrip all of these. It wouldn't be as lavish, as Kevin was a very quiet person, but in her eyes it would be the best wedding ever. Cathy would always live on in Kevin's heart, but it would be her who would be by Kevin's side until one of them died. Life was wonderful. The only fly in the ointment was the way that he stared at Rosie; it was unsettling at times but then she realised that she was being silly. It was just Rosie's resemblance to Cathy that made Kevin stare at her. Smiling, she picked up another magazine and thumbed through it.

'Fit as a fiddle,' said Doctor Lloyd, 'things are fine. I take it that you and Mr Fowler still use condoms.'

'Yes.'

'Good, you'll need to right to the end.'

'But how am I supposed to get pregnant?'

'You'll have to revert to adoption unless Mr Fowler has stocked up any sperm bank before he got ill. He may have done, my patients don't tell me everything. Personally I thought that he'd never settle down, let alone want to bring a child into the world; it's too risky.'

'Risky?'

'Yes, for you and the baby.'

'But I didn't realise that I was at risk; I almost put holes in the condoms.'

'Well I'm glad that you didn't, you would have signed your own death warrant.'

'I don't understand.'

'Surely he's given you leaflets to read; I gave him plenty. You need to be kept informed.'

'He said that there was nothing that I could do and it was enough for him that I'd be around at the end.'

'He should have involved you; you need support yourself. There's a group that meets in the town centre once a week on a Tuesday morning. You should attend. You will have people around you that are facing the same difficulties, and you all support each other. Here is a leaflet for you, just give them a call.' Ellen's eyes grew wide as she took the leaflet from the doctor, and then she fled the doctor's room sobbing.

Outside in the waiting room, Candy surveyed her tear-stained friend. Her mascara had run, giving her panda eyes. 'What's wrong?' cried Candy.

'Let's get out of here, I need a drink,' replied Ellen, dabbing at her eyes with a tissue. Together the girls left the surgery and headed for the nearest pub. Ellen was like a broken woman. 'He lied to me,' she cried, 'the bastard isn't dying of motor neurone disease, he's dying of Aids. No wonder he didn't want a baby, he must have had this for years. The only time that we've been apart has been when he's guested with Z Tones, other than that, we've always been together. He wasn't himself when he returned from Los Angeles. I was going with him, and then my father died and my mum needed me. He must have caught it then. Through the years, he's got sicker and sicker. What a fool I was. When was I going to find out? Was he ever going to tell me? Would it be on his death bed, or was he going to pay someone to write on his death certificate that his cause of death was motor neurone disease, hiding the truth? If he'd told me, I would have nursed him to the end; it's the lies that I can't take. I'm going to play along with him until next month. He's booked into hospital then. I'll go with him on the day that he's admitted, and then I'm leaving.'

'But you'll have to tell him that you know.'

'Why should I? He's destroyed me, and I'm about to return the favour. The wedding's off; don't tell anyone about this because I want him to suffer. Thanks for coming with me today, I do appreciate it. I could have signed my own death warrant. How I hate men; I'll never trust another one.' Candy felt helpless; there was nothing that she could do apart from console her friend as best as she could.

Ellen was as good as her word and, a month later, when Romany was admitted to hospital for treatment, Ellen went with him, kissed him, and said goodbye. Back at the mansion, she packed her bags and left. Romany couldn't take in what had happened; throughout his stay, Ellen didn't visit once. He rang Kevin and Candy, and they both said that they had no idea where she was. Desperate, he rang Rosie and got the same reply.

He wondered if she'd gone away for a few days to get her head together; he'd been a bit of a pig of late. Expecting her to turn up on his date of discharge from the hospital, he was once more disappointed; Ellen seemed to have disappeared off the face of the earth. Ordering a mini cab, he went home where he found an empty house, plus a letter. With a sinking heart, he opened the envelope, settled himself onto an easy chair and read the letter:

Dear Romany,

You were and always will be the love of my life but I have to leave, if you'd only told me about the true nature of your illness, I would have been there at the end. How could you treat me this way? The only crime that I'm guilty of is falling in love with you. I had no idea that you had Aids. Do you think that I would have pestered you for a baby if I had? I believed what you told me, I almost pierced the condoms a couple of times, thank God that I didn't.

I went with Candy to the doctor's to make sure that my health was good enough to carry a child. The doctor assumed that I knew about your illness and gave me a leaflet for a group that meets once a week in town. As soon as I read the leaflet, I realised exactly what your illness was. Night after night, we've made love, I wonder if at any time, one of the condoms could have been faulty. I've even given you oral pleasure, I wonder if it's possible to contact your illness this way. Am I in the clear, or did you consider ending my life too?

I've spoken to Candy about this and we've come to the conclusion that you must have become infected whilst you were in Los Angeles, oh, how is Rick? Is he dying too? I've spent five years with you, hanging onto your every word, wanting to please you in any way that I could. I should have seen the signs when you insisted on wearing condoms, you told me that you wanted me off the pill as you'd just lost a friend with a pulmonary embolism caused through taking it, you'd told me that over the phone so obviously you realised that something could be wrong. You wore a condom on the night you returned saying that you couldn't bear it if I died. I honestly believed that you meant it and stopped taking the pill straight away.

Once a player, always a player or so the saying goes, it's true in your case. Apart from Candy, nobody else knows about your guilty secret. I think that maybe Rosie might have an inkling but she's never said anything. You and her go back a long way so she had to put you first, you should remember that as nobody wants to die alone. Women will come and go but at the end, they will desert you.

Don't lose touch with Rosie, she has a heart of gold. Also, don't try and contact me, I won't come back, I deserve better. Whatever happens, I will always love you.
All my love
Ellen

Romany read the letter over and over again. He was stunned, he'd lost everything. Taking to his bed, he stayed there, only getting up to eat and drink. He felt as if his life was over right now and the thought of overdosing entered his mind several times, but one thing made him stop. Someone else had played a part in Ellen's escape. When Romany had asked Candy on the phone if she knew where Ellen was, she'd said no and even if she hadn't known where she was, she did know that Ellen had left him. It had probably been her idea in the first place; he could imagine her egging Ellen on. The bitch had probably told her to leave him. Boiling up with anger, Romany made a decision; if his life was over, so was hers. He needed to get onto his medication and fight back. Reaching for the telephone, he dialled Rick's number. A slurred Rick picked up the receiver. 'What the fuck do you want, I'm occupied, can't you ring back later?'

'No, this is important, what are you doing on April the fifteenth?'

'Fuck knows, I thought that you were getting married on the sixteenth?'

'The wedding's off.'

'Oh, woken up at last, have we, well, if it's off, you won't need me to come over to England.'

'On the contrary, namby pamby Kevin is still getting married and his stag night is the fifteenth.'

'I ain't coming over for that nonce's stag night.'

'We're going to the hen night.'

'Fuck off.'

'Listen, if we do attend the hen night, we get to fuck the bride. It'll be a night to remember, and we can fuck her this way, that way, upside down, inside out, whatever way you want; you can even film it if you like.'

'She's agreed to this?'

'She doesn't know about it, but I've got a score to settle with her, and I think that you'll enjoy helping me to settle it.'

'Sounds good, I'll ring nearer the time, gotta go, I've got two hot chicks creaming themselves here. Yeah I'll come, we'll have ourselves a party, just like we did with Cathy.'

'Better than that bro, I promise.'

'Great, speak to you later.'

Romany replaced the receiver, revenge was sweet but at the moment he needed to get laid. Thumbing through the local paper, he scanned the escort and massage services; the old Romany was reborn. The massage girl would be infected but he couldn't care less about her. She was a professional and was paid to take risks. 'Fuck all women,' shouted Romany. He intended to, as many as possible before he died.

Chapter Thirty-Two

Six months later

1989 became 1990, a new era was born. Vic was a happy married man; Lop did everything for him. He'd sacked his secretary and left his wife in charge. He was now putting his feet up and loving every moment of it.

Susie was pregnant; she was delighted about this, because, since she had married Vidal, she'd had to work part time whilst staying in Tenerife. The Costamar was now rented out on a permanent basis so she had to settle with living in the Torres Del Sol in very cramped conditions. Everyone was falling over each other, and her husband had found her work in the restaurant where he worked. She hated it, but Vidal and Luisa loved it; it allowed them to have passionate love making sessions in Susie's absence. Washing up, preparing vegetables, and cleaning was not Susie's idea of wedded bliss; she'd thought that Vidal would keep her. Her savings were dwindling, and her parents were unsympathetic to her needs.

They told her that they'd completely revamped Walton Road, plus they'd got the builders in to reconstruct the concrete slabs with bright red brickwork. It had cost about £2,000 as they'd managed to get a grant on Susie's behalf. Inside the house, the carpets were top of the range, curtains very expensive, and with the very pricey furniture that Ray and Rosie had also provided, the place resembled a little palace. Susie was a snob though. She still didn't like living in an area that was part council owned, and repeatedly asked her parents if they could sell the house and put down a deposit on Norma's property. The answer was a resounding no, so was the suggestion that they could move back in with Ray and Rosie, and rent Walton Road out. She was told to grow up and appreciate what she had. This was echoed by Vidal. Luisa was now a regular visitor and stayed with Susie and Vidal for weeks at a time. Resigned to it all, Susie went out with Luisa looking at prams and top-of-the-range baby equipment and designer clothes.

Candy herself was now pregnant, and Kevin was over the moon about it. He'd kept to Cathy's wishes, and was raising Eddie to the best of his ability, but a child of his own would make him the happiest man on the planet; he couldn't wait for the birth of his baby.

Deanne was becoming a problem; she was almost thirteen and well aware of her attraction to the opposite sex. She'd rebelled against her parents, as they'd stopped her sleeping with Eddie. She'd started her menstrual cycle at the age of eleven and, although Rosie had been pretty flexible until her daughter had started her periods, she felt that this was the cut-off point. Deanne ranted and raved, but to no avail, so did Eddie; they didn't want to be split up and sleep alone.

After many sulks and tantrums, both Eddie and Deanne realised that they had to cave in on this matter. They only had one ally, and that was Uncle Rusty who lived a nomadic lifestyle and was an ageing hippy. He was Ed's older brother, and to him it was a case of anything goes. If the children wanted to sleep together, that was fine by him. They were only eleven so nothing was going to happen; they were too young. Suddenly, both Deanne and Eddie wanted to spend weekends with Uncle Rusty, and Ray and Rosie, believing that the children would be sleeping separately, let them go. Now, as the teenage years approached, Deanne flaunted herself at any boy who wanted to take notice. She was a hit in the playground, but worse was to come; she had a target in her sights, the new maths teacher.

Candy's hen night had arrived. She set off to the venue, accompanied by Rachel, Susie, and Luisa. She was wearing a short black dress, high heels, a wedding veil and L plates. Rachel looked stunning in her little black number, but Susie felt frumpy in her red outfit. She was heavily pregnant and had had a row with her husband just before she had left. Vidal had instructed her not to drink or speak to any men, and Susie had retaliated, saying, 'I don't suppose that the same goes for you.'

'It is different for men, so just remember that you are carrying my child; behave with dignity, you look like a slut.'

There had ensued a full scale row, and Susie had yelled that she would speak to whomever she wanted. Vidal had seen red and had grabbed her by her throat, telling her that if she hadn't been pregnant, he would have beaten her. Luisa intervened, telling Vidal that she would take care of Susie and that they wouldn't be home too late.

Satisfied, Vidal headed for the shower, wondering if he'd get lucky that night. Kevin was a boring fart, but Ray was quite lively. The downside to that was that Ray was his father-in-law. Still Ray couldn't watch him all night; it was a stag do after all.

Candy thoroughly enjoyed her hen night; she'd had a great time and had had several slow dances with a well-dressed man with long grey hair and an American accent. He was charming and told her that he was a photographer who had just flown in from Los Angeles with his wife. 'We specialise in wedding photos,' he said, 'and are looking for English brides for our portfolio. I would love to take some of your wedding tomorrow.'

'Oh but we've got two photographers; one is professional and the other is a teenager called Michael, who's a brilliant photographer. He's only eighteen but he's got a great career in front of him.'

'But if I took some, they would be all over America; I won't charge you anything because you'd be helping me. I've got this contract in the States, and I have to supply at least twenty English brides, but so far I've only found five and they're pig ugly; you are a very pretty girl, and your photo would grace all the top magazines.'

'Well, I'd like to help but...'

The man threw back his head and laughed. 'Oh, you think that I'm spinning you a line and that I'm up to no good. I assure you, my dear, that I am married to one of the most beautiful models in the world; I worship her, and if you can find it in your heart to help me, you will be helping her too. She has to have surgery next month, that's why we're over here. It's a pretty big op and I promised her that I'd bring her over here to see her parents before she has her surgery. This project is more hers than mine and I would like to see her succeed at it. Just think, my dear, tomorrow is going to be the best day of your life, so you need to be able to look back on it. Come home with me and you can meet my wife, then you can see my work and hers. Who are you marrying?'

'Kevin Howard.'

'Not *the* Kevin Howard?'

'That's right.'

'You have surprised me. Everyone thought that he'd never get wed. He was involved with Ed Gold's wife before her death, wasn't he?'

'Yes, but she was a widow.'

'Oh, I wasn't casting aspersions, my dear. I just meant that I had heard that she'd become the love of his life; it was very sad. I never had much time for her or Ed Gold. I used to work in the world of rock and roll, but I gave it up in the end. There are too many nasty people involved in it. Photography's much nicer.'

Candy didn't know what to do. She wanted to help but wasn't sure if this man could be trusted; she didn't know him from Adam.

Suddenly the man burst into tears. 'My poor Crystal,' he sobbed. 'I so want her to succeed with this project. Are you sure that you won't come home with me? A wedding like yours would make her day. She's always loved Kevin Howard.'

'Then maybe you could show up tomorrow and I'll introduce you both to him.'

'Thank you so much, my dear, you have a very kind heart but I would love you to see some of my work. I have some photos in the car; come and look at them.'

Candy felt so sorry for this man; obviously he adored his wife and wanted her to succeed with her project. Smiling, she said, 'Okay, you can take photos tomorrow. I'm sure that Kevin won't mind, especially when I explain the circumstances.'

'Wonderful, I'll give you some photos to take with you, just so he can see that I'm genuine; everything is in the car.'

'My friends are getting ready to leave. I'll have to be quick.'

'Five minutes.'

'Okay,' and Candy got to her feet and followed the man outside to his car. He opened the car door, got in and opened the passenger door. 'Get in,' he said.

'Oh, but can't you show me out here?'

'Lighting's not good enough, get in, you can leave the door open if it makes you feel better.'

Candy got into the car, he seemed all right and he'd just picked up a photo album to show her. She took the album from him, leaving the door open. She flicked through the album; there was only one photo in it. 'It's empty,' she cried.

'So is your brain,' said a voice behind her, a voice that she recognised. Romany had been crouched down in the back on the floor. The grey haired man grabbed her arm and held her fast as she screamed, 'Let me go.'

'No chance,' replied Romany, 'you destroyed my life, now I'm about to destroy yours. Kevin won't want you after we've finished with you.' Candy continued to scream and struggle until she felt a cloth being pressed over her face from behind, and knew no more.

'Well, where is she?' cried Susie. 'I thought she'd gone to the loo, but we've been waiting almost half an hour.'

'I hope she's all right,' replied Rachel. 'I'll go and look for her in the loo. You go and ask the bar staff if they've seen her.'

'Better do it the other way around, this baby's pressing on my bladder.'

'Okay,' and Rachel approached a plump auburn-haired barmaid who was clearing glasses and wiping tables.

When asked, the barmaid replied that she'd gone outside for a smoke and seen Candy get into a car.

'You're sure that it was her?'

'Had to be, she was the only one here tonight wearing a wedding veil and L plates.'

'So she actually got into the car of her own free will?'

'That's right, the passenger door was open for a while, and she started to get a bit agitated, but then the door was closed and they drove off together, probably a lover's tiff or something.'

'What car was it?'

'One car's the same as another to me, it was quite flashy though.'

'Kevin drives a Volvo. I'd hardly call that flashy.'

The barmaid returned to the glasses. 'She's probably fine; maybe they've decided to abort the wedding and get married without any fuss. It wouldn't be the first time.'

Luisa wandered over. 'She did mention that her brother might be coming to the wedding; they didn't get on but she had sent him an invite.'

'But surely she would have come back and told us?' said Rachel.

Luisa frowned and yawned. 'Well we can't stay here all night; if she comes back, she'll have to get a mini cab. If it was her brother, they've probably gone off for a chat and then he'll take her home.'

'But it's out of character,' said a worried Rachel.

'Maybe she had a lover,' quipped Luisa, 'and they were saying goodbye for the last time.'

'Rubbish,' snapped Rachel, 'you've got nothing good to say about anyone.'

'Still waters run deep; it happens in Spain all the time.'

'Well this isn't Spain, it's England.'

Susie returned from the toilet. 'We need to order a mini cab; I'm tired and it's going to be a long day tomorrow. My back's killing me, I think this baby's going to be enormous,' she said. 'I'm leaving even if you're not, Candy will be fine, she'll walk down the aisle tomorrow with a huge smile on her face, wearing her expensive wedding dress. She's not going to miss her own wedding, is she?'

'Suppose not,' replied Rachel, still feeling that something was amiss. 'Okay, I'll ring for a cab.'

Candy awoke in a strange room. She was lying on a king sized bed and feeling very groggy. Her eyes refused to focus and her body felt heavy. Seconds later, she found a drink being thrust into her hand, and she gazed up into the eyes of the man that she'd met at the club. 'Where am I?'

'In my humble abode. Do you want a look around? It's a nice pad; I'm renting it while I'm here. I didn't introduce myself before, did I? My name's Rick, Rick Fowler. I believe that you know my brother Roy, otherwise known as Romany?'

Candy's memory was coming back slowly. Romany had been in the car, and she was terrified. 'You won't let him touch me, will you?' pleaded Candy, 'he scares me.'

'Of course I won't, my dear, I'm a gentleman and my wife is in the next room,' said Rick in a soft voice, and then his expression changed and he snarled, 'now get your fucking clothes off before I rip them off.'

'Why are you doing this to me?'

'Well, sweet lady, you appear to have upset my brother, and if he's upset, so am I. He's decided that he wants to fuck the life out of you.'

'But he's got Aids.'

'So have I, so neither of us gives a fuck what happens to you. We caught this poison from some whore in Los Angeles, fucking bitch. I hope she dies in agony; she's wiped us both out.'

'I'm marrying Kevin tomorrow.'

'Well, you'll have a nice wedding present for him, won't you? A nice dose of Aids.'

'Please let me go, I won't say anything.'

'Too true you won't; you won't be able to.'

Romany entered the room and gazed at his prey. He leered, and then stood over the girl, saying, 'You made Ellen leave me, so you've got to pay.'

'I didn't. All I did was accompany her to the doctor's. It was her decision.'

'But you didn't exactly talk her out of leaving me, did you? I can hear you now, "he's lied to you, Ellen, leave him, he's no good".'

'I didn't, I told her to stay and tell you that she'd found out, but she refused to stay.'

'But you must have known that she was planning to leave me, so why didn't you let me know? I might have been able to talk her out of it.'

'Please let me go, Romany, I want Kevin.'

'Kevin, eh, I remember in 1983 how you followed him around like a puppy until Gary Grayson came onto the scene and then you became an item. I'd been after you, and you knocked me back several times, still everything comes to those who wait.'

'I'm pregnant.'

'Shame, your baby will become infected too. Did you know that the female body is geared up for HIV, whereas a man has to be unlucky.'

'Please let me go, I'm begging you.'

'No chance.' Rick removed the grey wig and shook his head, making his hair fall around his shoulders. The hair, although streaked with grey, matched his brother's.

'I want Kevin.'

'Hear that, Rick, it's déjà vu. Do you recall when Cathy was crying out for Ed? God that was some night, we gave her coke and rode her out for hours, even made a sandwich of her. What's your blow job like, Candy?'

'I don't want to die.'

'Oh that'll take years yet. I guess I've probably still got another four years left in me, so you'll have mega time; now, take your clothes off.'

'No.'

Rick made eye contact with Romany and then pounced on the girl. He ripped her dress from her, exposing her tiny bosom. 'Christ, I reckon that most men's gonads are bigger than your tits.'

Candy struggled as Romany tore her knickers from her. He watched as Rick filled up a syringe and then approached the petrified girl. 'What's that?' cried a terrified Candy.

'Nothing for you to worry about, you'll love it, just lay back and enjoy it.'

Candy cried as Rick shot the contents into her arm. Minutes later, Romany was astride her and, seconds later, Rick's penis was being forced into her mouth. She was as good as dead; she knew it, and so was her unborn baby.

Kevin wasn't enjoying his stag night; someone had ordered a stripper and she'd cavorted around him, peeling her clothes off until she was naked. She then invited men backstage, and several went with her. Ray was propping up the bar, and Vidal was making eyes at every girl in the room.

Kevin would be glad when it was all over; it wasn't his scene at all. He thought of his lovely bride-to-be who had replaced Cathy in his affections, and wondered if she was enjoying herself; he hoped that she was. He couldn't wait to get the wedding band on her finger, and by the end of the year, he'd be a daddy. He couldn't wait for that either.

For hours, Candy endured the violation at her captors' hands. She felt sore and dirty, and had no chance of escaping the HIV virus. Rick and Romany were thoroughly enjoying themselves; they were tanked up on drugs and loving the humiliation that their victim was enduring.

Rick looked at his watch. He was beginning to get a bit bored now, plus he was feeling tired; the illness was taking its toll on him. He couldn't keep going all night like he used to. It was time to wind the games up. He winked at Romany. 'Sandwich,' he said. Romany's eyes glinted with lust. He pulled the girl across him while his brother got behind her. Candy screamed with the pain; no man had done this to her before. Rick had his hands around Candy's throat as he thrust at her from behind, and Romany had his eyes closed and didn't realise that anything was amiss until Candy collapsed across him like a rag doll. His eyes snapped open. He'd heard the girl making gurgling noises in her throat but just put it down to Rick's sick game. Candy's face had turned blue.

'Fuck, man, what have you done? She's dead.'

'Don't be stupid, she can't be.'

'Take a look at her.' Romany disengaged himself from the lifeless body. He slapped her around her face but there was no response. 'You stupid bastard,' yelled Romany, 'the idea was to fuck her life up, not kill her. We'll be done for murder.'

'Dress her.'

'What?'

'Do as I say and then we'll take a drive; there's a shovel in the boot.'

'What are we going to do?'

'We'll drive to Epping Forest and bury her there.'

'Something will dig her up. Christ knows what lives in that forest.'

'People disappear all the time; come on, move it.'

'And then what?'

'We'll drive to your place. I'm over here looking after you; I'm your alibi. You were too ill to attend Kevin's stag night, remember; you were in bed, too ill to get up.'

'Shit, man, I didn't want this to happen.'

'Well at least she can't talk now, can she?'

'But that wasn't the plan. I wanted Kevin to think that she'd gone with us of her own free will. I wanted to fuck both of them up.'

'For fuck's sake, help me dress her; she'd have cried rape.'

'It would have been her word against ours.'

'Shut the fuck up, Romany, this way's better. Kevin will think that she's left him, now move your arse.'

The brothers dressed the girl and carried her outside to the garage, where they placed Candy in the boot of the car, then they made themselves presentable and drove off to Epping Forest. Romany was a bag of nerves. He was horrified; murder did not form part of the game plan. He hardly spoke on the drive to Epping, he was scared that Rick might get a pull; both of them were still high. If they did get a pull and the cops asked them to open the boot, they were done for. He couldn't understand how cool Rick was, and wondered if this had not been the first girl he had snuffed out. Nothing had fazed him, and her death just seemed to be a nuisance. Rick's driving was all over the road, and he was laughing as he said, 'Pity that we didn't rig a camera up, we could have made a fantastic snuff movie. It could have netted us a fortune.'

'And of course we would have been recognised.'

'Do you think that the kind of people that buy that stuff would have been bothered who we were, anyway they probably wouldn't recognise us, we're shadows of ourselves these days.' Romany flinched; Rick was scaring him. Closing his eyes, he tried to blot out the night's events.

The next day brought chaos to the Lynne household. Norma was playing up, Deanne was telling Eddie that he looked a right twit in his suit, and Bobby was dancing like a dervish and taking the proverbial out of Raydon who was dressed as a page boy. Rosie was tearing her hair out, and if things weren't bad enough, the bride was missing. Ray was staying with Kevin; he was the best man, although he didn't feel at his best, he'd drunk too much the night before. Vic and Lop arrived. Vic was giving Candy away as her father couldn't be found. Lop looked every inch a hooker with her split skirt and low cut top. Rosie was fiddling with her hat; she hated hats but as Candy was motherless and had chosen Rosie's outfit, she was trying to fill the breach of mother of the bride. 'Where's the bride?' asked Vic. He felt quite important at giving Candy away.

'I don't know,' replied Rosie, 'she didn't come home. How can we have a wedding without a bride; I wonder if she stayed with Susie?' There were new arrivals; it was Susie, Vidal, Luisa, and Rachel. 'Where's Candy?' asked Rosie, letting them in.

'Don't know, she disappeared at the end of the hen night. We thought she'd gone to the toilet but one of the staff said that they saw her getting into a car. We wondered if it was her brother's car. Is he here?'

'No, he rang to say that he couldn't make it. This is ridiculous, where is she?'

'Oh well, you'll have to take her place, Rosie.' Norma was trying to find a solution.

'Mother, I can't marry Kevin, I'm already married.'

'But you could pretend to get married. I love weddings; are my seams straight?'

'You're wearing tights, not stockings.'

'Oh, don't they have seams?'

'No, mother, what are we going to do?'

'Ring Ray,' said Susie.

Rosie shrugged her shoulders; she didn't know who else to call. Dialling Kevin's number, she got a very sleepy Ray. 'Ray, is Candy with you?'

'No, she's with you.'

'She's not, she didn't come home last night; what can I do?'

'Carry on regardless,' replied Ray, 'leave Vic behind to wait for her but get everyone else to the church.'

'Okay, Ray, see you later.' Rosie replaced the receiver and inspected her brood. Norma looked good in her floral two-piece plus pink hat, Deanne was the picture of innocence which made a nice change, Eddie looked embarrassed, as did Raydon, Susie looked like a pink beached whale, Vidal a spiv, Luisa untidy, Lop a streetwalker, Vic in the same grey suit that he'd had for twenty years, and Bobby, in his suit, was still dancing, trying to perfect a Fred Astaire routine.

She gazed at her own reflection in the mirror and decided that she didn't look too bad, but she hated her hat. Deciding to leave it off until Candy arrived, she removed it. 'That looks much better,' she said to her reflection. Her red knee length skirt looked good, as did the black blouse and red tight fitting jacket with a black fur collar; yes, she'd scrubbed up well. Putting on her red high heels, she muttered, 'Come on, Candy, time's marching on.'

Chapter Thirty-Three

At the church, Kevin stood nervously beside Ray. He was very impatient; he wanted to get the service and reception over so that he could begin married life with his new bride. 'Do you think that she will jilt me?' he asked Ray.

'Never in a million years,' replied Ray, trying to cover up his own nerves. Rosie hadn't got back to him, so what was happening?

The thought that maybe Candy had taken flight had crossed his mind, but then he felt that she would have informed Kevin so that he didn't have to stand around waiting for a no-show.

The Lynne family were out in force; Alf was in the same suit that he'd worn for every wedding he'd been to. Roland, Tim, and Martin had turned up in almost matching suits, and Ray had quipped, 'What happened, was it a case of buy one, get two free?' Neither of his brothers or their wives found Ray's remarks funny, and kept away from him. Ada, in her usual fashion, was wearing something rather colourful, a two piece lime green trouser suit with a bright pink hat and red shoes.

Rosie's party were the next to arrive, and Ray made his way over to her. 'Is she back at the house?'

'No, Vic's waiting for her. I'm beginning to think that maybe she's got cold feet.' Everything about Candy was cold, she was lying in a shallow grave in Epping Forest, unaware of anything.

As time wore on, it was obvious that Candy wasn't going to show. A humiliated Kevin told the vicar that the wedding was a non-starter, and people started to drift away. Everyone felt for Kevin but all he wanted to do was flee the scene. He told the crowd to go to the reception. 'It's all paid for, enjoy yourselves,' he said. 'I'm going home. Candy might be sick or even in hospital, I have to find out. She may even be waiting for me at home with an explanation. You can't blame her for jilting me if she has; if I were her, I'd jilt me too.'

People laughed at this attempted joke, and then headed for the reception hall; it was a sad situation but it would be plain stupidity to let all the food go to waste.

Back at Rosie's home, Vic was still waiting for Candy, and while he'd been waiting he'd been snooping around in search of those films, that Ray had mentioned, of Rosie and Ed in their own home movies. He looked everywhere, but the bedroom seemed the obvious place. Searching through the wardrobes, and fighting his way through a multitude of Ann Summers gear, he found nothing. There was no sign of a safe, and rummaging through the chest of drawers, he also found nothing apart from piles of lingerie and vibrators. He was about to give up when the phone rang; it was Rosie. 'The wedding's off, Vic, thanks for waiting. I don't know where Candy is. Kevin's distraught, so he's gone home. You might as well come to the reception, Lop's missing you.'

'Okay, Rosie, thanks for telling me, I'm on my way.' Vic had been sitting on the bed when he'd taken the call; his foot had knocked against something that was under the bed. It was a box, and Vic pulled it out. Opening it, Vic found that it was packed with films, homemade ones. He shuffled through them and stopped when he saw 'Ed and Rosie 1976', then he found another labelled 'Ed and Rosie 1978'. 'Eureka,' he shouted and, taking the two films from the box, he stuffed them into his jacket pocket and replaced the lid on the box. He was excited as he pushed the box back to its original place. He was about to get these films copied; this was wonderful. Al would copy them for a price, and then Vic would have something over Rosie. It needed to be done now, so he would leave the films with Al before he went to the reception. Then the next day, he would pick the copies up with the originals, and pay Ray and Rosie a visit. It would only take minutes to replace the originals; all he had to do was go upstairs as if he were going to the toilet and dive into the bedroom instead. Things were on the up. Candy seemed to have disappeared, leaving the way clear for him to push Rosie and Kevin together and earn him big bucks. Of course Ray was in the way, but he could be persuaded to move over slightly with the help of a few litres of spirits. The guy would be so pissed that he wouldn't see what was going on under his nose.

Kevin was a fighter, and he kept a brave face on his misery. Ray and Rosie asked him to move in with them for a while, but he declined, saying that he had to keep things as normal as possible for Eddie. The boy was confused; he couldn't believe that Candy had left Kevin.

'She wanted to marry you, I know she did; she wouldn't just leave without telling you, something's wrong.'

Kevin replied that he'd checked all the hospitals, and that she hadn't been admitted to any of them. 'Sometimes people change their minds, Eddie. I was going to marry your mother and then she took her own life.'

'But she was dying and in a lot of pain. She loved you but the pain got too much and she went to live with Daddy. Candy wasn't ill, and she wanted to marry you. Maybe someone's kidnapped her, can we find out?'

'I've done everything, Eddie, so have the police. Maybe she just doesn't want to be found; we have to face up to that.'

'But, Kevin, she wouldn't just leave, I know it.'

'Come here, let's have a hug.' Kevin's heart was broken but he had to be strong for Eddie.

Meanwhile, in Havering atte Bower, Rosie was having an almost identical conversation with Susie and Deanne. Deanne was adamant that Candy wouldn't have just upped sticks and left. 'She would have said goodbye, and how come that all her clothes are here, plus her bank cards?'

'I don't know, maybe she just got cold feet and she'll turn up in the near future,' replied Rosie.

'And maybe she's dead,' snapped Susie, 'she was seen getting into a car. Rachel and Luisa thought that it might have been her brother, but it couldn't have been because he phoned up and said that he couldn't make it for the wedding.'

'Don't say such wicked things, Susie,' cried Rosie, 'she'll come home in her own good time, you'll see. Don't forget that she's pregnant, so she'll have to come back once the baby's born so that Kevin can see it.'

But Candy was unable to return and, as time went by, Kevin and everyone else accepted the fact that she wasn't going to.

Susie gave birth to a baby girl and called her Maisie Rose; she was over the moon with her little girl. Rosie had been looking forward to being a grandmother, but she was still depressed from her abortion and, as the baby was put into her arms, she began to cry. Everyone put it down to tears of happiness, but Rosie wept tears of misery. The abortion had come back to haunt her and, two weeks later, she had a complete mental breakdown. She told everyone that she saw Ed all the time and that he was angry with her. Nobody believed her apart from Norma who believed that Ed wasn't angry with her, but warning her that something was about to happen.

The actual breakdown occurred over such a trivial thing. It had been a normal Saturday afternoon, and Eddie and Deanne were busy in the kitchen baking cakes and pastries. Norma decided to give it a whirl too. Susie and Vidal had come over for a visit with Maisie Rose. They'd had a dreadful row before leaving home, and Susie needed someone to take it out on. She chose Deanne as her target and criticised her every move. Deanne ignored her at first, but Susie was determined to upset her sibling and made fun of her efforts. 'If you've made fairy cakes, they'll be more like rock cakes,' said Susie, 'you're useless at cooking.'

'I'm not, and neither is Eddie, we're making tea for everyone.'

'Tea as in the cup?'

'Well, yes, but I meant a family tea of nice sandwiches, fairy cakes, pastries, and tea and coffee, Nana Norma has made some jam tarts too.'

'Wonderful,' said Vidal, 'you're a very clever girl, Deanne. You should give Susie some lessons.'

Angered by her husband praising her younger sibling, Susie made very snide remarks at Deanne. 'Stop it, Susie,' said Rosie, 'at least she tries. You rarely did when you were thirteen, so go and sit in the lounge and we'll bring the food through to you.'

Vidal hooted with laughter. 'She still doesn't try, if I want a decent meal I have to cook it myself; we live off takeaways.'

'Well, maybe if you got a full time job, I would make more effort.'

'Calm down,' cried Rosie, 'what's wrong with you, Susie?'

'Nothing,' snapped Susie, and stormed off into the lounge.

'Oh dear,' said Rosie, 'you'd better go after her, Vidal.'

Vidal got to his feet, saying, 'She is in a funny mood today. I will sort her out.' Then he laughed again and went in pursuit of his wife.

A little later, the food, tea and coffee were brought into the lounge. Susie stared at the teapot. 'Usually if the tea is made in the pot, it means that Deanne's made it.'

'So?' replied Deanne, placing a plate of fairy cakes onto the large coffee table.

'Well, your tea is like cats' piss.' Susie was enjoying ridiculing Deanne.

'Susie, enough.' Rosie was getting angry. 'You don't live here any more. You are a guest, so behave like one and apologise to your sister.'

'Yes, apologise,' snapped Vidal.

Deanne was close to tears; all she'd wanted to do was make a nice spread for everyone, and Susie was attacking her for nothing.

'Get her to pour it out then and I'll prove my point.' Susie was unrepentant.

'At least I'm making tea. I don't suppose you make it these days; I bet Vidal has to make it. When you were thirteen, you didn't do much apart from attempt the impossible.'

'And what's that?'

Norma came into the room with two plates of jam tarts. 'Would anyone like to sample some of my tarts?' she asked. 'I've made strawberry, blackcurrant, and apricot ones.'

'I would love one of each,' said Vidal, 'they look irresistible.'

Deanne picked up the teapot and poured out a cup of tea. 'See,' she said, 'its okay. How many sugars do you want, Vidal?'

'Two, please.' Vidal stared at the cup that Deanne was now giving him. Susie's description was pretty accurate; it didn't look too good but he accepted the beverage and, after a couple of sips, said, 'Beautiful, Deanne, much better than Susie's.'

'I asked you a question,' cried Susie, 'what is the impossible? I'm surprised that you can say it, I bet you can't spell it.'

Deanne left the room and returned minutes later with a writing pad. Then she wrote on it the word impossible and thrust in under Susie's nose. 'You must have looked it up in the dictionary,' Susie snapped.

Rosie's patience was wearing thin. 'For God's sake, what is the matter, Susie? She wouldn't have had time to find the dictionary let alone look up the word; pack it up or you can leave. I won't have my daughter verbally attacked in her own home when she's done nothing wrong.'

'Then make her tell me what she meant about me attempting the impossible.'

Deanne was now fighting back. 'I said that you used to lie around attempting the impossible.'

'I know, but what do you mean by impossible?'

'The impossible, is you looking beautiful; you were always putting stuff on your face, but it never worked, you're just plain ugly. You should try putting a sack on your head, that might work.'

Susie removed a floral cushion from behind her back and aimed it at Deanne. It missed, making Deanne chortle with glee. 'Stop it,' shouted Rosie, her face purple with rage, 'enough.'

Norma handed Vidal a plate with three jam tarts on. 'Would anyone else like one of my jam tarts?' she asked.

Susie hadn't finished, she got to her feet and flung herself at Deanne who knocked into Eddie who had just come in with two plates of salmon and cucumber sandwiches. He landed on the floor in a sea of them. The two sisters rolled around on the floor. Deanne had a handful of Susie's hair in her fist and was tugging on her scalp hard. Norma was in hysterics. 'The loser gets one jam tart and the winner two,' she cackled.

Rosie was on her knees, trying to help Eddie pick up the sandwiches. She felt strange, very strange. Eddie looked different, somewhat older. Then she gazed at her laughing mother; her face was changing. Gone were the lines and wrinkles; she was unruffled and pretty just like she had been in her younger years, her hair was light brown, her mouth was smiling, her eyes sparkling. What was happening? Vidal and Eddie were now separating the warring sisters. Why was Eddie staring at Deanne in that way? It wasn't the way that a brother looks at his sister; it was a knowing look, one that was wrong, and did Vidal slap Susie around her face? She didn't know. Rosie felt sick and she looked down, her stomach seemed to grow larger and larger, she was pregnant, was she about to give birth, was that Ed standing in the corner? From the next room, a baby could be heard crying. Was that the baby that she'd aborted?

'Where's my baby?' she cried.

There was a silence, and then Susie said, 'Raydon's upstairs.'

'Not Raydon, I want my baby, I can hear it crying.'

'No, Mum, that's my baby, I'll go and get her.'

'Then where's my baby?'

Vidal got to his feet. 'Senora, are you all right?'

Rosie's eyes were blank. Vidal waved his hand in front of her face, but she didn't blink. Then, turning to Norma, she said, 'Mum, I want to go to the sweet shop, Mr Jarvis has some new sweet tobacco and I want some cigarettes.'

Deanne and Eddie stared at each other. Who was Mr Jarvis? Susie entered the room with Maisie Rose in her arms; she'd heard her mother's last remark and knew exactly who Mr Jarvis was. Her parents had told her many times about their trips to this shop. Mr Jarvis had a barbers shop, plus he sold sweets. His shop was next door to Havering Road School, and was a magnet to the school children. Was her mother regressing?

'Mum, I think that you should go and lay down, you're tired, you've had a lot to deal with lately, what with Candy disappearing and other things. I'm sorry I taunted Deanne, this is all my fault.'

Rosie gazed straight ahead, apparently seeing nothing, then she turned back to Norma and said, 'Please, Mum, Ed will take care of me, we won't talk to any strangers. I love sweet cigarettes and you know how much Ed loves the sweet tobacco. I'll be really good if you let me go, I'll even bring you back some pear drops.'

Norma stared at her daughter; her short term memory was all but gone, but her long term one was perfect. 'If you go and have a lay down for a little while, I'll give you some money for sweets, let's get you upstairs.'

'Oh no,' replied Rosie. 'Ed will take me up,' and she headed for the stairs with her hand outstretched as if offering it to someone.

'Does she mean my father?' asked Eddie.

'She's tired and doesn't know what she's saying,' replied Norma, 'now let's go and get the rest of the cakes and sandwiches from the kitchen. I'm sure that Vidal and Susie would love them.'

'Okay, but Aunty Rose will be all right, won't she?'

'Of course she will, things have just got on top of her.' Deanne frowned; there was more to this than met the eye.

Chapter Thirty-four

Ray had been in the recording studio when he'd received Susie's frantic call. Immediately, he dropped everything and left with a worried Vic's words ringing in his ears. 'Take as much time off as you need, Ray, we all love Rosie. Send her my best wishes for a speedy recovery.' Ray was terrified. What did Susie mean when she'd said that she thought Rosie had had a mental breakdown. It wasn't possible; Rosie was a fighter. She wouldn't allow herself to have a mental breakdown.

Reaching home, he was confronted by Rosie's doctor who could make no sense of what Rosie was saying. He wanted her to be assessed at Warley Hospital in Brentwood, and Ray refused until the doctor said that her mental state was serious. The doctor made a phone call to the hospital, and pretty soon Rosie and Ray were on their way to Warley Hospital.

At the hospital assessment room, Ray watched as the doctor's fired questions at Rosie. 'What's your name?'

'Rosaleen Lynne.'

'What day is it?'

'I don't know.'

'It's Saturday, how many children do you have?'

'I don't know.' Rosie suddenly moved her legs and brought them up to her stomach.

'Why did you do that?'

'There's a snake under my chair.'

'Who is this?' the doctor pointed at Ray.

'I don't know.'

Ray now realised just how sick she was as she shrank away from the window. 'It's pouring with rain,' she cried, 'we'll all get wet. It's pouring down the walls.'

'But Rosie, it's a lovely sunny day.'

Rosie turned to Ray. 'Where's my baby?'

'Raydon's at home and he's not a baby any more.'

'Not Raydon, I want my baby.'

'Rosie, we haven't got a baby.'

'No, because you made me kill it. I want my baby, I want to die, I did a wicked thing. I want my mum.'

'Norma's at home.'

'I want my mum.' Rosie started screaming hysterically, making the doctors sedate her with an injection.

'We'll have to keep her in.'

'You can't,' replied Ray.

'You heard what she said, she wants to kill herself. She needs to be monitored.'

'I can keep an eye on her. My boss says that I can take as much time off as I need.'

'She needs professional help.'

'For how long?'

'A week, a month, six weeks maybe.'

'But she can't stay, this is a lunatic asylum, it will destroy her.'

'She'll be fine; she's not in the real world at the moment. As soon as she's well, she'll be allowed home and, as for your remarks about this place being a lunatic asylum, it's not true.'

'Well, Warley's well known for it.'

'Only to ignorant people. Yes we have schizophrenics and violent cases, but the majority of people here are like your wife, and are suffering from mental breakdowns. We even assess people to find out if they're suffering from Alzheimer's disease and dementia.'

'Her mother suffers with dementia. Surely Rosie's not going into that early?'

'I doubt it. I believe that she's suffered a trauma, and not a recent one either. She mentioned killing a baby; has she had an abortion?'

'Years ago, but she seemed to be getting over it.'

'She blames you for it, her words speak volumes.'

'I didn't want the baby. I'd had a vasectomy and I believed that she'd cheated on me.'

'How soon after your vasectomy were you having unprotected sex?'

'About a week later, am I on trial here?'

'Maybe, everyone knows that precautions have to be taken after a vasectomy. Was your first test clear?'

'I never went back.'

'Then it appears that your ignorance may be at the root of this.'

'Don't call me ignorant.'

'I didn't, but you were in this case. Probably the abortion has been playing on your wife's mind since she had it done, and it's simmered inside her until now. Obviously something's triggered it and now she finds herself in another world. Has someone recently had a baby in your family?'

'My step daughter.'

'And how did Rosie respond to the child?'

'She cried when it was put into her arms, but we all thought that she was crying with happiness.'

'Leave her with us, Mr Lynne; we will give her the attention that she needs.'

After several more protests, Ray conceded defeat, realising that the doctor did know best. Rosie didn't even seem to want him there. He kissed her, said goodbye, then left the building and drove home.

Back home, he let himself in. Susie and Vidal were still there waiting for news. 'She's had a nervous breakdown; I think that it's been coming for a long time,' he said, 'you might as well leave. I'll ring you if things change.'

'Okay, Ray,' replied Susie, and placing Maisie Rose into her small carrycot, she picked it up and left with Vidal. Ray sat down and sobbed his heart out; his Rosie was sick and it was all his fault. He sat there for what seemed to be an eternity until he felt a hand on his shoulder and a soft voice saying, 'Is there anything I can do, Mr Lynne? Is Mrs Lynne any better?' It was Mary the new nanny.

'She's spending a little time in hospital, Mary, she needs a rest.'

Mary smiled. 'I've put the boys to bed. I'll tell them in the morning. They must be wondering where their mother is.'

'No, Mary, I'll tell them, I'm taking a bit of time out from work, so I'll be around in the morning.'

'As you wish, well I'll be getting myself to bed if that's okay with you?'

'Fine, Mary.' Ray watched as the chubby little red-haired Irish girl headed for the stairs, and then broke down again. He closed his eyes, feeling guilty, and then he realised that he was not alone.

'This is all your fault.' Deanne was framed in the doorway, glowering at him.

'My fault?'

'Yes, you used to be a brilliant father, now you're the pits. I overheard your conversation with Mary. You've put my mother in hospital, you made her get rid of her baby, that could have been my brother or sister.'

'How did you know?'

'I live here. I used to hear her crying at night and pleading with you to let her keep the baby. She loves kids. It was bad enough when she lost Gary, but you made things ten times worse. My father would never have made her do it; he may not have been perfect, but he loved her. You're the one that should be in hospital and if I had a gun, I'd put you there. How could you treat her so badly? I'm ashamed of you.'

'Not as ashamed as I am. You're right, little lady, you always are, you've got balls just like your father. What do you think that he would do to me if he were here?'

'He'd kill you and I'd help him.'

'And I deserve it; God knows he beat me up enough times.'

'Good, I'm going to bed now. I hope you're proud of yourself.'

'Deanne, what triggered Rosie's breakdown?'

'Susie and I were rowing, and then she attacked me, then Maisie started crying and Mum kept asking where her baby was. After that, she got very confused and started talking about herself, Dad, and Mr Jarvis.'

'Mr Jarvis, I remember your mother and Ed talking about a Mr Jarvis who sold sweets next door to their primary school.'

'Then Mum asked for money to go and get some sweets, and Nana said that if she went upstairs for a rest first, she would give her some money for sweets.'

'And that was it?'

'Not quite, Nana wanted to go upstairs with her, but Mum said that my dad would take her up. She held out her hand to someone that nobody else could see. Do you think that maybe Dad was here?'

'Maybe. If he was, I'll probably be found dead in my bed in the morning.'

'Serves you right, like I said I'm off to bed.'

As Rosie was facing her demons, Romany was facing his. He couldn't get Candy's face out of his head; it haunted him. She'd turned blue before his eyes. He couldn't live with himself; he'd lost the taste for parties and orgies. A girl's life had been snuffed out. She was lying in a shallow grave in Epping Forest, unless she'd been found. Half of him wished that she had been found; everyone deserved a decent burial, but then if she had been found a forensic trail would lead to him and Rick, and then what? It didn't bear thinking about. What was it that Ellen had said in her letter: 'Rosie is a true friend with a heart of gold'. He needed to speak to someone, but then he might spill the beans or something else as he hid an even darker secret, and if Rosie found out about that, she'd probably never speak to him again, plus she may even turn him in. One thing was for sure, he'd have to make a written confession before he died.

Ray visited Rosie every day; he also began to take much more interest in his family. He listened to Deanne's teenage problems, encouraged Bobby with his dancing, spent more time with Raydon, and took Norma over to her home on Sundays. Rosie was slowly improving; she now knew who Ray was and he attempted to restore her memory loss. Vidal and Susie visited Warley Hospital once, but never went back as Rosie attempted to attack Vidal, yelling at Susie that he didn't want her, that he was cheating on her, and that one day he would kill her. Vidal told Susie that is was better if they stayed away. That however wasn't the reason; Rosie's words were too close for comfort.

None of her other children visited as Ray said that it wasn't a nice place to visit and that Rosie needed her rest. The place freaked him out; true, most of the inmates were suffering from nervous breakdowns or mental trauma, but there were some pretty violent cases there too. Obviously they weren't in Rosie's area, but he would often hear screams and cries of 'let me out' and other noises. One day he'd been about to get into his car when a man threw himself at a glass window and repeatedly head butted it. Another time an inmate had managed to get out and she threw herself in front of his car, screaming that people were trying to kill her. Ray had got out of the car and led her back to the ward. When he left, she was screaming that she wanted him to take her home and called him Uncle Alfie. No, this was not a place to bring children or impressionable teenagers.

He was now bonding better with Norma than he ever had. The trips to her home really helped her memory, and they would chat all afternoon about the old days. Sometimes the rest of the family came with them, but nine times out of ten, they stayed home wanting to do their own thing. Norma constantly rattled on about her night visitors, and to humour her he listened and agreed with her, saying, 'Well it's nice for you to have visitors, isn't it, Norma? At least you'll never be lonely; I suppose your husband Bob visits every night.'

'Not every night, but Ed does.'

'Really?'

'Yes, well he would do, wouldn't he? Rosie's got his babies. He needs to look over them, doesn't he?'

'Of course he does, he really loved Rosie, didn't he?'

'From the first day that he met her. He was a spoilt brat; his mother Jeanette ruined him, but then I suppose she thought that she was doing what was best for him. We all try to do our best for our children, don't we?'

'That's right.'

'You've been a good chap, taking on Rosie and her children; many men would run a mile. Step children can be a pain in the arse; when they don't want to do something they always cry 'you're not my real dad or mum', whatever the case may be, and it makes it hard for any step parent.'

'Then I've been lucky, because that's never happened, although Deanne's tried it a few times.'

'She would, got a lot to say for herself that little Madam, needs a good slap now and again. When Rosie misbehaved, she got a slap and, if she really misbehaved, her father would take his belt to her.'

'That's a bit extreme.'

'Maybe it was, but these days kids get away with murder; they need discipline and don't get it, a slap now and again never killed anyone. I've seen Rosie dish out a few to her kids. I think that they quite like being kept in line; it makes them know that they are cared about. Boundaries have to be set.'

'You are a very wise woman, Norma.'

'I don't know about that; I'm losing my marbles, but they say that if you know that you're losing them, it's okay, the real problem is when you don't know and think that everyone else is mad.'

'I couldn't have said it better myself. It's a lovely view from here, isn't it?'

'Yes, I love this place, but I can't take care of myself any more. I often dream of coming back here but I know that it will never happen.'

'Maybe when the kids are off hand, all three of us can move here. We won't need the big house then. I think that sometimes it crosses Rosie's mind.'

'Why do you say that?'

'Well, the house hasn't sold, and Rosie refuses to drop the price. I think that's why she lets it out, to give you a bit of income and stop it selling.'

'You've got a point, but by the time the children are gone or off hand, I'll be dead.'

'Not necessarily, Norma. Susie's gone, Deanne wants to move in with Eddie when she's old enough to leave, Bobby will most certainly go as soon as possible and, as for Raydon, there would be room for him here.'

'Wouldn't that be wonderful? I feel so close to Bob here. He loved this place. He'd always wanted to live in Lake Rise, and when Rosie started dating Barry Grayson it became a reality. Bob used to work with his band part time, as he needed a day job too, but Barry got the band loads of work and Bob's income soared. He was so happy right up to the time that he died. Many people would have gone under, suffering that massive stroke but he fought on right up to the end. Rosie taught him to write with his left hand, and he even played guitar with Ed; one would control the strumming and the other the neck of the guitar. He even walked with the aid of a three pronged stick. Ed was good to him; he still visited even after Rosie had returned to Los Angeles to Barry. Ed was a good boy really. I really don't know what went wrong with him and Rosie.'

'Water under the bridge, Norma. Shall I make us another cuppa?'

'That would be lovely.' Smiling, Ray went back into the house and put the kettle on.

Later that night, back at home, Ray made sure that all the doors were locked, and then looked in on his family. Norma had just gone to bed, and Ray went in to close the curtains. 'Night, Norma,' he said, walking over to the window.

Norma looked up and said, 'Don't close the curtains, Ray, I like to look at the moon, plus I can see my visitors more clearly.'

'I'll just close them a little bit, it's more cosy.'

'Oh okay, goodnight, Ray, thank you for taking me out.'

'My pleasure, Norma, goodnight,' and Ray left the room.

Singing to himself, Ray went into his bedroom and prepared for bed. He could hear Norma rattling off, she often did it. He could hear singing too and guessed that maybe Norma had put her radio on. Picking up his toothbrush, Ray began to clean his teeth. The singing grew louder, and Ray recognised the song. It was *Eden's Rose*, then the sound dropped slightly and Norma could be heard saying, 'I love this song and the title's perfect; well, she always was your rose in the Garden of Eden, wasn't she? Ray's a good man, but she'll never love him like she loved you. She's fooling herself that she does, but we both know better, don't we?'

Ray's heart was pounding. Rinsing his mouth, he replaced his toothbrush in its holder and left the en suite. Crossing the bedroom floor, he left the room and headed for his mother-in-law's. He'd left her door partly open as Norma never liked closed doors. Ray could see the moonlight streaming into her room through the gap in the door. He pushed the door slightly, making the gap increase, and from where he was standing, the bottom of Norma's bed was visible. She was humming along with the song, and then she

331

said, 'They all think I'm crazy, maybe I am, it's such a lovely night. I told Ray to leave the curtains open but he still half-closed them. I like looking at the moon, especially on nights like this.'

She got out of bed and pushed the curtains open, illuminating the figure sitting on her bed. This couldn't be happening; there was nobody else in the house apart from the family, but there was most definitely someone or something sitting on the foot of the bed. The figure was caught up in the illumination of the beam of moonlight and the background of the landing light. It continued to play, and then turned its head, making eye contact with Ray who by now was shaking. He knew who it was and then, in a blink of an eye, it was gone. Ray's legs were giving way. He staggered back to his room, threw his clothes off into a heap on the floor and got into bed with his mind racing. He could hear Norma waffling on again, and the singing resumed.

'I didn't see it and it didn't happen. Norma's sick, and Ed's dead, it's all in my imagination,' he said out loud. He blotted out the singing by putting his head under the bed clothes and, when he re-surfaced, the singing had stopped. A relieved Ray relaxed; it was just his imagination after all, and then a familiar laugh echoed through the hallway and the singing began once more. This wasn't happening; he'd had a few drinks before coming to bed, that was it, he'd had one too many. Closing his eyes and putting in some ear plugs that he kept by the side of the bed, he drifted off to sleep.

As Rosie drew up outside her home with Ray, she saw a huge banner strewn across her gates. 'Welcome home, Rosie' it displayed. 'This is so lovely,' she cried. 'I suppose this is your doing, Ray?'

'Well, the kids helped, we've all missed you so much.'

'I feel as if I've been away forever.'

'It felt like forever for us too; it's been over a month. I don't know how we've coped without you.'

'Can't wait to get inside.'

'Come on then.' Ray got out of the red Merc, held the car door open for Rosie, and then activated the electric gates.

Once inside her home, Rosie was swamped with people. Norma took her into her arms. 'My beautiful girl,' she cried, 'how we've all missed you.'

Bobby and Raydon rushed over and hugged their mother; both had tears of happiness in their eyes.

'Deanne, what have you done with your hair? It's so pretty.'

'Do you think so? I don't like it. I wanted to look nice for you, and that wally Bobby altered the clock.'

'Why?'

'Well, he realised that it was fifteen minutes fast, so he altered it and didn't tell me, so the colour was left on too long. It was supposed to be golden blonde but it's more like a strawberry blonde instead. Still, it's not permanent, so it'll wash out. We've all prepared a special tea for you. Susie and I did most of it and we didn't argue for one second.'

'Wonderful, where's my granddaughter?'

'Here she is,' replied Susie, 'do you want to hold her?'

'You bet I do, I need to bond properly with her.'

Maisie Rose was put into Rosie's arms, and once more she wept, but this time it was tears of joy. Eddie hung back with Kevin; he had a huge bouquet in his hands. He felt a bit silly, he was after all thirteen years old, and boys of his age didn't usually carry flowers. 'Are those for me, Eddie?' asked Rosie.

Eddie shuffled forward and said, 'Kevin and I bought these for you, we hope you like them.'

'Thank you both, they're lovely; could you put them in water for me, Susie?'

'Yes, Mum,' and taking the flowers from Eddie, Susie left the room.

Mary entered the room and began to put various sandwiches, cakes, pastries, and nibbles onto the coffee table. 'Welcome home, Mrs Lynne,' she cried.

'Thank you, Mary.'

'Are you feeling better?'

'A million times better, how I've missed you all.'

The evening passed in a flash. Rosie was amazed at all the flowers that were surrounding her; her home looked like a florist's.

Later that night, after making love to Rosie, Ray said, 'I guess that everything was my fault?'

'Yes, Ray, it was. We both murdered our baby, but it was at your bidding. I'm stronger now, so don't give me any more ultimatums, because you may find out that I may not choose you next time.'

'No more ultimatums, but plenty of orgasms,' laughed Ray.

'I'm up for that,' replied Rosie.

Ray gazed at his wife; this was never going to happen again. He'd learned his lesson and was now counting his blessings.

Deanne still had her sights on her maths teacher. All the girls in her form loved him; he was their form teacher too. Each girl tried to get his attention. He was twenty five, tall, dark and handsome, and had a fine muscular figure owing to his regular sessions at the gym.

Deanne got her kicks from getting her work wrong and suffering detention. Then, when everyone had left to go home, she would stare at her teacher who was checking essays and maths work, and then unbutton her blouse, making her cleavage visible. Then she would ask him to look at her work and show her where she was going wrong. He would leave his seat and walk behind her and then find himself staring at her work plus an eyeful of cleavage. When he'd shown her what she was doing wrong, she would gaze up at him and flutter her eyelashes, turning him into a quivering wreck.

Deanne found it hilarious, and occasionally she would go to the book cupboard to look for a book and tell her form teacher that she couldn't find what she was looking for. 'Could you help me, sir?' It was a very confined space, and Mr Pike had to squeeze past her to find the book. Her misbehaviour, plus badly done work, netted her at least one detention a week, and all the time she worked on seducing her teacher.

At one detention, she burst into tears, and when Mr Pike tried to find out what the trouble was, she clung to him crying that she'd lost her necklace the previous day up at Bedfords Park, and that she would get into so much trouble with her mother over it.

'Why?' asked Mr Pike, 'it's only a necklace.'

'Yes but it belongs to my mum; it's a golden necklace with a huge St Christopher on it.'

'But if she let you borrow it, it's partly her fault.'

'She doesn't know that I've borrowed it.'

'That's bad, Deanne, that's stealing.'

'I know but I need to find it. Could I skip detention tonight and go and look for it? I know exactly where I was sitting.'

'Not much point, it looks like it's going to rain.'

'But my mum will kill me.'

Mr Pike was a kindly man. 'Stop crying, Deanne, you can do your detention and then I'll take you to Bedfords Park and help you look for it. Sometimes two pairs of eyes are better than one.'

'Oh thank you so much, sir.'

Mr Pike disentangled himself from the nubile girl's grasp. This girl was too hot to handle and only thirteen. He was as good as his word, saying that if it rained, the necklace could get bogged down underfoot and never be found. An excited Deanne got into his car and together they headed for Bedfords Park.

After much searching for a necklace that never even existed, it began to rain and the couple got back into Mr Pike's car. 'It's very pretty here, isn't it?' said Deanne.

'Yes,' replied Mr Pike. 'I used to come here to pick bluebells with my sister when I was young; we took them home to our mother.'

'That's nice.' Deanne crossed her legs making her skirt ride up.

'Well I don't think that we are going to find the necklace.'

'I'll have to come clean with Mum unless you and I come back here tomorrow.'

'No point, the rain will have either washed it away, or it will have become bogged down.'

'I suppose you're right, well thanks for helping me look for it.'

'That's all right. I'd better get you home.'

'Can't we stay for a little bit longer?'

Mr Pike scrutinized his watch. 'Just for a little while if you like, then I'll drop you off at your home.'

Deanne uncrossed her legs, and then crossed them again, making her skirt ride up even higher. 'Oh dear,' she said. 'I'm almost showing my knickers; can't have that can we, or would you like to see them?'

'Deanne, you are thirteen.'

'I know, but there's no one else around.'

'Deanne, we're leaving.'

'Oh, don't be like that, sir.' Deanne took his hand and pushed it down the front of her blouse. 'Does that feel nice? It feels good to me.'

Mr Pike swallowed hard. 'You are still only thirteen.'

Deanne eyed his crotch; it was visible that he had a hard on and she relished the fact that it was she that had made it happen. She attempted to unzip his trousers and found her hand being slapped hard.

'That's it, we're leaving.' Mr Pike wanted to leave before he lost control; this girl was jailbait.

Deanne was gazing at him, pouting. 'Don't you want to touch me, sir? I'm gagging for it.'

'Deanne, this is obscene.'

'I know, it's lovely, isn't it? I've got a problem; I need someone to show me how to satisfy a man.'

'Do your seat belt up, girl, we're leaving.'

'But an older man could teach me so much, and you'd get something out of it too.'

'I said, do your seat belt up.' Mr Pike's voice was failing him. Deanne smiled and fastened her seat belt; it was just a matter of time, she knew it.

One person who was not smiling was Vic Lee; he couldn't make out where his money was going to. Lop seemed to know her job; she had a full rein on their accounts but something wasn't right. She certainly knew what she was doing. She'd opened a bank account solely in her name, and it was growing steadily each day. She was a good wife to Vic, but he disgusted her in many ways and she felt that she should be rewarded for putting up with him, so she creamed off as much as possible.

Many times, Vic questioned her about the money, but it was then that she became the subservient wife and gave him mind blowing sex. Constantly she told him to sell the agency and retire, but he dug his heels in and said that he'd be carried through the door feet first on the day that he quit.

Lop was having sex with several of the up and coming acts, lowering their fee, but Vic never knew about it and paid them their original fee.

There was one particular singer that kept pestering Vic; his name was Dylan and he came from Scotland. He was never away from the office, but Vic was unimpressed and he recalled a certain singer from the past called Derek Bodgers. He'd auditioned for years but, apart from a few working men's clubs and pubs, the guy had never taken off. Vic wondered if Dylan was related and avoided him like the plague. He'd just landed the Z Tones a contract in Germany, and they were headlining. That was a turn up for the books, so maybe things were on the up and he'd been mistaken about the accounts. After all he had the best possible secretary in his wife.

Luisa was getting impatient. 'You told me that you would divorce her, and now she is pregnant again.'

'Luisa, she tricked me, she told me that she was on the pill. I cannot abandon her while she carries my child,' replied Vidal.

'Why not? I think it is the lifestyle that keeps you together, not love.'

'It never has been love, you know that. You're the only one that I have ever loved.'

'I don't believe you; you now rub shoulders with a rich family and own your own house. You wear designer silk shirts, and Susie now owns a car even though she can't drive; you will never divorce her.'

'I will, soon. After she gives birth I shall file for divorce.'

'You are lying once again. You cannot leave a woman straight away after she's given birth.'

'Then I'll wait until the child is nine months old.'

'And then she will be pregnant again.'

'She will not and, anyway, I've been thinking of another plan.'

'Keeping me as a bit on the side as the English would say.'

'No, Susie has a lot of money coming to her on her twenty first birthday; she had a massive payout on her eighteenth, but this is much larger.'

'So?'

'Well if I stick around until then, it will improve our finances.'

'How?'

'She could have an accident at the Santa Cruz carnival; we haven't been to Tenerife for a while. There are many accidents at the carnival.'

'An accident.' Luisa was more than impatient now.

'An accident on my order. I will instruct someone to make sure that she has one, and then as her husband, I shall inherit everything.'

'You would kill the mother of your children?'

'Yes, they will have another mother, you, then after a period of mourning, I will sell the house, take the money and run back to Tenerife.'

'It could go wrong.'

'It won't, trust me, Luisa. Her birthday is in September 1991 so we'll have to wait a little longer. I promise you, querida, that my wife will not see her twenty second birthday, now come on let's make love. Susie has taken Maisie Rose over to see her mother; she won't be back for a while.'

Chapter Thirty-five

Vic was preparing to take Z Tones on tour. He'd asked Romany to do a couple of guest spots and got an emphatic no. The drugs that he was on were having horrible side effects. Fluid was building up around his heart and he was in hospital more than he was out of it. His muscles were wasting away and his kidneys were failing. He was too scared to look in the mirror now as his reflection horrified him.

Before embarking for Germany, the band had a week's work in Scotland, and it was there that Ray spotted a face that he'd rather forget. It was at the after show party. Ray had been chilling out and the normal entourage of groupies were in evidence. He felt a tap on his shoulder and a voice said, 'Hi Ray, I'd hoped to catch you.'

Ray looked the woman up and down, saying, 'You caught me once, you'll never do it again.'

'I'd hoped that you'd be pleased to see me.'

'I'd hoped that I'd never have to see you again.'

'How's Rosie? I bought a copy of *Eden's Rose*; it was a great video.'

'Don't speak her name, you're not fit to, anyway, what are you doing here? You're a bit old to be a groupie.'

'I told the roadies that I was an old friend and that you invited me to the party.'

'I wouldn't invite you anywhere.'

'Ray, you're so bitter. We were happy until Ed screwed everything up.'

'Screw being the ultimate word. He didn't even like you, you were just easy.'

'Surely you can forgive me after all this time?'

'The point is, if it hadn't been for you, Ed and Rosie would have married and so would you and I but you had to fuck everything up; you broke Rosie's heart and mine.'

'My husband was coming tonight, but he's too ill, he has cancer.'

'You can't hold on to anyone can you? Terry died of cancer, you miscarried my baby through stupidity, I left because of your affair with Ed who used and abused you, and now your husband has cancer.'

'I loved Ed.'

'He hated you after you split him and Rosie up.'

'Ed and I might have still been together had he not become famous and met that stick thin upper class Faye; she was a model, or claimed to be. Anyway they got engaged and I stayed on my own for a time as I knew that Cathy was back on the scene, then I moved to Scotland and met Duncan. We fell in love and got married.'

'He must be some stupid dumb prick to marry you.'

'Listen Ray, I'll never forgive myself for what I did, but Ed dazzled me and I was weak.'

'So now that you've finally found true love, your old man is going to kick off the planet in a few years' time; shouldn't you be at home looking after him? I know Rosie would if I had cancer.'

'Duncan told me to come. He loves your band; actually I was wondering if I could have a couple of photos to take home to him.'

'See that little bald headed fat man with the Thai girl who looks like a hooker?'

'Yes.'

'Well that's Vic Lee and his wife, not that you'd think that she was, she puts it about a bit, opens her legs to anyone.'

'Ray, you're so cynical.'

'No, just honest, now go and see him and he'll sort you out with some photos. He's my manager, now piss off and leave me alone.'

Hurt, Jenny wandered off and introduced herself to Vic who was intrigued as her story unfolded. This could be the first step to splitting Ray and Rosie up. Grinning, he said, 'Any friend of Ray's is a friend of mine. Lop, would you take care of Ray, he looks in need of a drink, and I'll join you both in a minute.' Placing his arm around Jenny's shoulders, he added, 'Come with me, my dear, and tell me more about yourself; this is going to be a great party. We leave for Germany in the morning. You can stay as long as you like, all night if you want to. Would you like a drink?'

Ray looked on, wondering why Jenny had let herself go. Her lovely hair was almost grey, her face was heavily lined, and she had a bad case of middle spread; how'd she's changed from the lovely young girl that he'd fallen for when they were both fifteen. Lop offered him a drink, followed by another. Ray had declined the alcohol at first, but temptation got the better of him and he ended up blind drunk. Everything was a blur as Kevin helped him upstairs to his room. They shared a room, and Kevin wondered how he was going to sleep with the racket downstairs getting louder and louder. Ray had no such problem; he was out for the count, fully clothed.

He awoke the following morning with an arm around his waist and a body snuggled up to him. 'Rosie, I'm so sorry,' he cried. 'I didn't mean to get drunk, it won't happen again.'

'That's okay,' said a voice behind him.

Ray turned round and beheld Jenny. 'Who the fuck let you in?'

'Nobody, I put you to bed and you asked me for a cuddle so I got into bed with you.'

Kevin awoke with a start and looked over at Ray and Jenny; he couldn't take in the scene before him. 'When I put you to bed, you were on your own and I locked the door; she must have had a pass key.'

'Vic gave me the key, I was worried, you'd had a lot to drink. People can choke on their own vomit.'

'I am aware of that, and also aware that I didn't invite you to my room, now piss off,' said Ray.

'You didn't say that last night when you made love to me.'

'I did not, I was incapable.'

'I'm not lying.'

'You already have, you've changed your story. First you say that you put me to bed, which is a lie, and then you say that Vic gave you a key because you were worried; you're a compulsive liar.'

'What does it matter? We made love, that's all that counts.'

'We did not, get out of my bed, look I'm fully clothed.'

'Let's cuddle, I won't tell Rosie.'

With a superhuman effort, Ray pushed Jenny out of bed saying, 'I suppose that's what you said to Ed.'

'What?'

'I won't tell Rosie.'

'Actually I did, but his reply wasn't what I'd expected; he said, "if you tell Rosie, I'll break your neck." I was hurt.'

'Get out.'

'But Ray, it was brilliant last night.'

'Nothing happened; there's no way I could have got an erection at the sight of you, and in fact if I'd already had one when I went to bed, the sight of you would have made my dick go limp.'

Kevin got out of bed and handed the naked Jenny her clothes. 'Better get dressed,' he said. 'Ray's a happily married man.'

Taking her clothes from Kevin, Jenny headed for the bathroom and dressed, then turning to Ray she said, 'Bye lover, and thanks for an incredible night. We must do it again; it was just like the old days.' She blew Ray a kiss and left.

If he thought that he was through with her, he was mistaken. Before she'd got into bed with him, she'd slipped a note into his jacket pocket which had been hanging on his wardrobe door. She felt certain that Ray was like most men and never checked his pockets, but she felt sure that Rosie would.

Deanne was still attempting to work her magic over Mr Pike. He was tempted; the girl was a little Lolita. He lay awake thinking of her, and it all came to a head after she'd picked a fight with a class mate and ended up rolling around on the floor with her. Both girls were sent to the headmistress and given detention. They were given lines to do, five hundred of them, saying 'I must not fight in the classroom and in future I will behave like a lady'. Corinne finished hers, but Deanne lagged behind on purpose; she wanted Mr Pike to herself. The girls also had to stack books on a shelf before they went home as punishment, and Corinne raced ahead of Deanne and left the classroom with a smug look on her face. Deanne finished her lines and, as soon as her classmate had left, unbuttoned her blouse and hiked her skirt up a little. She began to stack the books, leaving the top of the shelf until last.

'Have you finished, Deanne?'

'Nearly sir, just a few books to go.'

'Good, I want to go home.'

'I'm doing my best, sir.'

'I'm sure that you are.' Mr Pike walked over to the shelves. Deanne was standing on a stool and reaching up high. Mr Pike moved behind her, her knickers were visible beneath her short skirt. Slowly his hands moved over her thighs and Deanne smiled. She'd done it, she'd finally seduced her teacher.

The German tour was a success, and Ray was happy to be home. He'd totally forgotten about Jenny and looked forward to spending some quality time with his family. Therefore, he was surprised when Deanne's little indiscretion rocked the boat. Neither Rosie nor Ray had any inkling that Deanne was behaving so badly. It all kicked off when Rosie became suspicious that Deanne was having so many detentions. She wondered if she'd met a boy and was going around to his home for a little hanky panky. Deanne had said that she had to stay behind because her maths was so bad that she needed extra curricula tutoring. Rosie decided to follow this up; this had been going on for over two months.

The next time that Deanne was late home, Rosie decided to check up on these activities. Making her way to the classroom, she walked in on the studies. Her daughter was sitting on her tutor's lap, sharing a passionate kiss. Crazed, she rushed across the room and dragged Deanne from Mr Pike's lap. 'You disgusting creature, how dare you corrupt my daughter.' Rosie whacked Mr Pike around his head.

'It wasn't my fault, she tempted me,' he cried.

'That's what Adam told God in the Garden of Eden. I'm reporting you for this, and hopefully you'll lose your job.'

Deanne was downcast; she'd been enjoying herself until her mother had walked in. The following morning, Deanne was kept at home, and both Rosie and Ray went to the headmistress.

Mr Pike was suspended, but Rosie realised that not all was black and white when Deanne said, 'It's a shame that he got the sack. I did encourage him from day one; it took me a long time to get him but I did in the end. I'll miss our afterschool activities, it was good.'

'Did you have full sex?'

'No, but we did a lot of stuff.'

Rosie stared at her daughter. Mr Pike was gone, but who was next on Deanne's list? A man had been sacked, and Deanne was unrepentant.

Susie celebrated her twenty first birthday. It was a lavish affair, and she was now a rich young lady, with more money than she could spend. Vidal was excited and quite happy that Susie had miscarried her baby. At first, Susie didn't feel too bad, but after a while she became quite depressed, so when Vidal suggested taking a long break in Tenerife, Susie agreed, thinking that maybe the sunshine might help her. They left England just after the New Year, leaving Maisie Rose with Rosie.

'It will be our second honeymoon, Susie,' said Vidal. 'I shall spoil you until you get bored with it.'

'I could never get bored with being spoiled,' replied Susie. 'I love you so much, Vidal.'

'And I adore you, baby,' replied Vidal. He intended to spoil her as much as possible, as she wouldn't be coming home again.

Susie did find the climate helpful, and Vidal fawned around her like a little dog. Senor Martinez was in Spain, staying with his cousin. Pablo lived in Galicia, and the two cousins always got on well in each other's company.

The Torres Del Sol was a little less crowded with Vidal's father away, so that made life a bit easier too. Susie began to feel so much better; obviously the reason that she and her husband had drifted apart a little was because he felt pushed out by Maisie Rose. This was indeed like a second honeymoon.

As the date of the carnival approached, Vidal suggested spending some time in Santa Cruz in the north of the island so that they could watch the carnival up close, and maybe partake in it. Susie was thrilled. She'd never been to Santa Cruz before; this was new territory and, by all accounts, Tenerife's carnival was second only to Brazil's. Happily, she packed a bag and set off with Vidal and Luisa. Luisa had been taking Vidal's comments with a pinch of salt; she didn't believe that Vidal would divorce Susie, and was wondering if it might be a good idea to start looking for someone else.

At Santa Cruz, the trio hired fancy dress costumes. Vidal hired a matador costume, and the girls hired flamenco dresses. The girls' outfits were identical apart from the wigs and masks. Susie's wig and mask was pink, and Luisa's blue. 'Tonight's the night,' whispered Vidal in Luisa's ear. Luisa grunted; Vidal was full of hot air these days.

As they merged with the milling throng, Vidal wandered off.

'This bloody wig is too tight,' muttered Luisa, 'it's so uncomfortable.'

'Swap with me then,' replied Susie, 'mine's too loose.'

'Okay.' The girls swapped wigs and masks and then set off in search of Vidal. He was nowhere in sight, and with all the jostling from the crowd, the girls got split up.

Luisa passed an alleyway and caught sight of a figure dressed as a matador. He beckoned to her and Luisa entered the alleyway and headed toward him. Smiling, she moved closer to him, and it wasn't until she was a few steps away from him that she realised it wasn't Vidal at all. Backing away, she was terrified as the man advanced. Was she about to be raped? She needed to get back into the crowd again. The man was almost upon her. She saw a flash of steel as the man raised a knife and plunged it into her chest. Luisa fell to the ground, and the man plunged the knife in repeatedly. Satisfied that his victim was dead, the man ran off. Luisa wasn't dead, but she was close to it. She crawled out of the alleyway, collapsing just as she reached the crowds. She grasped a girl's ankle who was dressed as a cowgirl, making the girl scream.

The crowd clustered around the dying girl, and Vidal pushed his way through them and toward the girl who was face down. There was blood everywhere. Rolling her over and holding her to him, he cried, 'Oh my darling, what happened?' Then he turned his eyes on the onlookers and screamed, 'Help, help, my wife is dying, she has been stabbed, get an ambulance.' There was one parked nearby and the medics went into action. Blood was pouring from the victim's chest. Vidal kissed her on her lips and removed her mask, then let out a scream of agony. It wasn't Susie, it was his beloved Luisa. 'No, no, don't leave me my angel, I can't live without you. I want to die too.'

Susie forced her way through the crowds; she'd heard the screams. Seeing Vidal on the ground cradling Luisa, she cried, 'We got split up. Oh my God, who did this?'

Vidal flashed her a look of pure hatred and then returned his attention to Luisa. The medics prised Luisa from Vidal's grasp and felt for a pulse; there was none. He wailed even louder as her body was taken away. Susie surveyed her blood stained husband. 'It's all right, Vidal, I'm here for you. We all loved Luisa but together we can get through this.'

Vidal got to his feet and hauled Susie away from the crowd. 'But you see, that's it, isn't it, I don't want you around. Whose idea was it to switch wigs and masks?'

'Luisa's, why?'

'Because you see, my darling, if you hadn't, it would have been you that would now be dead.'

'Don't say such things, you're upset.'

'Yes, I'm upset. I've always been in love with Luisa; she wasn't my sister. I've never loved you; you've got nothing to offer, no sex appeal, no nothing, you're just a rich bitch.'

'You're scaring me.'

'I'm going to do more than that.' Vidal dragged Susie to his car.

'Where are we going?'

'Los Gigantes.'

'Why? You need to clean up, and our clothes are at the hotel.'

'You don't need clothes where you're going.' Vidal tightened his grip on Susie's wrist, 'Come on.'

'Let's get our things first.'

'I'll pick them up later.'

'I don't understand.'

'Of course you don't, you're too stupid.'

'I want to go home.'

'I want, I want, come with me Susie, Los Gigantes is waiting.'

'No, I'll scream,' and with that Susie let out a piercing scream. Vidal turned and dealt Susie a blow to her jaw, knocking her out, and then he picked her up and carried her to his car. Several passersby watched the matador carrying the Spanish lady. They laughed, obviously the senorita had had too much alcohol. Vidal joined in their laughter, saying that his wife was pissed and he was taking her home. He felt empty; the love of his life was dead, and soon Susie would be too.

Romany awoke in a cold sweat, another nightmare about Epping Forest. In this one, Candy was clawing her way out of her shallow grave; she was coming for him, her dead blue face staring ahead. He switched on the bedside lamp, which would be staying on for the rest of the night. He couldn't breathe, he was burning up. He buzzed for his live-in carer; he'd soiled the sheets in fear. Madeleine came into his room, helped him out of bed and ran a bath for him, then she helped him into it and set to changing the sheets. Romany was scared of dying, but at the same time, he was hardly living. His mouth was full of thrush again, his bronchitis had returned, and he seemed to pick up every infection going. After a long soak in the bath, Madeleine returned and helped him out of it, and towelled him dry. She helped him back to bed, tucked him in, and left, hoping he'd sleep. It wouldn't come, his heart beat wildly, he was getting chest pains and couldn't breathe. Reaching for the buzzer, he alerted Madeleine. She came in, took one look at him, and called an ambulance. Once more, Romany was on his way to hospital.

Chapter Thirty-Six

Deanne and Eddie had gone to London. They were both spoiled, and used to being chauffeured everywhere, so it was quite an adventure to use buses and trains. They were both discussing their futures. Eddie wanted to be a reptile vet, and Deanne was thinking about doing something along the same lines. It would mean going to college when they left school, but as neither of them wanted to do anything other than work with reptiles, college seemed the only way forward. They'd got on the train at Romford Station and disembarked at Liverpool Street Station. Then they hopped onto a number eleven bus which took then to Trafalgar Square. As usual, Deanne got her own way about everything, and Eddie fell in with her plans, but today, Deanne could not be satisfied. She found fault with everything that Eddie did, and kept picking arguments.

They ended up in Oxford Street, and repeatedly got bumped into by shoppers. Deanne wandered into several shops, with Eddie lagging behind and trying to make conversation. Deanne was getting fed up with his chatter, especially when he kept going on about learning to play the guitar.

'For Christ's sake, Eddie, stop going on about you playing the guitar, you've never been bothered before.'

'Well, I just thought that it might be nice to learn.'

'Shut up, you'd probably be useless.'

'Give me a chance; it might be fun. Why are you so wound up?'

'I'm not, just leave me alone.'

'But Dee?'

'I said shut up, go away. If you don't, I'll call a policeman.'

They were outside Selfridges when Deanne started to scream and rant at Eddie. Several tourists were getting a front seat, and one large Texan man was gaping and pointing at the warring teenagers.

Eddie steered Deanne away from Selfridges, where a crowd was gathering in a semi circle. 'I don't know what your problem is but we'll continue here,' he said.

'Get your hands off me. I told you before, I'll call a policeman.'

'You don't need to, the noise that you're making will have half a dozen of them running here; everyone's staring and most of them are tourists. They think that we're part of some street theatre company. They can't understand what we're saying but they think that we're performing for their benefit. Look at that Japanese guy, he's rummaging in his pockets for money to put in a hat, see, he's now looking on the pavement for a hat.'

The Japanese man walked over and doffed his hat. 'Good, very good,' he said.

Eddie addressed him. 'Speak English?'

The man shook his head and handed Eddie ten pounds. Eddie refused the money, but the Japanese man was insistent. 'You take, very good,' he enthused.

Never one to lose an opportunity of making money, Deanne tapped him on his shoulder.

'Don't go,' she cried, 'there's more,' then rushing to Eddie's side she said, 'sing.'

'I can't sing.'

'Neither can I, let's do that song that we did at Susie's sixteenth birthday party.'

'I can't remember what it was.'

'*Hello Goodbye* by The Beatles, you dummy, and we'll follow on with *Hey Jude*, ready?'

351

'Dee, we can't.'

'Eddie, just sing, then I'll do a bit of dancing and acrobatics. Use your head, if these people want to part with their cash, the least we can do is try to entertain them.' Deanne took her brand new shoes from their box and placed the empty container on the ground. 'Right, now sing,' she ordered.

The two teenagers attempted to muddle through both songs with Deanne chiding Eddie every time that he went wrong. The tourists loved it, thinking that it was all part of the act. Soon the cardboard box was filling up, and as soon as Eddie and Deanne had finished singing, Deanne gave a very showy performance of acrobatic dancing.

The box was more than half full by now and the teenagers finished by giving a rendition of *Get Back*. The crowd dispersed and Deanne picked up the box. She was about to start counting the money when she felt a tap on her shoulder. She froze, thinking that it might be the strong arm of the law but fortunately, it was a huge Texan.

'Honey, you are great, we have travelling shows back home but we usually have several players, as a duo, you were fantastic, you should come to the States. Which company are you with?'

'A company called Travelling Light; we're a new company,' lied Deanne.

The Texan was reaching into his pockets and produced a twenty pound note. Handing it to Eddie, he said, 'Where are you performing next?'

'Trafalgar Square in half an hour. We must rush, maybe you'll catch us there,' said Deanne, stuffing the money into her bag and replacing her shoes in the box.

The Texan grinned and shook Eddie and Deanne's hands. 'I surely will, what do you say, Momma?'

It was then that Deanne noticed the over-made up, over-dressed bleached blonde plump woman by his side. The lady nodded and then walked off with her husband. 'Come on,' laughed

Deanne, and together the teenagers made for a coffee shop to count out their spoils.

When Susie awoke, she was on the back seat of the car. It was dark outside and she couldn't see a thing. Her jaw hurt, she'd bitten her tongue, and the taste of blood was in her mouth. She could hear sobbing; it was Vidal in the front seat, and then everything came flooding back to her. She had to get away and return to England. Vidal's revelations defied belief; he'd been conducting an affair with a girl that he'd called his sister and all the time she'd been unrelated and his lover. What a fool Susie felt, and she was scared too. Vidal heard her movements and turned around.

'Ah, you are awake, do you believe in God?'

'Yes, why?'

'It's just as well, you will meet him soon.'

Vidal sneered at his terrified wife as she cried, 'Vidal, what about Maisie?' Susie needed to keep him talking.

'I will return to England, console your parents, and bring our daughter back to Tenerife. She will be raised here.'

'But she needs me; every child needs it mother.'

'Sometimes it is better not to have one; my mother was a pathetic drunk.'

'Vidal, take everything, the house, money, you can have the lot, but I need Maisie and she needs me.'

'You are a pathetic mother; your own mother sees more of her than you.'

'Vidal, I'm begging you, I won't tell anyone about this.'

'You won't be able to.' Vidal opened his door and moved to the back of the car. Opening Susie's door, he dragged her out. 'What a beautiful spot this is, Susie. People flock here every day; look at the moon reflecting on the water. Can you swim?'

'You know I can't, you always promised to teach me but you never did.'

'Well it would make no difference; there are many rocks beneath the surface. You will be dead before you have a chance to swim.'

Vidal dragged a screaming Susie backwards toward the edge of the cliff, when suddenly a light appeared, a small but bright light which scared her. It illuminated everything and was a large orb which was growing larger by the second. 'Vidal, look behind you.'

'There's nothing behind me.'

'There is, I'm scared.'

Vidal was feeling a bit uneasy. The night had been still and now, suddenly, a wind had got up which was increasing by the minute. It became gale force; what was happening? He let go of Susie and she fell to the ground, not wanting to focus on this bright light. It also seemed safer as the wind was making it difficult to stay upright. Vidal was staggering around all over the place. Was it a UFO experience? Whatever it was, it was making Vidal freak out. Susie glanced up; the orb was taking shape, the shape of a figure. She cast her eyes onto the ground once more; maybe she and Vidal were both about to die. Vidal was terrified; he recognised the figure. This man had died years ago.

'No,' he screamed, 'get away from me, I was just playing with her, I would never have harmed her, I love her, she is my adored wife, it was just a game.' Vidal's face was a mask of terror as the figure moved toward him. There was no escape, only backwards, and that led to the edge of the cliff. 'Help me, Susie, he will kill me,' screamed Vidal.

Susie kept her eyes down. If this thing was going to kill Vidal, she'd probably be next on his list. It was no use trying to run; the wind was so strong now that staying upright would be an impossibility. She heard a long drawn out scream, and looked up just in time to see Vidal go backwards over the cliff. The man stood on the edge and then turned toward Susie. She glued her eyes to the ground once more, praying that the figure might just go now that Vidal had met a certain death. The figure drew level with her and suddenly the wind dropped as if by magic. Susie felt a hand in hers and the figure helped her to her feet. The terrified girl held her breath and kept her eyes on the ground, too scared to make eye contact. Then she found herself being held in an embrace, a loving one. Scared, Susie looked up into the eyes of someone that she knew only too well. She drew back, believing that she was dreaming and, just as suddenly, the man released her and pointed an accusing finger at her, crying, 'You stupid girl, you have let me down.'

Choking back her tears, Susie sobbed, 'I'm so sorry, Daddy.'

Then the figure became blurred and began to lose its form, becoming a bright orb again and finally disappearing across the sea. A shocked Susie made her way back to the car. Vidal and Luisa were both dead, and her dance with the devil was over. Opening the car door, she removed her bag and then walked on foot until she found a road. It had been the obvious thing to do, abandoning the car. If the car remained behind, it would appear that Vidal had driven to this romantic spot and committed suicide. Luisa wasn't around to dispute it.

Susie's plan was clever, she had to return to the hotel in Santa Cruz, pick up all of Vidal's, Luisa's and her own personal effects and clothes, and return to the Torres Del Sol. Once inside, she would deposit both Vidal and Luisa's belongings, pack her suitcase, and leave for the airport. She couldn't wait to see her family again.

Lop was desperate to sell the agency. She rang Barry Grayson, saying that she thought Vic was too old to run an agency any more. 'Would you be interested in buying him out?' she asked.

'No,' replied Barry, 'but Rosie might be interested in buying a half share. She's had years in front of the desk, and behind it. She's the ideal candidate. Her kids are growing up and she's got time on her hands, plus money in the bank, but what is Vic's take on this?'

'He is a stubborn old goat and his eyesight is failing, plus he is being screened for cancer of the stomach. I think he should retire.'

'Best thing you can do is ease him out gently, suggest making Rosie a partner; it would take some of the work load from Vic and I know that he would work with her because she knows the business inside and out. Then at a later date, when his health gets worse, Rosie could buy him out completely. Think about it.'

'Maybe,' replied Lop, who had other things on her mind. There was a young man coming in to audition for her in fifteen minutes. She didn't know if he could sing, but he was a hunk, and Lop wondered if his talent may lie in other directions.

'You bastard.' Rosie was throwing verbal abuse, plus half of the kitchen at Ray.

Terrified, he cried, 'I haven't done anything.'

He was ducking pots and pans which were flying past his head. Rosie screamed, 'You ask me to take your jacket to the cleaners, so I emptied the pockets and guess what I found?'

'I don't know.'

'A note saying: "thank you for an incredible night, it was just like old times, when can we meet up again? love from Jenny, please ring me." I can only think of one Jenny that dates back to the old days. I heard that she'd moved to Scotland.'

'For God's sake, Rosie, do you think I would have left it in the pocket if I'd known it was there?'

'So, how did it get into your pocket? Did you sleep together?'

'No, she was at a party that Vic threw, ages ago. We went to Scotland for a few gigs just before the German tour. I'm afraid I was pissed, and she must have slipped the note into my jacket pocket while we were standing at the bar. You know I can't stand her, I told her to piss off.'

Another pot flew past Ray's head. The cupboard was almost empty, and pots and pans were strewn all over the floor. Ray wondered what was coming next; he was distracted as the buzzer was going off. He headed for the intercom just as Rosie was aiming her heaviest pot at him. This time the pot clouted him on the side of his head and he saw stars. 'Rosie, pack that in, there's someone outside.'

'Well it's too early for my mother, so find out who it is and then I'll finish you off with the wok.'

Cursing Ray, Rosie hurried upstairs; she was fuming. She'd thought that Jenny was history, and now the bitch had raised her head once more. Ray had really done it this time. He'd omitted to tell her about this meeting with Jenny, and as he'd said this meeting was ages ago. There was more to this than met the eye. She was going to pack his bags and throw him out. He'd probably been paralytic when he'd met Jenny, so God knows what might have happened. He'd kept it all secret and they'd never had secrets. Enough was enough.

'Rosie, come downstairs.'

'I'm packing your bags, you're leaving. You can go back to Scotland and shack up with your precious Jenny.'

'Rosie, will you please come downstairs.'

'In my own good time; I hate you Ray Lynne, and I wish that I'd never met you.'

'Rosie, this is important.'

'Really, has Jenny turned up?'

'No, this is really important, you're needed down here.'

'Damn.' Rosie ran downstairs, still cursing her husband.

Ray was not alone. Beside him stood a young woman with a bruised face and an unkempt appearance, a woman that Rosie hardly recognised. She drew in her breath as the woman said, 'It's me, Mum, I've come home, Vidal and Luisa are both dead,' then she burst into tears.

'Susie,' cried Rosie, 'oh my God, what happened?'

Romany had had a stroke of luck. Ellen had made contact; she had rung his number and got Madeleine. After identifying who each other was, Ellen headed for the hospital. Romany was overcome with emotion when he saw her and broke down in tears. 'I thought I'd lost you,' he cried.

'You never lost me, but I was very hurt. I would never have left if you'd just come clean with me, it was the lies that destroyed me.'

'Will you come and visit me again?'

'Visit? I'm moving back in with you. I'll be with you right up until the end.'

Romany was overjoyed. With Ellen around, he would fight this disease even harder.

Rosie opened her arms to her daughter. 'When did you last eat?'

'Yesterday. Vidal tried to kill me; he said that he'd never loved me and it had always been Luisa that he wanted.'

'His own sister?'

'She wasn't,' and Susie slowly divulged her nightmare to her horrified parents. They didn't know what to say; Jenny was no longer an issue. Rosie cooked Susie her favourite meal, chicken and chips, and watched as her daughter devoured it. Her face was badly bruised, and Rosie wanted a doctor called in but Susie declined, saying that all she wanted to do was relax with her family.

Norma arrived home from the day centre and viewed her battered granddaughter. 'He saved you, didn't he?' she crowed.

'He tried to kill her,' snapped Ray.

Norma turned to Ray and smirked. 'Not the gardener, I always knew that he was a bad lot, always full of promises, but fulfilling none. Susie knows who I'm talking about. I may be old and senile, but I still see and hear things at night. He told me that he'd saved her. Come to my room tonight, Susie, and you can thank him yourself.'

'Yes, Nana. Why are the pots and pans all over the floor?'

'A slight misunderstanding,' replied Ray, 'isn't that right, Rosie?'

'Yes, but things are okay now.' As far as Rosie was concerned, Susie was her priority today and she needed to see her settled, but the following day she was going to pay Vic Lee a visit. He had some explaining to do.

Rosie left home about nine o'clock the following day and made her way to London. She stormed into Vic's office and demanded to see him. Lop stared at her; she had been filing her nails. 'Anything that you want to say to him, you can say to me,' she said.

Rosie smiled sweetly. 'Really, do you know that I used to sit where you are now? Doug Trent used to run this office and he ran it well.'

'That was nice.'

'Nice doesn't come close, this agency was run with precision, but nowadays it's run by a pervert and a harlot.'

'I beg your pardon?'

'I want to speak to the organ grinder, not the monkey, now go and get Vic before I ram your nail file up where the sun don't shine. Mind you, it'd probably get lost considering how many pricks have been up there.'

Lop got to her feet and scurried away. Vic emerged from the back office. 'Rosaleen, my darling, how nice to see you.'

'Cut the crap, Vic, I want to know if anything happened between Ray and that tart Jenny.'

'I'm not a fly on the wall. Don't you trust Ray?'

'Yes, it's her that I'm bothered about. Next time you visit Scotland, I want her banned.'

'Well you see, Rosaleen, that will be difficult because I'm looking for a female vocalist for the band, and her voice is not bad.'

'Why do you need a female vocalist?'

'To complement Kevin; he works better with a female beside him. He used to sing with Cathy as Platinum; they really could have gone places.'

'Has Jenny signed a contract yet?'

'No, my dear, why, are you considering applying for the job?'

'I'll think about it.'

'Wonderful, I'll give you until the end of the month to decide, and if you say you don't want the job, I'll contact little Jenny Wren; that'll be her stage name.'

'Jenny Wren, more like a vulture. Okay Vic, I'll give it serious thought, but if I decide against it, I want Ray to leave the band.'

'Impossible, I've just renewed his contract.'

'Come to dinner Friday without Lop and we'll discuss it.'

'Wonderful, my dear, I'll look forward to it.'

Rosie left the office knowing that she was beaten. Resuming her career as a singer wasn't exactly top of her wish list, but at least she'd be able to keep her eye on Ray.

As she left, Vic called Lop in. 'How did I do?' he asked, 'did you hear everything?'

'Most of it, you were brilliant, you had her fooled. She really believed that you were taking Jenny on.'

'I'm the master of getting what I want.'

'I'm proud of you.'

'Talking of proud, I've got something in my trousers that fits that description. Could you deal with it?'

'I would love to,' replied Lop, revolted by the thought. Vic wanted a blow job. She locked door, and her thoughts switched to a young man that she was going to audition the following day.

'Lop.' Vic's voice was booming out of the back office.

'I'm coming.'

'So will I be if you don't hurry up.'

Lop sighed. Vic was pissing her off, but she smiled to herself. Her savings were growing, and it would only be a matter of time before she had cleaned him out. She wanted to bring him to his knees, and having no conscience made it easier. He was just a silly old man who had bagged himself a young Thai bride. She wouldn't have looked at him twice if he'd had no money. He was going blind so she signed everything for him; he trusted her implicitly, believing that she'd always be there for him. Vic had finally met his match.

Chapter Thirty-Seven

Three years later

1995 was a strange year. Rosie was singing her heart out with the Z Tones, Ray had controlled his drinking once more, and Susie was engaged to the long suffering Steven. Romany was dying; the doctors could do no more. His brother Rick had died a month previously but there was no way that Romany could go to the funeral; the flight to Los Angeles would have killed him. Ellen was a brilliant nurse and worked hand in hand with Madeleine. Romany looked like a skeleton; he'd ordered all the mirrors to be taken down as he couldn't stand the sight of his reflection. He rarely changed his clothes or bathed, and now he had bronchoscopy tubes down his throat.

'It is so degrading,' he told Ellen. 'I want to rip these tubes out but I can't.'

'Shh,' replied Ellen, 'come on eat some yoghurt; it will help with the sores in your mouth.' She felt his forehead, he was burning up. His temperature rarely fell below 106, and his emaciated appearance brought tears to her eyes. How he'd suffered: candidiosis, leukaemia, Karposi sarcoma cells, pneumonia, herpes, bronchitis, hepatitis, night sweats, mononucleosis pleurisy, cytomegalovirus, heart and kidney disease; he'd had the lot. Ellen never judged people, but according to reports from other people, Romany had been an expert at making others suffer. She was most surprised one morning when he awoke and asked for a bath. 'Are you feeling a little better?' she asked.

'No, but I want to see Rosie, and I don't want her seeing me like this.'

'But, darling, we can't remove the tubes.'

'I know but you could help me with a bath and give me a shave.'

'Okay, I'll ring her, do you want to see Ray too?'

'No.' Romany attempted to get out of bed but couldn't make it; he almost fell onto the floor.

'Let me help you,' said Ellen, 'that's what I'm here for.'

She got Romany's wheelchair, put him into it and pushed him through to the en suite. 'Can you sort out my best suit for me, Ellen? I want to look my best, if that's possible.'

'Of course I will,' replied Ellen, 'now let's organise this bath.'

Three hours later, Rosie arrived and flinched at Romany's appearance. 'Long time no see,' she said. 'I've brought you some fruit. Ellen said that you wanted to see me.'

'That's right, I do, and I've even put on my best suit for you. You're looking gorgeous.'

'Thanks, but I'm almost fifty, a bit long in the tooth to be fronting a band.'

'Rubbish, good singers go on forever. You're a good listener too, Ed told me. You've known me since I was in short trousers.'

'And afterwards when you couldn't keep your trousers on.'

'Those were the days.'

'Am I here to reminisce?'

Romany became serious. 'Rosie, do you think that Rick went to hell?'

'I don't know, none of us know where we're going. I think that God is good and he forgives us our sins.'

'So you're a believer.'

'Always have been, you have to believe in something.'

'But you've always been a good girl, and you've been treated badly. God will find a place for you. I've been downright evil at times. I didn't even know what love was until I met Ellen.'

'Well at least you've found it, some people never do. I found it twice, with Ed and Ray. I never really loved Barry. He loved me and I still feel guilty about it. I'm a grandma now; would you like to see some photos of Maisie?'

'Yes, I would.'

Rosie took some photos from her bag and handed them to Romany. 'Lovely child, she'll break some hearts when she's older, but then all of your children have been blessed with their looks. Susie's lovely, Deanne's a stunner, Bobby's gonna knock the girls dead when he's older, and Raydon's very handsome.'

'Thank you, Romany.'

Rosie stared at the emaciated figure whose suit hung on him. He had the body of someone who looked as if they had been held in a concentration camp. Even with the buttons done up on the suit, it looked in danger of falling off him. His teeth, what were left of them, were rotten, he was going gradually bald, and his eyes bulged from their sockets; he looked like a living corpse. Yes, Romany would have been a prime candidate for a horror movie.

Ellen entered the room. 'Would you two like a drink?'

'Just water,' replied Romany.

'An orange juice,' said Rosie, 'aren't you going to join us?'

'No, I'm very busy, and Romany has things that he wants to tell you in private. I'll get your drinks.'

Baffled, Rosie stared at Romany. 'What things?'

'Let's just say that I'd like some "you and me" time. I wish I'd had kids.'

'You've probably got them all over the world.'

'But none that I know of.'

'I bet they're all good looking; you always were the looker of the band.'

Ellen entered with the drinks; she gave Rosie hers and placed Romany's on a side table. She smiled and then left the room saying, 'See you later.'

'Great, isn't she?' said Romany. 'I can now see the error of my ways but it's too late.'

'It's never too late. Ed will be waiting for you on the other side and you'll have great times again.'

'That's what worries me. He found out about me and Cathy and almost beat me to a pulp.'

'The past is the past, and anyway they're together now.'

'You have the knack of making people feel better. You should have been a counsellor.'

'Maybe. Ed confessed all the last time that I saw him, so maybe I'm in the wrong vocation.'

'You're fantastic. I want you to do something for me. I can't trust anyone else.'

'Not even Ellen?'

'No. I'm at the end of my life; and I have maybe a week left. There's a package on top of the wardrobe addressed to you. I don't want you to open it until after my death. I've remembered your entire family in my will. I've no kids of my own so I want yours to benefit from my death.'

'But what about Ellen?'

'She's been well provided for. You've been a great friend, Rosie. In that package, you'll also find a letter. I've written my instructions in it; please carry them out for me.'

'I will.'

'I've finally sussed out why I screwed so many girls.'

'Really?'

'Yep, I was afraid of dying, so I wanted to screw as many as possible before I died.'

'Well you must have satisfied them, they always came back for more, not that you gave them a second chance.'

'Too busy moving onto the next one. I admire you so much. Tell me the truth, out of Ed and Ray, which one did you love the best?'

'That's not a fair question, Ed's dead.'

'But if he was alive, which one would it be?'

Rosie blushed. 'You know the answer to that, don't you?'

'Yep, no contest, you and Ed were made for each other. I've left Ray all my guitars, and I've signed them.'

'All of them; they're worth a fortune.'

'I know, and I can't think of a better person to leave them to.'

'He'll be made up.' Rosie gazed at the man who resembled a live skeleton. The tubes that were down his throat looked dreadful; he had no dignity in death, and now his eyes were drooping.

'Rosie, get that package and take it home. I'm so tired; I really do feel as if I'm knocking on heaven's door. Will you ask Ray to sing it at my funeral?'

'Of course I will. In fact, I'll pop back in a couple of days with him and then you can tell him yourself.'

'I'll be dead in a couple of days. Get the package and go home and pray for me. I'm ready to die, I'm so tired, really tired. Thanks for coming.'

'My pleasure.' Rosie got to her feet and retrieved the package, 'Bye, Romany,' she said. There was no answer. Romany had drifted off to sleep. Rosie found Ellen and then left, and began her long drive back to Essex; she wondered if she'd ever see Romany again. He looked resigned to dying, and at peace with himself. He had no quality of life left at all, and death would probably be a happy release.

The following morning, she relayed a dream that she'd had the night before to Ray. 'It was crazy,' she said. 'I'd gone to visit Romany and Ellen, and Ellen had gone out. Romany was back to full health and made me a coffee, but he spilt most of it down my dress. He suggested that I take a shower while he dried my dress. After my shower, I couldn't find my clothes so I wrapped a large brown bath towel around me. When I got downstairs, I told him that my clothes were missing, and he said, "Don't worry about it, we'll go shopping" and guess what, I agreed. When we got to the shops, they were just like they were in the sixties, and here I was shopping in a bath towel. We had lunch and then he went missing, so I got on a bus and went back to his house.'

'Buses don't run anywhere near his house.'

'I know, I told you it was crazy. Once I'd let myself inside the porch, I found it full of people all queuing up. I asked what they were doing and they said that they were waiting to use the toilet. His porch had been converted into a public loo.'

'Fantastic.' Ray was in stitches.

'Yes, but it gets crazier. I went inside the house and a man knocked on the door saying that he wanted to wash his hands. I told him that it was a private house, and he apologised and walked away.'

'And then what?'

'Nothing, I woke up; what a strange dream.'

'Dreams are supposed to mean something. You visit him, he makes sure that Ellen's out, he spills coffee all over you making you take your clothes off, he takes you to lunch with you still dressed in a bath towel because he's hidden your clothes, and then he disappears in order to screw the waitress. As for the bus, I don't know, but the porch being converted to a loo makes a lot of sense. Over the years, the number of scrubbers that have graced those doors would have made it into a cess pit, with a little help from him, of course. I suppose it's because you saw him yesterday and he's played on your mind, and that's why you dreamed about him.'

'Maybe, I wonder how he is today?'

'Who knows, who cares?'

'Ray, he's dying.'

'That's right, and throughout his life he's made people suffer, so now it's his turn.'

'Will you come with me in a couple of days to see him?'

'If it makes you happy.'

'Thanks Ray, I love you so much.'

The couple spent the rest of the day with their children and Norma. Deanne was missing; she was at college studying hard to become a veterinarian. Eddie was also at the same college. Rosie hardly ever saw Deanne any more; if she wasn't at college, she was staying with Eddie at the mansion. She was almost eighteen and had blossomed into a beautiful young lady. Bobby had a torn Achilles tendon, and for the first time in his life couldn't dance, so he joined in a game of Totopoly with the rest of the family. After dinner, Rosie and Ray chilled out listening to Dylan; he was great to chill to.

Rosie was snuggled up to Ray when the phone rang. It was Ellen, and her voice was breaking up as she said, 'I just wanted to let you know that Romany's passed away; the doctor's here now. I was holding his hand when he died. He looked up at me and said, "I love you Ellen, if we'd only met earlier things would have been so different, thank you for everything, you're so beautiful, come closer so I can see you better, it's getting dark and I'm so tired", then he closed his eyes and fell asleep. His pain is over now.'

'Shall we come round?'

'No, but I would like you at the funeral; he told me what songs he wanted played months ago. He said that he wanted Ray to sing one of them.'

'I know which one, he'll do it. Are you sure that you don't want company?'

'No, I just want to be here alone with my memories, besides, Madeleine is still here, and she won't be leaving until tomorrow.'

'Okay, but if you need anything, just call.'

'I will, bye Rosie.'

'Bye Ellen,' and Rosie hung up.

'Trouble?' asked Ray.

'Romany's dead; I guess I'd better open the package that he gave me.'

'What package?'

'The one on the sideboard that he asked me not to open until after his death.'

'Well, get it then. I'll open it if you like; you're shaking all over.'

'Thanks, Ray, I suppose I'm in shock.' Rosie picked up the package and handed it to Ray, then she sat down beside him and snuggled up close as he undid the package. Inside were two letters, one marked 'Rosie' and one marked 'to be taken to the police station', there was also a plain brown envelope. Ray handed the letter that was marked with her name on it to Rosie. She opened the envelope; it was a thank you letter and made several references to their youth. Some of it made Rosie laugh, and she was still smiling until she got to the last few lines which said, 'by the time that you've examined everything in this package, you will hate me. I'm so sorry. I've let you down badly, thank you for everything, love from Roy'.

'What does he mean?' said Rosie, handing the letter to Ray.

'Dunno,' replied Ray, 'open the brown envelope.'

Rosie opened it with trembling fingers, and recoiled in horror. A note dropped out onto the floor as she removed a wallet from the envelope, one that she recognised. It bore the initials GBG. Rosie flopped down onto the sofa. 'It's Gary's,' she cried.

Ray picked up the note and read it. He wasn't sure whether Rosie should read it; she'd probably find it too upsetting. He voiced his feelings, but Rosie demanded that he hand the note over. She was devastated as she read:

> *I swear that I didn't mean to kill him, I just*
> *wanted to teach him a lesson. I waited for him*
> *to come out to the car park and we scuffled, he*
> *fell and hit his head and I panicked and stole*
> *his wallet to make it look like a mugging.*
> *Before I left I saw Candy coming out of the*
> *building and knew that she would find him.*

I didn't know that he would die, please forgive
me, I've carried this guilt to my grave. I know
that this will cause a lot of extra pain to you,
but I felt that you had to know what really
happened.
I beg your forgiveness, Roy

At first, Rosie was struck dumb and then she clutched the wallet and fell to the ground with sobs wracking her body. Ray helped her to her feet and held her to him, soothing her. 'He'll be punished Rosie, he'll be judged, Gary will get justice.'

'I can't believe that he let me and Barry suffer for all of this time. He left my son to die, my son who was on the threshold of life; how could he do such an evil thing?'

'Evil was his middle name; he danced with the devil and in the end he lost. You're in shock, let's call the doctor.'

'I don't want a doctor, I want to get the remaining letter to the police station. I need to know what's in it. I suppose it's a confession to Gary's murder.'

'We could open it ourselves.'

'No, let the police deal with it.' She kissed the wallet, saying, 'I got Gary this wallet for his sixteenth birthday; how he loved it, he never let it out of his sight. Come on, Ray, let's go.'

'If you're sure that's what you want.'

'It is.'

Ray drove Rosie to Romford Police Station which was in the main road, and once inside the station, Rosie handed over the letter at the desk. A large police officer opened it as Rosie said, 'A so-called friend has just confessed to a crime that was committed in 1983, and I believe that this is a written confession. Unfortunately, the coward waited for his own death before I was allowed to open a package that he'd given me. I wish I'd opened it before his demise so that he could have been thrown in jail and the key thrown away.'

The officer read the letter. 'What was the victim's name? The writing is very shaky.'

'Gary Grayson, he was my son.'

'That's not the name on here, and the date's not 1983, its much later. The victim's name is Candice Ryan, and apparently she was murdered by two brothers in a sexual frenzy; their names are Rick and Roy Fowler.'

'What? Both of those men are dead.'

'Apparently the victim's body is buried in Epping Forest; they made that her last resting place.'

'No,' screamed Rosie, as the room was spinning. She felt Ray's arms around her and then she was engulfed in darkness.

Chapter Thirty-Eight

Barry flew over to give Rosie support. He was broken-hearted, but at least the truth was out. It had appeared much earlier that Gary had been mugged by a stranger, when in fact the killer had been someone who had mingled amongst everyone as a friend. Vic had been horrified, but not completely surprised as he'd recalled the hatred that Romany had shown toward Gary. He attended Romany's funeral, but none of the Lynne family attended so Romany's request for Ray to sing at his funeral was thwarted. Ellen was devastated; she was trying to come to terms with Romany's death and now she was being questioned by the police. She could tell them nothing of importance, so they left her to her misery. Rosie was like a walking zombie, so was Kevin. It had been hard enough to believe that Candy had stood him up on their wedding day, but to be faced with the fact that the poor girl and her unborn baby had been killed was too much. He could only guess at the horrific ordeal that his fiancée had been through.

Rosie hadn't wanted to attend the reading of the will, but Barry made her see sense on that one. 'He has robbed us of our wonderful son, but if you take what he has left you, you could put it to use, make a positive out of a negative. He had no real friends, nobody stuck around Romany for long and he'd amassed a fortune; take it Rosie, he owes it to you.'

Rosie had thought hard about Barry's words; to her it was blood money, but Barry was right, life had to go on. Her so-called friend had committed two heinous crimes, maybe more, and maybe with Romany's money she could bring Vic to his knees; the world needed him gone.

She attended the reading and sat around the table with Ray and Barry. Vic was there, wondering if his lead guitarist and so-called friend had left him anything. Ellen was supported by her mother; she was an innocent victim in all of Romany's evil doings, but she felt responsible even though she hadn't been around when either of the crimes had been carried out. The solicitor cleared his throat and began.

> This is the final will and testament of Roy Fowler.
> To my friend Ray Lynne, I bequeath all of my guitars
> most of which are signed. To Susie, Deanne, Bobby
> and Raydon, Ray's children, five thousand pounds
> each, to Eddie Gold, ten thousand pounds.

Rosie held her breath, she had to come next.

> To Mrs Rosaleen Lynne, my friend and confidante
> a much larger sum, one that she will not be expecting,
> she has always been there for me, never judged me,
> helped and advised me and been the best friend that
> I could ever have wished for. Therefore I bequeath
> to her the sum of one million pounds.

Rosie was pleasantly shocked, she was already a wealthy woman, and now her finances had rocketed. Had Romany really valued her that much, or was it the guilt factor? Whatever it was, she knew what she was about to do with the money. Ellen amassed millions, plus Romany's house, although she had no intention of living in it. She was going to get it put on the market and move abroad with her mother. She needed a new life. A new identity. Her love for Romany would never die but she would never be able to forgive him for the pain that he had inflicted on Rosie and Barry, or the death of her closest friend Candy.

Six months later, Rosie had bought into Vic's agency; she was now a joint partner. Vic would never walk all over her or Ray again. Kevin clung to Rosie like a limpet; he'd always had feelings for her but their joint suffering had brought them much closer. To Kevin, Rosie was like a breath of fresh air. They duetted on stage and bloomed in each other's company. She inspired him, and when she wasn't around, he felt lost.

Deanne's eighteenth birthday went well. She hadn't celebrated her sixteenth, as she'd been away at college, so plans had been set in motion to make her eighteenth exceptional. Her parents had bought her a car, and the Lynne household was full of A listers, plus every celeb that was available. Kevin serenaded her; he announced that Deanne was a very special young lady. 'When this beautiful young girl was born, her father, who was my predecessor with the band, began performing this song on stage. It was because she was his little princess, and she meant the world to him. I'm going to attempt to sing this song, but I doubt that I'll do it as well as he did, or the original singer, the great Reg Presley, but I'll do my best.' Then he led Deanne up onto the stage and serenaded her with the Troggs *Little Girl*.

It brought tears to Deanne's eyes, and Rosie's. She knew just how much Ed had adored his daughter, but as he'd been married to Cathy at the time of Deanne's birth, both father and daughter saw very little of each other.

Ray was okay at the beginning of the night, but as it wore on, he became increasingly inebriated. Soon he was incoherent, and Rosie's heart sank. Ray had fallen off the wagon again. Rosie felt sick; this was Deanne's eighteenth birthday and she knew that she should be feeling happy, but once more Ray had plunged her into the depths of despair. Walking out into the garden, she sat on a bench and sobbed her heart out.

On the drive outside, Eddie was admiring Deanne's new car, He smiled and gave her a hug. 'You lucky thing, good thing that you've passed your test.'

'I love it, the car will give us much more freedom, and I don't need to come home at all now. It's great, I can move in properly with you.'

'I'll have to ask Kevin.' Eddie ran his hands over the car bonnet.

'Kevin can't say much, he's got the hots for my mum. When they're on stage together, his tongue's almost hanging out,' said Deanne.

'But she's married.'

'I know, but Ray's hitting the bottle again; he went back onto it after Mum found out the truth behind Gary's death. He's been no support at all; anyone would have thought that Gary was his son.'

'Grief affects people in different ways, Dee.'

'Maybe, but Kevin and Mum have had to support each other. I reckon that he could do himself and my mum some good, and I doubt that Ray would even notice.'

'Dee, you're terrible.'

'I know, but that's why you love me.'

'Dee, what we're doing is wrong.'

'I know, but if I move in with you, we'll be out of sight, so stop feeling so guilty. We need to go back inside, Bobby's doing a special routine for me.'

'Okay.' Eddie followed Deanne back inside the house.

'Rosie, are you okay?' It was Kevin's voice that broke into Rosie's reverie.

She wiped her eyes. 'I'm fine, just needed some air.'

'I've just helped Ray up to bed; he's out of it again.'

'Thanks, where will this all end? He does so well and then he falls off the wagon. Maybe it's because I haven't given him much of my attention lately, I've been too sunk in my misery over Gary.'

Kevin sat down and placed his arms around her shoulders. 'Maybe you should think of cutting loose.'

'I'm fifty, and my kids need stability. Susie's left, I hardly see Deanne, she's always at your place, so they're off hand, but Bobby and Raydon still need me and they love their father.'

'And what about you, do you still love Ray?'

'Of course I do, but when he's down, he brings me down with him. I'm so tired, what with working in the office and touring, I'm exhausted.'

'And you need a shoulder to cry on now and again.'

'Ray's my rock when he's sober.'

'But he hardly ever is, thanks to Vic.'

'I can't watch him twenty four seven.'

'And Vic knows that. Come on let's have a cuddle, I'm here for you.'

Rosie cuddled up to him and rested her head on his shoulders. 'That feels nice,' she said.

Kevin stroked her hair. 'I'd look after you if you'd let me.'

They remained like that until Rosie said, 'I have to go, I'm all right now. Deanne will be wondering where I am, and Bobby must be almost ready to perform.' Kevin kissed her forehead and then moved to her lips slowly. Rosie responded with a passion that almost knocked Kevin from the bench. Pulling away, she cried, 'I'm sorry.'

'Don't be, I'm not, I've always wanted you.'

'I'm married.'

'Yes, to a drunk; leave him and come and live with me.'

'Ray needs help, not abandoning, besides, we all work together in the same line-up.'

'And how long do you think that Vic will put up with Ray's drunken antics?'

'Well, he encourages him.'

'I know, because he wants him out with the rest of the band; he only wants you and me.'

'The evil bastard.'

'But you and I could work. If Ray gets tanked up again

tomorrow, come over to my place and I'll get Mrs Shores to cook us something nice, then we can chill and see where things lead.'

'It's not fair on Ray.'

'And he's not fair to you; you've only got one life, so why stick with someone who drags you down?'

'I'll think about it.'

'Please do; call me tomorrow night and let me know what you decide.'

'I will, now let's get back to the party, Bobby's going to perform *Mr Beaujangles*. He's worked so hard on perfecting it and I don't want to miss it.'

'Just one more kiss, please.'

The couple shared a fervent embrace, and then Rosie got to her feet and wandered back to the party with Kevin at her heels.

Chapter Thirty Nine

Someone else whose life was becoming a nightmare was Jenny Brown; her husband Duncan was very sick and had had several operations recently. The surgeons had told her that the surgery, plus chemotherapy, would extend his life for about another two years. It was good news, but obviously the end was in sight. Jenny had lost her looks and almost her mind. Ray had been right, she had screwed her life up, but she knew that things would have been so different had her first love Terry not died at the age of fifteen.

Towards the end of his life, Jenny had mucked in, helping Terry's mother cope. She had willingly cleared up puke when Terry had been sick; in fact the aroma of Dettol was a regular smell that got up her nose as she scrubbed away. The house was full of love, and Jenny could recall every detail about the lounge where she'd spent many hours with Terry, laughing, fooling around, and doing all the things that teenagers do. The polished sideboard was full of family photos, the heavily stained beige carpet had seen better days, the well used red and grey three piece suite was inviting, and the dining table with its wobbly leg was always covered with a pretty lace tablecloth. In the corner of the room stood the rented television set, and on the window sill stood a vase of colourful imitation flowers. She could even recall minor details like the drawing pins in the ceiling where the Christmas decorations had been taken down. That room was imprinted on her memory, and would be until the day that she died. She had not seen Terry at the end as she'd caught chicken pox, and by the time that she'd recovered Terry was dead. Jenny had felt dead too; as far as she was concerned, her life was over until Ray had picked her up and made her happy again.

Ray opened up a new world for her; he was kind, funny, and adored her. He'd taken her virginity just before her sixteenth birthday and, sexually, she couldn't have asked for anyone better. Later, she'd become pregnant, but after a fall in her ballet class, she'd miscarried their baby. Ray still wanted to marry her, but by now she had another man in her sights, Rosie's boyfriend Ed. He was in a different league as far as Jenny was concerned. Jenny had carried on an affair behind both Rosie and Ray's backs, believing that Ed loved her; she was besotted with him. Ed in turn didn't really like her at all, but she'd put it on a plate and, being a man, he wasn't about to turn her down. It all went sour when Ray and Rosie found her in bed with Ed, and on that day both men had finished with her, Ray because he'd been humiliated, and Ed because he'd lost Rosie. What a fool she'd been. Ray had really loved her, and would have laid down his life for her, and she'd cheated on him with a man that couldn't care less if she was alive or dead.

Then there had been Tommy, a drifter who was her son's father. Their time together was very short, but he'd managed to get her pregnant. She had drifted in and out of communes until she'd met Duncan, and her problems all seemed to be over. He was a good man. He even adopted Dylan, who by now was a real handful, but now her happy ending was drawing to a close. Duncan would be dead in two years, maybe less; she really loved him and would miss him greatly.

She wondered what had happened to the note that she'd put in Ray's jacket pocket. It had been years since their last meeting, and Ray's marriage looked as solid as ever. Maybe she'd put it into the wrong pocket, after all, Ray and Kevin had shared the same room. One thing was for sure, as soon as Duncan died, she would be returning to Seven Kings and move in with her mother. Havering wasn't far from Seven Kings, so Ray and her would practically be neighbours. She wanted him back and, if only she could split him and Rosie up, they could sail off into the sunset together. Duncan was still in hospital, but Dylan had rung earlier and said that he was on his way. Making herself something to eat, she sat down in her armchair and switched on the television to await Dylan. As the clock struck ten o'clock, Jenny decided to go to bed. Obviously Dylan had been delayed, but just as she was about to go upstairs, she heard the front door slam and was confronted by an angry Dylan.

'Nobody fucking listens, nobody cares. I've done the rounds again today, but those agents living in the smoke wouldn't know talent if it jumped up and smacked them in the face. Vic Lee sits there taking the piss with a tart that looks as if she's just stepped out of a brothel, and Rosaleen Lynne.'

'Rosie works there?'

'Dunno, she might have just popped in I suppose, but she was behind the desk.'

'Really, then give it a couple of weeks and then try and arrange an audition with Rosie; we used to be best friends.'

'Yeah, and you fucked that up just like you fuck everything up.'

'I'm trying to be constructive.'

'I'd rather use a gun.'

'You and guns don't mix. If Rosie can't help you, I'm sure that she'll know someone who can.'

'Okay, I'll give it a try but if that fails, I'm gonna get a gun and blow the whole fucking lot of them away, including your precious Ray Lynne.'

The day after Deanne's party, Ray couldn't remember anything about the night before and, after breakfast, Rosie left for work leaving him to watch television, have a bit of lunch, and then later report to the whiskey bottle. By the time Rosie returned, he was inebriated and, after dinner, became aggressive. Rosie called Kevin. 'I'm on my way,' she said.

'Great, you can stay as long as you like.'

Rosie didn't tell Ray that she was going out; he didn't even know that she was around. Mary would take care of Norma and the boys, so Rosie didn't have to worry on that score. Leaving the house and getting into her car, she headed for Surrey.

Kevin was overjoyed to see Rosie, and his eyes lit up when he saw that she was carrying an overnight bag. Mrs Shores had prepared a banquet, and Rosie and Kevin tucked into it. Neither of them had eaten, Rosie because of Ray's aggression, and Kevin because he felt sure that Rosie would visit him.

After dinner, they chilled out with a few drinks and a couple of smooch dances. They cuddled up on the sofa, neither of them wanting to make the first move. It was Kevin who finally said, 'We'll be here all night if you don't make the first move, I'm scared of a knock back.'

Rosie placed her arms around his neck and said, 'I'm getting a bit old for this, Kevin, I'm fifty.'

'I'm forty, what's ten years? I'll be your toy boy.' They both fell about with laughter and then made their way upstairs.

Upstairs, Rosie sprawled on the bed. She was more than ready for Kevin, as these days Ray was too inebriated to get a hard on. Kevin knew that he had to get inside her before his cock exploded, if he didn't, things would be over before they'd begun. He wanted to impress Rosie, not embarrass himself. Rosie wrapped her legs around him, her body was screaming out to him to take her. Kevin spread her legs and entered her; he rode her slowly, wanting to savour every second. Rosie was moaning and crying out to him over and over again.

'I love you, Rosie, I really do, I always have.'

Rosie didn't reply, she just urged him on. Kevin couldn't believe that it had finally happened; his dream had come true. She was sensual, very sensual, a pleasure giver. She was loving this, and so was he. This was no grand passion, just slow waves of pleasure which lifted them to alarmingly beautiful heights. Kevin had never been with a woman that gave herself like Rosie did; they were on the same wave length and thriving on the sensuality of it.

'Rosie, you're beautiful, this is out of this world, you're making me feel beautiful too.'

Rosie gazed up at him; she was experiencing the same feelings. Slow and beautiful sensations were overtaking her; she was arching up towards Kevin as the orgasm swept over her. They clung together, reaching a simultaneous orgasm, and then sank. Afterwards, cuddled up to Rosie, Kevin said, 'Just as I knew it would be.' Rosie said nothing, all of the tension within her had evaporated. She felt beautiful and loved; it was a beautiful feeling.

The following morning, things were completely different. Rosie awoke and flew out of bed. Kevin was dismayed as he'd hoped to make love to her before she left for work, but she was on a mission; one to get out of the house as soon as possible. Kevin got up and followed her to the en suite. He sneaked up behind her and placed his arms around her waist. 'Will you come back tonight?'

'No, I need to check up on my family.'

'You could come back later; I'll even pick you up if you like. You could stay over and then I could take you to work the following morning.'

'No, I'm busy, can't stay out two nights in a row, maybe next week, I don't know.'

'Next week, but last night was perfect.'

'Last night was a mistake; we were both feeling down and we spent a nice night together.'

'Nice, how can you say nice? I'm in love with you.'

'I'm married.' Rosie switched on her toothbrush and began to brush her teeth.

'But you don't love him, he treats you like shit.'

Rosie continued to brush her teeth and, as soon as she'd finished, rounded on Kevin. 'I love Ray, like I said it was a mistake.'

'Don't you have any feelings for me?'

'Yes, but I'm not in love with you.'

'So you were just playing with me.'

'You invited me, remember, it wasn't the other way around.'

'Then maybe we can meet up now and again. I'll settle for that until you're ready to leave Ray.'

'God, its déjà vu.'

'What?'

'Ed asked me the same question years ago when I was married to Barry.'

'So what happened?'

'I agreed, but there's one major difference here, I never loved Barry but I'm still in love with Ray.'

'So will you?'

'Will I what?'

'Come and stay with me now and again?'

'Haven't you listened to a word that I've been saying? I'll think about it as long as you realise that any relationship we may have will exist entirely on sex. I've got to go, I'm never late for work and now that I own half of Vic's agency, I'm not about to break the pattern.'

'I might call in later.'

'Please yourself, I'm going to have a coffee, then leave.'

'I'll make it.'

'Stop fussing, I'm perfectly capable of making a coffee.' Rosie was angry, not with Kevin, but with herself. How could she have let herself get into this situation? After drinking her coffee, she pecked Kevin on his cheek and left for work.

When she arrived home that evening, Ray was in his usual state, half cut. He didn't ask her where she'd been the night before; it was obvious that he hadn't realised she'd been away. He was unshaven and wearing clothes that he'd obviously slept in. Rosie gave him a kiss and then recoiled; his breath was stale.

'I'm going to make dinner, Ray, and then I think that we should have an early night, there's nothing on television.'

'Good idea.' Ray shuffled around in his armchair. Rosie looked gorgeous but then she always did. He grinned and then said, 'You're looking great, Rosie, I'll go and have a shower, then we'll have dinner, chill for a while and then go to bed.' He ran his hand over his chin saying, 'I'd better get rid of this stubble too, unless you like to feel prickles on your body.'

'No, I don't. I'll give you a shave; you'll probably cut yourself in your state. I'd better come up and help you shower too, otherwise you'll probably fall over and knock yourself out. I really don't fancy a night in A & E. Just let me get dinner on the go and then we'll shower together.'

'Sounds good to me, I can't remember when I spoiled you last.'

'Neither can I, Ray, you view your world through the bottom of a whiskey glass.'

'I've got to stop, I know I have, but it's hard. I only intend to have one, then I have another and pretty soon, the bottle's empty.'

'Ray.'

'Yep.'

'I love you.'

'Love you too, baby, and I will till the day I die.' Rosie smiled. Kevin was just a silly mistake.

A month later, she was sat behind her desk auditioning Dylan. When he walked in, Vic went blood red. 'I told you not to come back,' he blustered.

Rosie smiled sweetly. 'Excuse me, Vic, he's auditioning for me, I'll decide if he's talented or not. Why don't you take Lop out for a coffee.'

'This is my agency.'

'And I own half. Now, young man, tell me what you are going to do for me today.'

'I'm going to sing you one of my own songs.'

Rosie stared at the ginger-haired, brown-eyed, bearded young man before her; he was very slim and had an angry look about him. 'One won't be enough, I need you to cover other artists' songs too. Do you play an instrument?'

'Keyboard, drums, and guitar.'

'Versatile.'

'He's shit,' snapped Vic.

'I'll decide that,' replied Rosie.

'Fuck this.' Vic got to his feet and dragged Lop from the office.

'Okay, Dylan, do you have a demo tape, or photographs, or portfolio?'

'No, just myself.'

'Okay, show me what you can do.'

Dylan sang one of his own numbers, accompanying himself on acoustic guitar. Rosie wasn't impressed. 'Very nice, what else are you going to do?'

'*Get Back* by The Beatles, *Like A Rolling Song* by Bob Dylan, *Brown Sugar* by The Stones, anything you like.'

'Can you do me a bit of each?'

'Sure.' Dylan launched into song.

When he finished, Rosie sat back in her chair and met the inquisitive stare of the young man before her. 'It's difficult to place you,' she said.

'Okay, I'll go, everyone else thinks I'm shit,' said Dylan.

'No, Dylan, I like you, but I would like to see you perform in front of an audience. You're versatile too, and I think you've got something. However, getting you the correct venues isn't going to be easy. I have a friend who is having a birthday party on Saturday. She has booked a band through me and I would like you to do three of four numbers with them; they have a keyboard and drums unless you want to use your own.'

'All I own is this guitar.'

'So will you accept this gig?'

'Sure, I haven't got any others.'

'Fine, do you like Bob Dylan?'

'I was raised on him. My mother loved him, that's why she chose my name.'

'She had good taste.'

Dylan looked down. If Rosie knew who his mother was, she'd drop him on the spot. 'Guess so, what time do you want me?'

'About seven so that you can have a chat with the band; where do you live?'

'Up north, I just came here today for the audition.'

'Really, you are keen. Here's my card, come down the day before and I'll put you up. If you give a good account of yourself, I'll sign you up straight away.'

'Thanks.' Dylan shook Rosie's hand; he was overwhelmed. Rosie was a nice lady and he'd never forget that she'd given him a break.

Chapter Forty

Thirteen-year-old Bobby now had a terrific vocal range, and his dancing was brilliant, but his voice was now rivalling it. Steven had his own band and would often let Bobby front it. As Bobby had grown older, he appeared even more like Ed, even though everyone told him that Ray was his father. The only one to dispute this was Norma who informed him that he shared the same father as Susie and Deanne.

Bobby knew that his grandmother suffered from dementia so put her theory down to that. He was going to be performing at the party where Dylan was going to make his debut. He was quite excited as he was going to be performing his *Mr Beaujangles* routine. He'd studied Sammy Davis Junior's routine and had polished it to perfection.

On the night of the party, Dylan was on a high. He'd stayed overnight at Rosie's home and had been in awe of it. Her family had been most accommodating, and made him welcome; he'd even got to jam with Ray. He travelled with the family to the party feeling on top of the world. The last twenty four hours had whetted his appetite even more to achieve recognition. Stepping out of the car, he turned to Rosie, saying, 'I'll try not to let you down, I really will do my best.'

'You'll be fine,' replied Rosie, 'now let's get inside and meet the band.' Dylan was introduced to the leader of the band, and as the night wore on, he grew more and more excited. When his name was announced, he stepped up onto the stage and went straight into his first number, *Mr Tambourine Man*. It got a warm response, but his next number, *This Wheel's on Fire,* literally set the house alight. Everyone loved him. He followed up with *Brown Sugar* and ended with a Beatles medley. As he left the stage, people flocked around him, wanting a part of him.

'Aren't I the clever girl?' said Rosie, leaning back onto Ray.

'Yes, you've got a star in the making there.'

'Vic said he was shit.'

'The only shit that Vic understands is the kind that comes out of his arse, and I'm told that he doesn't like parting with that.'

'Mum, when am I going on?' Bobby was growing impatient.

'You're opening the second half, you're looking dapper.'

Bobby flashed his mother a beaming smile. 'You don't look so bad yourself,' he quipped. He couldn't wait to get out there and perform; he was never happier than when he was performing.

Later when he began to perform, Ray watched him intently. 'His father would be proud of him,' he said.

'You're his father.'

'Oh come on, Rosie, every single mannerism reminds me of Ed.'

'You are his father.'

'Well, whether I am or not, I'm proud of him. Whoever would have thought that the child from hell would turn into such a polished performer?'

'Why don't you get a DNA test done?'

'Because while I'm not sure, I've got half a chance. If I found out that I'm not, I'm defeated.'

'But I will always love you.'

'I know and that's wonderful. I've been a bastard of late, and I'm ashamed of myself.'

'It's the drink talking.'

'I know, and I need to address it. I'm trying, Rosie, honest I am.'

'You'll get there.' Rosie gave Ray a loving hug, wishing she could believe her own words. Sighing, she returned her attention to her son on stage.

Vic was used to getting his own way, and Rosie was proving a hard nut to crack. He wanted to disband Z Tones. He'd already sacked Ray, who'd become an embarrassment and had fallen off the stage and broken his arm. 'He's a piss head,' he snapped, 'he can't work at all now.'

'You encourage him to drink.' Rosie was angry.

'It loosens him up.'

'Yes, so loose that he fell apart and into the audience. God knows how long it'll take to get his arm right, it's not just broken, it's broken in two places.'

'Well, I'm disbanding Z Tones; they've been around since the sixties, and we're more than halfway through the nineties. We change drummers more often than I change my underwear.'

Lop sniggered. She had to prise Vic out of his underwear; he hated changing it. 'Maybe you should retire and let Rosie buy you out, then you'll see her fall flat on her face.'

Rosie slapped Lop around her face. 'How dare you, you poor excuse for a hooker; what do you know about show business? The only show that you know is showing yourself up. Neither you nor Vic know what you're doing. Have you told the band yet, Vic?'

'No, but Gerry's wanted out for years. He'll get work as a session musician and, as for the others, I couldn't care less what happens to them, they're a bunch of tossers.'

'Oh well, I guess that Kevin will go solo and I'll stay behind the desk.'

'No, I've got plans for both of you.'

'What if we don't like them?'

'Kevin will love it.'

'Have you asked him?'

'We've spoken about it many times. Rosie, let's talk about this. Lop, could you go out and get us some lunch?'

'Of course,' replied Lop; she was angry. Rosie had slapped her and Vic just acted as if nothing had happened. Still holding her face, she left the building.

Rosie gazed at the leering lump of lard before her; he was a revolting sight. 'So,' she said, 'what is your devious plan?'

'Well, Rosie, we can do it the easy way, or the hard way,' replied Vic.

Rosie sat down behind her desk and started leafing through a pile of contracts. 'And what is the easy way, Vic?'

'Agree to work with Kevin and become mega famous.'

'And the alternative?'

'Well, Rosie, do you remember when we filmed *Eden's Rose*?'

'Yes, get to the point.'

'Well, everyone wanted to know if you were the inspiration for the song.'

'I remember. I had reporters and photographers scaling my walls and staring in the windows, terrifying my kids. That's why I did a few interviews to get rid of them.'

'I told them that you and Ed had been childhood sweethearts, as you were, but we both hid the fact that your daughters had Ed as their father. As far as the press is concerned, your children have other fathers, Susie was Barry's, and the others were Ray's.'

'Yes, I did appreciate that, Vic.'

'Well you see, I could always call them back and give them the real story because when I launch you and Kevin, they will rear their heads once more and maybe the truth may emerge.'

'Before you go any further, Bobby is Ray's. I know what you've been saying to people.'

'Rubbish, Ray's a mine of information when he's drunk. Everyone knows whose Bobby's real father is. Does Bobby know, because if the story leaks, it might affect his friendship with Eddie? I gather that they're quite close. If Eddie found out it could cause all sorts of problems. How would he feel if he discovered that he has a talented half brother who was born the wrong side of the blanket? It would prove that Ed was fucking you whilst professing total dedication to his mother. I think that he might see you in a different light. By the way, how are he and Deanne getting on?'

'What's that got to do with you?'

'Well according to Kevin, she's moved in with Eddie.'

'They've always been close since they were children.'

'Maybe a bit too close, incest is not a pretty word.'

'How dare you, what has Kevin been saying?'

'Good headline though, Ed has sold more and more albums since his death. Just imagine picking up the newspaper and reading Eddie and Deanne Gold in sex scandal.'

'You bastard, it's all lies.'

'Maybe you don't watch your daughter close enough. I recall an article in the papers about a girl getting a teacher sacked.'

'She wasn't named.'

'Who?'

'The girl in the article.'

'You nearly tripped yourself up, you and I both know that it was Deanne. I know the reporter that did the article; right little Lolita, wasn't she?'

'You're lying.'

'Am I? Ray's very chatty when he's drunk. All your family secrets come out after he's had a few.'

'Deanne and Eddie wouldn't do such a thing. They know that they can't indulge in sexual intercourse.'

'And sometimes being told that you can't do something makes it all the more interesting and attractive. I think that Deanne could become a real little celebrity, and the press would thrive on an article like that. Ed would sell even more discs.'

'You would do that just to get me on board with Kevin?'

'I'd do more than that. You think I'm bluffing, but I assure you I am not.'

'More?'

'Yes, do you recall me being Candy's best man?'

'Yes.'

'Well I stayed around to wait for her because she hadn't come home and you thought that she might still return.'

'What's Candy got to do with it? The poor girl was lying in a shallow grave in Epping Forest.'

'No, but you see, my dear, previously Ray, in a pissed stupor, had told me about some home movies that you made with Ed.'

'That's in the past and private property.'

'It could be made public property. People would pay a fortune for footage like that, seeing as Ed's in it with his *Eden's Rose,*' laughed Vic. He had her licked.

'Surely Ray didn't give you the footage?' Rosie's heart sank.

'No, my dear, but while I was waiting for Candy, I had a look around and found a box full of films under your bed. I was intrigued, Ray had made them sound fascinating. I couldn't resist peeping.'

'But the films are in the box. Ray often watches them, it seems to turn him on in a strange way. I'll keep the box locked in future. Better still, I'll burn them, and that'll foil your sick plan.'

'Too late, I took them while everyone was at the church.'

'You're lying; they're still in the box.'

'And also in my possession. I didn't come straight to the reception, did I? I popped in to see Al Simpkins and got copies done, and then the following day I visited you and put the films back. Boy, what a sex life you and Ed had; there's even Ed referring to your teenage years. You must have been red hot for each other in those days. This is class stuff, and I love all those outfits that you were wearing, they were very titillating. There were some great close ups too, and I'm not talking about your face. As for the oral sex and the sixty nines, what can I say.'

Rosie stood up and whacked Vic around his head, knocking his glasses from his face. He staggered around disorientated and then flopped down into his chair. 'You can slap me around all you like, but one word from me and those films go public. I might even send one to Eddie and Deanne; they could learn how to improve their lovemaking by watching it.'

'Vic, that's obscene.'

'So are the films; they're the best that I've seen, and could make me a fortune. I doubt that your family will talk to you for a while, it could cause a rift.'

'Vic, please don't do this.'

'I won't, my dear, I don't want you upset, I want the best for you. I need you and Kevin on board, you'll be the greatest thing since sliced bread.'

'How long will this contract run for?'

'As long as I want it to. Kevin's a nice guy. It must be so miserable for you being married to a drunk; most drunks can't get it up and I don't suppose Ray's any different. Actually, when Lop returns, I could send her home after lunch and we could close the office. I've got some tablets in my drawer that help me to maintain an erection.'

'You are disgusting.'

'I've been called worse, that's mild.'

'I'll speak to Kevin and make sure he never signs for you again.'

'Please yourself, but if you talk him out of signing, your films will go public faster than you can say Jack Robinson. Ah, here's Lop, she's laden with goodies.'

The conversation ended, and after lunch, Rosie approached Lop. 'Can I have a word in private?'

'Yes, I need to freshen up.'

Vic stared at the two women. 'Off to the khazi again? You women spend most of your time there, you're not having girl on girl fun are you?'

'If we were, we wouldn't tell you, sicko,' retorted Rosie.

Jenny was at her wits end, Duncan was dying slowly and very painfully. Dylan was now making a mint, thanks to Rosie's faith in him. He had work abroad, work in London, and a recording contract. For years, Dylan had never got on with his mother; he was the son of a drifter who had disappeared without a trace. His mother was stupid. For years he'd watched as Ed had used and abused her. He'd blamed Jenny for splitting him and Rosie up and had never forgiven her. Often Dylan would cower in the corner of his bedroom in the caravan, listening to the verbal abuse hurled at his mother. Ed terrified him and, in the end, Jenny sent him to live with her parents so that she could continue her affair with a man who would never love her. Once Ed had gone out of her life, Dylan had resumed living with his mother, but he never forgave her for choosing Ed over him. As he'd grown, he'd got into a shed load of trouble, and if there was a fight, he'd be in the midst of it. He beat a school mate to within an inch of his life, and had attacked a school teacher.

When Jenny met Duncan, it was the first time that Dylan had had any stability in his life. At first, he rebelled about someone giving him orders, but as time passed, he gelled with his stepfather, realising that the orders were for his own good. However, it wasn't long before Dylan ended up in jail for beating a man up and being in possession of a fire arm. He'd have used it too, had it been loaded. Now his life was on the up, but Jenny had to be kept in the background, because if her identity was found out things could change, and Rosie might withdraw her support as Dylan's manager.

Jenny wondered where her life was going. Her husband was dying and her son didn't want to know her, plus she still pined for Ray. She'd written to him every day and sent them to the office, but Vic had been told to destroy anything with a Scottish postmark on it. At first, Ray had returned the lot, but as time passed he allowed Vic to deal with things, and Vic returned every letter without a stamp and wrote across each one, 'not at this address'. In the end, Jenny got the message and stopped writing for a while until she came up with another plan. She was determined to get back into his life one way or another.

Chapter Forty-One

'You're not happy working here, are you Lop?' asked Rosie.

'No, but it's what my husband wants and I must obey him. He should retire; he can hardly see and he will need surgery soon.'

'I would like to buy him out; can he be persuaded?'

'I doubt it, but I wish that he could. We could enjoy his retirement and travel, maybe even move to Thailand. I miss my family so much.'

'I'll pay you the asking price, plus more, so we could both benefit from this.'

'I could ask him again.'

'When he loses his eyesight completely, he won't know what he's signing, he trusts you.'

'It's underhand.'

'Lop, Vic's name is underhand, think of yourself, he's had his life and fucked it up; you have your life in front of you. Shall we shake on it?'

Lop extended her hand, and Rosie took it; both women intended to bring Vic to his knees. They would have to wait until he was completely blind, but they could wait, revenge was sweet. They returned to Vic, and Rosie asked if she could leave early. 'Why?'

'I need to see Kevin. You've got a short memory, Vic. How can we get an act together if we don't meet up?'

'I could get him to come here.'

'It's more comfortable at his place, if you know what I mean.'

Vic went red in the face. 'Oh yes, you go, I'll ring him and tell him you're on your way.'

'Thanks, Vic,' and Rosie picked up her bag and coat and left the office.

Rosie's visit to see Kevin was anything but putting a repertoire together, she wanted to check up on her daughter. Kevin was overjoyed to see her. He had worked with her on stage since their night of passion but hadn't tried his luck again as he hadn't liked being branded a mistake. He knew that Ray had been sacked, and wondered if Rosie's visit was just to cry on his shoulder. He'd offer it if another night of passion followed. Rosie relayed Vic's suggestion of a duo, and said that she'd agreed to give it a try. She also mentioned Vic's remarks on Deanne and Eddie, and Kevin was horrified.

'Lies,' he snapped, 'do you think that I would allow it?'

'No, but where does Deanne sleep?'

'At the end of the corridor, next door to Eddie.'

'He used to sleep next door to you.'

'Yes, but he moved when Deanne moved in, saying that as they kept late hours, they didn't want to wake me. I thought that was considerate.'

'Or crafty, you seem to forget who their father was. He was the craftiest thing on two legs.'

'Surely you don't think...?'

'I don't know what to think any more, I need to find out if Vic's rantings are true.'

'You can't believe anything that he says.'

'Well, I need to put my mind at rest. I'll ring Ray and tell him that I won't be home tonight.'

'Ring him later, by then he won't even know his own name, let alone yours.'

'Don't mock, it's not funny. Ada's staying with us at the moment, as Alf's in hospital.'

'You're wasted on Ray; what the fuck's up with him?'

'He's an alcoholic who has now become impotent, plus he has a broken arm.'

'Shame' replied Kevin, the night ahead looked promising.

Deanne and Eddie arrived home about three in the morning. Rosie heard the car door slam and, soon after, the front door open and close, followed by two sets of footsteps ascending the stairs, and laughter. She lay beside Kevin who was sleeping like a baby owing to the fact that his night of passion had worn him out. Deciding to give the couple time, Rosie lay on her back with her mind in turmoil. For several years, Norma had said that Ed was angry, and when Rosie had asked why, Norma had replied, 'He's doing her.' At the time, Norma's words hadn't made sense; who was doing who? Obviously, Norma's dementia had moved on to another stage. Rosie had shrugged it off until now, but Norma's words were sending chills through her.

She waited another twenty minutes to let the couple settle, and then got out of bed and tiptoed down the corridor towards Eddie's room. At first there was silence, and then Deanne's voice could be heard crying, 'Harder, harder.' Rosie froze. Maybe Eddie hadn't returned, and Deanne had brought someone else home with her. If that was the case, then Rosie had no right to spy on her daughter. She was above the age of consent, but then why was she in Eddie's room? Eddie's door was part open and a bedside lamp with a pink shade was still on. Rosie could see her daughter's face reflected in the mirror that was just above the headboard, her eyes were closed and she was straddled across a man that Rosie couldn't see. Kevin crept up behind Rosie just as she stepped back intending to return to his room. She cried out, and Deanne's eyes snapped open, she turned her head and locked eyes with her mother, but she wasn't about to stop what she was doing for anyone and continued to ride her lover out.

Rosie withdrew and returned to Kevin's room, sobbing. She threw herself across his bed crying, 'Does she usually bring men home?'

'No, Eddie always brings her home; he likes to make sure that she arrives home safe.'

'Then who's she with; is there anyone else living here?'

'No.'

'Then Vic was right.'

'Calm down, Rosie.'

'Calm down.' Rosie fixed her eyes on the huge blow up photo of Cathy above the headboard. 'Are you proud of your son; is this what you want for him?'

'My mother was always proud of me,' said a voice from the doorway. Eddie stood framed in the doorway with his arm around Deanne who looked anything but guilty.

'How could you both?' cried Rosie.

'What do you mean?' snapped Deanne. 'The words pot and kettle come to mind. Ray's at home with a broken arm, probably pissed to the hilt, and you're sharing Kevin's bed.'

'But you share the same father; you know you can't have sex.'

'Why not? We've different mothers.'

'Let's take this downstairs,' said Kevin, 'this is getting us nowhere; you two should be ashamed of yourselves. Rosie's got enough on her plate without you adding to it.'

'Then she shouldn't snoop,' cried Deanne, folding her arms.

'Dee, stop it, Kevin's right, your mum has had a shock.'

Deanne shrugged her shoulders. 'Okay, but I'm not ashamed, you can't choose who you fall in love with. I love Eddie and he loves me.'

Eddie said nothing. Deanne didn't feel guilty, but he felt as guilty as sin.

Downstairs, things were stalemate. Deanne was unrepentant as her mother said, 'When did this all start?'

'At Uncle Rusty's caravan; you split us up and we wanted to keep sleeping together.'

'Russell let you share a bed? No wonder you wanted to visit him at weekends; he told me that you'd have separate beds.'

'We did, but I used to get out of mine and get into Eddie's. One night when we cuddled up, I could feel that his thingy was hard so I put my hand down the front of his pyjamas and he had an accident.'

'Dee.' Eddie was wishing the ground would swallow him up.

'Well, she wants to know so I'm telling her, and after that we stopped visiting the caravan as Uncle Rusty went to Ibiza with his family and stayed there for a few months. Anyway, we didn't need him any more because when Eddie stayed with us, I'd wait until everyone was asleep and then tiptoe across the landing into his room. I'd set the alarm clock and, as soon as it went off, I'd go back to my own room.'

'So it was going on under my own roof?' Rosie was stunned.

'Yes but we didn't do much, it wasn't serious stuff. Then a while later I had my little scene with Mr Pike; shame he got the sack. I was thirteen then and I learnt a lot from him, and Eddie enjoyed himself when I tried it out on him.'

'Dee, shut up.' Eddie now wanted to die as Deanne continued.

'When Susie got back with Steven after Vidal had died, we started double dating with Steven's younger brother Michael. I experimented a bit with him. He knew plenty but I didn't have sexual intercourse with him; it was Eddie that I loved and I wanted him to be my first. I waited and it was worth it.'

Rosie's head was spinning. 'I didn't even know that you'd dated Michael, so how long did you wait before you had full sex?'

'I was fifteen, and Eddie was still fourteen.'

'Oh God, I feel ill.'

'Well, you did ask me. Look, I know that this has been a shock but I've no intention of getting pregnant; I'm on the pill. I had been thinking of getting sterilized, but Eddie said not to just in case anything happened to him and I met someone else and wanted a family. He offered to have a vasectomy but I told him the same thing. We do know what we're doing, we love each other, always have, so surely you can forgive us? You can't choose who you love in this life, and I know that if my dad were still alive, and Cathy was dead, you and he would have married by now, Ray or no Ray.'

'I'm really sorry,' said Eddie, 'but I do love Dee, and I don't want anyone else. We didn't mean to cause you any pain.'

'I should have seen this coming and stopped it,' replied Rosie. 'I'm the one who should bear all the guilt.'

'You couldn't have stopped it; we can't live without each other, and wouldn't want to. I'm tired, and we should go to bed. We've all got work in the morning, except Kevin. Tell you what, Mum, call in sick in the morning and spend the day with him. He'll put a smile on your face and then when you go home to misery guts, you'll be refreshed. Come on Eddie, bedtime.'

The couple went upstairs, leaving a dazed and confused Rosie. 'I'm a hypocrite,' she said. 'I did all sorts of things with Ed when I was a teen. Deanne is indeed her father's daughter; she sets her own rules and is not for turning. Where do we go from here?'

'Bed, you're tired and in a state of shock.'

'But I was eighteen when I lost my virginity, and I was out of it when it happened. In some ways I can identify with my daughter. Ed was my first and I wouldn't have wanted it to have been anyone else.'

'But you weren't related. If Eddie had been my son, I would have given him a good hiding.'

'It wouldn't have done any good, you heard what they said. God help them in their future; if anyone finds out, it'll be plastered all over the newspapers.'

'But nobody will find out; we're the only ones that have been told. I'm not going to say anything, neither are you, and as for Vic, he's just guessing.'

'I should go home.'

'No, you're not in a fit state to drive. Come on, let's get back to bed. Take the day off tomorrow and I'll spoil you, God knows you need it.'

'You reckon?'

'Yes I do, you look shattered, I'll carry you up to bed,' and with a sparkle in his eyes and excitement over what tomorrow could bring, Kevin swept Rosie up into his arms and carried her upstairs.

Chapter Forty Two

Two years later

Ray now drank all day, and Rosie and Kevin were conducting a full on affair behind his back. Vic had been right about the couple being a smash, everyone wanted them. Rosie found it rather funny; she was now fifty-two and Kevin forty-two, so they were hardly young jet setters. Kevin was on cloud nine, believing that at some stage Rosie would leave Ray. He regularly sang Dan Hartman's *I Can Dream About You,* and relayed to the audience that that was what he did when his girlfriend was absent. He also performed *Time After Time*, and sang it to Rosie both on and off stage. He'd never felt better in his entire life.

Jenny was still watching her husband clinging to life and reading her son's reviews; he wasn't in the big league but Rosie had certainly helped his career along. Sometimes Jenny thought about ringing her up and thanking her, but she resisted as she realised that it could jeopardise his career and, besides, she hadn't given up on Ray, so Rosie was still her rival.

Time after time, Rosie arranged for Ray to get help, but although she arranged appointments for him, he never showed up for them. She was more like his carer these days, when she wasn't touring, as he rarely did anything for himself any more. Several times, Rosie had accompanied Ray for doctor's appointments, but as soon as his name was called, he would refuse to go in.

Vic had had surgery for bowel cancer, and his health and eyesight were failing. Lop was his eyes, and she now had power of attorney which she abused, making her bank balance grow even larger. It was now only a matter of time before Vic would be cleaned out completely and, before long, she was going to put the wheels in motion for Rosie to buy him out.

Bobby now fronted Steven's band on a permanent basis; he still worked in musicals but always found time to fit gigs in. He was in great demand and still only fifteen. Fourteen-year-old Raydon was studying photography, and was benefitting from Michael's help who was now working for a top magazine. Raydon took many photos of Ray when he was paralytic, hoping that it might shame him into giving up alcohol, but even that didn't work. Nothing got through to him apart from a deluge of phone calls from some lady who repeatedly told him that Rosie was having an affair.

About the same time, flowers began to get delivered to their home and, at first, Ray took it all as a joke, but after a while he began to wonder if there was any truth in it.

One morning, when a delivery of flowers arrived, he questioned Rosie. Slumped in his chair with a glass of whiskey in his hand, he muttered, 'Are you having an affair? I'm getting dozens of phone calls from a woman saying that you are.'

'Who's the lucky man then?'

'I don't know, you tell me.'

'Would it matter if I was?'

'Of course, we've got a great sex life.'

'You haven't touched me for years.'

'Rubbish, we had a good go last night.'

'Last night, I was working, and when I came in you were blind drunk.'

'Don't tell me what I did; I'm not losing my marbles.'

'We're ex-directory, not many people have this number, you're imagining it.'

'I'm not; maybe Vic gave it out. This woman keeps banging on about you having an affair. She says that she's a friend.'

'Some friend, thanks for the flowers.'

'I didn't send you any. I don't go out and I certainly wouldn't buy over the phone; there's enough credit card fraud going on.'

'Really, maybe it's a fan; there are good and bad ones, Ray.'

'Or maybe it's your fancy man.'

'I haven't got one.'

'You must have. If you're right and we haven't had sex for years, I can't imagine you going without it for that length of time, although I think you're lying. We had a great session last night.'

'We didn't. You haven't changed your clothes for a week, and you've even slept in them.'

'I change my clothes every day.'

'If you don't change the ones that you're wearing soon, they'll walk away from you on their own.'

'Fuck off, I'll change them when I'm ready. Why do you need a fancy man, wasn't I good enough last night?'

'Ray, when I came in last night, you were watching an episode of Eurotrash that you'd recorded weeks ago.'

'I don't watch Eurotrash.'

'You did last night,' said Mary, walking into the room, 'you even asked me to watch it with you.'

'I did not, you're both trying to belittle me in front of Raydon. He sat up with me last night, didn't you, son?'

'No,' replied Raydon, 'but you were watching Eurotrash.'

'What is it with my family, and why aren't you at school?'

'Free period.'

'Didn't have them in my day, kids are spoilt nowadays. I was working at fourteen; why don't you get a job in a cobblers like I did? It's a good job, you meet lots of people, especially birds; stupid idea this photography lark.'

'Michael does well out of it.'

'The cobblers was good enough for me, should be for you too.'

'Shop's probably closed down now,' said Rosie.

'That's it, stick your fucking nose in; who asked you?'

'Don't talk to Mum like that.'

'I'll talk to her how I like. Did you send her flowers?'

'No.'

'Must be her fancy man then.'

'She hasn't got one.'

'How would you know?'

'Because she loves you, can't think why though, she could do so much better.'

'You cheeky little bugger, I'll whip you for that.' Ray attempted to stand up and fell to the floor. 'Help me up Rosie,' he cried.

'No way, you're drunk already and it's not even midday.'

'I'm not drunk, I'm suffering from vertigo, I need a doctor.'

'You need to stop drinking,' cried Rosie, heading for the kitchen. Ray partly crawled to the kitchen and hauled himself upright by leaning on the kitchen units. He managed a few steps, then fell forward smashing his head against the tiled wall. Blood spurted from his chin, and Mary, Rosie, and Raydon helped him to his feet and supported his weight as they led him back to his armchair. Raydon picked up his camera and began taking photos.

Ray swore as the camera repeatedly flashed. 'Bloody, fucking kid,' he yelled, 'why don't you go and get Bobby to come and dance round me, you'd get a better shot.'

'He's at school.'

'Schools wasted on him. He can't add up without a calculator.'

'Neither can most kids these days.'

'It wasn't like that in my day.'

'Those were the days, my friend, we thought they'd never end,' sang Raydon.

'Will you stop flashing that camera in my eyes?' Ray cried. He attempted to stand up once more, lost his balance, half spun round and crashed to the floor with his full weight on his shoulder. He cried out in agony, 'Rosie, I've broken my arm again.'

'It's your own fault.'

'You callous bitch. That's it, walk away to your fancy man, see if I care.'

'Okay, I will.'

'Rosie, come back. I didn't mean it, my arm's broken.'

'Okay, I'll ring for an ambulance.'

'I don't want one, just get me to my chair. Raydon, be a good boy and help me up.' Raydon helped his father up and back into his armchair, and then he burst out laughing.

'What's funny?' cried Rosie.

'His biceps moved, he looks like he's been doing weights, it's in the wrong place.'

Ray looked down at his arm. 'Get the doctor,' he screeched.

Rosie was now heartily sick of all this and was about to pick up the receiver when the phone rang. 'Mr Lynne, your wife is definitely having an affair. You deserve so much better; you could be with someone who would care about you, someone who would never cheat on you.'

Rosie had had enough. Ray hadn't been imagining it after all. 'Now listen to me, you conniving bitch, Ray is very sick and doesn't need the likes of you making him worse. Nobody is having an affair, so why don't you reveal who you are, you coward, and who gave you this phone number? Do you live in Scotland, because if you do, I've got a pretty good idea who you are? Ray is not interested in you, and our marriage is rock solid. I'll tell you one thing, if I ever come face to face with you, I'll rip your heart out, and by the way, this line is tapped, now fuck off.'

Ray could be heard in the background shouting, 'Go Rosie, go, put a few fucks into her whoever she is, the evil bitch.'

The caller hung up and Rosie called the doctor who arrived about thirty minutes later. He viewed his patient. 'You've been in the wars, Ray,' he said.

'I know, I'm suffering from vertigo but everyone says that I'm drunk.'

'You are drunk, Ray, and your face is cut too. One day, you'll fall down and not get up again, and your liver must be suffering with your alcoholism. I've made several appointments for you to help you with your drinking and you never turn up for counselling. This is ludicrous. If you can't do it for yourself, do it for your family.'

'What family? Rosie's always in the office or touring, my eldest daughter is shacked up with her boyfriend, or should I say fiancé to use a better word, my youngest daughter has moved out, Bobby never stops singing and dancing, and Raydon thinks that he's David Bailey, plus the mother-in-law is nuts and the nanny is Irish.'

'Well I can't fix your bicep, Ray, you've ruptured it, so you need to visit the trauma clinic. You could have surgery, but if you're not prepared to give up the alcohol, no surgeon will touch you.'

'Will it repair itself?'

'No.'

'So I've got to walk around with my bicep in my elbow for the rest of my life? Can't you strap it up?'

'It wouldn't work, the bicep will go back if you follow exercises at the trauma clinic, but it will continue to pop out at any given time.'

'This is bad, the next thing that I'll know is that my arse will fall off and I'll be wearing my bollocks in my socks. Look at my bicep, Charles Atlas eat your heart out, have you got anything to put lead in my pencil? I can't get it up lately.'

'Lately, it's been two years,' quipped Rosie.

'It's alcohol that gives you brewers droop, you need to give it up,' said the doctor.

'I will, but I need to do it myself, I don't need a counsellor.'

'You can't,' snapped Rosie, 'you've tried and you always end up falling off the wagon.'

'I can, I'm just not ready.'

'Well I can't do anything, my hands are tied.' Ray's doctor shook his head sadly.

'So's my bicep, it's in knots, fine doctor you are.'

'I could give you pain killers, but it's not a good idea as morphine and alcohol don't mix, sometimes the combination becomes like a form of poison.'

'I don't care, you've got to give me something.'

'Be this on your own head then. Rosie, you're my witness that I warned him; if he gets ill, take him to hospital, and they'll sort him out.'

'Message understood, he told you to do it,' said Rosie, wishing that she was in Kevin's warm embrace.

The doctor took a syringe from his bag and seconds later pumped Ray full of painkiller. 'You'll sleep well, Ray, but don't attempt to go upstairs.'

'Not much point if I can't get it up.'

'Ray, stop being so crude. Don't worry, doctor, I'll make him a bed up down here; we don't want him breaking anything else.'

Raydon was chuckling away. He'd carried on taking photos, and even had one of the doctor administering the pain killer to Ray. 'People will think I'm a junkie,' snapped Ray, 'if I could stand up, I'd break that camera.'

'I'm off,' laughed Raydon, 'free period's over.'

Jenny was fuming. She'd thought that the phone calls were a good idea, and had persuaded her neighbour to make them while she had listened in on the extension. She'd been shocked when Rosie had picked up the phone, and was infuriated that Ray had been egging Rosie on in the background. Dylan had unwittingly supplied both Rosie's address and phone number. Jenny had been tidying up his room and had gone through his desk. She'd found his address book and copied the details down. Duncan was now at death's door, and as Jenny was his sole beneficiary, she would cop everything. Once the grieving period was over, she'd hand the cottage back to the landlord. She smiled to herself and arranged for more flowers to be sent to Rosie. She needed Ray to believe that Rosie had a lover; it was paramount if she was ever to get him back. Rosie had incensed her by saying that she'd rip her heart out, and she'd pay dearly for that remark. Her life was forfeit, she would suffer greatly and then so would her daughters; they were Ed's and she now hated him too for ruining her life. She was fifty two years old and living in the past. In her sick twisted mind, she wanted two things, Ray in her arms, and Rosie in her coffin.

A month later, Duncan passed away leaving Jenny financially secure. Part of her mourned him, and part of her felt relief; his illness had destroyed both of them. Duncan had been her saviour until the illness had taken him over and, just like in her teens, Jenny had to watch him slip away like her first love. Terry had died within a year of contacting the cancer; his young life had been snuffed out just before his sixteenth birthday, but with poor Duncan, he'd lingered for years and decayed before Jenny's eyes. After the funeral, Jenny stayed on for a month and then left Scotland. She rang her mother, saying that she felt they both needed each other and wanted to come home. In truth, her obsession with Ray was consuming her, and drawing her to her home town.

Rosie's patience had reached the end of the line; Ray had sunk to an all time low and refused all counselling and medical help. Rosie still loved him, but realised that now was the time for drastic action. Her cousin who lived in Spain was coming to England to look for a house. Rosie extended an invite, saying that the house would be empty as she was taking her family to Tenerife for a break; she hadn't been out there for eighteen months and wanted to check on her properties. 'When you get your flight dates, let me know, I'll book my flights for the same day. How long are you staying?'

'About a month.'

'Fine, I'll lap up the sunshine for a month.'

'Thanks Rosie, you're a gem; it'll be great being the lady of the house in your place, and my girls will be so excited.'

'My pleasure, bye.'

'Bye, Rosie.'

Placing the phone back onto its cradle, Rosie gazed at Ray who was slumped in his armchair with a bottle of whiskey by his side. She nudged him, 'Lynne's coming to stay for a month.'

'The fuck she is, I can't stand her. She hasn't got a pot to piss in, and she puts on all those airs and graces. I can't stand having her around, and as for those two stuck up daughters of hers, well they need a good fucking.'

'No doubt they get it now and again; anyway you won't be here.'

'Why, where am I going?'

'You can either come to Tenerife with me and the family, or go and stay with Ada.'

'How can I fly like this? I wouldn't make it.'

'You've got a few weeks before Lynne arrives, so there's plenty of time to sober up.'

'You bitch. All you think about is yourself. Are you taking your fancy man?'

'Haven't got one.'

'Well, the house is like a florists.'

'I know, maybe they're from some crazed fan.'

'It's not funny, Rosie, you could be right. I'd kill myself if anything happened to you.'

'You don't even notice that I'm here most of the time.'

'Because you're not, you're either at the office or touring.'

'Work is good therapy. If you could sober up, you could join me every day at the office. I could find you work; I do own half a share in the place, and Vic is practically blind.'

Ray sat up. That appealed to him; he hated being out of work. Since Z Tones had disbanded, he'd hardly worked at all, and nowadays he was too drunk to function. He staggered as he got to his feet. He recalled having a massive row the night before with Rosie, although he couldn't recall what it was about.

Rosie remembered it only too well; she'd gone to bed and drifted off to sleep. A few hours later, she'd heard a crash downstairs and went down to investigate. Ray was in the kitchen, surrounded by broken crockery. Rosie was angry as Ray was protesting that he hadn't eaten for weeks and wanted a plate. She had retorted that he'd polished off a large roast dinner a few hours earlier, but Ray denied it and continued searching for a plate. Rosie wasn't too bothered about the plates. Ray smashed everything these days, and she had a cupboard full of them as they owned a dish washer. And then she saw it; her beloved Pyrex 'Country Rose' gravy boat which now had a broken handle. She burst into tears; it couldn't be replaced.

Norma had had a full set of the Pyrex design in the sixties, and Rosie had loved it and bought a plate a week to add to her mother's collection. The line had been discontinued, and neither Norma nor Rosie had been able to purchase the gravy boat. It was Gary who had found one and presented it to her. She'd been overjoyed and had added it to the set which was now completed. Now it lay on the floor broken, and Ray's excuse that he needed the plate that the gravy boat stood on was a feeble one. Ray had yelled that he'd buy Rosie another one.

'Not possible,' cried Rosie. 'Gary bought it for me, it's a discontinued line. Can you get him back for me too? You're a lost cause, Ray, I want a divorce.'

Ray's reaction to that was to walk over to the washing machine, open the door and relieve himself in it. Then he let out a yell; his bicep had popped out again. He dropped to the floor clutching his arm and sprawled on the floor. Rosie gazed at him with disgust, and then left him to it. She needed sleep, lots of it. About an hour later, she was lying in bed, unable to sleep, when she heard Ray coming up the stairs. Then there was another yell, obviously the bicep had popped again. There was the sound of someone falling down the stairs so, getting out of bed, Rosie went to the foot of the stairs where Ray was lying with a silly, happy look on his face. This was the final straw; she wanted out.

Chapter Forty-Three

Jenny wasted no time after her return to Seven Kings; she made a few phone calls to various nasties and met them in a local pub. Most of them were lowlifes with no principles or consciences, but even they shied away from the type of killing that Jenny wanted, branding her a sicko. Then one night in a boozer in Whitechapel, she ran into Adrian and his brother Larry. They couldn't help her but they knew a man who could. His name was Luke; he was a butcher by day and a hit man by night. 'We've worked with him a few times,' said Larry, 'but most of the time he works alone. However, I think he would need our help on this one because you need a lookout, someone to knock the old man out, someone to lock the boys in their room, or tie them up, and Luke to do the bloody stuff. We don't mind cutting the girls' throats but dissection does not form part of our line of work.'

'The thing is, can you find the money for all of this? Luke doesn't come cheap, neither do we for that matter, but we get pleasure from our work so we don't expect top dollar,' said Adrian. 'I reckon this will come to thousands, many thousands.'

'I have been left a lot of money. My husband died a short while ago and he has left me comfortable.'

'Why can't we kill the lot of 'em? It would make more sense.'

'Because Ray and the boys are not to be harmed; deal with them as nicely as possible.'

'Nicely! We're hit men.'

'I know but they are not to be harmed.'

'So, if you're serious about this, I'll make a phone call. Are you?'

'Deadly serious.'

'Fine.' Adrian picked up his mobile phone and dialled a number. Minutes later, he finished his phone call and said, 'Okay, let's go.'

'Go where?'

'To meet Luke, but you'll have to be blindfolded.'

'Why?' Jenny's nerves were wavering.

'Because he doesn't want anyone knowing where he lives.' Larry raised his eyes to high heaven, wondering if this woman knew what she was doing. If she didn't, her life would be forfeit as well as her victims. They walked outside to the car park and, once inside the brothers' car, Jenny was blindfolded and the car drove away.

The Lynne family left for Tenerife, minus Ray, on the day that Lynne and her girls moved in. Ray moved in with Ada and Alf, telling Rosie that he would call time on his drinking. 'I know you will. Your parents won't put up with the shit that you've given me. You'd better get your act together, Ray, or I will divorce you. This is not fair on anyone, especially Bobby and Raydon, who witness your behaviour daily,' said Rosie.

'We'll sort him out,' said Alf, 'he'll be a new man by the time you return.'

'I'll settle for the old one, the one I fell in love with,' replied Rosie. Goodbyes were exchanged, and Rosie and her entourage headed for Stansted Airport.

Kevin was mortified that he hadn't had an invite to Tenerife; he was obsessed with Rosie and had seen this holiday as a chance for them to be together for a whole month. Rosie had told him that if Ray didn't clean up his act, she'd be filing for divorce, making his heart sing, so why had she left him behind? The thought struck him that maybe she was thinking of getting rid of him as well as Ray and, ten days later, unable to bear the pain of separation, he booked himself on a flight for Tenerife.

Vic and Lop were studying Dylan's track record, or at least Lop was, Vic's sight was gone by now. Vic had hated Dylan on sight in the days when he was partially sighted. Rosie had overruled him and made him a star, but the whole thing had gone to Dylan's head and he was now buying into sex, drugs, and rock and roll. He loved the booze and these days was rarely sober. Bookings were falling; he was being turned away from venues, and the last straw came when he got banged up for beating up a security guard. Rosie was away and, as far as Vic was concerned, he was acting in the interest of the agency. He decided to let Dylan ride out the rest of his contract, and then end it; he had unwittingly signed his own death warrant.

Rosie and her family chilled out in Tenerife. The boys spent most of their days at the Aquapark, and nights at the clubs. Mary had come along for the ride, and the sweet Irish girl was overawed with everything; it was like another world for her. The climate, shops, and nightlife offered everything. She chaperoned Norma most of the time, and went out with the boys on her nights off, promising Rosie that she'd keep an eye on them.

Rosie found that funny. Raydon could be chaperoned, but Bobby, no way. He'd been sexually active since the age of twelve, pinning a class mate up against a wall behind the bike sheds and taking her standing up. Since that day, he'd chased everything in a skirt, especially the chorus line in musicals. Rosie knew that he was a chip off the old block, and it was now obvious who his father was. Introduce him to a pretty girl and it was only a matter of time before the girl was flat on her back. He was having a whale of a time in Tenerife, but just like his father before him, he had the sense to take precautions. There was no way that he was putting a girl up the spout, or catching a sexually transmitted disease.

413

On their stay, Rosie ran into an old friend in the shape of Mick Fraser. He was working the bars on the island. Rosie had always been attracted to him since the first day that she'd met him at her interview with Doug Trent. When the Shelltones were formed, Doug had let her make them her baby; she'd chosen their name, dressed their image and, overnight, made them stars. She'd been in contact with Mick right up to the time of his dreadful car crash, but then they lost touch. Ed replaced Mick as front man, and Rosie was married to Barry. Now there was nothing standing in their way. She was on holiday in the process of thinking about filing for divorce, and Mick was a free agent playing in all the bars. They lost no time in getting it on, until a week later when Mick left for Gran Canaria to fulfil a contract. They said their goodbyes, with Rosie feeling on cloud nine; Mick had been a brilliant lover.

Eddie and Deanne went to Lloro Parque to see Tom the huge tortoise, and Eddie now had dreams of opening up a tortoise sanctuary at his mansion. He'd taken the breeding programme back from Rosie three years ago. She'd done a brilliant job in hatching, raising, and selling the Sulcata babies, but what with the touring and working in the office, plus the fact that she was having difficulties with Ray, it made Eddie feel that she'd done more than enough. Wacky and Daisy were still breeding, and the mansion had huge grounds, just the place for a tortoise sanctuary. Eddie was now a fully qualified reptile vet, and the thought of many abandoned tortoises roaming the grounds filled him with excitement.

Susie and Steven were going through a bad patch; they hadn't married, even though they'd got engaged years ago. Susie felt that Steven was tight, but Steven believed that he was just being careful. Susie wanted to be spoilt, and although Steven did it with love, he didn't follow through with money. He'd had a pretty poor upbringing until Cathy had married Ed, and he'd not forgotten it. He was determined not to go back to those times; he'd known what it was like to go hungry and had installed this into Maisie Rose when she threw a tantrum. Susie didn't know what poverty meant. She'd been spoilt and indulged by Barry and Rosie, and later by Rosie and Ed, and she just looked on Steven as mean. Walking through the streets of Los Cristianos, she experienced déjà vu; she'd been fifteen when she'd met Vidal and began dancing with the devil. Vidal had consumed and nearly murdered her. Senor Martinez lived in Spain permanently, so there was no chance of bumping into him. The family had been strange. Susie had never met Vidal's mother, who hadn't even shown at her wedding, or even when Maisie Rose had been born. Senor Martinez had shown no interest in her. The only one that had stayed close was Luisa, Vidal's so-called sister, and she'd only hung around so that she could continue her love affair with Vidal.

Susie walked through Los Cristianos with Maisie Rose skipping along at her side. The child was a beautiful little girl with dark brown hair, a cheeky grin, and brown eyes that sparkled with fun. Susie, Steven, and Maisie Rose were staying in the Costamar for the month so they could have some privacy. She was happy about that as the apartment on Paloma Beach was very crowded.

It was Deanne who let Kevin in. She was surprised to see him, but relieved. Rosie's fling with Mick hadn't gone unnoticed, and she was a bit worried that her mother might bump into some other associate. With Kevin here, it couldn't happen. 'Mum's taking a nap,' she said, 'there's some champagne in the fridge, nod nod, wink wink.'

'Good thinking,' replied Kevin, and about five minutes later, headed for Rosie's room with the bottle in an ice bucket, and two glasses. He opened the bedroom door; the room was in darkness and he could make out the outline of Rosie's body in the bed. Stripping off his clothes, he got into bed after placing the champagne and glasses on the bedside cabinet. He nuzzled into Rosie's neck. 'That you, Ray?' she murmured.

Kevin was hurt; obviously Ray was still paramount in her thoughts. Undeterred, Kevin began to caress her. 'No,' he replied softly.

'I thought that you'd gone to Gran Canaria, Mick,' said Rosie, 'couldn't you tear yourself away from me?' Kevin felt even worse. Obviously she hadn't missed him at all. He rolled her over onto her back and her eyes flickered open. 'What are you doing here? I didn't invite you.'

'I missed you.'

'But I needed time alone to sort my head out.'

'Mick helped you, did he?'

'Actually he did, but that's got nothing to do with you.'

'Who is he?'

'A blast from the past, he used to front the Shelltones.'

'I know him well, he fucked Cathy too.'

'Really, well let's hope she enjoyed him as much as I did.'

'We've been conducting a love affair for years, I love you.'

'Drop the love; I'll own up to the word affair, you and I know that it's only happening because Ray's sick. If he recovers, you won't get a look in, you know that.'

Kevin was angry. 'I could tell him about us.'

'Waste of time, he probably knows anyway.'

'What's wrong with you?'

'Nothing, you're the one with the problem. How many times have I told you to find someone else? I'm not Cathy, I just look like her. I just want to have fun until Ray gets well.' Kevin had had enough, and ripped her chemise from her. He tried to assert his control over her, but all he succeeded in doing was to inflame her, making her urge him on, crying, 'Go on then, hurt me, Barry and I did this all the time, he had to get angry to get it up.' Kevin thrust at her as she orgasmed repeatedly; he was taking her body but he couldn't take her heart. His heart was breaking and he finally collapsed across her, sobbing. Rosie stroked the back of his head saying, 'Don't cry, I loved it, you were great and every bit as good as Barry, we must do it again.'

'You callous bitch, I would die for you.'

'Don't do that, we've got almost three weeks left.'

Kevin dried his eyes and started to laugh. Even in his misery, he found Rosie funny. Rosie got out of bed, threw on her wrap, and headed for the kitchen. 'Where are you going?' asked a puzzled Kevin.

'To the kitchen to make coffee.'

'But we've got champagne.'

'You need cheering up. I'm going to treat you to the best hot and cold blow job that you've ever had.' Kevin's head was spinning; he wasn't going to argue with that.

The following day, Susie bumped into Norma and Mary; she was delighted to hear that Kevin was on the island. She lost no time in going home, showering, and making herself beautiful, then she headed for Paloma Beach. A bleary-eyed Deanne let her in. 'What do you want?'

'Nice to see you too.'

'Mum's out. I'm going back to bed, but you can wait if you like.'

'Thanks,' replied Susie and walked out onto the balcony to sun bathe.

An hour later, there was no sign of anyone and she was about to leave when she heard movement coming from Deanne's room. Obviously her sibling was getting up. She waited for another ten minutes and then she heard Deanne talking dirty to someone, and the noisy movement of the bed. Deciding to leave, Susie opened the front door and was about to close it behind her when she heard Deanne cry, 'More, more, oh Eddie, you are the best.'

Susie froze. Deanne had just called her partner in lust Eddie. She couldn't be, no, it was impossible; she couldn't be having sex with her half brother. She closed the front door and went back to the balcony. This couldn't be happening, it was incest. Fifteen minutes later, Eddie emerged from Deanne's room looking flushed and happy. He didn't see Susie at first, and when she came into his line of vision, tried to cover up his nakedness. 'Sorry Suze, didn't know you were here.'

'My sister did,' and with that, Susie charged into Deanne's room. She threw herself at her, screaming, 'You dirty little cow, how could you? Wait till I tell Mum.'

'She already knows, so does Kevin.'

'I don't believe you.' Susie started slapping Deanne and pulling on her hair. Deanne was screaming, Susie was hurting her.

'I don't care whether you believe me or not. We're not harming anyone and we love each other.'

'But he's your half brother.'

Deanne knocked Susie from her bed. 'Well at least I haven't fucked up my life like you; your track record stinks. First you marry Vidal, then he commits suicide, next you shack up with Steven who's a very nice guy, and you're still not satisfied, and now you walk around with a face that looks like a slapped cow's arse.'

'Where's Mum?'

'Out with Kevin. I hope she ditches Ray and marries him; he adores her.'

'But she's married to Ray.'

'Who treats her like shit. He's always belittling her; she's too good for him.'

'He doesn't.'

'How would you know? Bobby and Raydon have told me plenty. Neither you nor I live at home, but they do. Her life's hell; the only one that's unaffected by it all is Nana because she's away with the mixer.'

'Where is Nana?'

'Out with Mary and the boys.'

'I'm leaving.'

'Good, give my love to Steven and Maisie Rose.'

Susie left and slammed the door in her wake; her day was going downhill fast.

As the weeks passed, Rosie began to get closer to Kevin. He was bending over backwards to please her. They had heady nights, walks along the beach, and once or twice had made love on it. Something was stirring inside her; she loved him, but wasn't in love with him. On their final night, Kevin took her out to a top restaurant and, in front of everyone, went down on one knee and proposed to her. Rosie gazed down on him and wondered if she should give up on Ray, thinking that even if he became sober, history could repeat itself and he could fall off the wagon again. Kevin loved her and was ten years her junior; at her age she wasn't going to get a chance like that again. They loved each other's company and were great on and off the stage, but at the core of this situation was Ray, and she still loved him.

'Kevin,' she said softly, 'if Ray has not conquered his drink problem when I go home, I will divorce him. I do love you, but I'm not in love with you. Once I set the wheels in motion for the divorce, I will move in with you, but you'll have to accept my sons and Norma.'

'I'll settle for that,' replied Kevin. As far as he was concerned, Ray was an alcoholic and always would be, but then he'd underestimated Ray's love for Rosie.

Chapter Forty-Four

Luke had terrified Jenny; he was a sinister looking character whose body was covered in cuts. It was a terrific shock to be confronted by him when Adrian removed her blindfold. The room resembled a dungeon, and on the walls were restraints, chains, masks, manacles, and hoods. There were many other things dotted around the room, but owing to the fact that Luke had no electricity and depended on candlelight, several other items were not properly visible. Luke leered at Jenny and then threw back his head and laughed at the woman before him.

'Is this a joke?' he said, 'because if it is, you may not leave here alive. I don't like sick jokes. The boys have informed me that you want three females murdered, one of them to be gutted.'

'It's no joke.' Jenny's nerves were wavering.

Luke wandered around Jenny in a circle; he had a cat of nine tails in his hand and ran it across her throat. 'Fine,' he said, satisfied that he was scaring the shit out of the woman, 'the boys can deal with the daughters, and I'll enjoy taking the mother apart.'

'I want her to suffer.'

'Oh, she will, and before I deal with her, I will let her see her girls with their throats cut; that should add to her suffering.'

'Good.'

Luke cackled. 'Are you sure that you have the stomach for this? I think you're a fraud, maybe a grass. I don't know if I can let you leave.'

'I'm not the one taking the risks.'

'No, but you'll be the lookout.'

'Why?'

'Because we need someone to take care of the sisters, someone to take care of the father and the sons, and myself to do the carving. We also need a lookout unless you want to pay extra for someone else. Actually we may need to enlist someone else to keep an eye on you and your mother.'

'What's my mother got to do with this?'

'Well, if you grass on us or disappear leaving us without transport, we will need to know what to do about her. I don't suppose she will offer much resistance because you're quite old, so she must be even older. I know where you live, you know.'

'How?'

'Do you recall those two men that called you a sicko?'

'Yes.'

'They followed you home. We all know each other, and it was only a matter of time before your path led you to me. I am the master of dissecting and gutting. I used to be a doctor but I got struck off, then I became a butcher, but I only do that part time as my night work is much more enjoyable and well paid.'

'You will be well paid if you do a good job.'

'I told you, I am the master. Do you like blood?'

Jenny was feeling faint, but managed to stutter 'y-yes', thinking that it was the right thing to say.

'Good, Lucy come here.'

A woman aged about forty walked over to them. She had been sitting in the corner but she'd blended in with the darkness. She was blonde, rather plump and, like Luke, had cuts all over her body. The woman spread a plastic sheet on the floor, and Luke stripped off. Now Jenny was wondering if she was to witness Luke fucking the woman. Lucy took off her clothes and picked up a long handled knife. Then Luke lay flat on his back and pulled Lucy down beside him taking the knife from her. Lucy straddled

421

Luke and he began to slice into her arms. Her blood flowed freely and dripped and trickled onto Luke who now had a massive erection. Obviously blood turned him on big time. Jenny stared in disbelief, and then felt her legs give way and knew no more until she came round in another room. 'I thought you said you liked blood.' Luke's face was inches from Jenny's.

'I do, but I haven't eaten today.'

'You're a fake.'

'I'm not.'

'Who sent you?'

'Nobody, can you do this job, or not?'

'Yes, and I shall enjoy doing it. I want one hundred thousand pounds; these two goons work for peanuts,' he indicated Adrian and Larry and handed Jenny a photo album, 'this is some of my work.'

Jenny scanned the album, the candlelight wasn't very good but from what she could see it was a macabre collection. She handed the album back to Luke, saying, 'If you do a good enough job, I will pay you one hundred and fifty thousand.'

'But how do I know that I can trust you?' Luke smiled and then laughed, revealing yellow and broken teeth.

'How do I know that I can trust you?'

'Because I am a man of my word. Why don't you show your hand?'

Jenny opened her bag and pulled out her purse. 'Here,' she said, 'take it' and she offered it to Luke.

'What do we have here?' Luke opened the purse and removed a wad of money. He counted it and whistled, 'One hundred thousand pounds,' he said, 'so how did you know that I would ask for that amount?'

'I didn't, but as I said, if you do a good job, I will give you another fifty thousand.'

'You really do want this family dead, don't you? It would be easier if we could wipe the whole family out though.'

'No, Ray and the boys must remain untouched.'

'Take your clothes off.'

'What?'

'Do as I say, I need to know if you're wired up to the police.'

'Do it,' snapped Adrian, 'we don't want Luke getting angry, you saw what he did to Lucy and they were playing; just think what he might do if you upset him.'

'Fine.' Jenny obeyed; this was turning into a nightmare. Somehow she felt that maybe she was in too deep with a man who professed to love carving people up and loved bloodletting.

Luke stared at her naked body. 'Pure white unblemished skin,' he said, 'have you ever cut yourself?'

'Only as a kid when I've fallen over.'

Luke laughed out loud. 'No my dear, I mean purposely cut yourself, it's a wonderful feeling, a release, you would enjoy it.'

'I think I'll pass on that one.' Jenny dressed herself and stared at Luke who she could see was mocking her.

Larry tipped her bag upside down, and her personal address book fell onto the floor along with makeup and several other things. 'No mobile phone?' queried Larry.

Jenny picked her things up from the floor and said, 'Never had one, don't want one.'

'Get one.'

'Why?'

'You'll need it, if we're inside the house and someone turns up, you'll be able to alert me.'

'Okay, can you do this next week?'

'I don't see why not, we'll meet at the Bull pub in Romford Market on Friday about eight, then we'll go for a drive to find the house. We need to see it to decide the best point of entry, and the safest. Then we'll carry out the actual murders on the following Monday. Oh and bring the other fifty thousand with you or the deal's off, and if you grass us up, both you and your mother will die in the most painful and hideous way, I promise you. Now I must ask you to leave as I want to play a little more with Lucy. You can join in if you like.'

'Just one last question.'

'Yes.'

'If you know where the house is, why can't you do it the same night or the following one?'

'Because on the Friday, we don't know who is inside the house, plus on Saturdays and Sundays there are more people on the roads, plus at the weekend, these two goons will be sat outside watching to see who goes in and out of the place, and creepy crawl the grounds at night and the house if someone leaves a window or door open.'

'That's a lot of pluses.'

'Yes my dear, but we're professionals, so the job will be carried out on the Monday. It's a quiet night, and there won't be so many people around. Has that answered your questions?'

'Yes.'

Luke extended his hand. 'It will be a pleasure doing business with you. Now boys, put her blindfold back on, we know where she lives but my address is top secret.'

Lynne had found her perfect home, and called Rosie straight away, she couldn't contain herself. Rosie was very happy; she loved her cousin dearly and as little girls they had played happily for hours. When Rosie married Barry, Lynne married her husband a week later. They looked very similar and had often been mistaken for sisters. Even their daughters had similar names, Rosie had Deanne and Susie, and Lynne had Suzanne and Diane. In fact, Lynne was a bit of a copy cat which irritated Rosie at times, but Norma had always said that it was a form of flattery.

Lynne's two sons had stayed behind in Spain with their father who was only relocating to England as Lynne had grown tired of Spain. He told her to find a house but that he didn't want to be part of the viewings and other razzamatazz, preferring to stay at home and lap up the sunshine. He also added that he couldn't really afford to take a month off work, but gave her the go-ahead to find the home of her dreams.

Lynne was enjoying her stay at Rosie's home, and on the Sunday night had thrown a small birthday party for her mother who was about to be taken on holiday by Lynne's brother and his two boys. It had been a noisy party, and an even noisier goodbye when her brother had left; they were all crazy. He'd brought his mother along too and you could hear her a mile off.

Adrian and Larry watched as the guests left the party, and they were delighted to see a man and two teenage boys accompanied by an old lady leave the property. The lady of the house had obviously had too much to drink and fawned all over the man and the two teenagers. It was music to their ears when they heard the woman shout, 'Have a good time, send us a postcard, I hope you don't have any flight delays.' Then she was prised from her guests by a young female who Adrian suspected was one of his future victims.

'Bingo,' he cried, 'the old man is going away with his two sons, so that will make life easier tomorrow night. I wonder who the old dear is?'

'Dunno, but who cares, this job will be a doddle.' Larry was already counting his cash and wondering what to do with it.

'Right,' said Adrian, 'we'll wait until the lights go out and do a bit of creepy crawling.' He couldn't wait for tomorrow night.

It was Monday night, and Lynne had three days left of her stay; she was missing her husband and decided to give him a call. She picked up the telephone and dialled his number, but there was no dialling tone. Dismayed, she tried a phone in another room but that was dead too and, after trying every phone in the house, Lynne gave up and decided to have an early night. Her girls were outside in the garden talking, so leaving the back door unlocked, she made her way upstairs to run a bath. The girls were in fact having a crafty smoke as they knew that their mother disapproved of it. After about fifteen minutes, the girls came back into the house and settled in front of the television. Suzanne decided to get herself a pineapple juice from the fridge and walked out into the kitchen.

'Get one for me,' cried Diane.

'Get your own.'

'Miserable cow, I'm going outside again for another fag.'

'Please yourself, I'm going to drink my juice and then I'm going to bed; it's late and Mum wants to go shopping for furniture tomorrow.'

'Why? We've got to go back to Spain before we can take the house over, that's just plain stupid.'

'Well, maybe Mum fancies a bit of window shopping.'

'Maybe, oh well, if you're going to bed, I'll see you in the morning, goodnight. I need another fag.'

'You're smoking too much.'

'Are you my mother all of a sudden?'

'No, oh well, it's your lungs that will pay the price.'

'Right, goodnight.'

'Goodnight, don't forget to lock the back door when you come back in.'

'I won't, goodnight,' and Diane flounced off into the garden, neither girl aware of the fact that three predators were already in the grounds. They slipped past Diane who was inhaling her cigarette, and entered the house, leaving the back door open. They stayed in the kitchen and viewed Suzanne as she ascended the stairs.

'Go and get her,' whispered Larry, and Adrian crept up the stairs behind the unsuspecting girl.

A short while later, after polishing off two more cigarettes, Diane returned to the house. She was about to lock the back door when she realised that the key was missing. Cursing, she went in search of her sister and barged into her room. The room was in darkness and, angrily, Diane switched on the light, shouting, 'How am I supposed to lock the back door when you've taken the key I...' Her sentence was cut short as the shock hit her, her sister was propped up against the wall with her throat cut and her clothes blood-soaked. She tried to scream but nothing came out and then an arm enclosed her from behind and she felt the blade of a knife being pressed against her throat.

Lynne had had a long soak in the bath and was drying her hair with Rosie's noisy hair dryer. She knew nothing until she was flung to the ground from behind. She landed face down and, craning her neck, stared up into the eyes of a robed man with an evil look in his eyes. 'Who are you?' she cried, 'what do you want?'

'I'm your worse possible nightmare,' laughed Luke. 'I want you, Rosie.'

'I'm not Rosie, she's my cousin, look, take what you want but please don't harm my girls.'

'Your girls look real pretty,' laughed Larry, 'we've given 'em a ruby necklace each, come and see them. You're not as pretty as your photos, are you, Rosie? I guess that you plaster your face in makeup; even Adrian would look good in makeup and he's an ugly bastard.'

'I want to see my girls,' cried Lynne.

Luke yanked her to her feet and dragged her to Suzanne's room. She screamed in horror, crying, 'Why have you done this? I have no money, and my girls are guilty of no crime.'

'They're Ed Gold's kids, that's enough.'

'They're not, their father lives with me in Spain, and his name is Ray Carpenter. I'm Lynne Carpenter, and my girls' names are Suzanne and Diane, how could you do this?'

'Steady, Rosie,' chuckled Larry, 'lying won't save your skin. Luke's got something really special lined up for you.'

'I'm not Rosie,' sobbed Lynne as the door closed behind her, leaving her in the room with Luke and her two deceased daughters.

Luke stripped off, and Lynne seized her chance. She opened the door and ran through it right into the arms of Adrian and Larry. They pushed her back into the room where she faced an angry Luke. He was brandishing a long handled knife, and by his side was a collection of knives and a sword. 'Take off your clothes and lay down,' he ordered. Lynne obeyed; there was nothing she could do. Gone were her happy plans for tomorrow when she was going to spend a fun filled day with her girls. She would never see her husband or her sons again; her life was over, all because of a case of mistaken identity. At least Rosie was safe; obviously she'd become the target of some twisted mind.

Naked, she stood before Luke as he added, 'Lovely.' Obviously she was going to be raped before he killed her as he had a massive erection; she took another look at her daughters. She should have protected them; it was a mother's job to protect them and she'd failed. 'Spread your legs,' yelled Luke with a crazed expression on his face. Lynne gritted her teeth and closed her eyes, unprepared for the gruesome ordeal before her. Luke smiled as he moved closer with his long knife. She opened her eyes and stared up at her evil tormentor, who was laughing, and then passed out with the excruciating pain.

Ada and Alf had worked hard on Ray, and it had had the desired effect. He had cut down dramatically on his drinking with the doctor's help. The doctor had said that, at this moment in time, he would need to be weaned off the alcohol, as absolute abstinence could kill him. Over the month, Ray had taken an interest in his personal hygiene, and was determined to prove to Rosie that his drinking days were over.

Twenty four hours before Rosie's return, Ray had returned to his home with Alf. He knew that he'd have to suffer Lynne and the girls, but he'd suffer anything to get Rosie back. Alf and Ray pulled up outside the house and Ray activated the electric gates. 'Sounds quiet,' said Alf, 'unusual for Lynne, she's usually such a noisy woman, so are her girls.'

'Probably gone shopping for things to take back to Spain,' replied Ray pulling into the drive.

Both men got out of the car. 'You okay, Ray?' said Alf, 'does it feel good to be home?'

'It will do when Rosie gets back,' replied Ray, putting his key into the front door lock. It opened on the first turn of the key which surprised Ray. 'It's not double-locked,' he said, 'what's Lynne thinking of? Anyone could open this with a credit card.' They entered the house and Ray walked through to the kitchen to make coffee. It was then that he noticed the back door was wide open. 'What's going on?' he cried, 'she hasn't even closed the back door.'

Alf walked through to the lounge. 'You've been burgled,' he said.

Ray walked through and stared at the mess, drawers had been pulled out, scattering their contents all over the floor, the sofa was slashed, the television screen had been shattered, and what appeared like red paint had been poured over one wall. 'I'll call the police,' said Ray, and picked up the phone, but there was no dialling tone. 'Shit,' he added, 'the phone's dead. I'll use my mobile; fine homecoming this will be for Rosie, obviously someone's seen Lynne go out and broken in once she's left.' He rang the police from his mobile phone and was told not to touch anything, so he and Alf made a coffee and awaited the police, staying downstairs.

'There's always the chance that they might still be upstairs,' said Alf, 'and if they are, we'll be waiting for them.'

'Fine,' replied Ray, thinking that things were anything but fine.

Fifteen minutes later, the police turned up and viewed the scene. 'Have you touched anything?' asked Sergeant Bates.

'No, and we haven't been upstairs either. I suppose that you will want a statement. Will it take long? My wife's coming home tomorrow and I need to get this place sorted out.'

'We'll be as quick as we can. Could you take a look around upstairs, Paul?'

'Yes,' replied his companion and went upstairs. When he got to the landing, he said, 'There's an awful stench up here.'

'Probably Lynne,' said Alf, 'never remembers to flush the toilet.'

Paul went from room to room, and the stench was getting stronger. He'd need a gas mask if it got any worse. None of the rooms so far had been ransacked. There was just one more room to check, and that was where the stench was coming from; it was unbearable. He went back downstairs where a fingerprint expert was looking for clues. 'I need a mask,' he cried, 'there's a smell coming from the back room; it's horrendous and making me feel nauseous, my eyes are stinging too.'

His superior got to his feet. 'I'll sort it out,' he said, 'you young police officers are lightweights, probably a blocked drain or something. I'll be back in a trice, Mr Lynne.'

'Okay,' replied Ray. He couldn't smell anything, and watched as the two men went upstairs.

There was silence for a while, and then the sound of someone retching. Paul appeared at the top of the stairs and leaned over the banister. 'It's horrendous,' he wailed.

'I'll say, I can smell it now.' Ray was feeling nauseous.

An ashen-faced Sergeant Bates appeared and came downstairs. Collapsing onto an armchair, he asked, 'How many people were staying here?'

'Three, why?'

'There are three decomposing bodies in the back room. Whoever did this has made Jack the Ripper look like a poor amateur.'

'What?'

Ray got to his feet, wanting to go upstairs, but Alf stayed him saying, 'Leave it to the police, Ray, we'll go back home. You'll have to pick Rosie up from the airport tomorrow and take her somewhere else. She can't come home to this.'

'I agree, sir,' said Sergeant Bates, taking out his notebook, 'but before you leave, I need a statement from Mr Lynne.'

Ray put his head in his hands and wept. Rosie was going to get some homecoming.

Jenny had been very stressed on the night of the murders. She was acting lookout, and Luke had brought along his brother Max to keep an eye on her in case she did a runner and left them stranded. He was a large sweaty man who had brought along a box of sandwiches and regularly offered some to Jenny. She didn't know how he could eat at a time like this, and would be glad when Luke returned with his henchmen. She'd brought along her headset, not wanting to hear any screams coming from the house.

When Luke finally did return with Adrian and Larry, he was carrying a bag full of his knives and a bucket covered with a towel. Getting into the car, he handed Jenny the bucket. 'What the fuck's this?' she cried.

'Evidence that I've done my job properly,' replied Luke, 'they're my souvenirs.'

'What, I didn't ask for souvenirs, what are they?'

'Look inside. I always take home souvenirs from my work.'

'I don't think I want to.'

'I said, look inside,' ordered Luke, 'if you don't I'll push you face down into that bucket.'

Trembling, Jenny removed the blood-stained folded bath towel and looked inside. She screamed, and then opened the car door and threw up onto the grass verge. The men all burst into laughter at Jenny's distress, and Luke took the bucket from her and gazed inside. 'Lovely,' he cried. 'I had a shower after I'd gutted her and thought that I'd keep the towel as a souvenir too. I can use it when Lucy and I indulge in our playtime.'

Everyone laughed except Jenny, who was shaking, half with fear and half with joy. Ray was finally hers, and Rosie was gone. She knew that as soon as Ray had got over his grieving, he would come looking for her and fall in love with her all over again.

The press were out in force as Rosie touched down at Stansted Airport with her family. They were minus Kevin who had returned forty eight hours previously owing to work commitments. Rosie and her family knew nothing of the gruesome events at their home, as the story had leaked when they'd been in midair. Ray was waiting and ushered his family from the airport, telling them that they weren't going home at present and would be staying with Kevin for a while. Rosie was uneasy; something was wrong and Ray seemed very nervous. They made small talk on the drive to Surrey, with Rosie finally nodding off into a contented slumber as she knew that she had her Ray back. He looked great in his new suit, and he smelt of expensive aftershave. She knew that his days of dancing with the devil were over.

The following morning, the bombshell dropped. Rosie couldn't believe what had gone on in her absence. The news on the television and in the newspapers was grim. Headlines read 'Ritualistic Killing in Quiet Location' and 'House of Horror' amongst others. Rosie broke down in tears. 'How could someone do this to Lynne?'

'Rosie, it was a burglary gone wrong,' replied Ray.

'So why didn't they just tie her up? They didn't have to kill her.'

'Maybe she saw their faces and they panicked.'

'But whoever did this has taken body parts away with them, and it says that Lynne was disembowelled. Why would someone do such an awful crime?'

'Maybe Lynne had enemies.'

'But they would live in Spain, not in Havering. I'm scared Ray, I can't go home, not ever.'

'Rosie, its early days.'

'They say that Lynne's heart and uterus are missing; how sick is that? And that her girls had their throats cut and their hearts removed. Why did they target her? How did they know that she was there?'

'Rosie, it was a burglary gone wrong. I agree with Ray,' said Kevin, not wanting to admit that he thought that Rosie along with her daughters was the real target. He wanted to take her into his arms and soothe her, but he couldn't as she appeared to be back in Ray's arms once more now that he had sobered up.

'It's a lovely day today,' sang Norma, skipping into the room. 'I like this place, Rosie. Can we move in here or is this just another holiday home? Oh look, there's a house on the television that looks just like ours.'

Ray switched the television off. 'What do you want for breakfast, Norma?'

'Well, sausages would be nice and some streaky bacon, and I'd also like a couple of eggs on toast too.'

Kevin extended his hand. 'Come with me, Norma. You can tell my housekeeper what you want and she'll cook it for you.'

'Will she? I do like this place. Oh look, there's a huge tortoise wandering around outside; maybe he wants some breakfast too.'

Rosie laughed. Even at this low ebb, Norma had the power to make her laugh. Her mother was lost in her own little world, but happy. Norma walked with Kevin to the kitchen and was greeted by Ada Shores. 'What would you like, Norma?' she asked.

'I don't know, what did I ask for, Ed?'

'I'm Kevin.'

'Well, you look like Ed, but you've got better manners.'

'Norma would like sausages, streaky bacon, two eggs and toast,' said Kevin.

'Coming up,' replied Ada.

'Fancy you remembering. I don't remember anything these days. Oh look, there's another tortoise, I suppose he's come to see his friend.'

'That's right, Norma.'

Wacky mounted Daisy and began grunting as they mated. 'Oh dear,' said Norma. 'I think he's hurting that other tortoise, it's crying.'

'He's the one that's crying.'

'Is he, well I don't see why, he could crush that other one with his weight, he's a bully.'

Kevin laughed. 'We're opening a tortoise sanctuary here. Eddie wants to rescue tortoises.'

'Well, he'll need to split those two up, they'll kill each other. My goodness, that tortoise is noisy, it could keep you up at night.' Norma turned her attention to Ruby the housemaid, adding, 'that bacon smells delicious, are you having some Ed?'

'I'm Kevin.'

'Oh of course you are, where's Ed then?'

'He died, Norma.'

'Did he? He used to keep me awake at night; he'd give that tortoise a run for its money. I used to lay awake at night listening to him and Rosie, God what a racket. I used to think that he was killing her.'

Ruby set Norma's breakfast on the table and pulled a chair out for her. 'Thank you,' said Norma. 'I do like this place. I would love to live here.'

Kevin sighed; he was all for that because if Norma lived here, it would mean that Rosie would too. He'd have to wait now to see what materialised. Rosie was in no fit state to make decisions. His only hope was that at some stage Ray would fall off the wagon once more.

It was the following morning when the awful truth hit Rosie. Once more the story was front page. There were photos of the room where the three women had died, showing the blood-soaked carpet where Lynne had met her end, and there were many more references to the missing body parts, one stating that the assailants must have ripped the women's hearts from their bodies. The penny dropped and, turning to Ray, Rosie said, 'Oh my God, that's what I said to that woman.'

'What woman?'

'The one that kept phoning. I told her that if I met her I would rip her heart out. This is her, she's done this or got someone to do it, it was me that she wanted.'

'Rosie, that's not true.'

'Isn't it? Well, if you want more proof, look at the photo at the bottom right of the article.'

'You're talking in riddles.'

'I'm not, there are twelve red roses on the floor which the police say were laid across the corpse, and there are several things written on the wall in blood.'

'It means nothing, Rosie.'

'Really, then explain this.' Rosie had turned the page over and handed the newspaper to Ray. Ray stared at the article, and then back at Rosie. On the wall, daubed in blood, were the words *Eden's Rose*.

Chapter Forty-Five

Jenny had been shopping. She flicked through the newspaper but didn't read it properly. The fact was three corpses had been discovered in Rosie's house and Jenny knew who they were. She'd bought herself a new wardrobe of clothes and was feeling on top of the world. When she arrived home, she found her mother Brenda reading the newspaper. 'Poor Rosie,' she said, looking up from the paper, 'these murders are horrific.'

'Yes I know, I must get in touch with Ray; he must be devastated.'

'Shouldn't worry about the husband. What about the two boys? They'll never see their mother or sisters again.'

'Ray will look after them. I really should go round and see him.'

'What's the point?'

'He might need me.'

'Do you know him?'

'Of course I do, don't you remember him? We were engaged once.'

'Oh, that Ray, he'll probably be comforting his family. It must have been a shock discovering those three dead bodies.'

'What do you mean, that Ray, who did you think I meant?'

'Ray Carpenter.'

'Who's Ray Carpenter?'

'The husband of the woman that was murdered. Didn't you read the article?'

'Yes, but I thought...'

'Lynne Carpenter was Rosie's cousin; she'd been living in Rosie's house while Rosie was away.'

'What?'

'Oh Jenny, what a kind-hearted girl you are, you thought that Rosie had been murdered and that Ray needed consoling. He won't need you, dear, he'll probably be joined at the hip with Rosie; he won't let her out of his sight. The theory is that this could have been a case of mistaken identity. I wouldn't be surprised if Ray and Rosie leave England and retire to their holiday home.'

Jenny was seething. She'd paid a fortune to get rid of Rosie, and she was still alive, so were her daughters. As soon as her mother had left the room, Jenny picked up the paper and read it thoroughly. The photo of Ray crying, was him crying with relief that Rosie hadn't been in the house at the time of the murders, and the photo of Rosie further down the page was not of Rosie as the victim, it was one of her at the airport when she'd touched down at Stansted.

Jenny wanted to scream. Her plans had backfired, and later that day she rang Larry. 'You fucking imbeciles, you got the wrong woman,' she screeched.

'Calm down,' replied Larry, 'we did what you asked, and Luke carved the body up real good, her body was unrecognisable. The woman wasn't as good looking as Rosie but then we put that down to lack of makeup, plus her hair was wet, and all birds look different when their hair's wet.'

'I want my fucking money back. Did the woman speak at all?'

'Yes, she said that her name was Lynne and she was Rosie's cousin; she also said that her daughter's names were Suzanne and Diane.'

'And you still went ahead.'

'Of course, her daughters were already dead so there was no turning back. Anyway, we thought that she was lying because she didn't want to die. As for your money, you can forget it,

437

you're not getting it back, and don't even think about grassing on us, or you may end up looking like Lynne. You don't know the full facts yet. She was completely gutted, and she wasn't dead when Luke did it; she kept drifting in and out of consciousness, begging for mercy. Luke did it for fun, so don't get any silly ideas. Don't forget, we know where you live. Maybe one morning you may not wake up; it was nice doing business with you, Jenny, bye.'

Jenny replaced the receiver. She was beaten and scared but paramount in her mind was the problem of Rosie. She would now have to deal with her herself, that way there would be no mistakes.

For the following three months, Ray hardly left Rosie's side. He took her to work, worked alongside her in the office, attended all of her gigs, and engaged the services of Canny Kenneth. Ken was Rosie's bodyguard; he was a happy-go-lucky sort with a thick Geordie accent and was a little bit slow at times. He was built like a brick shit house and certainly knew how to handle himself when danger threatened. Maisie Rose loved him, mainly because he smiled like a Cheshire cat, revealing dazzling white gnashers. The grin was a bit scary at times because, as he smiled, he'd utter a long drawn out 'Eeeee'. Raydon was tinkering around on the piano one night, with Ken looking on interestedly. He gave up after a while saying, 'I'll never make a piano player, I'll stick to photography.'

As he stood up to leave, Ken seated himself at the piano, saying, 'It's easy, young Raydon, I'll show you how,' then he proceeded to play *Chopsticks*.

Raydon looked on in amazement. 'Not bad,' he said.

'Not bad, not bad, I'll hava you know I'm greet, man, top drawer that's me. I can also play "Keep your feet still Geordie Hinny or I'll cut the Buggers Off". Do you know that one?'

'No,' replied Raydon, backing away. Ken flashed him a beaming smile, and Raydon fled the room. Ken continued to finger the piano, and when Rosie came downstairs he was playing and singing *When the Boat Comes In*.

'I didn't know you could play,' said Rosie.

'I canna, I was just showing young Raydon how to play, he's got real talent, Missus, just needs a bit more confidence. How are you, me little chicken? You're looking well.'

'Fine, just a bit tired.'

'Well, we canna have you wearing yourself out, can we, pet; what time are we leaving for the concert?'

'In about thirty minutes.'

'Greet man, you get your feet up and I'll treat you to some of me favourite Geordie songs. I come from Newcassel, me mother and wor brother used to sing these songs around the piano when I was a nipper.'

'Lovely,' replied Rosie. She found Ken so funny. She was returning to her own home in the morning and wasn't looking forward to it. She had to return sometime, and now, with Ken protecting her, felt ready to do so. He was moving in with the family. He was to get a full salary, plus board and lodgings; the only problem though was where to put him. The only vacant room was the room where the murders had occurred. Ken wasn't fazed, saying, 'The dead canna hurt me, all the room needs is a lick of paint, I'll do it meself. I'll have it up and running in no time at all if that's all right with you.'

'Of course,' replied Rosie. 'I just thought that...'

'Dinna worry your pretty head, pet, I'll be fine in there. It's kind of you to put a roof over wor head. It'll save me a fortune in rent, and I'll be able to watch over you twenty four seven, it'll be greet man.'

Rosie was relieved, she loved her home and felt reassured that Ken would be on the premises.

Lop had finally talked Vic into retiring, and a party was going to be thrown in his honour, but a week before that, Z Tones were going to reform for a one-off performance. Ray's arm was now better after an operation, so he no longer had to suffer the jibes from Bobby, Raydon, and Norma, such as the Incredible Hulk and Popeye the Sailor Man. Vic sat out front on the night of Z Tones' performance and used Lop as his eyes. He couldn't see any more, but recognised the songs and voices.

All went well until Kevin began to sing *Go Insane* by Lindsey Buckingham. Rosie had been in the wings at the time, taking a break, and felt quite unsettled by the looks that Kevin was shooting her. He played this number on acoustic guitar while the rest of the band fell silent. As he gradually built the song up, his voice began to break up as he was pouring every part of himself into it. He finished the song with tears falling from his eyes, and left the stage to wild applause. Rosie smiled and applauded, but was unprepared for what happened next. Kevin grasped her hand and dragged her to the dressing room. The band was confused; what was happening? Ray wanted to leave the stage, but couldn't as his was the next number and the band had already begun the introduction.

'What's happening?' asked Vic. 'Kevin sounded like he was breaking down.'

'Don't know,' replied Lop, 'but he's just dragged Rosie off to the dressing room.'

'Probably giving her a good seeing to,' laughed Vic, 'wonderful.'

Lop shrugged, wonderful wasn't exactly how she would have described things. Ray was getting edgy, and kept casting his eyes to the wings, knowing that the intermission was a long way off.

In the dressing room, Kevin was venting his lust on Rosie. She was horrified, believing that he'd accepted that their affair was over. He was like a crazed person, and the more that she protested, the more he forced himself on her. Unable to stop him, she let him get on with it, and once he'd finished, pushed him away, crying, 'What did that just prove, that you're stronger than me?'

'Rosie, I love you, I can't go on like this, I'm going to tell Ray, I have to, my life's meaningless without you.'

'Then maybe what you've just done has given it meaning to you, but it meant nothing to me.'

'Rosie, just give me a chance. Ray will fall off the wagon again, you know he will.'

'Then if he does, that's my problem.'

'But I can give you everything.'

'So can Ray.'

'Okay, I concede defeat but let's have a proper final farewell. I'll book a hotel and then after a night of love with you, I'll back off, I promise.'

'You really will back off and leave me alone.'

'Yes, I don't want to. but I promise that I will.'

'Fine, I'm taking over from Vic soon. I'll dissolve your contract and then you won't need to see me any more.'

'No need to, you have my word. Give me a hug and then we'll shake on it.'

'Okay.' Rosie embraced him, shook his hand, and went to clean herself up, leaving Kevin to do the same, then five minutes later, they returned to the stage.

Back on stage, Kevin addressed the audience. 'I apologise for my mini breakdown,' he said, 'it's just that sometimes songs as beautiful as *Go Insane* get to you. There can't be a guy here who hasn't found himself in that position. You break up because she wants to, and move onto someone else hoping she will get you back onto your feet, but sometimes you can't, and because you haven't stopped thinking about your previous love, you call out her name because you can't forget her. Anyway it's a beautiful song by a fantastic composer and I hope that I did it justice.' The audience cheered, and Kevin went into *Big Love* by Fleetwood Mac.

During the intermission, Ray took Rosie to one side. 'What happened to Kevin; one minute he's giving the performance of his life, and the next he's rushing off stage dragging you away.'

'The song reminds him of Cathy, he got very emotional.'

'Shouldn't sing it then, I don't know why people do it, look at Ed. Gerry told me that one night he attempted to sing Rod Stewart's *Sonny* and broke down in tears. He never sung it again after that night I'm told.'

'Oh yes, but I know why.'

'Do tell.'

'Well, you're a Rod Stewart freak, you must have listened to the words. The guy is singing to his ex and telling her that his current girlfriend looks like her, and does everything like her, but isn't her. To Ed, that was me and Cathy.'

'I never knew that.'

'You do now.'

'I'm quite enjoying this gig, it makes me nostalgic. I'd like to get back on stage again.'

'No reason why you can't, I shall be the sole owner of Vic's agency soon. I'll be choosing all of the acts, and my word will be final.'

'So I'll be married to the boss. I'll have to watch my P's and Q's. Guess what, boss, I've got a huge snake down my trousers, can you help me?'

'My pleasure, Mr Lynne. Let's go and find an empty dressing room.'

Chapter Forty-Six

A week later, Rosie made her way to the hotel that Kevin had booked. She had a mixture of emotions coursing through her, guilt, lust, excitement, fear of getting caught out, just about everything. She pulled up outside and checked in knowing that Kevin was already upstairs waiting for her. It was seven o'clock and he'd told her that he'd be there a couple of hours earlier to make sure that everything was perfect for their night of passion. Ray was going to a stag night so Ken had been given the night off, but instead of going out he stayed in, promising Norma and Mary a night of greet laffs, as he put it.

Rosie made her way upstairs and tapped on the door of their allocated room. There was the sound of things being shuffled around, and then Kevin opened the door, with hair wet and a white towel draped around his lower half. Rosie closed the door behind her feeling very wicked.

There were scented candles burning, champagne on ice, rose petals on the bed and, in a vase, a dozen red roses. Rosie put her bag down and started to undress, but Kevin took her into his arms saying, 'Let me do it, I want to.' They kissed passionately and then Kevin picked her up and deposited her onto the bed. He spread her legs and went down on her, bringing her to orgasm over and over again. All guilt was gone as Kevin devoured her. Her body was impossibly sensitized and she jumped as the heat built up in her once more.

'I can't,' she cried, 'not again, I can't.'

'You're so beautiful.' Kevin was feasting on every inch of her skin and Rosie was discovering erogenous zones that she didn't know she had; she'd come so many times that she'd lost count. 'Just one more,' said Kevin, 'and then I'll stop.'

'I can't.'

Her clitoris was a swollen nub and he was suckling on it, a raging inferno was searing through her body, making her scream. She thought she could see a huge spider's web and was tangled up in it, then suddenly she burst through it and rocketed over the edge; she was dying and didn't even care as she toppled into the abyss.

Kevin kissed her and she could taste herself on his lips. He felt the rush of blood in his ears; desperation was taking over and driving him on. He adjusted her hips and thighs as he thrust deep. Her flesh closed around him as his hips pistoned, and everything was forgotten as his orgasm roared through him. He called her name as he felt his release, the euphoria rushing through him like a violent thunderstorm.

Rosie felt defenceless, something that she'd never felt before. Kevin was stroking her hair. 'Look at me,' he said. Rosie made eye contact. No man had ever looked at her that way; it was full of need. He kissed her and then poured out a couple of glasses of champagne.

'Susie and Steven have split up,' said Rosie, 'he and Bobby are just like Romany and Ed reincarnated. Steven's a nice guy but he's got sucked into the whole world of sex, drugs, and rock and roll. Susie won't put up with his womanising. She forgave him the first time and then he got a girl pregnant, but the final straw came when he gave her a sexually transmitted disease. She's kicked him out.'

'Poor kid, she's such a lovely girl.'

'And she adores you, she always has; you could do a lot worse.'

'She wouldn't want me.'

'She would die for you; she cried her eyes out when you got with Candy.'

'Hold on, when I started dating Candy, Susie was just fifteen. I knew that she had a crush on me but I didn't realise that her feelings went any deeper. Anyway, that would have been cradle snatching. I respected her, and you and Ray were my best friends, it would have ruined everything.'

'I told her that you respected her, but she still cried her eyes out every night.'

'Would you still leave Ray if he fell off the wagon?'

'Yes,' replied Rosie, taking the glass of champagne that Kevin was offering her, 'but he won't. What time are they kicking us out of here?'

'Midday tomorrow, how long can you stay?'

'Midday tomorrow, Ray's sleeping at his friend's house tonight.'

'Wonderful.'

'Wonderful, to what, me staying for the whole duration, or Ray staying at his mate's?'

'Both, what time do you want to eat? I can get room service.'

'We'll eat later. Is there a kettle here?'

'Yes, over there in the corner, there's tea, coffee, milk, sugar, and biscuits. Why?'

'Need you ask, we've got champagne on ice and hot coffee, fancy a blow?'

'Sounds good to me.' Kevin feasted his eyes on the voluptuous woman before him; he wanted her forever but midday tomorrow would have to suffice.

Lop's plan was working perfectly. Vic's party was arranged and she'd stirred up Dylan in more ways than one. She'd seduced him and promised him fame, fortune, and a new life in Thailand. He was fuming that Vic had ended his contract, and wondered why Rosie hadn't intervened, but he guessed that she was probably shot to pieces over the gruesome murders, plus the police theory

445

that this was no burglary but a case of mistaken identity. That was enough to send anyone over the edge.

Lop had mentioned that the only thing standing in their way was Vic, and she had provided Dylan with a gun to do the awful deed. Dylan had no conscience on this matter, for it had been Vic who had given him grief from day one and he hated him. The thought of himself and Vic's widow sailing off into the sunset excited him. The woman was an expert when it came to sex, and she was liberal with the money and gifts that she bestowed on him. This was his final chance to leave all of the shit behind him. Lop had stated that the best time to get rid of Vic was at his party. He was not a well man these days, and would retire to bed early. Once he was in bed, Lop would make sure that the coast was clear and then Dylan could go in and blast his brains out. The wheels were set in motion and all they had to do was wait.

Jenny had noted the party in the papers and, seeing that waitresses were required, applied for the job under the name of Kay Green. She was hired and immediately changed her appearance, dyeing her hair jet black and donning glasses with clear frames. She also went on a crash diet, which was agony as she loved her food but it was paramount that she wasn't recognised. Dylan was playing at Vic's party, courtesy of Rosie, so Jenny decided to turn the heat up. She rang Dylan, asking him to visit her for dinner. Dylan wasn't exactly pleased to hear from her. 'Suddenly remembered that you've got a son, have you? It might have been nice if you'd said, 'hello son, how are you?' but then that wouldn't cross your mind, would it?'

'I've got something to tell you, something that I should have told you years ago.'

'Oh, am I Rosie's son and she abandoned me? I couldn't be that lucky. Who was my dad, Ed Gold? Because you told me once that he was, and then when I tried to contact him, you admitted that you'd lied.'

'Dylan, this is important.'

'Nothing you say is important.'

'This is.'

'Okay, what time shall I come round?'

'Five thirty, I'll cook us something nice, your gran's going out. I don't want her around when I tell you my secret; we'll have the place to ourselves.'

'I don't care if the whole fucking army's there, see you later.'

Kevin and Rosie were in the bath. Kevin lifted a sponge from its dish by the side of the bath and dipped it into the water. He stroked the sponge over Rosie's breasts, making her nipples harden. She sighed and let out a cry. 'Getting turned on again, are we?' laughed Kevin, 'you are something else.'

'I'm a middle-aged woman, that's what I am.'

'But it doesn't matter.' Kevin got out of the bath and towelled himself dry, then taking another fluffy white bath towel from a rail, ordered 'Out.' He handed Rosie the towel.

'What?'

'I want to taste you again.'

Rosie obeyed, she was so turned on. This was crazy, she felt like a teenager. Wrapping herself in the towel, she blushed as Kevin played with the rigid peak of her nipple; this was exquisite torture.

After towelling herself dry, she got back onto the bed and lay back as Kevin pleasured her once more. After yet another earth moving orgasm, Kevin rolled her over. 'Get on your hands and knees,' he cried, getting behind her. Rosie shook as his hard member touched the swollen folds of her genitalia; she moaned as he sank into her. He was getting harder and harder, and she cried out as ecstasy built up inside her. Kevin grasped her hips harder and Rosie soared upward, the waves of pleasure engulfing her, throwing her down into sheer oblivion in a single moment of pure rapture.

Chapter Forty-Seven

'So what did you want?' Dylan was angry.

'I'll tell you over dinner, we've got corned beef, boiled potatoes, and baked beans.'

'No change then. When I was a kid, I recall being raised on this shit, plus barrels of lentils. Why are you still eating like this? Duncan left you a fortune.'

'I like it.'

'Nobody else does. I've got a hot date, so I can't stay long.'

'Sit down.' Jenny dished up their meal and then sat down facing him. 'It's about your dad.'

'Tommy the drifter.'

'He's not your dad.'

'Then who the fuck is?'

'Ray Lynne.'

'Shut up, don't you ever stop spinning lies? When I stayed with Rosie, Ray didn't say anything.'

'Well he wouldn't want to upset Rosie.'

'She doesn't know?'

'No, Ray left us in the sixties; Ray never married Rosie until the eighties.'

'So he left us to fend for ourselves.'

'He didn't have any money in those days.'

'Kids need love and two parents, not money. He's loaded now, he owes us big time.'

'Maybe he forgot us.'

'Then he needs his memory jogged.'

'Dylan, I've got a job working at Vic Lee's party. We could tackle Ray together.'

'Well I doubt that Rosie will recognise you looking like that. I did a double take when you opened the door; you looked ugly before, now you look pig ugly.'

'Dylan, I'll help you with Ray, but I don't want him harmed, or the boys. Just a talking to will suffice.'

'I'll kill the bastard.'

'No dear, Ray's your father, and the boys are your half brothers. We'll be one big family soon with Rosie out of the way.'

'You're nuts. Fuck the lot of 'em.' And with that, Dylan threw his dinner up the wall and stormed out.

'Straddle me,' ordered Kevin. Rosie cried out as she impaled herself on his huge erection; the room now smelt of sweat and sex. She rode him out to completion and then collapsed on top of him. 'Time to eat, I think,' said Kevin. 'I'll ring for room service.'

'Good idea,' replied Rosie. 'I've worked up an appetite; I'm not used to this.'

'We've had long sessions before.'

'Yes, but not like this, you're doing all the giving.'

'You deserve it; I'm going to spoil you all night long.'

'I hope my body's up to it.'

'You're better than a woman half your age. I can't get enough of you. Would you like some more champagne?'

'Love some, and then we'd better decide what we want to eat.'

'Your wish is my command. I love you, Rosie.'

Ray was having a whale of a time at the stag night; his entire family were there apart from Ada. The liquor flowed freely, so did the filthy jokes. Alf watched his son carefully; he didn't want Ray falling off the wagon. Ray indulged in a few pints but steered clear of the spirits. He eyed the strippers up, one had a face like a pig but the other one was quite attractive. She invited the men to perform a sex act with her and a few accepted the offer. Ray declined, telling his mates that he had the real deal at home. However, when the girl left, he followed her outside and allowed her to give him oral sex in his car. As far as he was concerned, that wasn't cheating.

Jenny had acquired guns; Duncan had taught her to shoot for her own safety. The area in which they'd first lived had its fair share of druggies, thieves, and guys that would do anything for a few quid. She'd been burgled three times in six months, and was elated when they'd moved a few months later to a much safer, quieter area. Since then, she'd not needed a gun but now she needed to remove Rosie and her girls from the mortal coil and she was going to enjoy it.

Rosie was getting second wind; she'd had a lovely hot meal and was snuggled up to Kevin watching the television. Kevin had brought a selection of music with him, mainly Barry White and Marvin Gaye tracks, but the one that amused her was *Freak Me* by Another Level. Kevin had played it many times, and even had it playing on Rosie's arrival when he'd opened the door to her. Rosie thought that she'd never be able to listen to that song again without recalling her night with her lover in the hotel. It was wrong being here with Kevin, but it felt so right, and after tonight their affair would be over. Smiling, she kissed Kevin and then worked her way down his body.

'You're funny.' Maisie Rose was in fits of laughter. Susie was out and Ken was babysitting. Susie had turned up unannounced, expecting Rosie to baby sit, and was narked when she realised that her mother was out and Ray was at a stag night.

She was about to leave when Ken said, 'Ah'll babysit for you man, Maisie's a canny lass. It'll be a pleasure to look after her, I love bairns, I've two of me own, all grown up mind, I'm proud of them, lovely lads they are.'

'Well if you're sure.'

'Waye aye man, we'll have a greet time, won't we, Maisie?'

Maisie nodded, and watched as her mother left; the child was mixed up. She didn't remember much about her real father, but she'd loved Steven and now he was gone. Now all her mother did was spend all day in front of the mirror and moan about everything. She liked Ken; he had a funny accent and made her laugh. As the evening had progressed, they'd watched television, played noughts and crosses, and listened to Ken's tales of the old days.

'Kids now days are spoilt. When I was a bairn, we had an outside toilet with cut-up newspaper hanging on a spike.'

'Why?' Maisie's eyes were like saucers.

'Well, we didn't have posh toilet paper, so we used the daily paper once Dad had read it. It was freezing some nights and we had to go outside if we wanted to use the lavatory. I hate spiders and every time I went outside, there was always one waiting for me, it was always a big bugger too, I'd rather face a bloody great anaconda than a spider.'

'What's that?'

'A huge snake.'

'Raydon's got a spider.'

'Well I hope he keeps it away from me, I'll bolt me door in future in case it gets out.'

'It's a friendly spider, I've held it. A huge snake could kill you.'

'So could a spider if it gave me a heart attack.'

'Have you remembered that poem yet?'

'Which poem's that pet?'

'Abu Ben Adam.'

'No pet, it starts, "Abu Ben Adam awoke one night with this thought", but I canna remember the rest.'

'What about, "It was Christmas Day in the Work House"?'

'Now let's think, "it was Christmas day in the work house, a terrible time of year" ooh noo, I've forgotten that one now. Wait a minute though, some of it's coming back, "up spoke some brave old porker as bold as brass, he said you can keep your Christmas pudding..."?'

'Stick it up your arse,' interrupted Norma.

'Norma, I'm ashamed of you; in front of the bairn too.'

'Well that's what you were going to say.'

'I wasna, the final line goes, "give it to wor lass" and I'm telling you, if you were a fella, I'd hang a one on ya.'

'What does that mean?' giggled Maisie.

'It means that if your greet grandma was a man, I'd have given her a smack, you canna go around talking like that in front of bairns, it ain't fitting.'

Maisie giggled some more. 'The next time Raydon annoys me, I'm going to tell him that I'm going to hang a one on him.'

'Not a good idea, he might not like it.'

'He definitely won't like it when I actually do it, but if he gets nasty, I'll let his spider out.'

'That's a terrible idea. I think it's time for bed.'

'Will you sing me that song?'

'What's that, pet?'

'The fishy on a dishy.'

'Well, I will if you go straight to bed after, is it a deal?'

'Deal.'

'Right, here we go.'

'I'm off,' said Norma. 'I can't take any more, even Mary's fallen asleep. You remind me of that man on Auf Weidersen Pet.'

'I'll take that as a compliment unless you mean Oz.'

'No not him, I mean the foreman.'

'Oh Dennis, he's canny man.'

'I think that's his name. Goodnight to you both, tell Mary that I said goodnight.'

'I will, goodnight Norma.'

'Nite nite great Nana. Come on Ken, you start and I'll join in.'

Back at the hotel, Rosie was holding up two garments. 'Which one?' she asked.

Kevin's eyes were like spirals, he'd hoped to exhaust and dazzle Rosie with his love-making but she'd reversed the situation. His penis was getting extremely sore with all this action. At the beginning of their affair, they'd made love about five times a night, but Rosie was turning this into a sex marathon. 'That one,' he replied, pointing to the naughty nurse outfit. He desperately needed a nurse, his legs had lost all feeling and he had to look down to make sure that they were still there.

He glanced at his watch; it was four fifteen in the morning and they'd been at it since seven the previous evening. Was there no stopping this woman? She was ten years his senior and putting him to shame. Still he had to keep going as he was hoping that Rosie would be so pleased with his performance that she might leave Ray. He watched as Rosie headed toward the bathroom with the nurse's outfit, then laid back and closed his eyes and dozed.

About five minutes later, he awoke with Rosie kneeling across him. 'Do you want to sleep?' she asked.

Kevin gazed up at her; she was clad in a short white nurse's outfit with white stockings, suspenders and high heels. 'No,' he cried. 'I just closed my eyes and drifted, I must have dropped off.' He felt as if his penis was about to drop off, but the stupid thing had raised its head at the sight of the vision before him. He'd be mega sore tomorrow, and this wasn't over yet. He had hours to go unless Rosie wanted to sleep, and she was showing no sign of that. 'How come you don't dry up like other women?' Kevin asked as Rosie raised herself above him.

'Dunno, I guess I'm turned on all the time. I thought I'd need help by now at my age, but I don't.'

'Lucky me,' replied Kevin, but at this moment his body felt anything but lucky.

Vic wasn't feeling lucky; he didn't understand how he'd been frozen out of the agency. 'I'm retiring,' he said, 'not giving up the agency.'

'That's right,' replied Lop, handing Vic a brandy, 'it's still your agency but Rosie will be running it.'

'I want the final say in things.'

'And Rosie knows that, she's agreed to everything.'

'Well from the way the solicitor was talking, it sounded as if I'd sold my share to Rosie.'

'You're tired and unwell. Rosie's running things until your health picks up. Would I lie to you?'

'No, but I don't know what I'm signing, I'm blind.'

'That's why I'm here. We will have a wonderful retirement; we can travel the world and see things that we've never seen before.'

'Well I won't see it, I'm blind.'

'So I will be your eyes, I'll always be here for you.'

Vic sighed, 'I'm a lucky man to have a wife like you. Where would I be without you?'

'I'm your wife, nurse, and whatever else you want me to be.'

'I think my colostomy bag needs emptying.'

Lop flinched. She hated this job but made herself attend to his needs. He was a very sick, very nearly bankrupt man, and now that Rosie's money had been transferred into his account, it would be only a matter of time before she moved it into her account and became a very rich widow on a flight to Thailand. Dylan was not part of her plan, but she'd made him believe that he was part of her future, and spurred him on to rid the world of Vic Lee forever.

Chapter Forty-Eight

'What time's breakfast?' Rosie was getting hungry.

'Between eight and ten.'

'I'm starving, maybe we should grab a couple of hours' sleep, as it's only five thirty.'

'Good idea.' Kevin was relieved; maybe they'd both oversleep, giving him time to rebuild his strength.

'On the other hand, we could keep going till breakfast if you want.'

'No, sleep's a good idea, then when we wake up, we can have a shower and a good breakfast. God only knows how I'm going to cope without you.'

'I'm getting old, Kevin, I keep telling you but you don't listen.'

'Rubbish, you'll never get old.'

'Nice of you to say so, but my mirror tells me differently; now let's get some shuteye.'

Kevin cuddled up to her, feeling so secure in her embrace. His eyes began to droop, and soon he'd drifted off into the land of nod.

Lop had already started packing her case in readiness for her escape. She couldn't wait to leave England and the slob that lay beside her every night snoring his head off. She despised him; he'd been a means to an end but it had been a long time coming. He was blind, needed a colostomy bag, and was a bully, besides being tight. She aimed to clear Vic right out so that he ended up with nothing. The house was of no importance; it was spectacular, but rented, so she couldn't gain from that. Vic wouldn't need money where he was going, so everything that he had was hers.

Dylan would take the rap for Vic's murder. It would be his hand that fired the gun, and she would have no part in it. She would be the innocent party, living a life of luxury surrounded by young virile men; she'd had enough of old ones. She also intended opening up a brothel that would be the best in Thailand. It was her turn now.

Rosie awoke at about ten to eight; she could hear footsteps outside in the corridor as people made their way down to breakfast. She got out of bed and headed for the shower. The sound of the water cascading down woke Kevin and he joined her under the shower. Once they'd freshened up, Kevin rang room service and, thirty minutes later, their breakfast arrived. Rosie felt as if she hadn't eaten for a week, she was starving. Her body had become like a raw and pulsating nerve, and she was aching all over. Kevin on the other hand wasn't hungry at all. Every part of his body throbbed, especially his manhood. Thank God for the little sleep that he'd had, and the breakfast before him; if he ate slowly, it would delay the inevitable. Rosie was playing footsie under the table; obviously she was ready to resume their activities.

They watched a little television and waited for their food to go down and, by nine fifteen, Rosie was raring to go once more. She was fuelled by lust, as Kevin was by love. During their passionate encounter, they'd gone just about every position possible. Kevin only had to look at Rosie to make the trouser snake rear its head. Rosie had surrendered to his will; her flesh had become a slave to the insistent strokes of his tongue. He had felt several aftershocks of a brutal climax; at one stage she had experienced a raging inferno within her, and found herself sobbing as her inside had burst into flames, rocketing her over the edge and into the abyss. Neither Rosie nor Kevin would ever forget their night of passion.

At eleven forty, they showered once more and packed their things into their bags. Kevin watched as the French maid, air hostess, pirate, schoolgirl, nurse, secretary, cowgirl, and serving wench outfits were packed away with many pairs of stockings and suspenders. They'd gone through the lot, and he thought it was a miracle that he was still standing. He felt sad that he was going to lose her, and took her into his arms, begging her to give him a chance to make her happy.

'You do make me happy, but I love Ray and if we continue to see each other, you'll never move on.'

'But I want you, and only you.'

'Kevin, you asked me for a final night of passion and I think I've delivered, so please let me go with a good heart.'

Kevin gazed at her, he couldn't resist her. Wiping the tears from his eyes, he smiled and then picked her up, depositing her back onto the bed. 'Just once more,' he cried, 'and then I'll let you go.'

Unfortunately, it wasn't just once, and at one o'clock the cleaners were knocking on the door. Kevin opened it and slipped the girl fifty pounds. 'Take it and come back in an hour,' he said. The girl happily took the money and moved off to the room next door. She returned in an hour and found the occupants ready to leave. Rosie laughed as they made their way down the corridor, and Kevin said, 'Best fifty pounds I've ever spent.' The skin on his penis had split open and he was bleeding, but to him the pain had been worth it. Rosie had plenty of stamina and had made him feel like the greatest lover in the world. He was buzzing, and now the only thing that he needed was sleep. They said their goodbyes and went their separate ways, both reeling from the experience that they'd had.

Reaching home, Rosie was greeted by Ray. 'Hi, Rosie red,' he said, 'did you have a good time at the party?'

'You haven't called me that in years; yes I had a good time. How was your night?'

'Okay, they had a couple of slappers there; they were ugly but then when you're married to the most beautiful girl in the world, every other woman looks like a slapper. I bought you some roses on the way home, a rose for my rose. Let's have a coffee and then we'll spend the rest of the afternoon in bed.'

Rosie's heart jolted. Her body was aching and sore but she couldn't refuse him or she'd give the game away, and he had bought her some flowers after all, so he was obviously expecting something. What she didn't realise was that Ray felt guilty after letting the stripper give him a blow job, and needed to make love to his wife to make him feel better.

'Fine,' replied Rosie, 'it's a long time since we've done that, sounds good to me,' and hurrying to the kitchen she put her bag down and proceeded to make some coffee. Back in Surrey, Kevin was sleeping like a log.

It was the day of Vic's party, and Lop had spared no expense. The caterers were top notch, as were the marquees and entertainers. Dylan was doing a few numbers, and Bobby was going to perform with Steven's band too. His latest show stopper was Van Halen's *Jump*, when he literally did jump, plus turn somersaults and belt the song out. He'd watched the video footage and followed it as closely as possible. Jenny had arranged with Lop that she could stay overnight. She said she'd been going to stay at a guest house but the place had double booked, and that she would pay Lop well if she could find her somewhere to sleep. 'I only have one guest room,' said Lop, 'so it won't come cheap.'

'How much do you want?'

'Two hundred pounds.'

'I'll give you two hundred and fifty for your kindness in helping me out.'

'Wonderful,' replied Lop, 'but I want it in cash.'

'It will be.'

'Then come and see me as soon as you arrive and you can move in straight away.'

'Thank you, Mrs Lee.'

'My pleasure.' Lop replaced the receiver knowing that she only had to suffer being Mrs Lee for less than twenty four hours.

Deanne had travelled with Kevin, minus Eddie who was laid low with a virus. They chatted away about things in general, and were having a good laugh when out of nowhere appeared a car. As this was a country lane and one way only, they were terrified. The car was heading straight toward them, there was no escape. It gathered speed and headed straight for them. Deanne screamed, the car was just feet away and then suddenly it passed straight through them. Kevin was sweating. This was unreal, one moment the car had been bumper to bumper, and the next it was gone. 'Jesus,' said a shaking Kevin, 'where did he go?'

'Straight through us,' replied Deanne.

'It's not possible.'

'Well I saw it too. Come on, let's get moving in case it comes back.'

'Good thinking,' and Kevin speeded up his car.

At the party, they relayed the incident and everyone laughed except Rosie. This had happened to her the week before, but she'd not spoken about it, thinking that people would laugh at her. 'What colour was the car and what make?'

'A canary yellow Lamborghini, wasn't it, Kevin?'

Kevin nodded.

'You didn't imagine it, Deanne, I experienced the same thing with the same car, it's the car that your father crashed in.'

'Then why is Dad trying to scare us?'

'He's not, darling, I think he's trying to warn us about something, and telling us to keep our eyes open; we need to be vigilant. Maisie Rose keeps going on about a yellow sports car too, and so does your grandmother.'

'God, that's creepy, I need a drink,' and Deanne wandered over to the bar.

Dylan was an angry young man. Jenny had fired him up, telling him that she'd received a letter from Rosie saying that she'd found out about his wild behaviour and that she had no intention of renewing his contract, and that she'd make sure that he'd never work for anyone else. Therefore, he was surprised when, on arrival, Rosie threw her arms around him saying, 'I've got such plans for you, I'll tell you about them later, must rush, I've got to run through some stuff with Bobby and run through some songs with Kevin. I hope we're paying you enough for tonight; let me know if we're not, see you later.'

Confused, Dylan went in search of his mother and found her laying tables. 'I want to see that letter,' he cried. 'I've just seen Rosie; she didn't sound as if she'd sacked me.'

'It's in my bag; I'll show it to you later.'

'I want to see it now. You're such a lying bitch; how do I know that I'm not being set up?'

'Oh all right.' Jenny went to the cloakroom and retrieved her bag. She took the letter from her bag and handed it to her son. 'There,' she said. Dylan walked away with it and, finding a chair, sat down. His heart lurched as he read it. His mother had been right; how could Rosie be so two-faced? He wasn't the brightest of buttons, and neither was his mother, so he'd overlooked the fact that there was no letterheading, no phone number, plus Rosie's name was misspelt, or the fact that the letter was addressed to a Mrs J Brown and had no stamp on it.

'What's that?' said Bobby, creeping up on Dylan, 'a love letter? I bet you have lots of girls after you.'

'It's nothing important.'

'Fancy a drink? Mum's got some great bookings for you, and there's even a stint in LA. She's worked her socks off to get that one for you. Her ex-husband is Barry Grayson; he's great, and he'll have pulled a lot of strings for you. You'll be a superstar in no time.'

'I've never met him.' Dylan's head was spinning. Was his mother lying, or was Rosie lying to her son? He had a drink with Bobby and then once more went in search of his mother. He found her walking around with canapés on a tray. Sidling up to her, he said, 'If you're lying, I'll put a bullet straight through your treacherous heart.'

'It's Rosie who's the treacherous one; she'll build you up all night and, then later, show you the door.'

'Well, I've warned you, I'm going to confront Ray tonight. If he is my father, he needs to be taught a lesson.'

'I don't want him harmed, or the boys.'

'Just watch your own back,' and Dylan stormed off.

Vic was trying to enjoy himself; he didn't feel well and could only distinguish people by their voices. Lop was by his side all night, fussing around him, her suitcase already in the boot of her car. She wasn't going to drive, she'd ordered a cab but at least the case was out of the house. Her idea of not driving was because she wouldn't need the car any more and, if it remained on the drive, it would appear that she was in bed with Vic and not at the airport.

Dylan went through his routine, and everyone loved him, apart from Vic who was furious. 'I sacked that cunt ages ago,' he yelled, 'get him out of my house and, furthermore, he's not getting paid for tonight.' Dylan was unphased as Rosie stepped up to the mic.

'Thank you, Dylan,' she said. 'I'm sure that Vic is out of sorts, he's a grumpy old soul at times. As for him sacking you, Dylan, he can't because you're my protégé; the only one that can fire you is me. I'm not stupid enough to do that, you're a star.'

'He's fucking shit,' yelled Vic. 'I own half of the agency, so you'll do as I say.'

'Not any more,' replied Rosie. 'I own it outright; ask your wife if you don't believe me. You've had your time, Vic, and I intend to recruit new blood and get things back on track. I will be collaborating with Barry too.'

'What the fuck's she talking about?' snapped Vic. 'You told me that she was just running it.'

'Its better this way,' replied Lop. 'I wanted to surprise you.'

'Well you've done that, you stupid cunt, cancel the contract.'

'Too late, Vic,' said Ray, 'you've had a good innings, mate, and I'm sure that Rosie will ring you if she gets stuck.'

'Of course I will,' said Rosie, 'you're still the master; just think of the acts that you've made stars, especially Eden Gold. You made him famous, and you demanded his blood, heart, and soul. I'll never forgive you for that. Then there was Cathy who you used and abused until Ed married her, then there's Kevin, who you've manipulated like plasticine. You tried it with me too but it didn't work, Kevin and I are now a double act and...'

'In more ways than one,' snapped Vic, 'did you know that Kevin had been fucking her, Ray?'

Ray's heart sank and he shook his head. 'No, I didn't, but if that's true, I asked for it. I was an alcoholic, aided by you for years, and if it had to be anyone, I'm glad that it was him. Rosie and I are rock solid again and I intend to help her as much as I can with the agency.'

Jenny had been hovering nearby and, frustrated at Ray's comments, dropped her tray of sandwiches. She swore out loud and dropped to her knees to recover them. She felt sick as Ray approached the stage and kissed Rosie's cheek, saying, 'This woman is the best thing that has ever happened to me. I've been a complete arsehole to her, but she's stuck by me and I've turned a corner. I don't drink any more.'

'Where's Al Simpkins?' yelled Vic. 'I'll fix you, Rosaleen Lynne.'

'You won't. What you want, Al doesn't have any more.'

Vic rounded on Lop. 'You evil conniving bitch,' he snapped. 'I want you out of my house, and you're not getting a penny from me.'

'You're overwrought,' cried Lop, 'this is for the best.'

The DJ began to play once more, drowning Vic out, and Kevin

wandered over to Susie. 'Would you like to dance with me before your father flattens me?' he said.

'If you like.'

'You could sound a little more enthusiastic.'

'Why? I'm rescuing you, aren't I, and obviously there's no one else who wants to dance with you.'

'I didn't ask anyone else.'

'Really, come on then,' and taking Kevin's outstretched hand, Susie let Kevin lead her out to the dance floor.

'Wow,' said Bobby to Deanne. 'I can't believe this; did you and Sue know about Mum and Kevin?'

'I pushed them together. Ray was treating her like shit, and Kevin had the hots for her.'

'Didn't Dad take it well?'

'He's not your dad.'

'Well, who is then?'

'Come on, Bobby, it's not rocket science. I was only a little girl when my father used to visit, and there was an occasion when Ray was away and Dad turned up unexpected. He stayed the night and, after his death, Mum started throwing up in the mornings. You don't even look like Ray or Raydon; you're the spitting image of my dad.'

'So you could be my blood sister.'

'That's right, so could Susie, and Eddie could be your half brother.'

Steven was setting up on stage. 'Bobby, we're on in ten minutes.'

'Gotta go, we'll speak about this later,' and a confused Bobby headed in Steven's direction.

Deanne swallowed hard, she'd had to tell Bobby because it seemed as if no one else was going to and he had a right to know. Now came the hard bit, telling Eddie when she got home. That wouldn't go down too well, as it would prove that his father was cheating on his mother with his beloved Aunty Rose.

Vic was lost for words. He had no agency, his wife had lied to him, and his best friend Al Simpkins had parted with his trump card. 'I'm going to bed,' he snapped.

'Don't you want to watch Bobby and Steven perform?' asked Lop.

'Do you keep your brains in your cunt? I'm fucking blind.'

'But you can hear him.'

'That's a point, I'll stay and listen to them, and then I'm going to bed. You can sleep in another room tonight and we'll discuss things in the morning.'

'I thought that you wanted me out now.'

'I do, but I need someone to get me up in the morning. You can go once I've had breakfast, and Al can take over.'

'Of course,' replied Lop, knowing that Vic wouldn't be around much longer. He'd certainly be missing breakfast and would be in no need of anyone's care.

Jenny had slipped upstairs and was finishing off the trap that she'd begun earlier; nobody was going to miss her, as the revelations made by Vic had begun a talking point amongst many. Entering the room, she took the gun from her case and began to put her evil plan into motion, copying the diagram she had seen in a book about assasination methods. Armed with fishing line and weights, and plenty of duct tape and adhesive, she began to laugh hysterically.

Dylan was completely fucked up; he didn't know who to believe any more. Rosie seemed genuine, but then there was the matter of the letter. Was that genuine or had his sicko mother written it? There was only one way to find out. Earlier, Ray had slapped him on his back, saying, 'Great performance, son, welcome to the family.' What did that mean, was he taking the piss?

Bobby passed by looking jubilant. He'd performed brilliantly and the thought that he may be Ed Gold's son had lifted him to alarming new heights. 'I feel fantastic,' he said. 'I've had some great news.'

'What's that?' Dylan was intrigued.

'Ray might not be my dad.'

Dylan was really pissed off now; Ray had deserted him and maybe raised another man's child. 'You can't tell without a DNA test,' said Dylan.

Bobby was unphased and continued to babble. 'Deanne said that Ed Gold's my dad. I guess I've always known it. Ray treated me different to Raydon. It must take a lot to bring up someone else's kid; Ray's a real diamond.'

'He's not so good at raising his own.'

'I don't understand, he's been a good dad to Raydon.'

'Get a DNA test, your sister could be wrong,' and an even angrier Dylan walked away. Bobby had really fucked things up now with his revelation that they might not be related now, and Raydon could be his only link. His only thought now was to kill Vic and fuck off to Thailand with Lop.

Chapter Forty-Nine

Lop had put Vic to bed, and came downstairs to tell everyone that the party was over. Ray had wandered off, telling Rosie that he needed a little time on his own. 'Big boys don't cry,' he said, 'but I need to and I don't want anyone seeing me.'

Rosie put her arm around his shoulders. 'I'm so sorry, Ray,' she said, 'can you forgive me?'

'Nothing to forgive, it was all my fault, I just need to be alone for a while.'

'I understand,' Rosie replied. 'I'll wait for you here.' She indicated the sofa that Ray had just vacated. She watched as he walked away, her guilt consuming her.

'Where's Dee?' asked Susie. 'I haven't seen her for over thirty minutes. Kevin wants to leave and he's told me that Maisie Rose and I can stay at his place.'

'Sounds promising.'

'He loves you, Mum, not me.'

'No he doesn't, he just thought he did. It was a fling, nothing more, nothing less.'

'Maybe,' replied Susie, 'maybe, now where is my little sis? If she's left in a cab I'll kill her, it would be just her style.'

Dylan was waiting on the landing for Lop. His trigger finger was itchy, and he wanted to get this thing done and dusted. Five minutes later, Lop appeared. 'Do it now,' she ordered. 'I'm leaving, here's your flight ticket.' She stuffed it into Dylan's pocket and kissed him.

'Why can't we leave together?' asked Dylan.

'It would look suspicious if we're seen together; I'll meet you at the airport. I'm going outside to wait for my cab, see you.'

Dylan walked into Vic's room. The bedside lamp was still on and he could see Vic propped up in bed. Vic awoke. 'Is that you, Lop? I told you to stay away from me until morning, so piss off.'

'No, its Dylan, just come to say goodbye.'

'Go to hell.'

'That's where you're going, bye,' and raising the gun, Dylan fired. The bullet literally blew Vic's brains out, and the blood splattered up the wall and headboard. As he left the room, he collided with Ray who was just walking past. Dylan saw red and, pointing the gun at a bewildered Ray, yelled 'Inside.'

'Was that a gunshot?' cried Susie, 'or was it an explosion?'

'Probably Vic blowing up the television,' laughed Kevin.

Canny Ken awoke with a start. These show business gatherings did nothing for him; the people were full of fakes or sickos. He'd rather be at home watching the television with a bottle of Newcastle brown ale in his hand. His immediate thoughts were for Rosie. He was here to take care of her and he'd committed the cardinal sin of falling asleep. 'What was that noise?' he cried, sitting upright.

'Nobody knows,' replied Susie, 'nobody knows where Deanne and Ray are either.'

'I coudna help overhearing the accusations made by wor Vic. Ray must be feeling a bit sick about them, and Deanne is probably with him, consoling him. I'll go and look for them. Look at the bairn stretched out there sound asleep, nothing disturbs her. Didn't she do a brahma rendition of *When the boat comes in*, I were proud of the lass. I'll just go upstairs and find the missing persons and then we can all go home to wor beds.' He left the room singing, 'dance to your daddy my little laddie, dance to your daddy hear the mummy sing thout shall have a fishy on a little dishy, thout shall have a haddock when the boat comes in.'

467

'He's a one off,' laughed Kevin.

Another ten minutes passed, and now Ken was missing. 'This is ridiculous,' said Rosie, 'where is everyone? You stay downstairs with Maisie, Bobby. Kevin, Susie, and I will form a search party.'

It didn't take long for the trio to discover the first casualty. Ken was sprawled face down on the landing. Vic's door was open and the bedside lamp was on. 'Phone the police, Susie,' cried Kevin, 'there's a phone in Vic's room. Something very heavy must have felled Ken; this is no accident, the back of his head's bleeding.'

Susie ran into Vic's room and then let out a piercing scream. Vic was propped up dead in his blood-soaked bed. He had a hole in his head and his eyes were wild and staring. Kevin and Rosie rushed to Susie's aid, not knowing what she'd seen. They both gasped in horror as they surveyed the scene before them. Rosie looked to her left; Ray was bound and gagged to a chair. 'Do come in, Rosie,' said a voice that Rosie recognised only too well, 'come and join the party. I heard you singing earlier. You were very good but then you always were, now close the door behind you unless you want me to shoot every member of your family.' Jenny stepped out of the shadows, waving a gun around. Although Jenny's appearance had changed somewhat, Rosie could now put a face to the voice.

'What do you want, Jenny?'

'I want you and your fucking daughters dead, so that Ray and I can start our new life together.'

'Let Susie go, your fight is with me, not my daughters, and where is Deanne?'

'She's okay at present, but look through that mirror.'

'Through it?'

'Yes, it's a two way mirror. The dead sicko has been perving through it for years, take a look.'

Rosie obeyed; the gun was pointed in her direction. Gazing through the mirror she beheld her daughter trussed up to a chair and staring down the barrel of a gun. It appeared that an elaborate system of wires and weights had been set up to pull the trigger when the door was opened. 'She's been waiting for you, Rosie. I wanted to make sure that you witnessed her execution. I want you to suffer, how I want you to suffer.'

'But she's innocent.'

'She's the spawn of the devil, she's fucking Ed Gold's. You two were pure poison; he's dead and you and your girls are going to join him.'

Ray was trying to break free of his bonds, and it was then that Rosie noticed it was Dylan who held a gun to Ray's head. 'Why, Dylan?' she cried.

'Because you were lying earlier, and my mother was right about you.'

'Mother?'

'Yes, mother, she gave me the letter that you sent.'

'What letter, I've been working my arse off to get gigs for you, so show it to me. How could I send you a letter? I don't have a forwarding address for you. I have to rely on you ringing me or being able to contact you on your mobile which is usually switched off.'

Dylan was speechless. It was true, she didn't have a forwarding address. 'Show me the letter,' cried Rosie. 'I have your new contract in my bag. Why didn't you tell me that Jenny was your mother? I don't harbour grudges; we could have linked up again.'

'She's bluffing, she hasn't got a contract.'

'Shut your fucking mouth. Here's the letter, boss lady,' and Dylan threw the letter which landed at Rosie's feet.

Rosie picked it up and read it. 'No letterhead, my name misspelt, and no stamp on the letter which is addressed to a Mrs J Brown at an address that I didn't know existed. Dylan, back off now and we'll forget that any of this happened. Take Ray's gag off, and let him speak for himself. If he is having an affair with your mother, she can have him, if that's what he wants.'

'It's more than that, he's my father.'

'That's impossible, your mother and Ray split up in 1963.'

'Shut the fuck up.' Dylan removed Ray's gag saying, 'If you cry for help, I'll pick off your family one by one. Admit it, you are my father.'

Ray licked his lips. 'Unless you were conceived at the time that Rosie has just mentioned, it is impossible that you're mine. I walked out on your mother when I found her in bed with Ed.'

'Explain yourself, Mother.' Dylan was getting suspicious.

'He visited me at the commune.'

'I've never visited any commune.' Ray was shaking with fear; the gun was still pointed at his head and Dylan's hand was also shaking.

'Your mother is a liar. After I left her I returned to my parents' home and then moved to Brighton to find work. The last time I saw her was in Scotland at a gig a few years back.'

Dylan looked at Ray and then back at his mother. Ray was struggling to free himself, and the cords were loosening. Rosie was sweating; she was trapped with her ex-best friend who appeared to have lost the plot. She couldn't think of anything to say until she remembered the phone calls and flowers. 'Did you keep making anonymous calls?'

'Yes.'

'And did you keep sending me flowers?'

Rosie was playing for time, hoping that Al Simpkins might wake up, or Lop come back having forgotten something. She'd seen her leave, but she might return.

'Yes, I sent you flowers.'

'What?' Dylan was now confused. Where was this leading?

'And did you kill my poor cousin and her daughters?'

'I paid someone to do it and the goons got it wrong, but I'm not going to get it wrong, you and your girls are going to die and then Ray and I are leaving with Dylan to start a new life. I'll take care of the boys, they'll want for nothing.'

'You did what? That woman was disembowelled; you had a part in that? You spent your dead husband's money on killing three innocent people. I thought that tonight was all about scaring Ray into confessing that he was my father, not about murder. You've done it again, you've lied, you're evil, I'm out of here.'

'Stay where you are you, chicken, I'm sending Rosie to hell where she belongs and I'll send you there too if I have to.' She aimed the gun at Rosie's head, and then lowered it, saying, 'I've got a better idea, you can unlock the door next door, Rosie, and watch as Deanne's brains get splattered everywhere, and then I'll kill you. Just think, the last thing that you and your daughter will see is each other's faces.'

'I won't do it.'

'Then I'll kill you now, shame though.'

'Over my dead body,' said Kevin, shielding Rosie.

'It can be arranged, say your prayers, Rosie.'

No one was prepared for what happened next. Kevin pushed Rosie out of the line of fire, and Susie flung herself at Kevin knocking him and her mother to the floor. The bullet went into Susie's chest and she fell to the floor. 'No,' screamed Rosie, 'no.' She cradled her daughter in her arms. Ray's bonds were looser now, and Dylan was helping him although he was still holding the gun at Ray's head. But from where Jenny was standing, she couldn't see Dylan's free hand. Suddenly the door opened and Bobby stood framed in the doorway; he took in the scene in one glance. His heart was racing, his sister lay on the floor with blood pumping from her chest, Vic Lee had his brains splattered out all over his bed, and Dylan had a gun trained on Ray even though he appeared to be untying his bonds with one hand.

'Wow' said Bobby. 'I came up because there's a gale force wind blowing up outside. It's blown the patio doors open and I can't close them.'

'Go downstairs, I don't want you harmed,' cried Jenny.

'Why not, my sister doesn't look too healthy.'

471

'We need an ambulance for Susie; take pity on her, Jenny,' said Rosie.

'She won't get pity from me. I can't wait to see the look on your face when you open the door next door; opening it will blow Deanne's head off.'

'Okay, Jenny, you've won. I'll leave Rosie but let her and the girls go,' said Ray.

'I can't, they'll go to the police.'

'Sounds like a stand-off,' said Bobby. 'Do you know what I do when I'm unsure of my next move?'

'Will somebody call an ambulance,' screamed Rosie, 'my daughter is dying. Go with Jenny, Ray, do anything, but please save Susie.'

'I dance,' said Bobby, 'and then the answer comes flooding through.'

Bobby started dancing, confusing everyone. Jenny turned back to Rosie. 'Get up,' she screeched. Bobby saw his chance, he spun round and did a flying scissor kick, knocking the gun from Jenny's hand. Kevin grabbed it as it hit the floor, and Ray, who was now free of his bonds, threw himself at Jenny. Dylan picked up the phone and rang for an ambulance, and then fled the room. The wind outside had gathered impetus, and the struggling couple were caught up in a vortex as the windows flew open.

Dylan now hated his mother, and wanted to put her in the ground, but decided to let the Lynne family deal with her; dying was too good for her. He fled the building with one thought on his mind, the airport and Lop. He didn't get far. He was about to get into his car when he heard a familiar voice. 'Dylan,' said Ben, a known drug dealer, 'the boss is looking for you, you owe him big time.'

'I've been away.'

'We know, but you've had plenty of time to pay up since you've been back.'

'How did you know I was here?'

'The press and our spies.'

'Look guys, I'm leaving for Thailand tonight.'

'So?'

'I'll pay you when I get back.'

'Maybe you're not coming back, you need to come with us and see the boss.'

'But Vic's wife is waiting for me at the airport; she'll be able to pay you.'

'And maybe she won't.' Ben stuck a gun in Dylan's ribs, saying, 'you'd better come quietly.'

Chapter Fifty

The wind was like a vacuum; Jenny and Ray were caught up in it and getting suctioned towards the window. Rosie looked on in horror as both of them hurtled through the windows and out of sight. The wind dropped, and Rosie stared out of the window. Jenny was impaled on the spiked railings that were just beneath it. Ray had somehow missed them but he lay on the ground motionless. She broke down in tears, and Kevin took her into his arms. 'Why did she do it, Rosie? I'd already pushed you out of the line of fire.'

'I told you before that she'd die for you.'

'But she never...'

'Just be there when she wakes up. Bobby, I need you to get a ladder and break into the room next door through the window. You can't go through the door as that will activate the gun.'

'I'm on my way,' said Bobby.

Ken rubbed his head and stared up into the eyes of Maisie Rose. 'Eeeh man, I've had a nasty bump on wor head,' he said, 'help us up, lass.'

'Did you fall over?' said Maisie, giving Ken her hand.

'I must have done, pet. Is that police sirens I can hear?'

'Think so, I rang them because you'd fallen over and I couldn't find anyone. I was scared and thought I was on my own.'

'Well, there's no need to be scared now, pet, I'm here. Let's go and find the others, they canna be far away.'

'Do you think that Uncle Vic might know where they are?'

'I doubt it. Some bodyguard, I am, I've lost the body that I was supposed to guard.'

'Why do you have to guard Nana Rosie's body? She's fit enough.'

'Indeed she is, hen, she's a fine woman.'

'She can still do the splits and River dance, and I can't do either.'

'Maybe you will one day, pet, let's get some lemonade.'

'How did you get a bump on the back of your head when you were lying on your stomach?'

'Well, I guess I must have hit me head, got dizzy, and then spun round landing on me front.'

'You are funny. Look there's an ambulance outside as well as a police car.'

'Then we'd better go down and let them in.'

Bobby charged past both of them like a bat out of hell.

'Are you all right, son?' cried Ken.

'Fine, can't stop.'

Once downstairs, Ken opened the door, and the police and ambulance men charged upstairs. 'What room is the shot girl in?' asked a paramedic.

'Shot girl, I dinna know about any shot girl.'

'Up here,' shouted Rosie, running out onto the landing. The paramedic headed for the room that Rosie was leading them to and, once inside it, tended to Susie who was drifting in and out of consciousness. Now that her daughter was being tended to, Rosie rushed downstairs and out into the garden where Ray laid motionless. Jenny was firmly impaled on the railings, and blood was still dripping from her wounds. 'Ray,' cried Rosie. 'Ray, please speak to me.'

There was no response, and Rosie threw herself across his body, sobbing her heart out. Seeing Rosie run outside in a blind panic, Ken followed her. 'What's up, lass?' he cried. 'Oh my God, what happened and why is wor Bobby climbing up that ladder, look, he's got to the top and is now forcing the window. Is he training to be a cat burglar?'

'Deanne's in there and we can't go through the door as there's a gun rigged up to fire if the door opens; the only way in to free her is through the window.' A paramedic knelt down beside Ray, just as Susie was stretchered out.

Inside the house the phone rang, and Maisie Rose picked up the receiver. It was Eddie. 'Can I speak to Dee?' he asked.

'I don't know where she is. The police are here and Mummy's just been carried out on a stretcher; she doesn't look very well and she's wearing an oxygen mask. Nana Rose is in the garden, and Ken fell over but he's all right now.'

'Okay Maisie, I'll call back in thirty minutes.' Eddie was worried. He hadn't wanted Dee to go to the party, as he liked to be around to protect her, and he was on a sick bed. Kevin had promised to take care of her, but somehow she'd gone missing and her sister was on her way to the hospital. Vowing that he'd never let Deanne out of his sight again, Eddie turned over and tried to sleep, expecting to hear her key in the lock any second.

'I'm very disappointed in you, Dylan.' Andy Frasier was drumming on the table with his finger tips. He had piercing blue eyes, the kind that made you want to avoid eye contact at any cost. His nose was like a boxer's nose; it had been broken many times and never dealt with surgically. He'd lost two fingers on his right hand from a debt that he hadn't paid himself when he'd been a teenager, and he had thin lips with a mouth that turned down at the corners. Most of his hair was gone apart from a small patch at the crown and that was grey. His frame was slight and he walked with a limp, also a wound that he'd achieved by grassing someone up. They had fractured his leg and, as that hadn't been treated either, he now walked with a clumsy gait.

'I'll pay you back, I promise, just give me time.' Dylan was shitting himself.

'Too late for that, Dylan, we're going for a ride.'

'Where?'

'Your place. Is the rope in the boot, Ben?'

'Yes, boss.'

'Right then, it's time to take Dylan home.'

Bobby had got into the room and began to untie his sister. She was covered in duct tape; it bound her to the chair, and the chair had been affixed to the floor. Her torso was bound to the back of the chair, and her knees to the legs. Her arms had been duct taped to the arms, and the chair itself could not be moved. Jenny had put several layers of duct tape around the feet of it; it was like duct tape island. 'I'll have to cut you free,' said Bobby, 'good job I always carry an army knife with me, plus I nicked some scissors from the kitchen downstairs.' He removed the gag from Deanne's mouth and said, 'What happened?'

'I don't know, this lady was on the landing and she asked me if I'd help her find her earring. She said that she thought that it was under the bed but that she couldn't reach it if it was. She was one of the waitresses, so I didn't suspect anything. I looked under the bed and then I felt this blow on the back of my head. The next thing I knew was that I woke up trussed to this chair. I thought I heard a gunshot at one time.'

'You did, that woman was responsible for Lynne's murder. She'd paid someone to do it because she wanted Mum, you, and Susie dead, and the killers got the wrong people.'

'How did you find out?'

'I was standing outside the door when I heard her confession, so I went in, played the fool and, when she turned her attention to Mum, and wasn't looking my way, I kicked the gun out of her hand.'

'Where was Ray?'

'Tied up with a gun to his head.'

'Who was holding the gun?'

'Dylan.'

'Why?'

'Jenny was his mother and had told him that Ray was his father.'

'Where's Dylan now?'

'He did a runner, he knew nothing about the killings and was so disgusted that he untied Ray and left. I think he killed Vic though.'

'Vic's dead?'

'Yep, and Susie's on her way to hospital. Ray's lying out in the garden being tended to by paramedics; he fell through the window while he was struggling with Jenny. She's dead, impaled on the railings.'

'Good.'

'I'll have you out of here in no time,' and Bobby set to cutting through all the duct tape.

Maisie Rose had gone upstairs; she wondered what the policemen were doing and peeped in the door. A policeman spotted her and took her downstairs and out into the garden. 'I found this little one upstairs,' he said, 'can someone take her, we're busy.'

Ken took Maisie from the policeman and went back inside the house with her. 'Busy,' he said, 'why not look through the two way mirror and you'll see someone's who's busy.'

'Two way mirror, what are you talking about?'

'Maisie, just wait here for me, I've got to show this officer something.'

'Okay, don't be long.'

'I won't, pet.' Ken hurried upstairs with the officer and, walking into Vic's room, said, 'That mirror.'

The officer stared through it. 'Jesus Christ,' he cried.

'No, just wor Bobby freeing his sister, doing your job in fact.'

'Where's the key to the door?'

'You canna use it, if you look more closely, you'll see that there's a gun rigged up in there which will go off if the door is opened. That young lad had used his initiative and climbed in through the window. You lot don't even know what's going on cos you're too busy hovering around that piece of shit that's in the bed decaying.'

'This is a murder case.'

'Yes, and he deserved to die, but that lass in the next room doesn't. I'm going back downstairs to take care of the bairn.'

Rosie watched as Ray was put on the stretcher, still breathing but unconscious. She gazed around the garden; it was so still now. She was so glad that Norma, Raydon, and Mary hadn't attended the party; at least they'd been spared this ordeal. Then she heard a sound behind her. 'Is that you, Dylan?' she asked.

There was no reply so Rosie began to make her way back to the house. 'Rosie, Rosie, Rosie,' whispered a voice. Rosie could see no one until a bright light appeared in front of her. It was hurting her eyes so she raised her arm to shut it out. The light became much larger and was heading Rosie's way, then it began to take form. Rosie was transfixed and petrified at the same time; this was nothing beautiful or spiritual, it was pure evil. The form now blocked her path as the voice grew louder and louder, making Rosie think that her eardrums were about to burst. Then she saw it, a woman with glittery robes and a headdress, a beautiful woman with jet black hair that reached her waist. Around her waist was draped a huge snake.

'Francine,' cried Rosie, 'you're not real, go, you're not having my children.'

The figure threw back her head and laughed. 'You'll never escape me,' she said. 'I'm waiting.'

'Go back to hell,' screamed Rosie, 'you're just a bad dream.'

Inside the house, Maisie had given Ken the slip, and crept upstairs curious to know why she couldn't go onto Vic's room. The officers all had their backs turned to her and her eyes alighted on something shiny on the carpet. Tiptoeing past the officers, she picked the object up, it was a key. Putting it into her pocket, she slipped out of the room and looked out of the landing window. Nana Rosie was in the garden talking to a lady who had a huge snake wrapped around her. Deanne worked with snakes as well as tortoises, she would have loved to have seen this huge one. She thought that she could hear Deanne's voice and Bobby's, and it seemed to be coming from the room next to Vic's. She pushed the door but it was locked and, wondering if the key that she'd found might fit the lock, she inserted it.

'Maisie, you're a bad lass, you know that you're not to come up here.' Ken was huffing and puffing running up the stairs. He reached the landing just in time to see Maisie insert the key. 'Maisie, no,' he cried. It was too late. Maisie had unlocked the door and there was the sound of a gunshot.

Bobby had freed his sister. He wiped his brow; that had been a close call. The officers were looking through the mirror and sighed with relief. 'Come on,' said Bobby, 'we need to leave the way I came in. I'll go first, that way if you fall, you'll fall on top of me.'

'Okay,' replied Deanne as Bobby made his way to the window. Deanne stood up and stretched. She felt so stiff, she'd been in that chair for ages and she'd been so scared that she'd wet herself. Neither Bobby nor Deanne saw the door handle move, and Deanne knew nothing until the door opened and the bullet hit her in her chest. She stared in disbelief as blood seeped through her glittery top and then she hit the floor and passed out. Maisie stood framed in the doorway. 'I just wanted to tell you that there was a lady in the garden with a huge snake, I've never seen such a large one and thought that you... I didn't mean to...' then she burst into tears and ran from the room and rushed downstairs with Ken in hot pursuit.

Rosie had heard the gunshot and raced back inside the house without a backward glance to see if Francine was still there or not. She walked into mayhem. Ken was on the phone requesting an ambulance, and Maisie was screaming and crying. She ran up to Rosie screaming, 'Nana, I did a bad thing, I saw the lady with the snake and I thought that Deanne would want to see it. I could hear her talking to Bobby and I'd found a key. I opened the door and I think that Deanne's dead.'

Rosie's legs refused to hold her up and she collapsed onto the sofa. She could hear sobbing coming from upstairs and, regaining her composure, stood up and went upstairs where she found the police now clustered around Deanne and Bobby. Bobby was cradling his sister in his arms and sobbing, 'I got her free, Mum. We were just going to leave and the door opened. I did try, Mum, honest I did, will she be all right?'

'Of course she will,' replied Rosie. 'I'll take over until the ambulance gets here. You go downstairs and sit with Ken and Maisie, and get her to draw you a picture of the lady that she saw in the garden with the snake.' Obviously Francine wasn't an illusion after all, Maisie had seen her too. Cradling her daughter in her arms, she began to sing the Troggs *Little Girl*. Deanne had been such a pretty little girl, and was now a beautiful woman. The policemen backed off. There was nothing that they could do, so they left the room, leaving Rosie with her daughter.

Chapter Fifty-One

Ben was rifling through Dylan's wallet. 'Eight hundred quid,' he said, 'that won't even make a dent in what you owe us.'

'I've got a flight ticket; you could get a refund on that.'

'Let's see.' Ben took the envelope that Dylan was offering. He opened it and then laughed out loud. 'Are you taking the piss?' he cried, 'it's a one-way ticket, so how were you supposed to pay us when you weren't coming back? Not only that, it's out of date.'

'It can't be, I was supposed to be meeting Lop Lee at the airport tonight; we were flying together.'

'Oh, Vic Lee's wife, she's had more dicks than she's had hot dinners; she's been playing with you, the ticket's a month out of date. Where were you flying from?'

'Stansted.'

Ben laughed some more. 'It's even a different airport. She's really had you over, she didn't intend taking you with her at all.'

'Fucking lying bitch,' yelled Dylan, 'she's made a real fool out of me. I didn't have time to look at the ticket; I had other things to do.'

'Never mind, your worries will be over soon. Are you any good at writing?'

'Why?'

'Well, I need you to write a suicide note, apologising to everyone for taking your own life.'

'I won't do it.'

'Oh but you will, unless you want me to rip your guts out; here's a writing pad and pen, start writing.'

'You can have anything you want, but please don't kill me.'

'We will take everything, including your car. You were a big fish in a little pond, but now you're a little fish in a big one. Oh and by the way, your friends will be given time to clear their debts and, if they don't, they'll go the same way as you.'

Dylan took the pad and pen and started writing. The words were scarcely legible, as tears spilled onto the paper smudging the ink. His life was over. No one had really cared about him, and as for Tommy the drifter, he was probably unaware of his existence. The only ones that had shown him any kindness were the Lynne family and, egged on by his mother, he'd almost destroyed them. He continued writing with a heavy heart. Rosie had given him a chance and he'd screwed it up by mixing with the bad boys. He recalled his days on the commune. They were free and easy days; the hippies were kind to him and he had many friends, but the only thing that he'd ever wanted was for his mother to love him and to have a loving father. Now, he wasn't going to Los Angeles, he was going to hell.

Deanne was stretchered out, and was now on her way to hospital with her mother and Bobby. Once inside the ambulance, Rosie broke down. A month earlier, she'd been looking forward to owning her own agency, starting a new life with her non-alcoholic husband, and just living her life from day to day into her old age. She gazed at her daughter whose complexion was pallid, and prayed to God above. She didn't go to church very often but she was a believer and felt that God knew this. She hoped that he did, and resting her head on Bobby's shoulder, she sobbed as if her heart would break.

Dylan's girlfriend awoke the next morning and found his suicide note. She woke the other people that shared the squat and they tentatively made their way to the barn where they found Dylan.

He'd been hanged, and pinned to the wall was a note saying, 'Debt paid in full, this is a warning to you other piss takers, pay up or you'll get the same. You can run but you cannot hide'. Barbara collapsed in shock, but later that day she packed her bags and left the squat. She had friends in Spain and that was where she was headed. The other two occupants decided to sit it out.

'Dylan owed thousands,' said Pete, a bald headed hippy, 'we owe a few hundred between us; they won't kill us for that.'

They were famous last words as, a fortnight later, both men met the same fate.

Lop was reading a magazine. She was pleased with herself, and was now a wealthy widow. She guessed by now that Dylan would realise that she'd used him, but she wasn't worried, as there was little chance that their paths would meet again. The world was her oyster; she had her life in front of her and she was still young.

Halfway through the flight, there was a thunderstorm and the plane suffered turbulence. She fastened her seatbelt and sipped her Bacardi and coke. The storm was a small price to pay for the future that stretched in front of her. Then suddenly there was an explosion, followed by another, people started screaming and the oxygen masks dropped down. Lop was gripped with fear, the pilot was telling everyone to prepare for a crash landing. 'Get into the brace position,' said the stewardess, 'the captain is going to bring us down safely, keep calm.'

The plane was plummeting. Lop stared out of the window; she could see the sea getting rapidly closer. She was terrified, if she died now, all of her scheming and manipulating would have been for nothing. 'I don't want to die,' she cried out loud.

Then the plane hit the sea and sank within minutes. There were no survivors.

Susie's eyes flickered open, and the first thing that she noticed was the smell, a distinct hospital smell. She closed her eyes again and felt someone squeezing her hand. Opening her eyes again, she tried to focus. It looked like Kevin, surely it wasn't, what had happened? She couldn't remember anything. 'Hello, princess,' said Kevin.

Princess? It had to be Kevin. Susie didn't answer, her throat felt very sore; it hurt to swallow let alone speak. Tiredness was overcoming her once more; she closed her eyes and drifted back to a place that was dark and peaceful.

Ray had survived and had had surgery. Awaking from the anaesthetic, he found that he had no feeling in his legs. 'You gave us a real fright,' said Bobby, 'promise me that you won't go diving out of windows again.'

'Is that evil bitch dead?'

'Yes, she was impaled on the railings.'

'Good, even that's too good for her, how are the girls?'

'Susie drifts in and out of consciousness, but she's on the mend. Its Dee that I'm worried about, she's in intensive care. Eddie hasn't left her side since she was admitted here.'

'She's strong, Rosie, she'll make it.'

'Of course she will,' replied Rosie, wishing that she believed herself.

Susie had seen fuzzy shapes, bright lights, and heard strange voices, but now she felt different, more awake. She tried to sit up but flopped back onto her bed, her arms and legs felt like lead weights. Closing her eyes once more, she drifted back into that dark and peaceful place. An hour later she was awoken by a nurse. 'Are you back with us, Susie? It's time to change your dressing; your boyfriend's gone to get you a coffee.'

'Boyfriend?'

'Yes, Kevin, surely you haven't forgotten him. It's your chest that was operated on, not your head, come on sit up for me.'

Susie winced with pain as the bandages were removed to reveal the pus covered dressings. 'We'll need some warm water,' said the nurse, 'that will make the dressing come off easier.'

After removing the dressings and putting on new ones, the nurse asked Susie to lean forward. 'Why?' asked Susie.

'I need to dress the exit wound.'

'Exit wound?'

'Yes, the bullet passed straight through you. It's probably embedded in the wall of the room where you were shot. It missed your heart and spine, but it clipped your aorta and you lost a lot of blood.' Minutes later the procedure was almost over. Susie gritted her teeth; the pain was unbearable as the dressing was removed. 'All done,' said the nurse, 'you're a model patient. I'll send Kevin in now, he's outside.'

'Thanks,' said Susie. She felt dreadful but at least she was awake.

Kevin entered the room with a coffee in each hand. 'Hi princess,' he said, 'so you've finally decided to speak to me.'

'What are you doing here? I thought you'd be with Mum.'

'Your mother has been dividing herself between you, Ray, and Deanne, so she's worn out. Anyway it's you that I wanted to see, I owe you a lot.'

'You owe me nothing, but it's Mum that you want, it's obvious.'

'But she doesn't want me, she wants Ray, and I was just there when she needed me.'

'So?'

'So I wondered if you would like to go out with me for a meal when you're a bit better.'

'You don't have to do this.'

'You saved my life, and that's a huge gesture to make. You were a kid when I met you and you're now a beautiful woman. I spoke to your mother just a while ago, and I can't believe that I've been so blind for all of these years.'

Susie flinched as she took the coffee that Kevin was offering her. 'She told you. How could she?'

'Because she had to open my eyes. We've survived a horrific situation recently, and I figure that if we can conquer that, we can conquer anything.'

·'You'd have to take on Maisie Rose; she's half Spanish and a handful, plus she's hooked on Geordie songs. She speaks Geordie too.'

'No probs, I might take her on stage one night and do a duet with her, we could do *When the boat comes in*, she'd steal the show.'

'You might have to include Ken.'

'That's even better, he's been looking after Maisie Rose and Norma since things kicked off.'

'Where's Mary then?'

'She quit, she says that working for your family is fraught with danger.'

'How are the boys?'

'Bobby's still dancing. Raydon's writing a book, and he wants to go to college to study art and photography.' Kevin smiled and added, 'You were unconscious when Bobby came into the room and started dancing. He kicked the gun right out of Jenny's hand.'

'I always said that his legs would come in useful one day.'

'So how about accepting my dinner date?'

'I'd love to.'

'Shall we seal it with a kiss?'

'Yes.' Susie shuddered as Kevin's lips came down on hers; her mother had been right when she'd said, 'if you and Kevin are meant to be together, you will be'. It had taken a long time to happen but at last her dream had come true.

At the time of the shooting, Deanne had remembered Bobby untying her, the door opening, Maisie Rose's face, pain, and then looking down and seeing blood staining her top. She'd been horrified and had passed out with the shock. After that, she'd recalled a siren and then being stretchered into the ambulance. A mask had been put onto her face, and a paramedic was telling her to stay with him. Everything was floaty, a needle was being put into her arm, they were giving her something, and she could taste blood in her mouth. She'd been standing up and stretching when the bullet had hit her, and the force of it had knocked her back down into the chair that she'd been taped to for so long. Nothing was real; she was having difficulty breathing and then suddenly there was darkness.

Eddie was devastated; his beloved Dee was hovering between life and death. He blamed himself for her state. They'd always done everything together, except for this one time when he'd allowed her to go out without him as he was on a sick bed. If she died, he wanted to die; he'd dreamt of standing beside her when the tortoise sanctuary was opened. She was now a qualified reptile nurse, and they'd wanted to make this sanctuary the biggest and best in England. They'd intended opening the place to the public at the weekends, and charging a small entrance fee to help with the upkeep of the place. Now it seemed that their dreams had gone up in smoke and that he was about to lose the love of his life.

'I still can't feel my legs, Rosie, I can't walk. What the fuck is happening; am I going to be paralysed for life?'

'It's early days, Ray, give it time.'

'I'm in my fifties, time I do not have; supposing that I never get any feeling back?'

'You'll walk again, I know it.'

'You might as well go back to Kevin.'

'Ouch, are you still sore at me?'

'No, it was my fault, I was a piss head, and I neglected you and my family. Bobby bore most of the brunt of it, poor sod. I've been a complete arsehole. Once I get home, I'm going to make it up to all of you.'

'Bobby's outside, he wants to talk to you alone.'

'Send him in.'

'Okay, I think he wants to have a man to man chat. I'll leave you both to it and go and see Deanne.'

Bobby sat beside his father's bed. 'Feeling a bit better, Dad?'

'Yes, what a little hero you've been, rescuing your sister.'

'She still got shot.'

'Yes, but if you hadn't freed her, the bullet would have entered her brain, so at least you gave her a fighting chance.'

'A slim one.'

'Well I think that you were marvellous, and you saved your mother too.'

'It was only a scissor kick. I love my family, and I'd protect all of you, were it possible.'

'Son, I want to apologise about the way that I've treated you.'

'Forget it, I know why now.'

'You do?'

'Yes, for years Nana Norma told me that I was Ed's son, and I thought she was mad, but I believe her now because someone else has told me the same thing. I'm sorry for you, it must have been shit raising someone else's kid. My father was a shit; he was married to Cathy when he got Mum pregnant.'

'But when two people love each other, things happen, look at Dee and Eddie; it's wrong but to them it's right. Ed and your mother loved each other, they had done since they were kids. She was honest with me when she found out that she was carrying you. She gave me the option of walking away.'

'But you still married her.'

'I loved her, besides you didn't ask to be born and you could have been mine. I still don't know the truth.'

'Then let's do a DNA test. You'll still be my dad. Anyone can be a sperm donor, but it takes a man to be a father, so you're my dad whatever the outcome. You've raised me and I'll never be able to pay you back. I really would like to know, Dad, honest I would.'

'Is this really what you want?'

'Yes.'

'Okay then, we'll do it.'

'Thanks Dad, I'm a lucky sod, I've got the best mother and father in the world. Ed Gold's a non-starter.'

'Don't let Eddie or your sisters hear that.'

'Well, that's another thing, isn't it? My sisters could be my blood sisters, and Eddie a half brother.'

'You're right, this needs sorting.'

'Thanks, Dad, and what did you think of my performance at Vic's place?'

'Bloody brilliant, *Jump* was a revelation, shame that David Lee Roth didn't see it.'

'I wasn't that good.'

'How do you do those back flips?'

'Like this,' and Bobby stood up, walked to the foot of Ray's bed, and threw himself backwards, landing on his feet perfectly.

Chapter Fifty-Two

Al Simpkins was the only one to attend Vic's funeral; nobody missed him. Rosie sent flowers; she'd never liked Vic and had more pressing things to deal with at the hospital. She did however pay for his funeral; he had met a horrible end and was broke with no assets left. Al wanted Vic's ashes, but Rosie stated that he could have half as she wanted the other half for something else, and that the crematorium had been instructed to put Vic's ashes into two urns. Al was confused but agreed as Rosie was paying for everything. He'd lost his old sparring partner but life had to go on. He was astonished to find that Lop had cleaned Vic out; she'd seemed such a caring person. He wondered what had happened to her, unaware that she was at the bottom of the sea.

'You have to prepare yourself,' said the specialist, 'if she does wake up, she could be completely dependent on you for the rest of her life; we really should switch off the ventilator.'

'No way,' cried Eddie, 'she'll wake up, and I'll pay you whatever it costs to keep her on the ventilator.'

'There's no point.'

'There's every point,' snapped Rosie, 'you're not turning the machine off. My son was in this position and he was turned off; if we'd given him longer he may have woken up.'

'But someone else could have their life saved by this ventilator; these machines are needed urgently.'

'And my daughter needs it. If I find out that you've switched it off I'll sue. We'll pay whatever it costs even if we end up bankrupt.'

Ed's brother, Russell, and his wife had arrived at the hospital to see the victims of the siege concocted by Jenny. Fawn, Russell's wife, was intrigued by Norma's ramblings at night about Ed.

'Why does he visit you, Norma?'

'He has to keep an eye on Rosie and her children, and he's worried about Deanne. I don't see her these days.'

'She lives with Eddie in his house,' said Rosie.

'Oh does she, but why is he worried about her?'

'Well she's always been a bit headstrong, hasn't she?'

'Yes, just like you and Ed; why is Ray in a wheelchair these days?'

'He had an accident, Mum.'

'Oh drunk, was he?'

'No, Mum.'

'Well that's a first, I'm older than him and I don't need a wheelchair. Do you know what's on at the Rex Cinema tomorrow? Maybe we could all go there, I love the cinema.'

'Norma, do you think that Ed might come to me?' asked Fawn.

'I don't know, you could sit with me if you like.'

'Thank you.' Fawn needed contact, Deanne's life was ebbing away.

Later that night, Fawn sat with Norma. Nothing happened that night, or the following one, but on the third night, Norma suddenly sat bolt upright in bed and said, 'Oh, there you are.'

Fawn couldn't see anything, but it was obvious that Norma wasn't hallucinating; there was someone else in the room. An orb settled onto the bed and took shape, and Fawn recognised him immediately; it was her deceased brother-in-law. His voice was almost that of a bad reception on a radio but Norma understood him perfectly. Fawn left the room silently; she'd seen all that she needed to.

The following morning she relayed the news to Rosie. 'I saw him, I think that he's chosen Norma because she's confused, that way nobody will believe her and he's free to visit.'

'Would he come to me?'

'He may, but it could be dangerous, he would need to take over my body for a while and we can't do it to order. I did this for Kevin and Cathy, but in Cathy's suicide note, she stated that she would visit Kevin on a specific date so she wanted to show herself to him. In your case, no such note exists. He's tried to contact you many times but you've always closed your eyes to him.'

'I saw him once.'

'Yes, he showed himself to you just after the memorial concert, but you've never tried to contact him since. I will do my best for you but you have to accept that there's a slim chance that he may not want to show himself after all this time.'

'But if he comes to Mum?'

'He comes because she accepts his visits. I will sit with her again tonight and see if I can interact with him.'

'Please try, it's just that I believe the only one who can save Deanne is him with my help.'

'I will do my best,' replied Fawn, 'love conquers everything.'

'The next forty eight hours are critical, she may shut down by herself,' said the specialist, gazing at Deanne.

'She won't,' replied Eddie. 'I can talk her out of this, she'll come through.' His voice was interspaced with tears.

Rosie took hold of Deanne's hand and kissed it. 'I wish her father was here, he'd know what to do.'

'Ask him then,' whispered Fawn, 'you will see him tomorrow night at your home.'

'Wonderful,' cried Rosie, and then settled herself beside her daughter's bed, holding her hand and willing her to wake up. The machine was performing all of her bodily functions but still Deanne lay still as if waiting for someone to wake her up.

Fawn was a very experienced clairvoyant, medium, and healer, but for all her gifts, Deanne continued to slumber. A woman from the donor department approached Rosie and Eddie and made a suggestion that they may like to donate some of Deanne's organs.

'She's getting near the end, and once she's in the operating theatre, she'll be treated with dignity.'

Rosie's eyes blazed with anger. 'Go away, you callous bitch,' she cried, 'she's not dead yet.'

'But she's as good as dead, the machine's breathing for her.'

'Piss off before I gouge your eyes out.' The girl fled and Rosie broke down in tears once more.

The following day there was still no change and, as they left the hospital, Rosie asked Fawn about Ed's visit. 'What time will he come?'

'Midnight, and he'll only be with you for a brief while but at least you'll be reunited for a few minutes.'

Rosie sighed, she was pinning her hopes on Ed helping her, but maybe she was expecting too much.

Ray now slept downstairs; a stair lift had been suggested but he declined saying that he wanted to walk up the stairs and was determined to do so one day. Some nights, Rosie slept with him and some nights she didn't. Tonight was going to be the latter. She went upstairs with Fawn at a quarter to twelve and they both lay on the bed in Rosie's room. Rosie told Fawn about her vision of Francine on the night of the shootings.

'Where there's good there's evil,' slurred Fawn, 'but love conquers everything.' Her voice was fading and slurring until it stopped and Rosie felt warm arms around her. Looking up, she saw her beloved Ed who held and caressed her; they were loving caresses, comforting caresses.

'Ed, our little girl is dying, please help me, I can't lose her, and Eddie will die of a broken heart if she dies. Why can't God take me instead, she's so young and vital.'

'Would you die for her?'

'Yes, I'd do anything.'

Ed kissed away her tears. 'Everything will be fine, I promise.' He continued to soothe her for what seemed like an eternity and then he said, 'When you see her tomorrow, tell her that Daddy loves her. Goodbye Rosie, I love and miss you.'

The words didn't sink in straight away, then the arms around her went cold and Ed's face became grainy. In the blink of an eye he was gone, and Fawn awoke and stretched. 'I feel like I've been asleep forever,' she said, 'how do you feel?'

'Intrigued, he said tell her that Daddy loves her and that everything will be fine.'

'Then it will be. I'd better go downstairs to Rusty.'

'No stay here, I'll send him up, you can have my bed. I'm going down to see Ray, he needs love too.'

'Thank you, I love this bed, it's so comfy.'

'Be my guest,' and Rosie hurried downstairs.

At the hospital the following day, the doctors were clustered around Deanne's bed; there was no hope, the end was in sight. Rosie approached the bed, saying, 'Hello darling, everyone's routing for you and although he's not here himself, your daddy loves you.'

Eddie looked dreadful; his appearance was unkempt and he looked like a shadow of himself.

Deanne's doctor turned to Rosie. 'She had a visitor last night.'

'Who was that, did you see anyone, Eddie?'

'No, but I fell asleep a few times.'

'Well,' said Rosie, 'you'll have plenty of sleep tonight. I'm going to sit with her, things are going to get better, I know it.'

Following the doctor from the room she said, 'What did this man look like, and what time was he here?'

'About twelve fifteen. I'd been called to your daughter as she seemed to be slipping away, but when I arrived this man was sitting by her bed holding her hand. He looked like your son, but older. I turned to check my notes and he was gone, I don't know how he got past me. The thing was, Deanne actually had some colour back in her cheeks at that time but it's gone now. You do know that she could go at any time, don't you?'

'I do and that is why I'm not going home tonight. I need to be with her, and Eddie's exhausted, he needs sleep.' She smiled to herself, knowing who the visitor was.

The day sped over. More tests were carried out, and Fawn laid her hands on the girl trying to heal her. Everything was failing but Rosie had faith, Ed had told her that everything would be fine and it would be. Constantly she spoke to her daughter, played her favourite music, held her hand, talked about her schooldays, and repeated over and over that Daddy and Mummy loved her. By eleven o'clock she was flagging, and Eddie reluctantly went to bed in a room next door to Deanne's. Through the night, Rosie dozed off a few times, still holding her daughter's hand. She awoke at one time as the nurse was checking the ventilator.

'Would you like a cup of tea?' asked the nurse.

'Yes please,' replied Rosie, yawning.

'Would the gentleman like one...? Oh he's gone, maybe he went to the toilet, he was here a minute ago.'

'Do you mean Eddie? I wanted him to sleep.'

'No, the other man, he comes here a lot, but as soon as we speak to him, he just squeezes Deanne's hand and leaves.'

'Really, well if he comes back and wants a cup of tea, I'll get him to find you.'

'Okay, one cup of tea coming up.'

Rosie gazed at Deanne; she did have a bit more colour in her cheeks.

One cup of tea later, Rosie began talking to her daughter once more. It was going to be a long night but she wasn't going anywhere. She dozed off again about two thirty, and awoke with someone stroking her hand. Hoping that it was Deanne waking up, her eyes snapped open and she beheld Ed sitting opposite holding his daughter's hand. She gasped, this couldn't be happening.

'Tell her you love her and hold my hand,' said Ed, so over and over they repeated that they loved her with their hands joined. This continued for about three minutes and then Ed was gone.

Rosie called the nurse. 'Look, she looks so much better, she's got colour and she looks as if she's smiling.'

The nurse smiled, she'd seen this before. The girl was at death's door.

By four o'clock Rosie had nodded off again, and awoke to the strains of *Little Girl* being sung. Ed was back and singing Deanne's favourite song. Once more Ed and Rosie joined hands and repeated that they loved her. Although Rosie didn't know it, several other people were doing the same. Ada Lynne was talking in her sleep whilst cuddled up to Alf. 'We love you, Deanne,' she said.

In a caravan in Bacton, Fawn's daughters, Amber and Amethyst, were saying the same. Eddie was repeating the same words in his sleep, and at Rosie's home, Fawn and Rusty were sitting with their hands joined uttering the same words. Norma was wailing it at the top of her voice, and Susie awoke crying. Scared that Deanne was about to die, she knelt down and prayed to God, crying that she loved Deanne. Ken had awoken as Norma's wailing had scared the life out of him. Raydon had been awake all night writing his novel, and found himself repeatedly writing, 'we love you, Deanne'. Only Bobby came off worse. He'd been in bed with a girl called Claire who was not amused by him calling her Deanne; he got a slap around his face and was shown the door. He made his way home confused; he'd never got a girl's name wrong before.

Suddenly, Deanne levitated above the bed and stayed there. Rosie looked on in horror, wondering if all the attached tubes would fall out. Then she sank slowly back onto the bed and lay there motionless. Ed kissed his daughter on her forehead, and kissed Rosie on her lips, saying, 'It's all over, Rosie,' then he was gone.

Rosie broke down in tears. What did he mean, saying it was all over, was Deanne dead? She felt helpless and laid across Deanne's body, believing that her daughter was gone. Then she felt a hand stroking her hair, and heard the sound of coughing. Rosie pressed the buzzer and the nurses came running. Deanne's eyes were open and she was trying to remove the tube from her throat. Everything moved like lightning as Deanne was relieved of the ventilator.

'Mum,' she said, 'my throat's so sore. Where's Eddie?'

'Oh, my darling girl,' cried Rosie, and leaving the room she went to wake Eddie.

Eddie awoke with a start. Rosie was calling him. 'Come quick,' she cried.

Eddie's eyes filled with tears. 'Is she dead?' he cried.

'Come with me.' Rosie almost dragged him to Deanne's room where Deanne was sitting propped up in bed smiling.

'Dee,' cried Eddie, 'you've come back to me.'

Rosie wiped away her tears. 'I'll leave you two alone,' she said. Walking outside the building, Rosie looked up at the sky. 'Thank you, God, and thank you, Ed, she must have needed one on the earthly planet and one on the other side to stop her from crossing over.'

She felt a kiss on the back of her neck and turned around. There was no one there but she knew who it was. 'I love you, Ed,' she said out loud, and then hurrying back inside, she phoned home.

Chapter Fifty-Three

Ray picked up the receiver by the side of his bed; the call had to be from Rosie. It was five in the morning, and he was shaking. Obviously this was bad news. 'Ray, it's me.'

'I thought it would be, is it bad news? I should have been with you; I'm fucking useless and no help to you at all.'

'Ray, she's woken up.'

'That's fantastic, I'll have to wake everyone up and tell them. Oh I can't, can I? I can't walk. Oh Rosie, I'm so happy, I'm gonna ring everyone.'

'I'm coming home now. Deanne and Eddie need their privacy. I'm too tired to drive; I'll get a cab and pick up the car tomorrow.'

'Good thinking, I'll stay awake until you get back, you need one long loving cuddle.'

'You can say that again.' Rosie was exhausted and felt as if she'd sleep for a week.

Deanne had to remain in hospital for another six weeks, and Eddie returned to his job as a vet. The tortoise sanctuary was almost finished, and Susie and Kevin had got engaged. Susie had been uncertain at first, as she believed that Kevin was still in love with Rosie, but Kevin put her mind at rest by saying, 'When I lost Cathy, I found it hard to survive but when Candy came along, she started the healing process, and when she was murdered, your mother was there for me. I'd been in love with her for years, but if it hadn't been for Ray's drinking, we would never have became an item. Her heart belongs to Ray, as mine does to you. I love you princess; you're all I'll ever need. Will you do me the honour of marrying me?'

Susie threw her arms around his neck, crying, 'Yes, oh yes.'

They broke the news to Ray and Rosie the same night and they were overjoyed. Maisie took Ken to one side saying, 'I think that Mum might have a bun in the oven.'

'Well that would be wonderful, pet; you'll have a little brother or sister to play with.'

'Maybe we can teach it Geordie songs.'

'Well of course, pet, I love weddings.'

Ray was sunk into his thoughts. 'Oh no, my mother will wear the same hat that she wears for everyone's wedding, it stinks of mothballs. Oh well, here's to another knees up. I'll have to practise using crutches, Rosie. I can't take Susie up the aisle in a wheelchair.'

'My band can play at the reception,' laughed Bobby.

A DNA test had proved that Ray wasn't his father. Bobby had prayed that he was, but it didn't really matter because he adored Ray, and although Ed was his biological father, Ray was his true one. He'd always been there for him and he doubted that his real one would have been.

Six months later, Susie walked up the aisle with Ray who was on a Zimmer frame. Kevin had chosen Prince's *The Most Beautiful Girl in the World* instead of the wedding march as he knew that Susie adored Prince, and that song was her favourite. She hid her baby bump under a flowing gown, and at last she was truly happy. Her handsome bridegroom's face reflected the same emotion. Maisie Rose looked cute in her pink bridesmaid's dress, holding her posy, and Deanne and Rachel looked stunning in their dresses which were designed by Rachel herself. Ada Lynne had been persuaded to buy a new dress and hat. Rosie had taken her to Debenhams and kitted her out in a lilac creation. Norma wore yellow, she loved the colour.

'It looks like sunshine,' she said, twirling round in her two piece.

'You look a picture, Norma,' said Ken, 'would you like a toyboy?'

He was his usual happy self, and he'd fallen on his feet. He'd believed that Rosie would dispense with his services now that her sworn enemy was dead, but Rosie said that she still needed security as she now had her own agency and you always made a few enemies in that game.

'I want someone that I can trust,' she said, 'and Bobby will need security in time, besides, Maisie Rose would never speak to me again if you left,' and so Ken became another addition to the Lynne family.

The reception was a noisy one, and Bobby performed with aplomb when he fronted Steven's band that night. He was still in his teens, but swamped with work. Steven looked at Susie; she looked radiant, and he remembered their early heady days together. It hadn't exactly been a match made in heaven but he'd always remember her as his first love. Love was off the menu at present, he was too busy enjoying himself with any willing female. However he knew that one day the right girl would come along and that would be it, but until that day, he would be having fun with his best friend and vocalist, Bobby.

Raydon's novel was almost finished, and when Ray asked him what it was about, he'd answered sex, drugs, and rock and roll. 'Well I hope that I'm not in it,' he said. 'I recall all of those photos that you took of me when I was pissed, and I wasn't a pretty sight.'

'You're still not,' laughed Raydon, 'no, you're not in it, you're too boring, still you're looking well.'

'I'd clip you around your ear if I could get out of this chair, you cheeky little sod. Oh no, don't look now but my mother's doing her famed knees up again. She's hitched her skirt up and you can see her drawers. Where does she get her energy from? She's in her eighties.'

'So's Nana Norma, look, she's copying Nana Ada.'

'Oh Christ, how embarrassing. Look the other way, they're waving at us. There are times when being in a wheelchair has its benefits. I can't dance, but you can, they want us to join in. Oh, here comes Ken.'

'Ah were wonderin' if you'd like a turn on the dance floor with your mother and mother-in-law, I can whiz you around a bit in your chair.'

'No,' replied Ray. 'I'll leave them to you.'

'Well, if you change your mind.'

'I won't, I need a drink.'

'Well, not too much, mind, it's not good for you.'

'I've learned my lesson.'

'Okay, I'll get back to the ladies. Come on, Ada, get those knees up, lift your skirts up Norma; you've got a fine pair of pins.'

Tim, Martin, and Alf wandered over. 'How's it going, Ray, any change?'

'I've got a bit of feeling coming back into my right leg, but apart from that there's no change at all, still my middle leg's okay, I get Rosie to check it on a regular basis.'

'I bet you do,' said Eddie, pushing a leaflet into Ray's hand.

Ray read it out loud. 'Grand opening this weekend at the Eden Gold Chelonian Sanctuary, five pounds admission, food and drink available, everyone welcome'. Well done, Eddie, I'm glad that you've achieved your dreams. We'll see you there.'

As Eddie walked away, Ray sighed. 'I wonder what Ed would make of his kids; he was a hell raiser and steeped in rock and roll. Susie married that Spanish prat and had no inclination to tread the boards, Deanne is a veterinary nurse, and Eddie is a vet also, with no theatrical leanings; he must be turning in his grave.'

'But what about Bobby?'

'Yes, he danced before he could walk, drove me nuts, he never stopped dancing. His voice could shatter glass and, as for women, well look at him now, I rest my case. Yes, his father would be proud of him.'

Alf laughed. Bobby was seated on a sofa with a girl either side of him. Rosie was heading their way. 'Gorgeous, isn't she?' said Ray. 'How lucky I am, and to think that I almost lost her.'

'Hi everyone.' Rosie was beaming. 'What have you got there, Ray?'

'A leaflet, it's Eddie's grand opening of his sanctuary this weekend.'

'Oh, let me see.'

Ray stuffed the leaflet down his trousers. 'You can see it later if you can find it, my legs throbbing a bit.'

'Well maybe you're getting more feeling into it; which leg?'

'The middle one,' laughed Ray, 'can you check it out?'

'Later,' said Rosie, and wandered off in Susie and Kevin's direction.

The tortoise sanctuary was magnificent. Eddie had spared no expense; there were many outdoor runs, tropical houses, baby tortoise houses, and just about everything that a homeless tortoise could want. Wacky and Daisy still provided many Sulcata babies, but now Eddie had a collection of Mediterranean tortoises including Hermanns, Marginated, Radiated, and Spur thighed tortoises. In another tropical house, he kept leopard tortoises and, in yet another area, Burmese Browns, and an Aldabran tortoise with three legs owing to an accident. He'd also taken in a herd of Redfoot and Yellowfoot tortoises too.

Donations flooded into the sanctuary. Eddie was a happy man. He'd named the sanctuary after his father as he'd been the one responsible for Eddie's interest in tortoises. Ed had bought Wacky for him when he was just a child, and his interest had grown from there. Eddie felt as if he had everything; he had a career as a vet, a beautiful mansion which now housed his tortoise collection in its grounds, and his beloved Dee. He'd recently acquired another addition, a half brother. The discovery that Bobby was his half brother had at first upset him because now he knew that his father had cheated on his mother, but after a while he accepted Bobby and went in search of his beloved Aunty Rose. Rosie was uncomfortable when Eddie took her to one side.

'I guess you hate me,' said Rosie.

'No,' replied Eddie, 'my father could never keep it in his trousers, and you and he had history, lots of it. I've always liked Bobby, and I'm proud to call him my half brother, but there is one question that I'd like to ask you.'

'Fire away.'

'Do you think that I might have any more half brothers or sisters?'

'Absolutely not, your father may have been a lothario but he always took precautions, and it was only myself and Cathy that he rode bare back.'

'Phew, thank God for that.'

'I thought that you'd be angry with me.'

'I could never be angry with you; you came into my life when I was a kid and you've always been there for me. All I can say is thank you.'

'Thank you?'

'Yes for giving me support when I've needed it, for giving me a lively half brother and, last but not least, for giving birth to my beautiful Dee. I love you Aunty Rose and always will.'

Rosie could feel tears stinging her eyes. 'I'm getting all emotional,' she said.

Eddie smiled and gave Rosie a hug. 'Come and have a look at my three legged Aldabran tortoise,' he said, 'she was mauled by dogs but she gets around much better than the four legged ones.'

Smiling, Rosie took his arm and together they walked over to the enclosure.

It was New Year's Eve 1999. Rosie, Norma, and Ken were seeing the New Year in quietly. Susie, Kevin, and Maisie Rose were in Los Angeles staying with Barry. Bobby and Steven were out at a party, and Michael and Raydon were taking photographs at a celebrity party. Ray was in hospital, having just had another operation. The trio had played Trivial Pursuit and watched a bit of television. At eleven thirty, they had visitors in the shape of Bobby and Steven.

'Where's Mum?' asked Bobby.

'Upstairs, she's feeling a bit down, she'd hoped to have Ray home but the doctors said that he couldn't come home yet. She'd hoped to see the New Year in with him,' said Ken.

'Well, tell her to come down, there's someone to see her.'

'Who do I say it is?'

'Just tell her that I need her down here.'

Ken went upstairs. 'Excuse me, Mrs Lynne, sorry to trouble you, but young Bobby's downstairs and he says that you've a visitor.'

'Who is it?'

'He didn't say.'

'Okay.' Rosie followed Ken downstairs and saw Bobby with a huge grin on his face.

'Someone to see you, Mum,' said Bobby. 'I'll bring him in.'

Bobby went outside, and returned minutes later pushing Ray in his wheelchair into the room.

'Ray, they said that you couldn't come home, oh I'm so happy.'

'Well,' said Bobby, 'it's amazing what you can do with a couple of back flips, autographs, and backstage passes, and as we've delivered your New Year's present, we're going back to the party. See you.'

Bobby planted a kiss on Rosie's cheek and winked at her, the same wink that Ed had given her many moons ago. She threw her arms around her son, crying, 'Thank you so much.'

'Easy Mum, don't mess with the hair. Steve and I have a couple of real beauties in the car. See you tomorrow, I love you.'

As he left, Rosie turned to Ray. 'Come on Ray, we'll celebrate the New Year with a bottle of champagne.'

Ken turned to Norma. 'Well I guess it's you and me, pet. Would you like a game of tiddlywinks or a drink to celebrate the New Year?'

'Both, I'll have lemonade.'

'But Norma we're going into the millennium, you'll have to have something a bit stronger.'

'Okay, stick an orange juice in it.'

'But, Norma pet...'

'I don't touch the evil drink and, anyway, there's three of us.'

'Three?'

'Yes, you've forgotten Vic.'

'Oh yes, Vic, shall we put him on the coffee table so that he can watch the television when Big Ben chimes?'

'Yes, he always did like a bit of telly before he went blind.'

Ken picked up the giant egg timer that adorned the sideboard and placed it on the coffee table. Norma stared at it. 'It was a good idea of Rosie's, putting his ashes into that egg timer. He used everyone and controlled them, but now Rosie's in control of him; she uses that timer for many things.'

'That she does, Norma, that she does, now what about pushing the boat out and having a sweet sherry?'

'Oh all right, as long as you don't sing.'

'I promise, I think I'll have two drinks, one for me and one for Vic.'

'Okay, now how does that song go?'

'What song?'

'The one about fishes on dishes.'

'Ah, *When the boat comes in*.'

'That's it, well as I'm pushing the boat out, we might as well sing about boats coming in.'

'I thought you didn't want me to sing.'

'You can sing if you teach me the words.'

'Right Norma, I'll get the drinks and then we can serenade wor Vic.'

In Ray's makeshift bedroom, Rosie made him comfortable. 'I'm so happy; I thought that I'd be spending tonight on my own.'

'Bobby fixed it,' said Ray, 'he's a great boy. He wanted us to be happy and he'd made his mind up that it was going to happen; no doctor was going to stop him. You should have seen him chatting up the nurses, he's fixed a couple of dates for next week; he's his father's son all right.'

As the New Year chimed in, Rosie and Ray raised their glasses of champagne and clinked them together. 'Happy New Year, Ray.'

'Happy New Year. Rosie, my leg's throbbing again.'

'Which one?'

'Need you ask? The third one.'

A month later, Ray was back in hospital. He had complete sensation back in his right leg and was getting pins and needles in his left. He had another operation and, while he was in there, Fawn paid another visit with her daughter Amber and her new grandchild. One night Rosie was awoken by Fawn.

'Ed wants to see you,' she said.

'But I thought that it was dangerous?'

'It's different, he wants to see you, that's totally different, you don't need me. You're on the same wavelength now, he can appear to you at any time that either of you wants. He can take shape without me.'

'I dreamed about him last night; we were in our special spot at Bedfords Park.'

'He put that thought there; he wants to see you there.'

'Now?'

'Yes, now, he has something to tell you.'

'Okay, I'd better go then, are you coming?'

'Yes, I'll drive you there.'

Rosie dressed and then left the house with Fawn.

Once they were in Bedfords Park, with the aid of a torch, Rosie found the spot that she'd visited many years ago with Ed.

'We used to come here all the time,' said Rosie, 'it's just before you come into the clearing, we always called it our special spot. I've lain in his arms many times under that tree.'

Fawn backed away, saying in a very soft voice, 'Just sit down, Rosie, and close your eyes.'

Rosie did as she was bid and sat under the tree, and within seconds she could feel Ed's arms around her. She nestled into his chest, saying, 'Thank you for giving me Deanne back.'

'It was love that brought her back to you.'

'What was it that you wanted to tell me?'

Ed kissed her gently and said, 'Ray will be fine, and he will walk again.'

'How wonderful.'

'And your next grandchild will be a boy.'

'How lovely, Kevin and Susie will be very happy.'

'Whenever you need me, all you have to do is call my name; I'll be with you in two minutes.'

'You don't look any different from when I last saw you on earth.'

'We don't age, in fact we have no form, the only way that you see me is as you remember me, we produce a form that you recognise but we can't hold it for long.'

'I am ageing; I'll be fifty-five in May.'

'But you're still beautiful, beauty comes from within.'

'You make me feel beautiful.'

'I always did; we were good together until I ruined things. I was stupid and trusted the wrong people, and they destroyed me. I was selfish, self obsessed, drank too much, took drugs, and abused women; I was a fool. Bobby's nobody's fool. He has a lot to learn, but with you to guide him, he will become a much better person than I was. Watch him closely; he will become very famous, but keep the jackals at bay.'

'I will, you can count on it.'

'I'm glad that you came tonight, from now on you will not need to seek me out, I will come to you, your eyes are open now.

Things were different before, I needed you to seek me out, to show that you still wanted to see me.'

'I'll always want to see you, I still love you.'

They cuddled for a little longer and then Ed kissed her once more and said, 'I have to go now. Call my name and I'll come running,' and then he was gone.

Fawn walked over and helped Rosie to her feet. 'True love never dies,' she said, 'let's get back; you need some sleep, and so do I.'

Rosie walked beside Fawn in a daze, and once they were out of the park, they got into the car and drove home.

Six Months Later: Los Angeles

Bobby stood waiting nervously in the wings. This was his big moment; he was in Los Angeles. His mother and Barry Grayson had got their heads together on this tour. Steven was warming the audience up; he was a real whiz kid on lead guitar. Rosie gave Bobby last minute instructions, and then Steven announced him and Bobby bounded out onto the stage. His performance was electric, the crowd roared their approval and, for sixty minutes, he danced and sang his heart out. He glanced over at his mother. He was hitting the big time; he'd need all of the help that he could get. The girls were falling over themselves to get to him, and he'd just had his first number one hit which had stayed at the top of the charts for six weeks.

As he left the stage, Barry gave him a hug. 'Fantastic,' he said.

'Well done,' cried Ray, 'you're a star.'

Rosie gave him a hug, saying, 'You were terrific, they're screaming for more; you'll have to give an encore.'

'There's a guy at the back who is there one minute and gone the next; he looks a lot like Dad,' said Bobby.

'He'll always be around,' laughed Ray, 'do you want to see my party trick?'

'Yep.'

'Look,' and Ray stood up and did a couple of shaky steps before he tottered backwards and flopped into his wheelchair.

'Dad, that's fantastic,' cried Bobby, 'at this rate, you'll be joining me on stage.'

'Not if you do *Jump* I won't. Are you saving that one for your encore?'

'Yep,' and with that, Bobby and the band trooped back onto the stage as the cheers and cries of the audience grew louder. The opening bars of *Jump* echoed through the auditorium, and Bobby went into a perfect splits. He capered around the stage, somersaulted, back flipped, and performed amazing scissor kicks. He was on top form, and the guy at the back had returned and was giving him the thumbs up. Bobby spun faster and faster, kicked, and jumped higher, he was on a high from his own adrenalin. This was his night and nobody could take it away from him. He was Eden Gold's son, and he was eclipsing him. And with Rosie as his manager, he couldn't go wrong.

Earlier in the evening, he'd surprised everyone by having a chair put on stage and bringing his mother on.

'People say that I don't do enough love songs,' he said. 'This is a beautiful one, and was written by my father about my mother. He wrote it because he loved her so much. We've also got a copy of the video that was made of this song, and you'll recognise me as a little kid at the beginning of it where I'm supposedly playing with a little girl, but in fact I was tormenting the life out of her.'

He seated Rosie, saying, 'This beautiful lady is the inspiration for this number and I'd like to sing it to her tonight.'

Suddenly the video flashed up onto the large screens and, taking Rosie's hand, Bobby serenaded her. There was a hush in the room as Bobby delivered the song with his heart and soul. As the song ended, along with the video, the audience went wild. Bobby kissed his mother's hand and then led her back to Ray.

Back on stage, Steven and the band struck up the opening bars for Van Halen's *Running with the Devil,* and Bobby excelled in the number. He knew that all kinds of temptations were in front of him, but with his mother as his mentor, he would never be dancing with the devil.

Or would he?

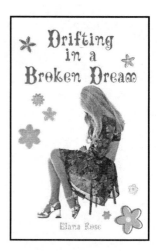

Books 1 & 2 of this series by Elana Rose

Written by a professional, speciality dancer who saw what sometimes went on behind the apparent glamour of the sixties pop scene, who witnessed the infamous drugs, sex, and rock 'n' roll at close quarters.

Eden's Rose: Rosaleen was seven years old when her new neighbour Ed Gold moved in. They become friends, eventually becoming teenage sweethearts. We follow their lives from the fifties to the eighties, dealing with childhood innocence, teenage sexual awakenings and deception.

They go their separate ways, with Rosie marrying a rich man and Ed becoming a gigolo in France, falling into the clutches of the beautiful Francine who heads a mysterious cult.

Drifting in a Broken Dream is a powerful novel of, and about, the 'swinging sixties', bringing back nostalgic memories of that era – a time of flower power, of hippies, of dancing to live bands, of peace and love, and ban-the-bomb idealism. This is Ed and Cathy's love story.

The author has produced an explosive and gripping account of her two leading characters who loved, and lusted after, each other through good times and bad – leaving in their wake a string of broken lovers, friends, and enemies – but always returning to each other, inseparable through a mysteriously sinister and secret bond.